A GLIMMER OF TRUTH

Dear Hugh,

My worst fears have been borne out . . . I beg of you, do not put yourself in jeopardy. God knows how many people have died over the past twenty years because of this monstrous thing, but sacrificing yourself will accomplish nothing. Telling you anything now would only put you in danger, but I can say that what I've discovered over the past few days is the stuff of nightmares. The implications of what has been going on here were bad enough before. But now I realize they are catastrophic!

Other Avon Books by
Christopher Hyde

JERICHO FALLS

CRESTWOOD HEIGHTS

CHRISTOPHER HYDE

AVON
PUBLISHERS OF BARD, CAMELOT, DISCUS AND FLARE BOOKS

CRESTWOOD HEIGHTS is an original publication of Avon Books. This work has never before appeared in book form. This work is a novel. Any similarity to actual persons or events is purely coincidental.

AVON BOOKS
A division of
The Hearst Corporation
105 Madison Avenue
New York, New York 10016

Published by arrangement with the author
Library of Congress Catalog Card Number: 87-91699
ISBN: 0-380-75371-5

First Avon Books Printing: February 1988

Printed in the U.S.A.

K-R 10 9 8 7 6 5 4 3 2 1

For Mariea as always,
and for Noah and Chelsea,
my own personal future

The large majority of global problems must be solved at the local level. Food shortages, sewage, water, recycling, pollution, and poverty cannot really be solved on a worldwide or even a national basis. They will be solved only when local communities become aware that they have real choices in how they shall live, and begin to act on those choices.

The Cold Mountain Institute, in planning and creating the community of Crestwood Heights, has tried to demonstrate that the choice is a real one. We have built a successful, future-oriented community that can give new direction to the architects and town planners of the world.

Crestwood Heights is more than just another suburb, it is an alternative to the large urban concentrations which have proven so inadequate in terms of quality of life for the people of America. More than that, Crestwood Heights affords us the opportunity to look into the future and see just how truly great this country of ours can be.

—Dr. M.P. Alexanian
Chairman, Cold Mountain Institute
Planning Director, Crestwood Heights Project
Architectural Review, July 17th, 1974

CHAPTER 1

Kelly Rhine leaned forward in the straight-backed bucket seat of the VW camper and rummaged around on the dashboard for her cigarettes. Lighting up, she vainly tried to drag a bit of pleasure out of the Kent III as she stared blearily out through the windshield. It had been a long drive. Ahead of her the highway snaked up and down the hills and valleys of upstate North Carolina, while behind her, crammed into the back of the camper, were the remains of eight years in Manhattan. It didn't seem like much, and more than once on the trip it had seemed to Kelly that living in New York had gone by like the blink of an eye. Before that it had been seven years with an alcoholic husband in L.A., and before that it had been San Francisco and the art school. Twenty years? More like yesterday. Her pseudophilosophical ex-boyfriend back in New York would have loved that. Life as an eyeblink.

She squeezed her eyes shut for a few seconds, testing the theory by playing blind chicken with the unfamiliar highway and trying to conjure up the past. She took another drag on the cigarette and shook her head. What a way to go.

She took a quick fix on herself in the rearview mirror. There were little lines at the corners of her big green Irish eyes, and the jet black hair was shot with gray here and there. Not bad though, not bad at all for a thirty-six-year-old broad playing Jack Kerouac. She could still get through life without an underwire bra, her MasterCard was a born-again virgin, and she didn't have a care in the world except for a balding left front tire.

"So tell me then, Kelly Kirkaldy Rhine, how did that state of affairs come about?" She spoke aloud, trying to defeat the vague sense of unease she'd felt ever since leaving New York.

She answered herself in a terrible brogue: "Faith and begorrah, it's like this then . . ."

Up until two weeks ago it had all been very different. Kelly Rhine had been senior illustrator for Murray Robbins Campbell and Orr. Her ex-husband was firmly in the past, her boyfriend—a mooching self-styled actor—was almost completely out of her life, and she had enough work on her big washable calendar to choke a horse. She had a thirty-seventh floor office in Midtown, a $1200 a month loft in Tribeca that was breaking her back, and a half-dead fern hanging above her drafting table. There was no window in her office and there were roaches in the apartment, but what the hell, you couldn't have everything—not in Manhattan.

Then Mort Robbins took her to lunch. Mort was a full partner in MRC&O and head of the art department. He was also a lecherous old bastard with a wife and two kids in Scarsdale and a key to the hotel suite a handful of execs kept at the Regency Hotel. According to Mort, when a female employee at MRC&O heard the phrase "Screw the company," she was supposed to ask which initial.

The free lunch was Mort's way of telling Kelly that she was next on the list and he made things even clearer by suggesting that they spend the rest of the afternoon between the sheets. From the way he phrased it, Kelly knew that it was an order, not a suggestion, and the implications were clear: play wee-wee games with Uncle Mortie or go look for another job.

For about thirty seconds Kelly thought about bringing up one fast booted foot and tipping him back to land where he kept his brains. Instead, she stood up without a word and left the restaurant. It took fifteen minutes to cab down to her building on Lispenard Street and by the time she paid the driver she'd gone through all her options. Mort wouldn't fire her, he'd strangle her. He'd funnel projects to other art directors, cut her out of meetings, and generally torpedo her career. Another six months and she'd be forced to bail out.

The only other course of action was quitting right now, for "personal reasons." A fast resignation, two or three months pounding the streets, watching the balance in her savings account dwindle, and she might land a job half as good. Things weren't booming in the advertising business, and it was already May. Not a good time to go job hunting. The smart money said she should grit her teeth and hang on to the job, hoping that Morty would leave her alone.

There were tears in her eyes when she opened the door to her apartment, and she wasn't sure if they were from anger, frustration, or self-pity. Maybe a combination of all three. Closing the door behind her, she let the tears flow uncensored. Griff, her actor boyfriend, had stripped the apartment down to the baseboards when he left and there was nothing in the little foyer except the phone, her answering machine, and a forlorn little pile of mail. Bleak end to a bad day.

"Griff." She said his name aloud now as she drove, then stubbed out her cigarette, eyes dropping automatically for a second to the bare ring finger on her left hand. She should have known not to get involved with someone with a name like that. He'd given her a ring to replace the wedding band she'd given up when she divorced and wouldn't you know it, the damned thing turned green within six weeks, just about the length of time they'd spent together.

The camper ducked under an enclosing stand of trees and then zipped out into the mid-June sunlight again. Kelly rolled down the window a little, letting in a buzzing rush of fresh air scented with clover. She sat back against the seat and let out a long breath. Getting the letter that shitty afternoon after lunch with Mort had almost been enough to make her believe in the I Ching all over again.

The thick, creamy envelope and the quartet of names in deep black italics in the upper left-hand corner were a dead giveaway. Barrymore, Nelson, Slater, and Soames had to be lawyers, and expensive ones, too, considering the Park Avenue address. The only thing she could think of was that the owner of her building was turning the apartments into condos and she was being offered first crack at buying her own place at some robber-baron price. The letter had been brief and to the point:

Dear Ms. Rhine:

Pursuant to proceedings in the Probate Court of Raliegh, North Carolina, and under the terms of the will of Mr. Nathan R.

Somerville, late resident of the village of Crestwood, North Carolina, we wish to inform you that as last surviving relative to Mr. Somerville's estate, you are its sole beneficiary.

The estate consists of business interests, several pieces of real property, a capital sum of money, and a small stock portfolio. The firm of Bekins Crawford of Crestwood Heights, North Carolina, acting as executors for the estate, has asked us to contact you concerning the disposal of these assets. We would appreciate it if you could give this matter your earliest attention by contacting this office as soon as possible.

Yours truly,
William S. Barrymore

Uncle Nat, her mother's half brother. She had a vague childhood memory of a short, ginger-haired man who put mustard on roast beef but that was about it. The only other thing she remembered was that he was involved in the film business.

A call to the lawyers led to a meeting, which in turn led to her whole life being turned upside down. When the lawyers, the Commonwealth of North Carolina, and Uncle Sam had finished with everything, she was left with $47,581.00, a fistful of penny stocks, a two-bedroom bungalow in Crestwood Heights, North Carolina, and a run-down movie theater in the old village of Crestwood.

Bekins Crawford, the lawyers in Crestwood Heights, had offered to dispose of the house and the movie theater property, and at first she'd been tempted. They already had buyers and for good prices, but in the end she decided against selling, at least for the moment. With Uncle Nat's cash in hand, she quit MRC&O, packed her bags, and left town. It was spring, after all, and time for a change. Avoiding the turnpikes, she'd been dawdling toward Crestwood for three days stopping when and where she wanted to, enjoying the first real sense of freedom she'd had in years.

A sign swished by, informing her that she was nine miles from New Hope. According to the woman she'd talked to at Bekins Crawford, that's where you took the turnoff to Crestwood. She was supposed to stop at the Chevron station at the crossroads and call the lawyers to tell them she was on her way.

Somehow, Kelly had gotten the feeling that Bekins Crawford wasn't too pleased that she'd turned down the offer to sell off Uncle Nat's assets, but that was probably just her imagination. Even if it wasn't, she didn't care. They'd lose a commission on selling the property, but she was getting a home and a business. If it turned out to be a pipe dream and she sold everything off in the fall, she'd still come out ahead. Three days on the road had proved to her just how badly she could use a rest, and maybe summer in a small town was exactly what she needed to get her life together.

New Hope was a grocery store, a church, a dozen weather-beaten houses and the Chevron station, all hunched in a dusty little trough between two scrub-covered hills. She'd spent the last week in New York boning up on North Carolina, but this wasn't the high-tech, twenty-first century Dixie she'd read about; this was the banjo-playing sequence from *Deliverance*. Bib overalls and white lightning. The air was sour, too, like old leaves in a graveyard.

She pulled the camper up to the pumps, told the tired-looking attendant wearing a too small baseball cap to give her five gallons and check the oil, then headed for the telephone. Surprisingly, it took her money and gave her a dial tone. She fished the lawyers' number out of her purse and dialed. She spoke to Mrs. Quinn, told her she was coming, and hustled back to the camper, keeping one eye on Baseball Cap, who was working away with a squeegee, chipping the dead bugs out of the front grill.

He had a face like leather, with just enough skin and flesh to cover the bones of his skull and jaw, and the deep-set dark eyes were blank, cold, and stupid. It was hard imagining him with a mother, and harder still to imagine a wife. She handed him the five dollars and then climbed up into the driver's seat again.

She slammed the door, locking it, glancing through the streaked windshield as a gray-bellied slab of cloud crossed the sun, throwing its shadow briefly over the cramped little valley. Shivering, Kelly fired up the engine and hauled the wheel around, taking her off the gas station lot. She took the right-hand fork and headed away. She knew instinctively that Baseball Cap was watching her go but she didn't check the mirror. A few seconds later New Hope was hidden by the dust plume she was raising on the oiled road and everything was all right again.

Crestwood was probably going to be pretty boring after Manhattan, but at least it would be safe—at this point in her life, she was willing to settle for that.

CHAPTER 2

Kelly Rhine came into Crestwood through the back door, taking County Road 26 from New Hope and following the snaking trail around the low, scrub-covered hills until she reached the flatlands close to the river. From the looks of things the farms hadn't been worked in years. Barns stood bleakly, gaping holes in their roofs, and tall grass grew up around the blind, blank windows of small, weather-beaten farmhouses.

The road itself was rutted and dusty, without any telltale slick of oil down the center to indicate its being maintained, and the timber snake fences on either side were tumbledown and almost invisible behind the jungle of weeds and wild flowers growing up from the ditches. With the window rolled down Kelly could smell the hot-sweet odor of marshland, cut with the deeper scent of the massed pinewoods on her right. Every now and again she caught sight of the twisting sun-bright ribbon of the narrow river, but nowhere was there any sign of human life and for the first time since leaving New York she found herself wishing she'd stuck to the main roads. This wasn't the romantic loneliness of the New Mexico desert or the enclosing solitude of the Rockies; this was Backwoods Alone, the kind of place were brothers raped sisters and strangers wound up with barbed wire tied around their ankles, tongues hacked off with a skinning knife so they couldn't scream when the swamp muck sucked them down and the leeches took hold.

''Jesus!'' she whispered, fumbling another cigarette off the dashboard. Back to the shrieking violins and Tony Perkins. It was just a bit of rural America and some failed farms, not the *Texas Chainsaw Massacre*. She knew perfectly well that any two-bit analyst in Manhattan would put it down to separation anxiety or something like that. Still, she let out a sigh of relief and toed the gas a little harder when she saw the silver-painted spire of the Baptist church peeking over the treetops.

County Road 26 had once been the main road into Crestwood, following the north bank of the river to the tobacco warehouses and cotton binderies of the eastern edge of town. The binderies were long gone, but the warehouses remained—long, windowless buildings, still reeking of nicotine even after lying empty for the better part of thirty years.

Kelly guided the VW over the level crossing just above the warehouses; once on the far side of the old rusted tracks of the spur line, she followed the now paved road up to Main Street and slowed, drinking in the scene.

Main Street was like something out of a Walt Disney movie. Walnuts and elms, all at least a hundred years old, spread their boughs in an arch over the street, dappling the sunlight over the wide sidwalks and the facades of the crisply painted buildings. Beneath the trees, cast-iron lampposts marched in rows on either side of the street for half a dozen blocks up to the clock tower, each one fitted with small tubular brackets holding an angled pair of small American flags. There were modern, concrete waste receptacles in the middle of each block, one on each side of the street, and the old-fashioned fire hydrants were painted the traditional cherry red.

Kelly smiled. The only things missing were a towheaded kid on a bicycle with fat tires delivering newspapers, and a milkman delivering clinking quart bottles. The violins faded and she could almost hear the theme music from "Leave It to Beaver."

The offices of Bekins Crawford, Attorneys at Law, were located in a two-story brick office building at the corner of Piedmont Street. The woodwork was painted a shiny black, the shutters on the second-floor windows were a deep green, and the company name was in a gold curve on the storefront window. Kelly found a parking spot directly in front of the office and climbed down out of the van. Locking up out of habit, she stepped up onto the sidewalk. Next to the law offices, a Baskin Robbins was doing business, disguised as an old-fashioned ice cream parlor, complete with a candy-striped awning and white, wrought-iron tables and chairs.

A small brass plate on the door to the law offices told her to WALK IN, so she did. She'd almost expected an interior as antique as the facade, with rolltop desks and a giant safe in one corner, but the reception area was stark white with thick, deep gray wall-to-wall carpeting underfoot. A secretary sat in front of a computer terminal and the telephone switchboard on her right was right out of an AT&T commercial. The secretary looked up as Kelly entered.

"May I help you?" The voice was cool and efficient.

"I have an appointment with Mrs. Quinn."

"You must be Ms. Rhine." The secretary reached out and tapped several buttons on the switchboard console. Kelly could hear a faint buzzing sound from the rear. The secretary looked up, flashing a quick, polite smile. "Go right in," she said. "Second office on the right."

"Thanks." Kelly followed the secretary's gesturing hand. She'd expected the secretary to have some kind of Carolina drawl, but the young woman's voice had been accentless and flat, as though any regional note had been surgically removed.

The door to Rebecca Quinn's office was open and Kelly tapped lightly on the doorframe before entering. The woman was on the telephone. She pointed to a chair in front of her desk and continued to listen, nodding occasionally, or putting in a simple *yes, no,* or *of course*. Kelly sat down and looked around the room.

The office was as white as the reception area. One wall was covered with bookcases, another was set with several large, framed prints. From where she sat Kelly could see that two of them were by Leger, while the third looked like a Renoir. The floor was varnished hardwood partially covered by a pale brown, hand-made rug, and a display shelf held several light brown pieces of pottery.

The desk was large, made of burled oak, with an inlaid leather top in dark brown. Everything looked expensive. Finally the lawyer hung up the phone. She extended a hand over her desk and Kelly took it. The grip was warm and strong, almost like a man's. She was wearing a dark blue suit with a ruffle-throated white blouse—a futile attempt at femininity. Rebecca Quinn was a lawyer first and a woman second.

"Kelly Rhine," the woman stated.

"That's right." Kelly fought off the urge to make a joke. First the secretary and now the lawyer giving her identity their seal of approval.

"We expected you sooner."

"I needed a bit of a break," Kelly answered. "I took the scenic route."

"So I gather." The lawyer pulled an inch-thick manila folder from a pile in her OUT basket. She flipped the file open and began leafing through the pages. "Presumably you haven't changed your mind about liquidating your uncle's assets."

"No."

"The prices I have for both the Strand Theater property and the Greenbriar house are more than generous. I may not be able to do as well later."

"I appreciate that," Kelly said, nodding, "but the money doesn't really matter too much. I've been hitchhiking around the advertising business for almost fifteen years, Mrs. Quinn. I need a rest."

"I see." The lawyer cleared her throat. "Do you have any experience managing a movie theater?"

"None at all." Kelly smiled. The woman wasn't giving up easily and it occurred to her that the people who wanted to pick up the Strand and her uncle's house might be clients of Bekins Crawford. One hand washing the other, collecting fees from both parties. "I'm a movie buff from a long way back, though."

"You would be in direct competition with the multiple theaters at the Crestwood Heights Leisureplex. Prior to his death your uncle was already experiencing financial difficulties."

"What, may I ask, is a *leisureplex?*" asked Kelly.

"The Leisureplex is a multiple-function facility used by the residents of Crestwood Heights. Indoor tennis, racquetball and squash, pools, health clubs, restaurants, that sort of thing. It's on Deep Wood Road—you'll see it on the way to your uncle's house."

"The theaters run first-release films?"

"That's right."

"Good."

"I beg your pardon?"

"I was thinking of making the Strand a rep theater," Kelly said. It was an idea that had been forming in her mind throughout the drive down from New York.

"And *what* is a rep theater?"

"Classic films," explained Kelly. "Oldies but goodies. A Bogart festival, a Roy Rogers festival, maybe a whole run of 'The Worst Films Ever Made.' "

"Are you aware that Crestwood Heights has its own cable operation?" Quinn asked. "I'm not sure you'll find enough people willing to support such a venture."

"You'd be surprised. Real buttered popcorn and corny old movies have an appeal you can't get sitting in front of a TV with a bowl of Newman's Own in your lap. There are a dozen repertory houses in New York."

"This isn't New York," Quinn replied dryly.

"I'm beginning to see that. It doesn't matter though. I'd like to give it a try." She paused and looked at the lawyer directly. "I'm *going* to give it a try."

"I see." Quinn opened a drawer and pulled out two sets of keys, which she placed in front of Kelly. "The set with the blue tag is for the theater. It's located a block west of here on the corner of Laurel Street. The electronic key-card is for the Greenbriar House."

"I'm pretty tired. I think I'd like to go to the house first," Kelly said. She picked up the keys, examining the thin plastic card for the house curiously. "How do I get there?"

"Go down Main Street to the clock tower and turn right," Quinn said crisply. "That's High Point Road. Follow the airport signs to Deep Wood Road and then turn left. Deep Wood runs into Greenbriar. Follow it around counterclockwise until you get to Fox Run, left on Fox Run to Erin Park. It's number 46."

"Could you write that down?"

"If you wish."

"What about money?" Kelly asked as the other woman wrote down the directions.

"That's been taken care of," replied the lawyer, handing the paper across to Kelly. "Your uncle's two accounts at the bank have been transferred into your name. All you have to do is go in and sign the signature cards."

"Fine." Kelly stood up and they shook hands again.

"If you want to reconsider selling, just give me a call," said Quinn.

"Of course." Kelly nodded and left the office, once again conscious of eyes on her back. A few moments later she was out on the street again. She thought about picking up a pint of Rocky Road at the camouflaged Baskin Robbins, but then decided against it. The meeting with Cold Fish Quinn had drained off the last of her energy and she suddenly realized just how tired she was. All she wanted was sleep.

CHAPTER 3

According to the sign on the edge of town, Crestwood had a population of 3,600, but as far as Kelly could tell it might just as well have read 360. Most of the angled parking spots along Main Street were empty and there were only a few people on the sidewalks. Driving slowly down the length of the business district, she realized that Main Street, Crestwood, was a tourist trap waiting to be baited.

The drugstore was called The Apothecary and came complete with a swinging sign in the shape of a mortar and pestle. The Open Cupboard Bakery had leaded glass windows blocked off by blue gingham half-curtains; an antique store called Yesterdays had a rocking chair outside the front door with a large potted plant sitting on it, and the card shop on the corner of Polk Avenue was called Paper Moon. Everything was done in black, brass, white, and pale blue, and Kelly was willing to bet that somewhere there was a committee of well-educated and well-meaning men and women who laid down the law of color schemes and ambience for the street.

She pulled to a stop in front of the Strand Theater. Uncle Nat had obviously not been on the committee.

The Strand was a monster of cracked, stained, medium brown stucco with a plain rectangular marquee supported on heavy rusted chains and decked out in Christmas tree lights. The four big doors were covered in quilted red vinyl and the glass was missing from one of the two outside display cases for posters.

Entranced, Kelly cut the engine and leaned forward over the wheel staring at the ugly old building. She'd kissed her first boy in a place like the Strand and sitting here now she could almost smell the stale popcorn and the liquefying chocolate-covered raisins clutched in a hundred little hands. Those were the days of double features and four-hit-horror marathons, and between features you'd head for the bathrooms to brush your hair, trying like hell to look like Annette Funicello or Sandra Dee. You religiously covered the toilet seats in the stalls with tissue because your mother told you to, and if you had the slightest chance of making out you didn't buy the licorice whips at the concession.

Grinning, she fired up the engine again and backed out of the slot, her eyes still on the crumbling facade of the theater. Any temptation to take Rebecca Quinn's offer had vanished. She'd been in the advertising business long enough to know when an idea was right. Owning the Strand would be like having a time machine; it was a chance to be a kid again and she was willing to bet that there were lots of people willing to pay the price of admission to get that same feeling. She slipped the van into gear and headed back up Main Street, turning right at the idiotic-looking clock tower and following High Point Road to the north.

Within three hundred yards she had reached the edge of Crestwood, but instead of the oiled dirt track she'd followed coming into town, High Point was paved and well maintained. To her left there was a low, tree-shrouded woods of mixed oak and elm, and to the right, on lower ground, rolling pastureland leading down to a narrow creek, and beyond that another screening bank of trees. Instead of run-down farms and tumbled fences, she saw well-maintained drainage ditches and eight-foot-high chain link. Apparently there really was a right and wrong side of the tracks in Crestwood.

A few minutes later she reached a T intersection and slowed. The signs were large and easy to follow. Ahead was Crestwood Municipal Airport and Deep Wood Park, the research enclave that had brought the town back to life. To the left along Deep Wood Road were the three satellite communities making up Crestwood Heights: Greenbriar, Colony Woods, and Orchard Park. Kelly swung the van to the left. Once again the road was paved, curves well marked and properly banked, the surrounding trees cut back just far enough to give good visibility without scarring the landscape. More money spent.

The Cold Mountain Institute had surveyed almost a score of sites during the late 1950s and early '60s, eventually choosing Crestwood. The town, with its lagging economy, was ideal, and the surrounding countryside was wide open for development. After assembling its land package, CMI began the first phase of its plan, building the core of the Research Park at the same time as the Greenbriar community was established. Some of the world's best-known architects and town planners were hired to work on the project and it was one of the first "new towns" in the United States to utilize passive and active solar techniques, computer-planned traffic patterns, core/collector site planning, and coaxial cable grids.

As Deep Wood Park expanded, more housing was built to accommodate the influx of new workers, resulting in the adjunct communities of Colony Woods and Orchard Park. At the same time, work began on the two-runway Crestwood Airport, designed mainly for use by the companies with research facilities in Deep Wood Park, but with the added benefit of providing air service to Crestwood.

By the late 1970s the total population of the combined communities had reached eleven thousand. The airport was finished and the five major medical facilities in Deep Wood Park joined together and established the Crestwood Heights Medical Center.

Once again there was a twofold benefit. The companies doing research in the Park had a facility for testing their research, and the residents of both the Heights and the old town had a hospital. The hospital had been built outside the Park at the intersection of Deep Wood Road and Crestwood Heights Road, and the following year the Leisureplex facility was put up, followed shortly by the offices of the Cold Mountain Institute.

The three buildings were built on the edge of a steep ravine leading down to Tryon Creek; the hospital, stepped in five levels almost to the creek itself, won several major architecture awards for its innovative design and imaginative use of the terrain.

In 1985, within the complex of workplace, residential units, and services completed, an entire issue of *Architectural Review* was given over to a retrospective examination of Crestwood Heights. The decision was unanimous and enthusiastically positive. Over a twenty-year period Corporate America had proved that it had a heart. The thirty-four companies in Deep Wood Park, under the management of CMI, had transformed a depressed and doomed backwater into a thriving, revitalized community that lived up to its motto: The Future Is Now.

At the intersection of Deep Wood and Crestwood Heights Road, Kelly slowed again, checking the signs. Crestwood Heights Road appeared to be a feeder to the Interstate while Deep Wood Road continued south. On her left, partially screened by a well-groomed stand of tall elm trees, she could make out the smoked-glass and brushed-steel shape of the Leisureplex and the step pyramid of the Medical Center. In five minutes she'd gone from the nineteenth century into Tomorrowland.

Crossing the intersection, Kelly guided the van through a series of pleasant, tree-lined curves as the road dipped down into what had once been called Honeyman's Hollow. Before the arrival of the Cold Mountain Institute, the hollow had been a barren mixture of broken, upslope farmland, brackish ponds fed by a halfhearted web of sluggish streams, bogs, briar patches, and deep-cut, slash-choked ravines. Even at the best of times, the people of Honeyman's Hollow had been dirt poor and by the time CMI arrived, the entire area had been almost completely abandoned.

Within less than a year the hollow had been transformed. The ravines became bicycle paths; drainage ditches were built to dry out the swampy areas; the ponds were cleaned up; roads were built, and the land was sodded. Stands of trees were judiciously thinned, while in other areas they were planted; and wherever possible, existing hedgerows and other environmental assets were maintained. It was a *Saturday Evening Post* cover by Norman Rockwell come to life, lush and green in springtime and a riot of color in the fall.

Kelly drove the van across the reconstructed covered bridge over Tryon Creek, bypassed the access roads to Orchard Park and Colony Woods, and eventually reached Greenbriar. The first of the three Crestwood Heights communities was roughly triangular, bounded by the tree-covered slope of Honeyman's Ridge to the south, a dense, boomerang-shaped tree lot to the north and a steep ravine leading down to Tryon Creek on the west side.

It was late afternoon and the slanting sun cutting down through the tall majestic trees along Greenbriar Drive had an almost magical quality. Kelly had her window rolled down and even over the whining rattle of the engine she could hear the high-pitched electric buzz of the cicada and the softer shuffle of the wind as it tumbled through the leaves. She could imagine the avenue between the trees in winter: stark, without being ominous, with a light dusting of frost on the hard ground, dried leaves swept into random banks across the forest floor, worthy of a painting. Now, *there* was a thought. She hadn't painted for her own pleasure in years.

She came out of the screening trees and found herself facing a large expanse of open parkland. There was a small pond, complete with a family of ducks, high-fenced tennis courts, swings, teeter-totters, a roundabout, and a wading pool. On one of the courts a couple in whites lobbed balls back and forth while a screaming tribe of three- and four-year-olds raced around the play equipment under the watchful eyes of several mothers. On the far side of the park she could see curving rows of houses and beyond that the humped shape of Honeyman's Ridge. Somehow, after the stage-set emptiness of the town and the open countryside beyond, the simple, well-populated surburban scene was almost shocking.

Following Rebecca Quinn's directions, Kelly skirted the park and turned onto Fox Run. The houses were large, contemporary ranchers with no attempt at colonial or Jeffersonian silliness, some of the roofs equipped with large solar panels, and without a single TV antenna to be seen. Kelly noted and approved of the fact that the houses had clearly been fitted into the existing landscape, and even in its earliest days the community hadn't been one of those flat, graded checkerboards with spindly maple saplings planted every fifty feet. In some places, large boulders had been left in the ground, incorporated into the landscaping; some of the houses stepped down inclines, while others were carefully placed among groups of long-standing trees.

Erin Park, her uncle's street, turned out to be a short cul-de-sac on the edge of the community, facing the L-shaped extension of the park she'd seen as she drove in. The houses here were smaller than the ones on Fox Run and from the absence of tricycles and other paraphernalia on the sidewalks, she guessed that it was a street reserved for older, or at least childless, people.

Number 46 was at the end of the cul-de-sac turnaround,

standing alone on a large lot that backed onto the Tryon Creek ravine. As Kelly pulled the van into the driveway and turned off the engine she felt a dreamlike uneasiness almost overwhelm her. She climbed down out of the van, her legs a little rubbery after the long day's driving, and studied the house. It was magic. Three and a half rooms in Tribeca transformed into this:

The single-story house was stepped back in three stages: garage, entrance, and then the main house. The main living section was windowless, earth bermed up to the roof level and thickly planted with shrubs. At the peak of the lightly pitched cedar-shingled roof Kelly could see a low, glass pyramid skylight. Considering the site, it was obvious that the windows in the house would all face the ravine, giving the best view. Turning away briefly, she banged down the stiff handle of the van's side door and slid it back. Ignoring the crammed pile of boxes, she pulled out her overnight case and slammed the door shut again. The rest of it could wait until tomorrow.

Reaching the front door, she put down the bag and dug out the electronic key-card Rebecca Quinn had given her. She slipped it into the door slot, and the door opened with a clicking sound. Picking up the bag, she stepped inside, startled as the overhead light in the foyer came on automatically. On her left was a door, probably leading down to the basement. On the right-hand wall there was some sort of electronic master control—lights, appliances, alarm system, sprinklers. Ignoring the switches, Kelly moved slowly through the house, turning the lights on as she went.

Beyond the foyer was a short central hall. To the left was a compact kitchen followed by a long, narrow dining room and living room; a glass wall ran the length of the house, with two sets of sliding doors leading to a flagstone terrace that looked out over the ravine. Part of the opposite wall was glass as well, facing into the atrium below the large skylight she'd seen outside. Flicking a wall switch, she drew in a breath. Her uncle had stocked the interior greenhouse with a hundred different kinds of tropical plants and let them run wild, creating a miniature jungle. She laughed. It was a long way from the half-dead fern she'd left behind in her office. On the other hand she had a notoriously brown thumb, so if the jungle was to survive she'd need expert help.

There were two bedrooms and a study, each one with a wall facing into the atrium garden. The largest, with a bathroom and dressing room, was obviously her uncle's and had the stark utilitarian fittings of a confirmed bachelor. The second bedroom was small and equally plain. Feeling a little queasy about sleeping in the bed in which her uncle may have died, Kelly dropped her bag in the smaller room and made her way back to the living room and the study leading off it.

Kelly had barely known her uncle, but the room spoke volumes about him. Three out of four walls were lined with bookcases crammed to overflowing with a hodgepodge of books on every subject imaginable, but heavily weighted toward film biographys, histories, and bound screenplays. Running the Strand had obviously been more than just a business for him.

From the look of things he'd been equally interested in computer technology. In addition to three full shelves of software packages, there was a large modern desk/work station in the middle of the room and sitting on it was a custom computer, printer, digitizer, and a telephone modem. Kelly frowned; the luxurious computer setup didn't seem to go with the kind of man who'd operated a run-down movie theater. She shrugged it off. She didn't know anything about computers, and even less about her uncle. She let out a jaw-cracking yawn and left the room, turning off the light and shutting the door. The sun was almost down now, long, butter yellow splashes of light filtering through the trees at the crest of the ravine and pouring into the living room.

Kelly went to the window wall and looked down into the ravine. There the light had already gone and everything was lost in dark green shadow. There was something primeval and almost frightening about the deep slash in the earth, like a wound that was a million years old and still lay unhealed. In daylight it would be a wonderful place, full of changing light and color, but now it was the first step into a child's nightmare, the real-life opening of Maurice Sendak's *Where the Wild Things Are*.

Not a bad idea. For quite a while now she'd played around with the idea of doing a kids' book and maybe this was it. She lit a cigarette and stood staring down into the ravine. Little girl moves from the big city to a new town in the country. Make it contemporary. Little girl's mother and father are divorced but they have joint custody. Little girl is with her mother for the summer holidays. Mom has a new job and ignores little girl. Little girl goes down into the ravine to play and . . . something happens. "You can play there when it's light, my dear, but don't stay after the sun goes down." Hey, not bad at all! She even had a title: *After the Sun Goes Down,* by K.K. Rhine.

The doorbell rang and she almost swallowed her cigarette. It was one of those triple chime things that sounded as though you were listening to an announcement in an airport and Kelly was completely unprepared for it. Flustered, she headed for the front door, threading her way through the unfamiliar pattern of furniture in the last dusky light. Reaching the foyer, she pulled open the door.

"Hi! My name is Carlotta Nordquist. Number 42." The bubbly voice was coming from the cupid's-bow lips of a woman in her late fifties. She was dressed in a tentlike Hawaiian print dress and her hair was the color of strawberry jam—a younger, chubbier Lucille Ball doused in far too much perfume. Not what Kelly needed five minutes away from a hot shower and a good night's sleep.

"Hi."

"You're—?"

"Kelly Rhine. Nat Somerville was my—"

"Uncle?"

"Right." Oh God. One of those women who never let you finish a sentence for yourself.

"It was terrible." The woman shook her head sadly.

"I beg your pardon?"

"Losing him. Nathan was a wonderful neighbor. You could count on him, you know?"

"I didn't know my—"

"Well, that's in the past now, isn't it. You've taken over the house?"

"Yes, at least—"

"Martin and I saw you arrive, of course. We're just a couple of old snoops. I suppose you'll be waiting for your furniture to arrive now, won't you?"

"No, I—"

"It doesn't matter. Nathan never kept anything in the house at the best of times, so I suppose your cupboard is bare. Martin and I insist that you come over for some dinner."

"That's very kind of you but—"

"I said we insist. You have your key?"

"Yes, but—"

"Reset the alarm?"

"Alarm?"

"Of course, dear." Carlotta Nordquist breezed by Kelly, the hem of her hostess gown billowing like a parachute. She examined the switch panel Kelly had seen when she arrived, tapped a couple of buttons, and returned to the doorway, taking Kelly by the elbow. "All set." The older woman smiled. "Not that we have anything to worry about in this neighborhood, although God knows you can't be too careful these days."

Not knowing quite how to escape, Kelly found herself wafted out of the house on a wave of Carlotta Nordquist's punctuation-free conversation, shrouded in a pungent cloud of My Sin.

CHAPTER 4

"*Hair*," Martin Nordquist said as he settled into the overstuffed, flower-printed chair in the small living room. Kelly eased herself down onto a suspiciously soft-looking couch with the same print. Around the corner in the kitchen she could hear Carlotta humming a vaguely familiar show tune while she made coffee.

"I beg your pardon?" Kelly said politely. There was a huge ashtray on the end table beside her, so she felt comfortable taking out her cigarettes.

"*Hair*," he repeated, waving a plump, pink hand around the room. "It paid for all of this."

"I thought you said you were a theatrical agent," Kelly said. Conversation over the surprisingly tasty Irish stew in the breakfast nook had revolved around the short, owl-eyed, bald-headed man's career as a booking agent in New York, and Carlotta's past as a show girl on Broadway.

"Sure." Martin nodded, beaming. "I had 'em all at one time or another. Everything from ventriloquists to dog acts. I was the best, and I got even better when I married Carlotta." He cast a proud glance back toward the kitchen and Kelly smiled. Tired as she was, she'd found herself enjoying the meal. It wasn't often you saw two people so thoroughly in love after so much time together. I Love Lucy married to a sixty-five-year-old Howdy Doody with a jaw-breaking Brooklyn accent.

"You were saying something about hair?" Kelly prompted.

"Right. Like I said, me and Carlotta were the best. Bar mitzvahs, trios for weddings, lot of variety acts for the Poconos, that kind of thing. Good steady money, enough to put a little away even—but nothing big, you know? All those years Carlotta and I dreamed of something big, like finding a Tony Bennett or maybe getting into something like 'Sid Caesar and the Show of Shows.' "

Carlotta appeared with a tray of coffee things and a plate of butter cookies. Kelly passed on the cookies but accepted a steaming cup of coffee. She could feel tiredness waiting in the wings and a shot of caffeine wasn't going to keep sleep at bay for long.

"Twenty years of Robbie the Wonder Dog and Marvello the Magician," Carlotta sighed, sitting down beside Kelly and crossing her legs beneath her on the couch. "You mind, dear?" She touched the package of cigarettes between them and Kelly shook her head. Carlotta tapped one out of the pack, deftly ripped off the filter, and lit up, sending out a gush of smoke from her pursed lips, followed by two snorting commas from her nostrils. Martin frowned, clearly not approving, but he said nothing. Kelly took the ashtray off the end table and put it on the couch as Carlotta leaned back and continued her story.

"Anyway, it was enough. We deserved better. I always told Marty that, but we just kept slugging away, you know? I thought to myself, What are we going to do when we get old? We had a shoe-box apartment in the Bronx and a hole-in-the-wall office on Broadway. Our neighborhood was turning into a war zone and the coffeehouses were stealing all the business away. I mean, what did me or Marty know from folk singers? Simon and Garfunkel? Lawyers maybe, or accountants.

"But Marty said we should just keep going and something would come along. I thought, I did vaudeville with my parents—may they rest in peace—I did burlesque, even USO, and then twenty years with Marty on top of that when I got varicose and had to retire. So what were we going to do? Put on Beatle wigs? I was worried, let me tell you, dear. But Marty was right, Marty was always right about those things."

"I still don't see what this has to do with hair," Kelly said, confused.

"Not hair, dear," said Carlotta. "*Hair*. You know: 'This is the dawning of the age of Aquarius . . . when the moon is in the seventh house, and Jupiter aligns with Mars.' God knows what *that* meant."

"The musical!" said Kelly, finally understanding.

"And what a musical!" murmured Martin. He bit into a butter cookie, ignoring the fallout of crumbs raining down onto his neatly buttoned cardigan.

"But who knew that back then?" asked Carlotta. "Nobody knew Ragni, and MacDermot was a Canadian, of all things. But Marty knew. They went everywhere trying to find investors. Marty comes home one night and says, 'Carlotta, I just invested our life savings in a musical about sex and drugs and draft dodging. It's going to be a hit.' I almost died."

"More than a hit," Martin said softly from the other side of the small room. "It was the Polaroid of musicals. And we bought five points. It took everything we—"

"A few weeks later he brings home the book and I read these lyrics and I almost die again," Carlotta interrupted. "You have to remember, dear, Lyndon Johnson is president and they've got songs about"—she hesitated, stumbling over the word—"masturbation. See? Even *now* I can hardly say it. Then I find out half the show is going to be done with no clothes on. I see our life savings flying out the window, the FBI coming to our door. My God! We lived through McCarthy. We knew what could happen. But Marty was right."

"You owned five percent of *Hair?*" said Kelly, astounded. She could still remember the words to most of the songs, even after all these years.

"Not *owned,*" Carlotta said, smiling happily. "*Own*. To this very day. We were one of the first investors. We got a piece of it all: the Broadway version, the album, the foreign runs, the movie years later—even the revival. I thought it was crazy. I told Martin, 'The kids who'll want to see this don't have the price of a bus ticket to Jersey, let alone a good seat in a Broadway theater,' but Marty had it figured out. It wasn't for the kids, it was for their parents and for all the ones who didn't grow their hair or drop out of school or take drugs or have sex with everyone including the milkman. Marty knew." She glanced fondly at her husband.

"We stayed two more years," Martin said. "After that it was ridiculous. We had more money than we knew what to do with. Carlotta saw an ad for Crestwood Heights and we came down to take a look."

"It was love at first sight," Carlotta said. "They took care of everything for you and it had everything we wanted. This whole neighborhood—eight blocks on the ravine and the park—was set aside for people without children—retired people. The Cold Mountain office even had an investment plan. A mutual fund, I think. We put our money into CMI and they guaranteed us a steady return on the investment, enough to let us do what we like. Late fall and winter we travel—Bahamas, Florida, once in a while even Europe. The rest of the year Marty helps with the Little Theatre and plays golf, and I teach tap at the school, garden a little, maybe change the furniture.''

''You've got a lovely house,'' offered Kelly, lying through her teeth. Her uncle's place was a bit too austere for her taste, but the Nordquists had gone overboard in the other direction. The house was a small one-story, with two bedrooms and a living–dining combination—every square foot of it covered with something.

The living–dining room had three stuffed chairs, three or four occasional tables, a coffee table, a dining room table and eight dining room chairs, two sideboards, and a china cupboard filled to overflowing. The walls were dotted with framed crewel work and dozens of photographs, mostly of people they'd booked through their agency.

''I think you'll like it here,'' Carlotta said, taking another cigarette. ''Everyone's friendly, crime's no problem, and there's lots to do. It's a happy place.''

''Surely not everyone is happy,'' Kelly said with a laugh. ''No matter where you live you find problems.''

''Not here,'' Martin said. ''It's a fact: Deep Wood Park employs just about everyone, there's no poverty, no slums, no crime, and the CHDC means most of the goods and services are cheaper than everywhere else.''

''What's CHDC?''

''The Crestwood Heights Development Corporation,'' Carlotta explained. ''Every home owner automatically has one share. Sort of a cooperative. A lot of big companies have research corporations in Deep Wood Park. The Development Corporation works with the Cold Mountain Institute and we pool resources.''

''I don't get it,'' Kelly said.

''It's not hard to understand really,'' Martin said. ''Take the telephones, for instance. One of the companies in Deep Wood Park is Intelecorp and one of the things Intelecorp sells is telephones. CHDC buys everyone equipment and service from Intelecorp and we get a big discount."

"It's the same with food," Carlotta went on. "Three out of four of the biggest food companies have research labs in the Park. They all banded together and came up with something called PETES—Product Testing Services. There's a PETES supermarket in each of the three communities. We get our food cheap, and they get their new products tested. All we have to do is answer the written questionnaires we get each month and the telephone survey."

"They seem to have thought of everything."

"Just about," Martin agreed.

"You know all those stories you hear about children being kidnapped?" Carlotta asked.

"Sure."

"Can't happen here." The older woman shook her head emphatically. "Every kid wears a PAL—Personal Alert Link. It's a little bracelet with some kind of microchip in it. If a child takes it off or goes outside the boundaries of Crestwood Heights, an alarm goes off. It's connected to the same system as the burglar alarms in all the houses. If a kid gets lost, you just call the PAL number and give them your child's identification number. They punch it up on their computers and locate the child."

"Pretty sophisticated," Kelly said.

"They live up to their motto, 'The Future Is Now,' " offered Martin, shifting slightly in his chair. "We were in here almost fifteen years ago, just when things were really starting up. They had cable long before anyone else and you can even get satellite service. HBO, Showtime, the Movie Channel—it's all state-of-the-art here."

"How well did you know Uncle Nat?"

"Just as neighbors," Martin said with a shrug. "He was like us, retired, but he ran the movie theater in his spare time."

"I thought the Strand was a full-time job for him," Kelly said.

"I guess it was," Carlotta said, "but he was working for CMI before that, I think."

"Doing what?" Kelly asked.

"I'm not sure," Martin said. "He never talked about it. But he was here before we were, and he sure didn't buy that house with what he was making showing movies at the Strand."

There was a long silence and Kelly barely suppressed a yawn. She put her coffee cup down on the end table and gathered up her cigarettes. "I really should get to bed," she said. "It's been a long day."

"We've kept you up," Carlotta said, frowning. Kelly stood up, shaking her head.

"No, really, I enjoyed myself. It's nice knowing I have friendly neighbors."

"Well, drop over anytime," said Martin, getting to his feet. He and Carlotta escorted Kelly to the door and stood watching as she cut across the lawn to her uncle's house. She found the key-card in the pocket of her jeans and popped the lock, then turned, giving the couple a friendly wave. They waved back and Kelly closed the door, finally letting out the yawn she'd been stifling. Nice people, but without too much prompting they'd be all over her, she decided.

She made her way to the guest bedroom, humming "Good Morning Starshine," then rummaged around in her suitcase, pulling out her toilet kit and one of her treasured and utterly sexless flannel nightgowns. She switched to "Black Boys-White Boys" in the shower and finished off with a garbled rendition of "Manchester England, England" while she was using her toothbrush and the bathroom's built-in Water-Pik. Back in the bedroom she hit the lights, slid under the covers, and sighed happily, letting her head fall back against the pillow. Home. It was an odd feeling. She spent almost thirty seconds trying to remember all the words to "Easy to Be Hard" but then gave up, gratefully allowing sleep to engulf her.

She knew who it was, even in the darkness; knew the soft smooth feel of his back and the thick urgent feeling between her legs as he moved slowly within her. How many years, how long ago? Even then she knew she'd never forget the smell of his hair—never shampoo, only soap—and the feeling of it against her cheek as he brought his mouth down on her neck, never slowing the movement of his hips. Silk.

Toby. Not the first—that had been Kirk Scottfield at fifteen on an air mattress in his garage with dust in the air and the smell of the gas from the power lawnmower. But Toby was first love, and that was 1967 in the Haight. The Mamas and the Papas? No, give it a second and she'd get it. There it was: Lovin' Spoonful, "Bald Headed Lena."

"Has anybody seen her, cute as she could be, cue-ball head as hard as lead, but that's all right with me, bop, bop, bop."

"What?" Out on the street. Main Street, and the light was very bright.

"You're having a dream dear." Carlotta, with a headband doing a little tap dance on the sidewalk. Martin, in a sheepskin vest and—my God!—hair on his head. Howdy Doody with long hair! This was no dream, this was an acid flash and she felt something tug deep in her heart, wishing she could have that moment with Toby again and wondering what had happened to him.

"She's right," bubbled Howdy. "Everything is perfectly all right here in Crestwood Heights. The Future Is Now, you know."

"You don't have to listen to him, dear," Carlotta advised. "You can listen to anyone you want as long as they don't get you."

"Who?"

"Them."

The walls of the corridor are shining white and she's running, three of them behind her, all with long hypodermics in her hand, and the public address system is firing out "Help!" by the Beatles and her heart is pounding.

Naked? Not quite. One of those hospital gowns, open at the back, fluttering like a tail, her bum in the breeze.

Strapped down. Now it's a nightmare. A face, covered in a mask, and the end of the hypodermic needle spurting something bright and glistening into the air.

"There, there, dear." Carlotta? "We just want to run a few tests and then we'll let you wake up. We just have to find out what you're all about. You'd like to know, too, wouldn't you? You'd like to know who you are."

"I want to wake up! I want to wake up right now!"

"I'm afraid that won't be possible, Ms. Rhine. There are rules in Crestwood Heights, you know."

"Now!"

"Just another minute, dear. You won't feel a thing."

And the needle comes down, slowly, heavy as lead, the

point breaking her skin, and she groans at the exquisite pain, pretending it's Toby, think of him and not the needle and maybe the nightmare will end.

But it doesn't. It goes on and on and on and then the blackness comes again.

CHAPTER 5

She woke up feeling as though she'd slept a million years, with only the faintest recollection of her dreams. Right eye closed and the left one in a squint, she stared up at the ceiling for a moment, letting her brain take out last night's garbage until she remembered where she was.

"Okay," she muttered, throwing back the eiderdown and swinging her legs over the bed. Question: Do unmarried ladies in their thirties wear jeans on a weekday in Crestwood Heights? Answer: Who cares?

After showering, she dressed in jeans and a favorite sweatshirt, bright red with NEW YORK splashed across the chest in white. She put on sneakers and went into the kitchen.

It was high-tech from one end to the other, all white, with European hinges on the cabinet doors, a built-in Jenn-Aire clone oven, and a microwave to boot. The dishes were all plain white, the cutlery was Swedish and the glassware was Corning. Nothing fancy, but all in good taste. She wondered if there might have been a little Zen in Uncle Nat's background.

Carlotta Nordquist had called it perfectly: there was virtually nothing to eat in the house and barely enough to make a cup of coffee. She made some instant, found and mixed some frozen orange juice, and with glass and mug in hand she went out to the flagstone terrace overlooking the ravine. Placing the glass and mug down on the circular patio table, she took her crumpled cigarettes out of her hip pocket and lit one. Picking up the coffee, she went to the wooden terrace railing and looked out.

Any sinister vision had vanished. According to her watch it

was just past eight and the sun was up in a cloudless blue sky. The thick undergrowth of the ravine was half in shadow, with little shattered glints of light blinking up at her from the burbling creek far below and just enough breeze to rattle the leaves pleasantly. She sipped from the mug and smoked, enjoying the play of warm sun on her face combined with the dew-cool morning air. Usually at this time of day she'd be right out there with the rest of the horde trying to rope and hog-tie a cab on Broadway.

So what *was* she going to do today? Play heiress for a little while longer and lounge around the house, maybe work out a storyboard for her kids' book project? It was an odd sensation having choices and it occurred to her that she hadn't had this much freedom in years. No man, no job, no worries.

Not quite. She did have a job, if she wanted to take it: running the Strand. She had something to worry about, too: if she didn't get some food in the house she'd either starve to death or find herself mooching off the Nordquists again. That was incentive enough—a trip into town to give the theater a preliminary check and then a shopping expedition.

She finished her coffee, downed the glass of orange juice, and went back to the kitchen. Glass and mug into the dishwasher for later, and cigarette butt into the sink. Tacky, but it looked as though Uncle Nat had been a nonsmoker because she hadn't seen an ashtray anywhere in the house. She made a mental note to pick up a few when she went shopping and then went outside, ignoring the switch panel in the hall. According to Carlotta there wasn't any crime in their little surburban utopia, so why bother with an alarm?

The Westphalia squatted in the drive, bug-eyed headlights staring at her. The rocker panels were starting to rust out, the front bumper had lost half its chrome, and the passenger side had a six-foot-long crease in it where a delivery truck had done a kiss-and-run a couple of years back. Not the trendy little Volvo or wood-paneled Country Squire Wagon that went with her new station in life.

She dug into her purse and pulled out the set of keys Rebecca Quinn had given her the day before: key-card for the front door; a tiny key that looked as though it might be part of the alarm system; and two others, one of which looked as though it might be for an ignition.

The garage door had the same kind of slot arrangement as

the front entrance and since there was no other electronic key she slid the one she had into the aperture. There was a whining sound and the door began to slide up. Kelly took a couple of steps back out of the way.

"Well, I'll be damned," she whispered. The garage was as neat and austere as the rest of the house, with none of the standard glut of lawn chairs, barbecues, and coils of garden hose. Standing neatly on the unstained concrete floor was a jet black, mint-condition Aston Martin DB5, the 1964 model used in *Goldfinger*.

Kelly walked into the garage, running the fingers of one hand along the classic lines of the car's body. She frowned thoughtfully. The more she found out about her uncle, the less she seemed to understand him. What kind of man leaves an obviously high-paying job to run a small-town movie house, lives in a designer house but furnishes it out of a catalog, and tops it all off by driving a collector's sports car?

It suddenly occurred to her that the car was now hers and she giggled nervously. She was instantly angry with herself—giggling was for teenage girls. She flipped through the keys and tried the smaller of the two standard ones in the door lock. It opened with a solid *click* and she smelled leather and oil. It was ridiculous; she felt like one of those idiot women on "Wheel of Fortune."

But that's what it was, of course. She'd just won the jackpot and like any red-blooded American woman she had giggled. The next stage was paranoia. Okay, guys. I won the house and I won the car, so what's the catch? But there wasn't one.

Kelly slid behind the wheel, feeling the deep bucket seat wrap around her with the same sensation she got when she tried on a really expensive pair of leather gloves at Saks. Not quite as good as slipping into bed with a man for the first time, but close—and without any of the performance pressure.

She placed one hand tentatively on the oversized steering wheel and slid the bigger of the two keys into the ignition. It was crazy, but somehow she knew that if she started up the car and took it out of the driveway, she'd be accepting everything. Somehow it was the last step bridging her old life with the new one. *Drive this car, honey, and there are no more excuses*. You've spent your whole damn life telling yourself that you're good, but not great. Last night you had a terrific idea for the kids' book you've always wanted to do, you've got the time and the money to do it, and now you've got this car. Take possession of it and you take possession of your life.

On the other hand she could take Quinn's offer, sell everything and put it into a retirement fund, and go back to work, maybe moving back to San Francisco or L.A. so she could fool herself into thinking she'd really changed her life. Take the risk or go for security, and it all seemed to focus down to the car.

"Screw security," she whispered, and turned the key.

The sound filled the garage with a deep, muscular burble that vibrated up through the seat and into the back of her thighs. She peered into the rearview mirror and saw that there was lots of room to get around the old bus. Looking down, she checked the gearshift pattern and depressed the clutch. It went down smoothly and she gingerly pulled the short-throw stick up into reverse. It engaged with a simple, definite *click* and she eased off the clutch, biting her lip. Too fast and she'd wind up on somebody's front lawn.

The car rolled easily out of the garage, and nudging the wheel a little, she maneuvered around the camper. There was a little bump as she went over the curb and then she was on the street. Putting the gearshift into neutral, she checked the instruments and saw that the speedometer went up to 160 and she knew it wasn't lying. Shifting into first, she headed off down Erin Park, getting the feel of the powerful vehicle as she drove.

By the time she found Greenbriar and the first of the morning traffic heading to work, she was feeling comfortable with the car; by the time she reached Deep Wood Road, she was in love. The independent front suspension and the live rear axle kept the car glued to the road and it accelerated magnificently for a vehicle that weighed almost two tons. She was doing seventy before she reached the high end of second gear and she was almost angry when she had to slow, turning away from the traffic heading up into the industrial park.

She followed High Point Road down into the town, retracing her route of the day before, dropping back into first gear as she turned onto Main Street, slipping into the shaded tunnel created by the overhanging trees. There were all sorts of parking spaces, so she pulled a tight U-turn in front of the

Strand, slipped the car neatly between a pair of white lines, and turned off the engine. She sat there for a moment, shaking her head and feeling the adrenaline tingle in her arms and fingers. It was a hell of a way to start your day and she loved every pulsing second of it.

"Uncle Nat, you must have been really something," she said, patting the steering wheel. She opened the door and climbed out of the car, locking it behind her. Crossing the sidewalk, she pulled out the second set of keys and opened up the theater.

The air inside the darkened lobby was stale and heavy—old popcorn, dust, and floor wax. She unlatched the other doors and left them wide open, letting the early morning air sponge away the cloying musty smell. Uncle Nat had died less than a month before, but it felt as though the Strand had been closed for much longer than that. If she hadn't known better, Kelly could have convinced herself that it had been shut down thirty years ago. It certainly *looked* like something out of the past.

The lobby was rectangular, forty feet by twenty or so. To the left was a glassed-in ticket booth with the manager's office tucked in behind it; to the right, a wide stairway leading up to the second-floor balcony and boxes. Beside the stairs was a pair of doors: GENTS and LADIES, separated by the standard water fountain. The walls were a dark green, picked off with lighter green lozenge shapes framed in yellow-white molding. The floor was heavy linoleum with a marbled pattern almost completely obscured by decades of old wax.

There were two big swing doors leading into the theater itself, and between them was the concession counter. The menu board on the wall behind it was blank, the glass shelves were barren, and the big popcorn maker beside the soda fountain was empty, the high glass bowl filmed with dust. The soda fountain itself was a collector's item, tall spigots made out of stainless steel and topped with Bakelite pulls. The word *Coke* was done in chrome and riveted to the front of the machine, the letters worked in the scrolling "classic" typeface. Between the fountain and the candy shelves was an old-fashioned hot-dog cooker, the kind with a paddlewheel rotisserie.

Kelly had been fascinated with those machines when she was a kid, and standing in line waiting for her popcorn and drink she used to watch the fleshy, sweating, bright red tubes of pseudomeat impaled on the long spikes. The spikes had heating elements built into them, so the dogs cooked from the inside out and if you waited too long they'd be charred in the middle and shriveled on the outside. God! What nostalgia.

Bypassing the counter, she pushed open one of the doors leading into the theater and used an overhead latch to keep it ajar. She stepped inside, letting her eyes adjust to the gloom and looked around, walking slowly out from under the low ceiling that was actually the balcony floor. She sneezed in the dusty air, the sound echoing around the cavernous auditorium. Once again there was a familiarity that took her back to her childhood.

Worn carpeting on the slightly sloping floor and a single block of seats with aisles on the left and right. At the far end of the big hall there was a low stage and beyond that a rippling, fake-velvet curtain in dark red covered the screen. There were two exits, their safety lights dark, tall speaker boxes mounted on the walls every fifteen feet or so, and a single gigantic chandelier hanging from the ceiling.

One of local theaters back in San Francisco used to have one just like it and none of the kids dared use the seats right underneath it for fear that enormous wasp nest of glass prisms and wrought iron would come ripping out of the ceiling one Saturday afternoon. It was the kind of childhood myth that went along with worrying about going blind when the lights went down or thinking about rats running around under the seats while you were watching Vincent Price up on the screen.

Kelly turned and peered up at the balcony. More nostalgia: a brass rail to keep you from falling over, ten steep rows going back to the rear wall, and the projection booth with its four rectangular holes. At fourteen the best seats in the house were back there where it was too dark for your friends to see you making out. She smiled. How many sticky hands had groped under how many sweaters and pure white double-A bras up there? And no matter what anyone said, she knew it rarely ever amounted to much more than that.

"Hello!" The voice came booming out of nowhere and Kelly jumped. Heart thumping, she looked back to the doors leading into the theater and saw a dark shape outlined in the light from the lobby. The figure stepped forward, lost in the darkness under the balcony overhang for a moment.

"Who is it?" Kelly asked nervously. The figure reappeared a few feet in front of her: a tall, balding, broad-shouldered man in his mid-thirties but wearing a tweedy business suit that made him look ten years older.

"Phillip Granger. Crestwood Heights Rotary Club among other things." She shook his extended hand. The grip was firm and dry, but the man held her hand for just a little too long.

"You scared me," Kelly admitted.

"Sorry." She could see his grin in the darkness, two gleaming rows of perfect teeth. Caps. "I saw you burning up the asphalt coming into town so I followed you in. Watching you handle that car was like seeing a ghost. Nathan used to drive it the same way."

"You were a friend of Uncle Nat's?"

"I knew him." Granger nodded. "We had some business dealings together."

"Oh." Kelly did not know what else to say. She began walking back toward the lobby and Granger came with her. In the light he turned out to be shorter than she'd first thought and quite good-looking except for a chin her mother would have called weak.

"I heard you were going to reopen the theater so I thought I'd come and talk to you as soon as possible."

"About what?"

"The Strand." Granger took out a pack of cigarettes and offered one to Kelly. They were Camel filter, her old brand. Feeling guilty, she took one and let Granger light it for her with an expensive-looking butane lighter.

"What about the Strand?" she asked.

"Your uncle was having trouble making ends meet. He and I were working out an arrangement just before he died."

Here it comes, thought Kelly. Maybe Granger was the interested party Rebecca Quinn had on the hook. "What kind of an arrangement?"

"I'm director of the Crestwood Heights Little Theatre," Granger explained. "We've got our own place at the Leisureplex, but we've been thinking about doing a summer festival. Shaw mostly."

"Here at the Strand?"

"That's right. We have several summer-stock directors

interested. We'd use some of our own people and bring in professionals for the summer."

"Sounds ambitious," said Kelly. "And expensive."

"I'm also on the board of the Crestwood Historical Society." Granger smiled. "We're the ones responsible for reconstructing Main Street. There are funds available for this kind of thing. I've gone over the statistics pretty carefully. Given the number of tourists coming through Crestwood between mid-June and September, I think we could do quite well, and it would be a welcome addition to the town."

"I have my own ideas about the Strand." Granger was pleasant enough, but there was something about him that she didn't like. He was too cool, too sure of himself.

"Such as?"

"I plan to open up a rep movie house," she answered, her tone making it quite clear that it really wasn't any of Granger's business. "I think you'd get more people coming to a Bogart festival than you would for *Major Barbara* or *Androcles and the Lion*."

"Perhaps. But I think Shaw would be more in keeping with the atmosphere we're trying to create here in town. I think the other members of the Historical Society would agree." He smiled coldly. "In fact, I can guarantee it." There it was, the velvet-veiled threat. Just as she'd figured, "we" was the local band of "ambience" vigilantes.

"Are you saying that I can't do what I want with the Strand?" asked Kelly, bristling.

"Not at all," Granger said, still smiling and showing his teeth. "But as I said, your uncle was having financial troubles before his death, and we were working on an arrangement. There's nothing to say that you couldn't have your movie theater during the rest of the year. The CHLT would only need it for the summer months and as I said, we're in a position to refurbish the theater completely."

"I haven't seen anything here that a little elbow grease wouldn't take care of."

"You might have a chat with the fire chief about that," Granger commented blandly. "According to my information you're going to need all new seating and a fire retardant curtain. Not to mention the lack of parking."

"There's enough parking for an army outside," Kelly said.

"Now perhaps." Granger shrugged. "Wait for a few more

weeks. By the end of June there are so many tourists in town you can barely get down the sidewalks. Crestwood has become quite the fashionable day trip from Durham and Raleigh. We're in all the tour books. They come by the busload."

"Great. And when they come, I'll give them Hitchcock, hot dogs, and popcorn with real butter. I might even put a sign up outside that says, 'Come on in, it's cool inside.' "

"Just think about what I've said, Miss Rhine. This isn't New York, and here you're an outsider."

"I'll think about it, Mr. Granger."

"Phil," the tall man said, his smile still intact. "Please." He turned on his heel and walked out through the main doors of the theater. Kelly stood where she was, back against the concession counter, and watched him go. Arrogant son of a bitch. She ground out his cigarette in one of the big sand-filled ashtrays, then looked around the lobby, hands on her hips.

Pretty dingy. Half a dozen of the big linoleum tiles were curling up, the walls had decades of nicotine on them and the outside of the theater was a disaster. If Granger was right and she did have to get new seats and a replacement curtain it would cut pretty deeply into the money she'd inherited. On top of that she didn't know the first thing about running a theater, and being a longtime movie buff wasn't going to get her very far.

"Welcome to Crestwood Heights," she muttered. She went out to the street, then locked up. She headed down to a place on the way in, Aunt Bea's Sweet Temptations Coffee Shop. Real coffee, another cigarette, and something made out of chocolate—three out of four major vices and all before eleven o'clock in the morning.

Aunt Bea's was just in from the corner of Piedmont Street between Yesterdays and the Open Cupboard Bakery. Neither the antique store nor the bakery was open and both had old-style wooden shutters covering their windows. In front of the open door to Aunt Bea's there was a life-size cigar store Indian, but instead of cigars in his hand, the wooden man held a large, imitation chocolate chip cookie.

Inside, the floors were stripped and varnished pegged softwood, the walls were papered in a blue-and-white print, and the furniture was reproduction bentwood. There was a glass display case against the back wall and a counter with stools running up to a cash register close to the front door. There wasn't anyone to be seen. Kelly sat down on one of the stools and waited, reading the hand-printed menu on the blackboard on the wall in front of her. Aunt Bea served everything from double espresso to mint tea, and peanut butter cookies to chocolate mousse.

"Anybody home?" she called out after a long moment.

"Be right with you!" The voice came from a doorway at the back of the store. A few seconds later a man appeared carrying a tray of butter tarts. He loaded them into the refrigerated display case and then came around behind the counter. Late thirties with a heavy shock of longish dark brown hair, shot with gray, medium height, and wearing a United States Marine Corps T-shirt. Muscles rippled under the thin cotton and the bare biceps and forearms were thick and corded.

Under the hair the man's face was lean and angular. He had the dangerous good looks of an actor, but the hardness was offset by the eyes—large, thickly lashed, and a strange silvery gray color that went with the salt-and-pepper hair. He also had a single earring, a tiny silver salamander. He was wearing a strange, musky after-shave and it took her a few moments to pin it down. It was patchouli oil, the kind of thing the guys always put on back in the sixties.

"What can I get you?" he asked. Nice teeth—not as perfect as Granger's, but the smile was a hell of a lot more sincere.

"Very strong coffee and something really caloric." She smiled back.

"Double espresso and a rum ball. How's that?"

"Heaven. Paradise if you happened to have a cigarette to go with it."

"Winston okay?"

"Perfect." He pulled out a red-and-white pack from under the cash register, plucked a book of matches out of a box, and slid them down to her. A moment later he was back with a cup of steaming aromatic coffee and an intimidating lump of chocolate on a small plate.

"No rum balls, so I brought you a chocolate mountain instead."

"What's a chocolate mountain?" she asked. He pulled out

a fork and napkin from beneath the counter and set them down beside her.

"Specialty of the house. Raw chocolate cookie dough dipped in one hundred percent dark swiss chocolate. Deadly."

"Wow," Kelly said, taking a tiny forkful and chewing on it.

"You bet. It's supposedly an aphrodisiac, but we sell to just about anyone. Good for days when you get up on the wrong side of the bed, menstrual cramps, and just about any mid-life crisis you could name. Speaking of names, you must be Kelly Rhine, Nathan Somerville's niece."

"I'm beginning to think this place is a goldfish bowl," Kelly said around another forkful of chocolate. "How did you know who I was?"

"Crestwood *is* a goldfish bowl, believe me," he laughed. "Especially when you come roaring down Main Street in Nathan's Astro Martin. My name is Robin Spenser, by the way. Mind if I join you?"

"Not at all." Spenser went back to the espresso maker, pulled himself a cup half the size of Kelly's, and sat down on a stool set behind the cash register.

"I saw you opening up the Strand a little while ago," Robin said. "And Phil Granger paying his respects."

"Good old Phil," Kelly said. She finished off the chocolate mountain, lit one of the Winstons, and sipped at the hot coffee.

"He has that effect on a lot of people," laughed Robin. "What did he want?"

"The Strand. He wants to start up a George Bernard Shaw festival."

"Oh God!" Robin moaned, shaking his head. "Not that again. He tried that on your uncle."

"He said they had an agreement."

"Horse puckies," Robin grunted. "Phil Granger is a bully. He's VP of Medtech Industries, director of the Little Theatre, on the board of the Historical Society, and plays organ for the Choral Society. If Crestwood or the Heights had a mayor, he'd be it. Not to mention the fact that he never sets foot in here. I'll bet you even money he was a gay-basher when he was a kid. He and Aunt Bea do *not* get along."

"Aunt Bea is gay?"

"I'm Aunt Bea." Robin grinned. "Old Phil thinks it's

sacriligious that a store run by a man should be named after a woman, especially when the man running it is a gay ex-marine. It upsets his view of the world."

"Screw Phil," Kelly said. Robin put one hand to his cheek in an exaggerated gesture of horror.

"What a thought!" he whispered, eyes wide. He dropped the pose and shook his hand. "I'm sure Phil thinks I'm bribing the children of Crestwood Heights with fudge brownies, but the truth is I've been a monk for the past couple of years. I was living in Florida, running a place pretty much like this, but it got to the point where having sex was like playing Russian roulette. Not to mention all the Colombians in sharkskin suits trying to buy my business so they could have a legit front."

"What made you choose Crestwood?" asked Kelly.

"They ran an ad in *Frobes*. 'The Future Is Now' and all that. I came up and took a look, liked what I saw. This place was up for sale and it has an apartment upstairs, so I cashed in my chips."

"Did you sell to a Colombian in sharkskin?" Kelly laughed.

"Two French-Canadians in leisure suits. They turned it into a donut shop." He shook his head and took a sip of espresso. "So what about you? Going to open up the Strand again?"

"Yup." Kelly nodded. "Not as a legit theater, though, Granger's right, there's not a big enough market and there's too much competition from the theater complex. I was thinking of a rep house."

"It might work." Robin nodded. "Nathan was leaning in that direction just before he died. He even had some leads out to distributors."

"You're kidding."

"He put a twist on it, though. Instead of the standard Garbo festivals and all of that, he wanted to bring back episodes from old television shows and run them in sequence. "Have Gun Will Travel," "The Millionaire," "Four Star Playhouse," that kind of thing. Stuff that's been out of syndication for a long time. He had the connections for it, too, of course."

"What do you mean?" Kelly asked.

"You don't know much about your uncle, do you?"

Kelly shrugged and shook her head. "Not much, except

for the fact that he had expensive taste in cars and that I was his last living relative."

"He was a big-time telecommunications engineer before he came to Crestwood, worked with one of the networks in L.A., and then he was with NASA for a while. From what I gather, he was right in at the beginning of the whole communications satellite thing. After NASA he worked for the feds in Washington and then Cold Mountain hired him to set up the communications system for the Heights."

"You seem to know quite a bit about him."

"He came in here a lot. We talked. I don't think you could say we were friends. He didn't have any."

"The house is like a hotel room," Kelly said, nodding. "Not much of his personality there."

"He was pretty private," Robin agreed. "Kept to himself. I've been here for two years and he only ever had the Strand open on weekends, and about a month before he died he shut it down completely."

"A little strange."

"I suppose. He made his pile long before the Strand, that's why he could give old Phil the finger. He bought the building for cash, so all he had to do was pay the taxes. It was a hobby more than anything else."

Kelly looked at her watch; it was after eleven. "I've got to run," she said. "It's been fun. Interesting. How much do I owe you?"

Robin put up a hand palm forward and shook his head. "First time is on the house, and anyway, we're fellow merchants in Crestwood. Which reminds me, there's a Main Street Businessmen's Association breakfast tomorrow. You should come."

"Really? It sounds ghastly."

"It is." Robin laughed. "But I think it would be a good idea; introduce you to the local folks. You're going to have to do it sometime."

"I suppose you're right."

"Come here around eight tomorrow and we'll go together. They have the meetings at the hotel. Two eggs over easy in real butter, bacon, and the best hash browns around. The food is worth putting up with Hugh Trask bitching about how the boys at Cold Mountain have destroyed the integrity of the community."

''Who's Hugh Trask?''

''Editor and owner of the *Crestwood Illuminator*, the local paper. He's the kind of guy who blames his hemorrhoids on fluoride in the water and thinks kids skinny-dipping in Tryon Lake is an abomination. He means well, though.''

''I like skinny-dipping,'' said Kelly. ''Maybe I shouldn't go to the meeting.''

''Eight sharp,'' Robin said, putting on a mock scowl.

''All right, all right.'' She gave the ex-marine a little wave and left the store, stepping out into the dappled sunlight. Her chat with Robin Spenser had taken away some of the bad taste left by Phil Granger, but looking up the length of the street, she had a brief uneasy moment.

She'd spent her entire life in cities, and she wasn't sure if she'd ever be comfortable with the incestuous closeness of a small town. In fact, she wasn't sure she *wanted* to be comfortable with it. She valued her privacy and respected the privacy of others, which, by the looks of it, was not how things worked in Crestwood Heights.

It wasn't until she was back in the enclosing luxury of the car that something Robin had said clicked in her mind. She sat for a moment, biting her lip, staring blindly through the windshield.

''Skinny-dipping,'' she said softly. She put the car in gear and backed out of the slot. She headed slowly up Main Street, thinking hard, sure that she was right. Last night she'd put on one of her most comfortable flannel nightgowns, but when she woke up this morning she'd been stark naked. Now, how the hell had *that* happened?

She swung the car around the clock tower and headed up High Point Road. She couldn't think of a reasonable explanation unless she'd suddenly taken up sleepwalking. She frowned and started to think about a shopping list instead. The mystery of the missing nightgown would have to wait.

CHAPTER 6

The Greenbriar PETES store was in an enclosed shopping mall just off Fox Run and adjacent to the park. There was an opening leading to an underground parking lot, but Kelly managed to squeeze into a space almost directly in front of the main entrance.

The main entrance was a false-front imitation of the stores on Main Street, discreetly landscaped with trees, but once inside there was no attempt to continue the nineteeth-century facade. Steps, an escalator, and a moving sidewalk led down to a below-grade, all-weather shopping concourse containing a dozen boutique-sized shops and the larger PETES supermarket.

At first glance it seemed as though the underground "street" was lit from above through a row of large skylights, but looking a little closer Kelly realized that the skylights were actually light boxes fitted with panes of opaque glass and lit from behind by high-powered daylight bulbs.

The mall was crowded and as Kelly moved down the concourse toward the PETES store, she spent a little time checking out her new neighbors. Mostly women in their middle and late thirties, at least half of them with preschool children in tow. Almost no blacks, even fewer Orientals, and no one of any color showing signs of economic distress. Greenbriar was a classic white Anglo-Saxon middle-class community, and proud of it. The closest the people of Greenbriar got to a ghetto was Oscar's garbage can on "Sesame Street."

The PETES store was like peeking into the future of food

marketing. Kelly had never seen anything like it in her life. Instead of rows of cash registers and fluorescent-lit aisles, there was a large room that looked like a well-designed waiting room in a modern bus terminal. There were several rows of comfortable seats, each with what appeared to be a television set on a swivel bracket. About half the chairs were occupied. The only other thing in the store was a circular workstation with a large sign that said INFORMATION. In the center of the workstation a young woman was staring at her own television. Confused, Kelly approached the information desk, where the woman looked up, smiling pleasantly.

"May I help you?" she asked.

"I was told this is a food store," Kelly said. "I wanted to do some shopping."

"PETES is a food store." The little tag on her dark blouse said that her name was Peg. "It's also a drugstore. You must be new here."

"I just moved in."

"I should explain then," Peg said smoothly. She launched into what was clearly a set speech for newcomers.

"Each one of those chairs you see has a data terminal and a light pencil. First you choose your method of payment. We accept most major credit cards and if you want to pay by check, you come to me. After you've chosen your payment method, use the light pencil to choose your food or pharmaceutical categories. Brands, sizes, and cost-per-unit are shown, as well as comparisons on a cost-per-unit basis between brands. Specials show up in yellow, regular prices are shown in red.

"As you proceed, you will notice a small square in the upper right-hand corner of the screen; that shows your running total. When you've finished shopping, use the light pencil on the total square. You'll be shown a total price as well as your delivery option. You can have your shopping taken to your vehicle if you're parked in the mall facility, or it can be delivered to your home. When you're all done you put your PETES card into the slot under the screen and that's that."

"I don't have a PETES card," Kelly said.

"You have a key-card for your residence." It wasn't a question.

Kelly nodded. "Sure."

"May I have it for a moment, and also the credit card you wish to use."

Kelly rummaged around in her shoulder bag and produced her MasterCard and the house key. She handed them to the girl, who in turn swiveled in her seat and began punching in numbers on a keyboard hidden under the workstation counter.

Watching over her shoulder, Kelly saw a stream of information come up on the data terminal. A few seconds later the woman turned again and handed back the key, the MasterCard, a third piece of plastic, this one in dark blue with the name *PETES* in white. "Thank you, Ms. Rhine. You're on the terminal now. If you'd like to take a seat you can begin shopping."

"May I ask a question?"

"Of course, Ms. Rhine."

"Where exactly *is* the food?"

"It's all warehoused underground." Peg was beaming. "Your order is assembled, bagged, and then delivered."

"But what if I actually want to see what I'm buying?"

"Well"—Peg frowned—"I suppose you could shop in Crestwood. They have a groceteria there, I think." She said the word *groceteria* as though it were a virus you could catch.

"I'm not in the underground parking lot. What if I want to take my groceries with me?"

"I'm afraid you'll have to have them delivered. We can only bring your order to the pickup in the underground lot."

"One more question."

"Yes?" Peg was beginning to sound a little annoyed.

"What if I want to pay cash?"

"We have no cash facility here. Check or charge only."

"Thanks."

"You're welcome." Peg went back to her terminal. Kelly crossed the pile-carpeted floor and took a seat, staring at the screen in front of her. She picked up the light pencil and hesitantly touched it to the START square on the screen, wondering if she was going to wind up with a hundred tins of cat food.

In the end she found the system quite easy to understand, and as she plowed through the seemingly endless screens of product information she realized just how shrewdly organized the PETES system was. By distancing the consumer from the product and providing a pleasant and comfortable environment, the chance of impulse buying was increased tremendously.

Even more useful was the fact that by employing data terminals PETES had a record of exactly what was purchased by whom and when. Beyond that, they could compute repeat purchases of products and by playing around with whatever demographic information they had, PETES, and the various companies providing the products, could make deadly accurate judgments concerning buying trends. It made the market surveying techniques used at places like MRC&O look archaic.

It took her less than half an hour to complete her shopping and when she finished and totaled she put her brand-new PETES card into the appropriate slot. The screen cleared, then put up the PETES name in bold blue letters for a few seconds. The screen cleared again and this time it filled with a message telling her that a single call to PETES/TELESHOP could bring PETES buying ability directly into her home. By using her television set and her telephone, she could shop at PETES, get prescriptions filled, and pay most of her bills. There was another brief commercial advertising an upcoming sale of garden furniture at PETES, and a personalized squib using her own name advised her that she could get her PETES nonfood item catalog from the information desk. Then the screen cleared and filled for a last time:

THANKS FOR SHOPPING AT PETES, KELLY.
HAVE A NICE DAY NOW, AND HOPE TO SEE YOU AGAIN SOON.

Cute but just a little bit presumptuous as far as she was concerned; Kelly wasn't sure she liked the idea of a computer calling her by her first name. No, strike that, she thought, as the machine spewed her card out of the slot. She didn't like the idea of a computer being *able* to call her by her first name. She dropped the card into her purse and stood up. She'd had enough high-tech culture shock for one day, not to mention her encounter with Phil Granger.

The groceries arrived at the house on Erin Park less than half an hour after Kelly did and by one o'clock she had everything stowed away. Feeling a little more at home with a full larder, she made herself a tuna fish sandwich and took it and a big glass of milk out onto the terrace. It was still spring-cool, but she could smell summer coming on the gentle breeze blowing along the ravine and it was hard to think about the obvious problems confronting her.

So far, Robin Spencer was her only ally in the town; Martin and Carlotta Nordquist, for all their good intentions and home cooking, didn't really count. According to Robin, Phil Granger was a big wheel in Crestwood Heights, and the ten minutes she'd spent with the man confirmed Robin's estimation of him as a bully. One way or another, Granger wanted the Strand and she hadn't forgotten the barely veiled threats about the parking and the fireproof curtain. The cap-tooth son of a bitch was going to try and sabotage her every step of the way, she just knew it.

She washed down the last of the sandwich with her milk and lit a cigarette, staring out over the ravine. The easiest thing to do would be to give up, of course. Shopping at PETES that morning had given her a taste of what living in Crestwood Heights would be like over the long haul. A safe, well-ordered community that, for all its obvious benefits, was really just an updated version of a company town. Nothing sinister, but nothing very uplifting either. Given enough time, she might even wind up being just like all those women she'd seen in the shopping mall—everyone trying to be just like everyone else, no one rocking the boat.

When, for instance, had a great American writer or great American artist ever come out of a suburban environment? Or even a great scientist, for that matter? She dragged on the cigarette and scowled. She'd seen it often enough over the past fifteen years. The friends she'd gone to art school with had wound up marrying chemical engineers and gynecologists, or taken jobs with Xerox and IBM, and when all was said and done it didn't seem as though anyone had really amounted to anything.

"Little boxes, little boxes, and they're all made out of ticky-tacky and they're all made just the same." Even after all this time she could still remember the words to the song. It had been a joke back in the sixties, a kind of reverse anthem of everything she and her friends would never do.

Which was all just a lot of elitist bullshit, of course. Had she fared any better? A free-lance illustrator who'd starved to death looking for supposedly meaningful work, baled into and out of a marriage, and finally wound up doing cutesy watercolors of kittens playing with unraveling rolls of pastel-tinted toilet paper.

The only difference was that now she had a second chance. Ever since she was a kid she'd loved movies and for a long time she'd thought she might get involved in the industry somehow. Now she had the opportunity. The Strand, firetrap curtain and all, was hers. So was this house and the Aston Martin in the driveway.

So quitting would be a rationale. Selling out would be just that, too; within a couple of years she'd be right back where she started, but just a little bit older. She frowned. For K.K. Rhine, Crestwood Heights was Custer's Last Stand. She'd give herself six months to make it or break it here, she decided, and if she failed . . . Well, hell, she'd find a gynecologist of her own.

She gathered up her plate and glass, put them in the dishwasher, and went on a detailed reconnaissance of the house. If she was going to stay on in Crestwood Heights, some changes would have to be made.

With her notoriously brown thumb any attempt on her part to keep the atrium/greenhouse going would be a disaster, but for the moment that could wait. She decided to switch bedrooms and moved her overnight case into the larger room with its picture window overlooking the ravine and its private bathroom. That done, she spent the next two hours unpacking the van, and removing the guest room furniture, which she stored in the rear of the garage. She set up her drafting table, lugged in half a dozen cardboard boxes of art supplies, and then spent another hour wandering from room to room with Uncle Nat's hammer, hanging up paintings, prints, and posters. By late afternoon she'd managed to give the house a little bit of personality; she'd also run out of steam. Ignoring the litter of boxes and crumpled paper that lay everywhere, she found a sketch pad and her favorite felt pen and escaped outside. She'd already lost too much light to go down into the ravine, so she decided on the park instead.

Erin Park Drive was less than a block long with no more than thirty houses. Kelly quickly identified six basic designs, noting that her uncle's house, *her* house now, was the only unique residence on the street. Most of them were variations on the Nordquist bungalow, some with additions, reverse plans, or carports instead of garages. Suburb or not, Kelly had to give the planners credit; it was obvious that a lot of effort had gone into working with the individual sites, and several houses had trees that were easily fifty or sixty years old.

Halfway down the street there was a gap between the houses on the east side and a gravel walkway leading into Greenbriar Park. Kelly followed the path and found herself in a sloping meadow that led down to the pond, children's area, and tennis courts she'd seen the day before. Farther east and almost hidden from view behind a magnificent stand of oaks was a low, redbrick building that had to be a school. To the west was another, lower stand of trees, and from the way they followed an erratic line at the top of the meadow Kelly assumed they marked the edge of the ravine that ran behind her house. Above it all, the sky was dotted with a score of picture postcard clouds and the air was filled with the sweet smells of freshly cut grass and wild flowers. Living in the suburbs might not be the best intellectual stimulus in the world, but if you were going to live an understimulated life, this was the place to do it. With her sketch pad under her arm, Kelly walked slowly down the path toward the children's area. If she really was going to do a kids' book she'd have to practice drawing kids.

She found an empty bench on the far side of the playing area and opened up her sketchbook. There were five children in the big sandbox, three girls and two boys, all between the ages of three and six. Beyond them were a trio of mothers talking together on a single bench, passing out Thermos cups and what appeared to be a bag of Famous Amos cookies. All three were wearing jeans, two of them were wearing tweedy jackets, and the third was wearing a battered fedora. It looked like a slightly updated Diane Keaton convention.

All three studiously ignored Kelly as she worked. She could almost hear the thought processes: she was a woman, which probably ruled out a sex pervert, but she didn't have a child with her so she was beyond the pale. Suburban sociology at work. Kelly lit a cigarette to alienate herself even more. To hell with them.

She chose the oldest of the children, a dark-haired girl wearing a quilted jacket with a vaguely Oriental look over a dark blue jumper. The child was playing alone, drawing little patterns in the sand with a stick. A study in boredom. Her mom had decreed that it was time for fresh air, so here they were. As she tried to get the child's expression down on paper, she noted that all of the children were wearing identical, dark green bracelets. The PAL devices Carlotta Nordquist had mentioned. Maybe it was a good idea—in theory, anyway—but she found the thought of bugging your own child slightly repellant, no matter how good the intentions, and even though she didn't know a whole lot about child psychology she was pretty sure that the children wearing the devices recognized the control mechanism implications. Kelly shrugged it off. Maybe in Crestwood Heights they'd turned it into some kind of rite of passage: "Well, dear, I guess if you're old enough to wear a bra you're old enough to go out without your PAL."

She concentrated on drawing the little girl, doing several quick studies of the face, then switching to full body drawings. She was vaguely aware that someone had sat down beside her on the bench, but she didn't pay any attention until the woman spoke.

"Not bad." Kelly looked up and turned her head. The woman on the bench was about her age, dressed in jeans and a navy blue turtleneck. Her hair was rusty blond, unfashionably long, and rubber-banded into a ponytail. She was also wearing lime green high tops. Not your average Lady of the Heights.

"Thanks." The woman smiled. She wasn't pretty, but there was something striking about her—large, intelligent eyes, set deep above high cheekbones and a mouth that was too wide. She had a Streisand nose and a broad, almost masculine chin. The resident dyke perhaps? Kelly stole a quick look at the left hand. The woman was wearing a gold band on the third finger along with a diamond engagement ring. Large, blue-white, emerald cut. High tops or not, she was out of Kelly's league.

"Doris Benedict," the woman said, extending a hand. Kelly stuck her pen between her teeth and shook.

"Kelly Rhine."

"An artist."

"Illustrator. Used to be, anyway."

"I haven't seen you around before. I walk through here most days. Visiting?"

"No I just moved in."

"Really?"

"Onto Erin Park."

"We're backyard neighbors," Doris said. "We live on Viewmount Crescent, that's the next street over on the ravine." She frowned. "I didn't notice anything up for sale on Erin Park. Which house?"

"Forty-nine," Kelly answered, putting a few finishing touches on her drawing. "It wasn't for sale. My uncle died and I inherited."

"Nathan Somerville?"

"That's right. Did you know him?"

"Cocktail party level. He worked for the competition."

"I don't understand."

"My husband is vice president of SCI, SatCom International. Nathan worked for Northeastern Telecommunication. Even after Nathan quit Nortel, Keith, my husband, kept on trying to get him to work for SatCom. He was supposed to have been quite brilliant. Keith said that if they'd given out Nobel Prizes for telecommunications your uncle would have had one. He could also tell terrific dirty jokes, which was a lot more important as far as I was concerned. Being the wife of a high-level executive is something like being a caterer at one long cocktail party. Gets pretty boring."

"Do you have kids?" asked Kelly.

"Banker's family. Boy and a girl. Both in school all day, praise Allah!" She looked up into the sky with a look of fervent thanks and Kelly laughed, already liking the woman. "Now I can get some work done at long last."

"What kind of work do you do?" asked Kelly. She glanced across the big sandbox at the three women on the bench. "I was beginning to think women in Crestwood Heights weren't allowed to work."

"I'm a consumer writer. I do a lot of free-lance stuff for trade magazines and I go into Raleigh twice a month to do a program called 'Marketplace' for the PBS station there."

"Sounds interesting," Kelly said. She decided not to mention her advertising background. Doris nodded.

"Crestwood's perfect for it," she said. "There are thirty-seven of the largest corporations in the United States represented in Deep Wood Park and their PR offices are usually falling all over themselves to help you out. It's also a target population; in fact, it was designed that way."

"Target population?" The phrase was vaguely familiar but she couldn't quite pin it down.

"Max Alexanian's ideal community," Doris answered with a dry laugh. "Max is the resident godfather type at the Cold Mountain Institute, sort of the guiding light behind Crestwood Heights. He wanted a bedroom community for Deep Wood Park, but one that reflected the national average as much as possible. CMI has an incredibly complicated computer program they use to vet employment applications for companies operating out of Deep Wood. The idea is to get a demographic cross section that CMI can use to predict trends. A test bed."

"PETES," Kelly offered.

"You've been there?" Doris asked.

"This morning. It was pretty bizarre."

"Terrific marketing tool though," said Doris. "And just you watch. You'll find PETES or something close to it right across the country within the next five or ten years. Food marketing on the outside is a good twenty years out of date. That's the whole idea behind Crestwood Heights. The research done here provides the basis for what will be happening for the rest of the country ten years down the line. It's kind of like peeking into the future."

"You sound like a booster," Kelly said with a smile.

"Not entirely. Not everything works." She laughed. "A couple of years ago Owens Crane, the big pharmaceutical company, tried out a line of antibiotics for kids built into a chewing gum matrix and there was an epidemic of the runs that had the filtration plant working overtime. On top of that it turned the kids' shit bright blue. There were lineups at the Medical Center. I was all set to do a story on it for my show but Keith convinced me that it would be bad PR."

"What did the FDA have to say about it?" asked Kelly.

"Food and Drug has a lab in the Park. They approved it."

"I'm not sure I fit in to the target population. Thirty-five, no kids, and self-employed."

"You can be our pet anomaly," Doris said, smiling broadly. "The exception that makes the rule. Speaking of which, how'd you like to come to one of my boring cocktail parties tomorrow night?"

"I don't really think—"

"Baloney. Are you married?"

"Not anymore."

"Even better!" Doris beamed. "You'll have all the wives nervous and all the husbands leering." She stood up. "Wear something revealing."

"But—"

"I insist. Seven-thirty, more or less, 34 Viewmount Crescent, the big Spanish-looking thing at the end of the street. You can't miss it, even in the dark. Bye!" She waved and trotted off. Kelly watched her go up the pathway toward Erin Park then disappear beyond the trees. She sighed and lit another cigarette. Tomorrow she'd get it from both sides: Crestwood Old Guard for breakfast and the Future Is Now team for cocktails.

She picked up her pencil again, hoping to get in a few more quick sketches, but the little girl and the other children had gone, and the bench with the three mothers was empty. She put the pencil back in her purse, closed the sketch pad, and headed for home.

CHAPTER 7

The following morning, expecting the worst, Kelly woke up early and prepared for her meeting with the Main Street Businessmen's Association. Going on the assumption that they would be conservative, tending toward the elderly and somewhat rurally oriented, she dressed in a simple, dark blue pleated skirt, off-white blouse, and a dark blue linen jacket. She slipped on low shoes, used almost no makeup, and kept her jewelry to a minimum.

It was a simplified version of her ''Old Fogey Ad Presentation'' outfit and made her look about as sexy as a quart basket of apples. She could have gone the Anne Klein route, topped off with a dash of Obsession behind the ears, but New York slick wasn't going to work on these people, and she was going to need their help if she wanted to get the best of Phil Granger.

She took the Aston Martin into Crestwood, keeping it down to a demure forty-five miles per hour, and pulled up in front of Aunt Bea's at exactly eight o'clock. Robin was waiting for her outside the shop and the only difference in his mode of dress from the day before was a token Harris Tweed sports jacket to cover the USMC T-shirt. The jeans and the battered suede desert boots were the same.

He greeted her with a broad smile and they headed off down Main Street in the crisp, early morning air, toward the clock tower and the Union Ridge Hotel. It was fun walking arm in arm with a good-looking man, even if he was gay, and Kelly couldn't help putting a bit of an extra twitch into her step as they strolled along the tree-canopied street. None of the stores were open and once again she had the feeling of being on a film company's back lot. Main Street, U.S.A., right around the corner from the parting of the Red Sea and not too far from Beaver Cleaver's house.

"You're looking good today," Robin commented as they crossed Laurel Street. "I hope you didn't dress up just for the breakfast meeting." Kelly glanced at her reflection in the window of Artemis Black, Boot and Shoe Maker. She could have been a minister's daughter.

"I thought I'd try to make a good impression. I'm the new kid on the block, after all."

"Don't sweat it." Robin smiled, gripping her arm a little tighter. "Any enemy of Phil Granger's is a friend of theirs and if they can accept a refugee from 'Miami Vice,' they can accept you. They're not quite the bunch of Southern crackers you might have been expecting."

They reached the clock tower and crossed Main Street to the Union Ridge. Kelly followed Robin through the ornate Victorian front entrance and across the wide, low-ceilinged lobby. A woman in her fifties wearing a frilly uniform and a look of utter boredom sat behind a high counter just inside the open French doors leading into the hotel restaurant and she nodded sleepily as Robin and Kelly entered.

The restaurant was decorated in neo-Ponderosa, complete with exposed barn-wood beams in the ceiling, fake oil lamps suspended from imitation wagonwheel chandeliers, and maple furniture everywhere. It was also empty, except for a long table in the far corner of the big room. Six men and one enormous woman were seated at the table. The men were smoking and reading newspapers and the woman was writing in a spiral bound steno book. The only vacant seats were on either side of her.

"Who's the woman?" Kelly whispered as they threaded between the empty tables.

"Laurel Hayes," Robin told her. "Laurel's Beauty Boutique just around the corner from me on Polk Avenue. Biceps like a wrestler, but she's a sweetheart. She's also chairman of the Association this year."

They reached the table and Robin made the introductions. There was a lot of chair scraping as the men rose to shake Kelly's hand and then the bored waitress appeared wheeling a food cart. She plunked down three big carafes of coffee and then started handing around plates. As far as Kelly could see there was no choice for breakfast—it was fried eggs, bacon, and hash browns or it was nothing. Another few minutes were taken up with passing around the ketchup and the salt and pepper and Kelly used the time to make sure she had the right names attached to the right faces.

Directly across from her was Dexter Carter, the pharmacist, sixties, bald with a too-round pink face that said something about his drinking habits. On his left was Cesar Rinaldi, owner of Rinaldi's Grocery, the last remaining food store in the village that wasn't a PETES, while on his right was Don Woodycrest, owner of the hardware store. On her side of the table were John Burtwhistle at the end, franchise owner of the Baskin Robbins; Charles Tennyson, the short, white-haired proprietor of the Open Cupboard Antique Store; and herself, Laurel Hayes, and Robin. At the far end of the table sat Hugh Trask, grouchy editor of the *Crestwood Illuminator*. Trask was an easy seventy, thin brown hair covering a speckled skull. He had a hooked nose, thin mouth, and piercing blue eyes that had none of the watery vagueness associated with old age. He was wearing a wrinkled, off-the-rack brown suit, white shirt overlaid by a thin knit cardigan, and a bow tie that matched his suit.

Eventually everyone began to eat and between bites Laurel Hayes got the meeting going. She had a soft, pleasant voice that didn't suit her massive body.

"I think I speak for everyone when I say welcome to Miss Kelly Rhine, the new owner of the Strand Theater. Miss Rhine recently inherited the Strand from her uncle, Nathan Somerville. I'd like to take this opportunity to offer Kelly our condolences. Not only was Nathan a member of our association, he was also a friend." The fat woman looked down at the notebook beside her plate and flipped a page, preparing to go on with her speech, but Hugh Trask interrupted, staring at Kelly over an uplifted forkful of hash browns.

"Do you intend on reopening the Strand, Miss Rhine, or has that little ferret Granger already got his hooks into you?" The man's voice was like broken glass, harsh and sharp-edged.

"Please, Hugh, I hadn't finished what I was saying," blurted out Laurel Hayes.

"Yes you had," Trask said. "Well?" He put some hash browns into his mouth and chewed, his eyes still on Kelly.

"I intend reopening," said Kelly. "I think I'll be changing the format, though."

"Oh?" Dexter Carter, the pharmacist, said, startled. "You were thinking of changing the theater somehow?"

"Porno perhaps?" Trask asked, cocking an eyebrow. "Or are we talking an art house with subtitles?"

"Neither," Kelly answered. She took a sip of coffee. "I was thinking along the lines of a repertory theater. I haven't gone over my uncle's books yet, but from what I understand he was having trouble competing with the movie complex in Crestwood Heights."

"What is this *repertory?"* asked Cesar Rinaldi. The barrel-chested Italian, napkin tucked under his chin, had already worked his way through most of his breakfast and was mopping up escaped egg yoke with a piece of toast.

"Classic films," Kelly explained. "Old favorites you don't often see on television and that rarely get into theaters a second or third time around."

"Interesting," Trask said, slightly mollified. "Festivals of old actors, that kind of thing?"

"Actors, specific themes, different kinds of films. Works by specific directors."

"I hate the Movieplex," said Laurel Hayes. "The seats are too small. And all the movies seem to be for teenagers these days."

"Will you be able to stay open year-round?" asked Trask.

"I'm not sure. I'd have to see how things went for a while. From what I understand, everyone in town does their best business during the summer."

"Hugh thinks we've become a tourist trap," offered Burtwhistle, the Baskin Robbins owner.

"Whores!" Trask snapped. "There's nothing left of the real town. We're nothing but one of Max Alexanian's pet projects."

"Oh, come on, Hugh!" groaned Tennyson, owner of the Open Cupboard. "You can't always make Alexanian your scapegoat. This town would be dead on its feet without Crestwood Heights and the Cold Mountain Institute. You know it, too."

"What I know is that you had a perfectly good office supply business before Alexanian's people put you out of work. You run that silly little shop of yours on his sufferance.

If Cold Mountain had any interest in running an antique store, he'd swallow you whole.''

''But he hasn't,'' Burtwhistle said. ''And the tourist trade is what makes this town tick.''

''It makes what's left of the town tick,'' snorted Trask. ''Every year that goes by, the Crestwood Heights Development Corporation buys up more and more property in town. If we let it go on much further, we'll all be Alexanian's tenants.''

''CHDC was responsible for getting us the grants to restore the street,'' Dexter Carver offered.

''For whose benefit?'' asked Trask. ''And I'd hardly call it restoration, Dexter. Carver's Drugstore has been in your family for almost a hundred years and you can't show me one piece of evidence to prove that it was ever called an apothecary. It's all codswallop.''

''Mr. Trask, please!'' said Laurel. ''We're off the agenda.''

''As usual,'' Tennyson muttered, pouring himself some more coffee.

''May I ask a question?'' said Kelly.

''Of course,'' said Laurel Hayes, relief in her voice.

''Is this the entire membership of the Association?''

''We're it,'' Robin answered.

''What about the other merchants on the street?''

''Ah!'' Trask said. ''You've noted the splendid apathy of our citizens.'' The elderly man pushed his plate away with the boney fingers of one hand. ''The truth of it is that once upon a time everyone with a store or office on Main Street was a member of the Association, but few feel the need now. Most of our functions have been usurped by the Main Street Restoration Society and the Crestwood Chamber of Commerce.''

''Isn't there a town council?'' Kelly asked.

''Not anymore,'' said Dexter Carver, shaking his head. ''Hasn't been one for three or four years now.''

''It started with the sheriff's office,'' Laurel explained. ''The Crestwood Heights Development Corporation thought that the Heights should have its own police authority and the town couldn't afford it, so the council ceded Crestwood Heights and Deep Wood Park to the CHDC. After a while it seemed stupid to have a sheriff's office here and the Crestwood Heights Police Department as well, so they merged. The

CHPD had better equipment, better communications, and paid higher salaries so the sheriff's office was swallowed up."

"Just like everything else around here," Trask said. Laurel ignored the comment and went on with her explanation.

"After that, things just seemed to flow naturally. The largest sector of the tax base comes from Deep Wood Park and the population of Crestwood Heights is ten times that of the town. Eventually the Crestwood Town Council dissolved and the local government reformed as the Crestwood District Municipal Association."

"Which just happens to have its offices at the Leisureplex," grunted Trask.

"It's not as though the town doesn't have representation, Hugh. I haven't missed a meeting yet," Laurel said.

"Tokenism," Trask snapped, glaring at the fat woman. "There are eight men on the executive board and you. It's all very nice and democratic but it doesn't mean a hill of beans when all is said and done. Max Alexanian runs the Cold Mountain Institute, CMI runs the executive board, and the board runs the town."

"Is Phil Granger on the executive board?" Kelly asked.

"He's the chairman," Trask told her, laughing dryly. "Are you beginning to get the picture, Miss Rhine?"

"He mentioned that the seating and the curtain at the Strand might not be up to scratch," said Kelly. "Does he have the authority to make that kind of thing stick?"

"I'm afraid so," Laurel Hayes said.

"Everything is pinned to the North Carolina Building Code and Trades Commission," Trask explained. "Which means that virtually no buildings in this town conform. He could pull the plug on all of us anytime he wants."

"But he hasn't," Tennyson commented. "Quite the contrary. With the exception of your newspaper all of us have had an increase in business, seasonal or not."

"The circulation of the *Illuminator* has nothing whatsoever to do with my feelings," Trask snarled. "The fact that Alexanian and his crew don't choose to exercise their power isn't the point. I don't like living under the aegis of a dictatorship, benevolent or not."

"I'm not an expert in municipal politics," said Kelly, "but

wouldn't it be possible for the town to re-form the original town council and take back some of its own power?''

''A bold idea, Miss Rhine,'' Trask said with a sour smile. ''But a white hope I assure you.''

''I'm afraid it wouldn't work,'' sighed Laurel Hayes. ''In fact, the idea has come up before. The demographics simply wouldn't support it.''

''Demographics my ass,'' said Trask. ''It's apathy again.''

''There are some seven hundred and fifty people living within the town limits of Crestwood,'' Laurel said. ''Most of them are . . . advanced in years.'' Here she shot a quick glance at Trask. ''The majority are content to let things go on as they are.''

''They all want bed and board at Alexanian's fancy funeral home,'' Trask said, leaning back in his chair.

''Pardon?''

''He's referring to Crestwood Lodge,'' John Burtwhistle said. ''It's a large geriatric facility CMI is building just north of Tryon Park. CMI is offering long-term discounted accommodations and care to Crestwood residents who want to move there when they retire.''

''Sign over your property to Cold Mountain and they give you a free wheelchair,'' Trask complained. ''It's an obscenity. And if you dig deep enough, you'll probably find out it's also illegal land assembly.''

''You're making this Max Alexanian sound like Attila the Hun,'' Kelly commented.

''More the Assyrian coming down like a wolf on the fold,'' answered Trask, ''and we're the fold.''

''Well, I don't see what all the fuss is about,'' said Dexter Carter. ''Things don't stay the same forever. Why do we have to assume that Crestwood Heights eventually taking over the town is necessarily a bad thing? It's not as though Mr. Alexanian has brought in prostitution and organized gambling.''

''No,'' Trask said angrily. ''He's imported a much worse form of corruption.''

''Nice melodramatics, Hugh,'' Burtwhistle said. ''But what exactly do you mean?''

''Nothing I'd talk to you about,'' the editor said. He pushed his chair back and stood up. ''I think the meeting is over. Good day to you all.'' He looked down at Kelly. ''And good luck to you, Miss Rhine. You're going to need it." Stiff-spined, Trask gave the other people at the table a curt nod, turned on his heel, and left the dining room.

It took less than twenty minutes to go through the rest of the meeting's business, most of it to do with a cooperative advertising campaign Laurel Hayes wanted to launch in the Raleigh newspapers. There was a few minutes of chitchat after that, and then Kelly and Robin followed the others out of the hotel.

"Well, what did you think of that?" asked Robin as they made their way back to Aunt Bea's.

"You were right, they weren't what I expected. Your Mr. Trask is a bit of a fire-breather."

"I don't know what to think about him anymore," Robin admitted. "He's been getting worse the past few months. He makes some good points, but I'm not sure if a lot of it isn't just sour grapes."

"Falling circulation, like Burtwhistle mentioned?"

"That, and just simple old age. He sees Crestwood Heights taking over the town and it's his past being chewed up and spit out. He's lived here all his life and it's changing. Visions of mortality."

"I know that feeling," Kelly said, smiling. "I suppose it's one of the reasons I'm here when you get right down to it. I'd like to actually do something with my life, not just go along for the ride."

"You've got more time left in your logbook than Trask does though." They reached the shop and Kelly's car.

"Well, that's enough for me," she said. "I think I'll go home and go back to bed." She unlocked the car door.

"Too bad. I thought we could have lunch together," Robin said. "I had some ideas about the Strand."

"Hold on to them. I've got to do some thinking on my own though. On top of that, I've got a party to go to this evening."

"That was fast!"

"A woman I met in the park yesterday while I was out sketching. Doris Benedict. She seemed nice enough and I thought it would be a good idea to get to know some of my neighbors."

"Boy, you sure can pick 'em!" laughed Robin. "First it's Phil Granger and now Doris Benedict."

"You know her!"

"She's the director of the Historical Society. I think she rates about number three on Hugh Trask's shit list."

"Oh God!" Kelly groaned. She flopped down into the front seat of the car. "Bad to worse."

"Don't worry about it. If Doris is having a party, every wheel in CMI will be there. You'll probably get to meet the great Max Alexanian himself. It'll be an education." He shut the car door and crouched down by the open window. Kelly fired up the engine and dropped the transmission into reverse.

"I'll give you a full report tomorrow," she said. "We'll have breakfast—alone."

"It's a date. Good luck tonight."

"Why does everyone keep on wishing me good luck?" Kelly muttered, and Robin backed away from the door as she wheeled the car out onto the street.

Kelly had shifted the camper into the garage the previous evening and the driveway should have been empty, so she was surprised to see a yellow and black Econoline van parked close to the garage doors. She was even more surprised to find the front door to the house unlocked. She'd taken enough time to familiarize herself with the control panel in the front hall, and like any good New Yorker she'd double-checked both the alarm and the lock on her way out that morning.

Stepping cautiously into the hall, she paused, listening. Vacuum cleaner noises from the back of the house and the sound of running water in the kitchen. Burglars cleaning up after themselves? It didn't seem likely. Leaving the door wide open behind her, she tiptoed down the hall and peeked around the corner into the kitchen.

A man in his late twenties wearing blue jeans and a yellow and black T-shirt was filling a plastic bucket at the sink. His hair was blond, slightly on the long side, and kept out of his eyes by a terrycloth headband. Spotting Kelly, he turned slightly and gave her a bright, frank smile.

"Morning ma'am!" The black letters on the yellow T-shirt spelled out MAID TO ORDER.

"Uh, good morning." The young man turned off the tap and dragged the bucket down to the floor.

"Pretty good weather we're having, so early and all."

"Yes," Kelly said. "Look, can I ask what you're doing?" The boy looked surprised.

"Cleaning."

"I can see that, but why? And how did you get into this house?"

"We've got a key."

"A key?"

"Sure. We can't get in to clean if we don't have keys."

"But how did you get a key to *this* house?"

"The boss gave it to us. You're on the list: 49 Erin Park."

"That's the address, but I didn't give anyone any key."

"You just move in?" asked the boy.

"Yes, but—"

"That explains it." The boy nodded. "We're working on the old owner's contract, I guess. Probably hasn't run out."

"Oh." It was beginning to make sense. Her uncle had a weekly cleaning service. "Okay. Well, I guess you'd better get back to work."

"We should be done in about twenty minutes or so. Just the bathrooms left now." He picked up the pail and disappeared.

Letting out a long breath, Kelly went into the kitchen, reminding herself that Crestwood Heights wasn't New York.

She filled up the coffee maker, took a half-pint carton of cream out of the refrigerator, and went to the cupboard for the tin of ground Colombian she'd bought the day before. Reaching blindly, trying to locate the tin, she felt a terrible stabbing pain, and jerked her hand back.

For an instant she thought she'd been stung by a wasp, and then she saw the blood and the curved, razor-sharp spear of glass still hanging in the soft flesh between the middle and index fingers of her left hand. Dumbfounded, she stared at her hand silently for a split second, and then she began to scream.

CHAPTER 8

Seen from the main entrance, the Crestwood Heights Medical Center looked like a one-and-a-half-story modern medical facility, pleasantly landscaped with trees, shrubs, and a stainless steel fountain set in the middle of a reflecting pool between the half-moon drive and the main road.

In fact, the Center was a full-sized hospital, and the building visible from the road was actually the top floor of a much larger facility built into the side of the Tryon Creek Ravine. The second, third, and fourth floors of the Center had been cut deeply into the steep bank of the ravine, each floor jutting out beneath the one above in a series of steps dropping right down to the creek itself.

The Center was almost three times the size necessary for the local population but it had been licensed by the North Carolina Medical Services Commission and approved by the AMA on the basis that as well as being a local health unit, it also qualified as a medical research facility. The approval was granted on the understanding that the Crestwood Heights Medical Center would give graduates of the University of North Carolina Medical School priority for the Center's residency program rather than going outside the state.

This suited the Center's administration since it gave them what amounted to first-draft choice of graduate students, both for research as well as general residency. Given the state-of-the-art facilities and much higher than average salaries and benefits offered by the Center, they had no trouble skimming the cream from the top of each graduating class. It was also rumored that UNC Medical School was attracting premed students from all across the country because of the school's association with the Crestwood Heights Center. By any standards then, if you were in need of medical attention, Crestwood Heights Medical Center was the place to get it.

Still in excruciating pain and with one of her uncle's handkerchiefs wrapped around her hand, Kelly had allowed herself to be bundled into the Maid to Order van by Randy, the boy she'd met in the kitchen. He drove her to the Medical Center, parked, and helped her into the main waiting room. He apologized for having to get back to work, but he told her that there was a taxi stand right beside the main entrance, and promised to lock up when he and the rest of the Maid to Order crew had finished at the house.

Even with her mind dulled by shock, Kelly was astounded by the efficiency of the Medical Center. Within less than a minute of arriving at the Center, a triage nurse carrying a clipboard had examined her wound and taken her name. Three minutes after that her name was called and she made her way weakly to the admissions desk, expecting the standard barrage of questions and a long wait as blood continued to drip into the already sodden handkerchief.

Instead, the admissions clerk asked for the card-key to the house, slotted it into her computer terminal and logged the information. At the same time the computer created a CHMC identity card, with Kelly's vital information tagged to it in the form of a bar code, as well as the name of her assigned physician. The clerk returned Kelly's key card, pinned the freshly minted ID to her blouse, and then called for an orderly with a wheelchair. A few seconds later she was being transported down a wide, softly lit corridor and into one of several emergency care cubicles.

The room was small, the walls a pale, soothing blue. It was equipped with an examining table, a small desk with a computer terminal, and a wall of glass-doored supply cupboards. Next to the examining table was a squat, black plastic taboret on casters fitted with a rack of odd-looking instruments on curly cord cables.

Kelly barely had time to look around the room before the doctor appeared. He was relatively young, no more than thirty-five or forty, wearing jeans and a light blue oxford cloth shirt under the regulation white coat. The name on his breast-pocket badge identified him as Stephen Hardy. He was good-looking with a pleasant, open face and a shock of black curly hair that tipped down over his forehead, giving him a boyish look. Kelly could see the classic stethoscope stuffed into the pocket of his coat and he carried a clipboard in his right hand.

"Hi. I'm Doctor Hardy," he said. He tossed the clipboard onto the examining table, plucked the ID off Kelly's blouse and slid the card into the computer terminal. He glanced at the screen as it filled with information, then pulled his chair around to face Kelly. Taking her damaged hand gently in his own, he carefully peeled away the handkerchief. "How'd you manage this?" he asked softly.

"Stuck my hand into a cupboard," answered Kelly. She tried not to look at the wound but she couldn't resist. She'd managed to get the large blade of glass out of her hand before coming to the Center, but she could see smaller pieces gleaming wetly. She tasted bile and looked away, swallowing hard.

"Nasty, but you'll live." The doctor smiled. "Hang on for a second." He stood up, went to the supply cupboards and returned with a loaded tray. Still feeling a little nauseous, Kelly watched as he loaded a small glass ampoule into a stainless-steel, pistol-gripped device. It had a science-fiction look to it, like something out of an episode of "Star Trek."

"What's that?"

"My version of a stun gun. A new toy from the boys at Deep Wood Park." He took Kelly's wounded hand again and gently pressed the flat-nosed end of the device against her skin an inch or so away from the wound. He flicked a triggerlike stud on the pistol-grip and Kelly felt a brief tingling sensation. Almost instantly her entire hand went numb and the pain began to recede.

"That's amazing."

"Iontophoresis," said the doctor. "It's just a simple anesthetic, but the stun gun carries charged ions of the drug under the stratum corneum. That's the outer layer of your skin. No needle trauma, no tissue bruising and the Novacain gets right into the stratum granulosum. That's why it acts so quickly."

"I can't feel a thing," said Kelly, surprised.

"Good." The doctor smiled. "Because now I'm going to practice my chain stitch on you. You mind if I do some other stuff while I'm sewing?"

"Like what?"

"You've got an almost blank chart," he said, jerking a thumb toward the computer screen. "I'd just like to get some updated information."

"Sure." Kelly nodded. "Anyone who can make the pain go away like that can do what he wants."

Working with practiced efficiency, the doctor detached several of the devices on the taboret beside her wheelchair and got to work. Rolling up the sleeve of her blouse, he fitted her with a cuff and three separate rubber suction cup electrodes. Pushing his chair around to the base of the taboret he flicked several switches and then turned his attention to her hand.

"The machines do basic diagnostic work," he explained, delicately swabbing the blood away from the gash. Reaching out without looking, he plucked a short wand on a cable from the taboret rack and eased the tip between the ragged edges of torn flesh. Using his thumb he tripped a small microswitch on the wand and Kelly heard a brief crackling sound and then smelled a tart, burning odor.

"What was that?" she asked weakly, not daring to look.

"A bit of cauterization," said the doctor. "And a blood analysis at the same time." Turning to the tray he selected a small curved needle and a roll of surgical thread. Deftly, he twisted the needle through the wound, pulling the edges together neatly into a short, puckered line. He put in six stitches, tied them off and then swabbed the wound again. "Almost done," he murmured. He chose a pair of scissors from the tray, tore open a flat, sealed package and removed a three-inch-square patch of pale pink material. Kelly spotted it out of the corner of her eyes and frowned.

"Is that a bandage?"

"Sort of," said the doctor. "Another wonder toy. It's called Proderm. Two layers, just like human skin. The top layer is a silicone–rubber–nylon compound to keep out germs and the second layer is artificial collagens and proteins to promote healing. It's less than one-sixtieth of an inch thick and you don't have to change it. When the wound is healed it'll just peel off in the shower, and the bottom layer will take what's left of the stitches with it."

"Interesting."

"It comes in all sorts of flavors too," offered the doctor, finishing up. He began unstrapping the cuffs and electrodes on her bare arm. "You can impregnate the material with quite a few drugs and use the patches to deliver medication. We're doing a series for diabetics and another series with clonidine, a drug for high blood pressure. NASA has been using the patches for three or four years now to prevent motion sickness in astronauts." He patted Kelly on the shoulder. "There you go, all done." He pushed his chair around to the computer terminal again and tapped out a set of instructions on the keyboard. The screen cleared and then began to refill with information.

"According to this you seem pretty healthy. Good blood pressure, nice heart rhythm."

"Gee, thanks," said Kelly, smiling.

"How about a few verbal questions just to fill in the blanks?"

"Sure."

"Age?"

"Thirty-five."

"Usual childhood diseases, nothing special?"

"Everything, including scarlet fever."

"Medication?"

"Aspirin."

"Normal menstrual cycling?"

"Like a clock."

"Do you use the pill?"

"No."

"IUD?"

"Not anymore."

"No birth control at all, then?"

"Not at the moment."

"Known allergies?"

"No."

"Smoke?"

"Yes. Not a lot though."

"That's what they all say. How about family history. Heart, cancer, stroke?"

"Not that I know of. My parents died in an automobile accident."

"Next of kin?"

"Nothing close. Some cousins. A great aunt in Arizona."

"Have you ever been pregnant?"

"Why?"

"For the record. You don't have to answer if you don't want to."

"Yes, once."

"Abortion?"

"Yes."

"How long ago?"

"I was eighteen."

"Okay, that should do it." He hit a few more keys and swiveled around in his chair again as the information was coded onto her card.

"How's the hand?" he asked.

Kelly lifted it and gently tried to flex her fingers. The hand was stiff and still partially frozen but the pain was at bay. She could barely see the bandage between her fingers.

"Pretty good," she told him.

"It was peanut butter, by the way," the doctor said. "That's what you cut your hand on—a jar of peanut butter."

"Your machines told you that?" Kelly asked, amazed. The doctor smiled. He was really *very* good-looking.

"No, I told myself that," he answered. "I could see it on a few bits of glass I removed. You should be more careful."

There was a whirring noise and then a click as Kelly's card was cycled out of the terminal. The doctor handed it to her along with a small vial of pills.

"Keep the card in your purse and if you're ever in here again just give it to the admissions clerk. And take one of the pills if the pain starts to come back."

"Okay."

"Now I'll wheel you back to the lobby."

"I can walk on my own," Kelly said.

"You'd deny me the pleasure of wheeling you?" the doctor said, smiling. "It's policy anyway. Saves on lawsuits." He grasped the rear handles of the chair and guided Kelly out into the corridor.

"I guess if you're going to be sick, this is the place to do it in," Kelly said as they headed for the lobby. "You wouldn't get this kind of service in New York, let me tell you."

"We try to please," said the doctor behind her. They reached the doors leading out to the lobby and they swung open automatically. Kelly found herself thinking about Hugh Trask and his feelings about Crestwood Heights.

"What do the people in town think of this place?" she asked as they headed across the lobby to the main entrance.

"I haven't had many complaints. I don't see many of them here, but I've got an office in town as well."

"How come?"

"Tradition," the doctor explained. They reached the main entrance and Kelly stood up, feeling a little wobbly. The doctor took her by the arm. "My father was a doctor in Crestwood for almost forty years."

"You're a local boy?"

"And proud of it." He smiled. "Let me get you into a taxi." He led Kelly out into the sunlight, and they walked slowly down to the cabstand. She let herself lean into his arm a little more than she really had to, enjoying the feeling of hard muscle under the white labcoat.

"I'm supposed to go to a party tonight," she said weakly. "I don't know if I'm going to be able to make it."

"Doris Benedict's?" the doctor asked. Kelly stopped in front of a waiting taxi and stared at the man.

"Now, how did you know *that?*"

"Simple deduction. Keith Benedict is my racquetball partner. We were playing this morning across the way at the Leisureplex and he mentioned that Doris had invited Nathan Somerville's niece to her party. When I was running through your chart, I noticed that the address on it was the same as Nathan's. I was his doctor. Simple."

"Are you going to the party?" she asked, wondering if she was being too obvious.

"I'll go if you will." He smiled, eyes twinkling.

"If I didn't know better, I'd think this was a setup," she answered.

"Not a setup, just a conspiracy." He laughed. "Every time Doris finds an unmarried woman she trys to matchmake me. I'm one of her pet projects. By the looks of it, you're next on her list."

"Okay, I'll go," she said, nodding. "I mean, we wouldn't want to disappoint Doris, now would we?"

"Absolutely not." He grinned. "I'll pick you up around eight."

"Okay." Kelly gave him her best smile and climbed into the taxi. She gave the driver her address, waved to the doctor, and then drove off. On the way back to the house she found herself wondering if Dr. Hardy's questions about what sort of birth control she used were entirely official, but she quickly banished the thought from her mind. In the first place it was wishful thinking and in the second place the pain in her hand was coming back and more than anything else all she wanted to do was take a pill and get into bed.

She slept through the afternoon, waking up just after six, feeling groggy but refreshed. The pain in her hand was there but it was nothing more than a dull ache. She could feel the tug of the stitches when she flexed her hand, but the wound itself was almost invisible, masked by Stephen Hardy's magic bandage.

Kelly got out of bed, threw on a bathrobe, and wandered into the kitchen. The boys from Maid to Order had done a good job, and there was no trace of blood on the floor and no remains of the broken peanut butter jar in the cupboard. She made herself a cup of tea and carried it back to the bedroom, mentally doing an inventory of her clothes, trying to come up with something to wear to the party.

Doris Benedict had been wearing lime green high tops in the park, but the party was probably going to be along more conservative lines. Suburban ensemble time. She settled on her only true cocktail dress, a basic black Anne Klein, sleeveless, low in the back and demure in the front, then added a pair of Maude Frizon pumps with low heels and a bow on the front. Sheer black hose, the diamond bracelet that was the one and only icon left from her marriage, and a pair of simple diamond studs.

With the clothes laid out, she ran herself a steaming hot bath and climbed in, careful to keep her bandaged hand out of the water. She allowed herself the luxury of a long, leisurely scrub, wondering what the good doctor would say if he could see her stark naked, lobster red, and wearing a pink-and-green plastic shower cap. Eyes half-closed, she smiled, idly running a washcloth up and down between her breasts. Sex was rearing its ugly head and she liked what it was doing to her.

It had been a couple of months since she'd gone to bed with a man, and up until this afternoon any desires she might have felt had been securely tucked away in a shoe box in the back of her mind. It was something she'd learned to do when she was married. Her husband, faithfully wedded to an infinity of Australian sherry bottles, had wanted sex about three times a year at best, so Kelly had learned how to turn lovemaking into a memory trick. Taking a lover probably would have been easy enough, but it had been easier still to live on the past, feeding her own diminishing sex drive with memories of lovers and affairs she'd had when she was younger. For a little while after her divorce, she'd wondered if she was ever going to make love again and then Griff had come along.

He'd been good for that at least and for a little while working life was nothing more than punctuation marks between marathon sex-bouts. But that's all it was, and it didn't really take her very long to realize that being impaled on Griff's admittedly enormous wang every three or four hours wasn't enough to keep a relationship going. The man was ruled by his glands and all his talent was in his penis.

Dr. Hardy, however, was something else again and even when she'd been bleeding all over the linoleum in his examining room, she'd felt a strong attraction. Smart, good sense of humor, *very* nice hands, and enough little crinkles around those bright blue eyes to prove that he'd been around the block a few times.

She felt a warm, fluttery feeling in the pit of her stomach and shifted the washcloth lower, making little circles around her waterlogged belly button. It was one of those night-of-the-big-dance, will-I-won't-I feelings that she hadn't felt in years. Butterflies.

Which was absurd. She was a grown woman who happened to be going to a cocktail party with a handsome doctor. Spend enough time in a hot bath and you could come up with all sorts of fantasies, but there was no need to be adolescent about it. Stephen Hardy was a nice guy, she was a nice woman, and that's all there was to it. She wasn't about to force the issue with him, not by a long shot. Still . . .

Annoyed at her own childishness, she popped the drain button with her big toe and levered herself up out of the tub one-handed. She didn't need a hot bath, she needed a cold shower. She was in Crestwood to get herself together and figure out what she was going to do with the rest of her life, she wasn't here looking for a man. In fact, a man was the last thing on earth she needed right now. A business manager was more like it, or, at the very least, someone who knew something about operating a movie house.

By 7:30 she was fully dressed and daubing on the last of her Rive Gauche in all the right places, and by 8:00 she was ready and waiting for Dr. Hardy, the butterflies dancing no matter how hard she tried to keep them quiet.

He arrived right on time, pulling in behind the Aston Martin in an equally exotic Citroën CX in fire engine red. The big four-door rolled to a stop and then slowly dropped down onto its frame as the hydraulics lowered it. Kelly had seen the fat-backed, shark-nosed automobiles often enough in Europe, but they were still a rarity in the United States.

She met him at the door and went down to the car, letting him take her elbow as she dropped down into the spaceship interior of the automobile. He climbed in on the driver's side, spooled up the big engine, and backed out onto the street in the dusky twilight. He was wearing a perfectly tailored chalk-stripe suit and he smelled of Lagerfeld. The butterflies switched from waltz time to a full tilt boogie.

"I'm beginning to think everyone in Crestwood Heights drives fancy cars," she said, trying to get a grip on herself as they cruised slowly up Erin Park to Greenbriar.

"That's not too far from the truth," Stephen answered. "No matter what you say, the Heights is a suburb, and people try to individualize themselves whenever they can here, I guess. Keith Benedict drives an MG TD, Doris drives a Jag, a lot of their friends drive BMWs, Audis, that kind of thing."

"What about the mysterious Max Alexanian?" asked Kelly. "What kind of car does he drive?"

"A Coupe de Ville Caddy. Ten years old," Stephen laughed. "Max doesn't spend much time worrying about his image."

"Will I meet him at the party?" she asked. "I've been hearing a lot about him."

"He'll probably be there. For a little while, at least. Keith's company was one of the first to build in Deep Wood Park. They're old friends."

"What about Phil Granger?"

"Most likely. Why, do you know him?"

"Not well. From what I gather, he's got his fingers in a lot of pies."

"He's got his fingers in every pie," Hardy said. "Not the

most likeable guy in the world, but I think he's pretty harmless."

Kelly almost brought up Hugh Trask's opinion of Granger and Alexanian, but she stopped herself. Stephen Hardy might be the son of the old town doctor, but he had an office in the Crestwood Heights Medical Center, too, and taking sides so soon after moving here might be socially fatal. Better to sit on the fence for a while until she made up her mind which team to join.

They reached Viewmount Crescent and turned up the low hill. The houses here were a lot bigger than the ones on Erin Park, and done in a mixture of styles. They were all obviously expensive, and each one occupied a lot twice the size of her own. She was in executiveland.

Stephen slithered the big car up onto a wide driveway already jammed with cars and pulled up behind a classic Mercedes gullwing 300SL that one-upped Kelly's Aston Martin. Ignoring the car, she looked up at the house. Doris Benedict wasn't kidding: you really couldn't miss it.

The house was enormous, a sprawling, Spanish stucco split-level with tile roof set well back on a triangular lot at the head of the crescent and dramatically lit by half a dozen spotlights hidden in the shrubbery. The garage looked as though it could accommodate half a dozen cars on its own and there were twice that many parked in front of it. They got out of the Citroën and went up the broad flagstone pathway that led to the front courtyard. Behind the stucco arch was a small ornamental pool and clusters of blooming shrubs beneath a row of multipaned leaded windows. Set to one side was a huge front door sheathed in hammered copper with an Aztec sunburst design blossoming out of a large pull ring.

There was no need to pull the ring because the door was already wide open, people spilling out into the courtyard and creating a wall of sound that was a mixture of light laughter, tinkling ice cubes, and muted speech. Somewhere from the depths of the house Kelly could hear music, but it was nonspecific without any identifiable genre. Cocktail Muzak.

"I'm not very good at this kind of thing," she admitted as they went into the courtyard. In fact, what she really wanted to do was get back into the car and leave.

"I don't like it much either," he confided, holding her elbow and whispering into her ear. "What you do is get the food, stuff yourself, and then find a quiet corner. And smile. Look as though you're having a good time and no one will bother you.''

They headed into the main body of the party with Stephen running interference, politely elbowing and shouldering his way through the crowd in the high-ceilinged foyer, then veering left up three wide steps into the main salon. The room was gigantic, the Spanish motif carried through to the stucco and beamed ceiling and the rough concrete fireplace set into one corner. The back wall of the room was an oversized rendition of the living room wall in her uncle's house, the combination picture windows and sliding glass doors leading out to a large terrace overlooking the ravine. There was, however, the addition here of a large oval swimming pool.

The furniture in the big room was expensive and authentic, a pleasantly skewed mixture of Chippendale and Federal with some Chinese thrown in as well as contemporary. The huge carpet on the floor was a Laura Ashley flower pattern, the knickknacks on an assortment of shelves and sideboards were mostly Oriental and the paintings on the wall went from Jackson Pollack–style splashes of color to a framed and individually lit series of English hunting prints.

They finally reached a long refectory table loaded down with dozens of trays of finger food. They loaded up plates and zigzagged over to a relatively private niche beside the fireplace. Kelly had trouble balancing the plate in her good hand and eating with the wounded one and eventually she gave up and allowed Stephen to feed her tidbits.

"I feel like a bird being fed by its mother,'' she said, chewing on a piece of battered shrimp the doctor had popped into her mouth.

"Just establishing a good patient–doctor relationship,'' he answered, smiling.

Doris Benedict appeared, dressed in an ankle-length concoction in midnight blue, a triple strand of pearls and earrings to match. She had a highball in one hand and a portable telephone in the other, the antenna extended like a fairy godmother's wand.

"Well, would you look at this!'' she said, spotting them in the corner. "I had all sorts of plans for introducing the two of you and now you've ruined it. Shame on you, Stephen." She tapped him on the shoulder with the end of the antenna.

"What's with the telephone, Doris?" asked Stephen Hardy.

"Tracking down a missing case of St. Emilion." She scowled. "The damn liquor store in town shorted me again, I'm sure of it."

"Why didn't you order from the PETES?" he asked.

"You know as well as I do that all they have in stock is that tepid California Chablis." Using the palm of her hand, she slapped down the antenna. "Oh, to hell with it!" She looked at Kelly. "So how did you meet Crestwood Heights most eligible single parent?" she asked. Kelly turned to Stephen, frowning. He hadn't mentioned anything about being married, let alone having a child.

"We met at the Medical Center," he answered. "Kelly cut her hand and I sewed it up. We compared notes and realized we'd been invited to the same party, so here we are." He turned to Kelly. "And I'm not a single parent," he explained. "I've been taking care of my goddaughter for the past few months. Her parents died in a boating accident on Lake Michigan. Her name's Lizbeth Torrance."

"She's a living doll," said Doris. "Smart too." She waved the phone. "Enough of that. I want Kelly to meet Max." She put the telephone down on the mantel and slid her arm into Kelly's.

"Can I tag along or is it a private audience?" asked Stephen.

"The more the merrier," Doris told him. "He's holding court out by the pool. Come on." Arm still hooked in Kelly's, Doris led the way across the room to the open doors leading to the pool, the chattering crowd parting easily before her.

Max Alexanian was seated in a wrought-iron pool chair, a tall glass of mineral water and lime beside him on a round, glass-topped table. There were four or five others seated around him, including Phil Granger, but Alexanian was definitely the center of attention.

He was a man in his mid to late sixties, his thick hair iron gray and almost a perfect match for the suit he wore. The face was square, the upper lip and chin covered by a neatly trimmed mustache and beard, the eyes deep blue beneath bushy gray eyebrows. He had a perfect, even tan to set off the crisp white of his silk shirt, and he wore a large, square-cut emerald signet ring on the pinkie of his right hand.

He sat comfortably, left leg crossed over the right, the left hand holding the long crooked stub of a chocolate brown cigarillo, the French cuff of his sleeve shot back just enough to expose the gold bracelet and oyster shape of a Rolex. Everything was in perfect taste, but something about the whole effect of his presence made Kelly think of a snake, coiled and poised to strike. Omar Sharif playing a Greek tycoon.

"Max, this is Kelly Rhine, Nathan Somerville's niece."

"Good evening, Miss Rhine," said Alexanian. His voice had a faint accent that she couldn't quite place. If his name was any indication, he was probably Turkish or Armenian by birth. "Phillip has been telling me something about you." He gestured toward an empty chair and Kelly sat down, relieved as Stephen Hardy took up a position just behind her, one hand on her shoulder.

"That's nice," she answered, glancing at Granger. "Not that he knows very much about me."

"Well said." Alexanian nodded, smiling. The teeth were as white as the shirt and just as perfect. Another case of caps, Kelly decided.

"I've just been talking to Max about the possibility of turning the Strand into a legitimate theater," said Granger smoothly. "He thinks it's a wonderful idea."

"It has potential," Alexanian acknowledged.

"I don't think Kelly has decided what she wants to do yet," broke in Doris Benedict. She reached down and plucked a celery stalk from the glass dish on the table beside Alexanian. "She's barely been here for two days yet."

"Surely you must be interested, Doris," Granger said, smiling coldly. "After all, you are one of the directors of the Historical Society."

"All Kelly has to do is apply for a grant to refurbish the exterior of the theater," Doris answered. "That doesn't mean she has to start putting on your plays, Phillip dear."

"I don't think Kelly came to the party to get into a discussion about her plans for the future," put in Stephen Hardy, using his hand to gently pass along a message to Kelly. "Speaking as her doctor I'm prescribing a pleasant evening among her new neighbors." He used his free hand to pluck a glass from a tray being carried by a passing waiter and handed it down to Kelly. "And a wine cooler," he added.

"You know Dr. Hardy?" asked Alexanian.

"I had a bit of an accident today," Kelly explained. "I was bitten by a peanut butter jar. Dr. Hardy was kind enough to repair the damage."

"Dear me," said Alexanian, frowning. "Not a pleasant introduction to our community." He paused. "Mind you, there are almost twice as many accidents in the home as there are in the workplace."

"Max could give you causes and numbers for every state in the union, too," laughed Doris. "He's just a little bit obsessed by statistics."

"Not obsessed," said Alexanian, smiling at Doris. "Just passionate. Used properly, statistics can be as much a creative instrument as the brush in an artist's hands."

"For instance?" Hardy prodded, giving the man his cue.

"Miss Rhine, for example. Simply by her age and sex we can deduce a great deal."

"Really?" said Kelly. There was something almost repellant about the man, but at the same time she found herself fascinated by his self-possession.

"Certainly," the head of the Cold Mountain Institute returned. "You are—what, thirty-five or so?"

"Close enough."

"You smoke, but you have tried to quit several times. You are almost certainly divorced and your average salary has been in the twenty-five- to twenty-eight-thousand-dollar-a-year range. You still have your appendix?"

"Yes."

"Then you were not born and raised on the Eastern seaboard. If that is the case, then it also follows that you do not wear dentures, which in turn means that you were raised in an urban area with a population over one million in which the water system has been fluoridated since 1960 or before. On that basis, the logical assumption is that you were born and raised either in California or the state of Washington. My own feeling is that it was probably California, and most likely San Francisco. How am I doing so far?"

"Hundred percent," Kelly laughed. "That's amazing."

"No. Simply a knowledge of statistics. Furthermore, I

would go so far as to say that you moved from the West Coast to the East after your divorce and as a result of it. Mr. Granger tells me that you came to us from New York. Knowing that, I can say that you have either witnessed or been involved in a criminal act of some kind within the last twenty-four months. The most likely type of crime would be theft in the home."

"My apartment was broken into about a year ago," Kelly confirmed. "That really is quite astounding."

"It's my business." Alexanian smiled. "That kind of statistical analysis is what Crestwood Heights is based on. North Carolina, for instance, has the lowest crime index trend in the United States: 1.7. New York is 6.9. By definition, it is safer to live here than it is to live there."

"Nice to know," Kelly commented. "But it takes more than statistics to make a community." She was damned if she was going to sit there at the feet of the master without putting up a fight.

"Quite true. But we are all statistics, whether we like it or not. We can all be put on the curve somewhere."

"I don't agree," said Kelly, shaking her head. "What about the odd man out? The exception that makes the rule?"

"In my experience there is no such thing," replied Alexanian. "Even the oddballs can be categorized."

"That sounds a bit Orwellian," Kelly said.

Alexanian shrugged. "Perhaps, but it is nevertheless true."

"That doesn't make Crestwood Heights sound very attractive then. You're saying that everyone here acts, operates, and lives according to a presupposed line of existence."

"Crestwood Heights is only a microcosm," Alexanian said. "There is room for creativity and individualism within a statistical framework. For me, Crestwood Heights provides a statistical cross section on which trends and policy can be based, but the analysis only describes options, it doesn't make the rules or the laws by which we live."

"Good," said Kelly. "I'd hate to think I was living in a conform-or-else community." She glanced at Phil Granger and gave him her sweetest smile. Take that you smooth bastard!

"Let me make one more deduction, Miss Rhine." There was an edge to Alexanian's voice that hadn't been there before. "You are approximately thirty-five, which means you were a teenager during the sixties. You also lived in San Francisco, something of a radical hotbed during those years. Is it safe to say you were of the beads-and-sandal generation?"

"Sure. You could say that if you wanted. There was a lot more to it than that, mind you."

"Be that as it may, Miss Rhine, I detect a certain unease in you. Perhaps a twinge from those years, a left liberalism that perhaps gainsays much of what I stand for."

"Maybe."

"Just bear in mind, Miss Rhine, that Crestwood Heights and the people who live here are responsible for doing a great deal of good in the world. Research done in Deep Wood Park has done more to save lives and make this a better world to live in than any number of peace marches. You come from a generation that did a great deal of talking, but not a lot of doing. The people here aren't like that. Our medical research has already created a score of lifesaving drugs and technological innovations, our efforts in the field of telecommunications and computer research have expanded man's knowledge enormously. On a strictly human level, our own Crestwood Infertility Clinic has been responsible for providing almost a thousand young married couples with healthy children they were incapable of having. The list goes on. We're trying to do something for the world here in Crestwood Heights, Miss Rhine. I'm proud of that."

"I feel as though I've been scolded," Kelly said, smiling weakly. Alexanian would have made one hell of a prosecuting attorney.

"I'm sorry for that," the man said, waving a hand. "I spend a great deal of time in Washington lobbying for research funds; sometimes I wax somewhat bombastic. You must excuse me. I meant no offense."

"None taken."

Alexanian uncrossed his legs a little clumsily and rose to his feet. For the first time, Kelly noticed that he used a thin, gold-handled walking stick for support. He bowed toward Doris Benedict.

"I'm afraid I must be off, my dear," he said quietly. "Would you be so kind as to accompany me through the hordes in your living room?"

Kelly watched as Alexanian limped off with Doris, followed by Phil Granger. She turned her head and looked up at Stephen.

"I've been roasted," she said, laughing. Stephen patted her shoulder.

"You did better than most," he said, smiling. "Not everyone would have tried to keep an argument going with Max like that."

Kelly stood up and together the two of them walked to the edge of the terrace, skirting the pool. Looking out over the low stone wall, Kelly stared down into the impenetrable darkness of the ravine.

"He makes it sound as though I don't belong here," she said quietly.

"Don't be silly," scoffed Stephen. "He's like that with everyone. The Heights is his version of utopia and anyone taking any kind of potshot is automatically the enemy."

"He hit some pretty raw nerves," said Kelly. "I really haven't done a whole hell of a lot with my life up until now."

"Maybe that's about to change," said Stephen, slipping his arm around her waist. He looked at her. "Anyway, we've done our duty and you look tired. Why don't I take you home?"

"Okay."

He drove her back to the house on Erin Park and walked her to the door. Standing with him under the porch light Kelly had a brief urge to invite him in, but she fought the feeling. It was too early for anything serious. Instead, she thanked him for taking her to the party and gave him a quick kiss on the cheek. In answer he kissed her back, this time on the mouth, and then turned away. She watched him get back into the Citroën and drive off, then let herself into the house.

The pain wrenched her out of sleep at three in the morning, a deep agonizing sensation in the lower right abdomen. She sat up and gagged, overcome by a sudden nausea. She barely had time to reach the bathroom before she vomited. It didn't help, and each time she took a breath it seemed to make the pain even worse.

She dragged herself back into the bedroom and managed to reach the telephone and tap out 911 before another wave of pain consumed her and she slipped down onto the floor, unconscious.

CHAPTER 9

Kelly Kirkaldy Rhine, Crestwood Heights Medical Center Active Chart number R-2428(AB/PER/SP/SPH), lay at the bottom of a deep well lined with thick black velvet. Some part of her brain recognized that all was not right with her body, and for the moment at least, sensation of any kind was being held at bay. Natural endorphins, triggered by the shock of acute peritonitis had been augmented by an artificial hormone called Endformaline, which successfully blocked pain signals from the brain. Endformaline, under the trade name ENDREX, was manufactured by the Owens Crane Pharmaceutical Corporation of Deep Wood Park and had been approved for limited use by the Federal Drug Administration.

The drug had been delivered using a dense polymer film rolled into a gelatine capsule. Once swallowed, the gelatine capsule was dissolved by the stomach's acids, allowing the film to unroll. The film was made up of two parts, a drug carrying matrix layer and a bubble containing barrier film. The barrier film allowed the matrix layer to float in the stomach and the endorphins were released slowly and absorbed into the bloodstream at a constant rate.

Although she was unaware of it, Kelly was also connected to a PCA dispenser at her bedside. PCA, or Patient-Controlled Analgesia, was another novel technique being used at the Center. Simply by pressing a button on the end of a cord, the postoperative patient could administer a painkilling analgesic through an intravenous tube. A timer on the machine, keyed to the specific painkiller being used, prevented overdosage while ensuring continuous relief.

Statistical analysis at the Cold Mountain Institute had proven that PCA overcame several drawbacks of standard scheduled analgesic injections: less time was required from the attending nurse; there was no pain created as a result of the injection itself; since the drug was introduced intravenously, relief was immediate, avoiding the twenty- to forty-minute delay with injections; and, finally, there was none of the sleepiness that resulted from large intramuscular doses.

Tests had also shown that PCA patients recovered from surgery more quickly and used less medication overall, desirable results both from a practical and economic point of view. PCA units had been placed in all of the 122 private rooms and there were also units for each of the sixty-four semi-private beds in the Medical Center.

Not that Kelly really gave a damn. As far as her limited consciousness was concerned, the universe had contracted to the inky cocoon she now occupied. As time passed though, the cocoon began to expand and awareness slowly returned. First sound, hollow and distant; then smell, familiar and antiseptic; and finally sight as her eyes fluttered open.

"Unh." There was enough of the synthetic endorphin in her system to make the pain no more than a deep, distant ache, but she knew it was there. Someone had taken a pointed stick and rammed it into her stomach. On top of that her mouth tasted like the bottom of a bird cage and someone had crazy-glued her lips together.

"Wake up." The voice was firm and insistent. Masculine. Kelly squinted but everything was too bright.

"Wha—?"

"Wake up, Kelly. It's Stephen Hardy."

"Dry," she managed. A few seconds later she felt the end of a flexible straw being inserted into her mouth. She sucked on it weakly and felt a trickle of room temperature fluid on her tongue. She sucked again and tasted a faint lemon flavor.

"Better?" Stephen's voice again.

She nodded. The straw was withdrawn. She opened her eyes and got a wavy, tilted impression of a room before dizziness overcame her and she shut them again.

"O God."

"Dizzy?"

"Umm."

"That'll pass. I want you to concentrate on waking up. I'm going to go away for a little while but I'll be back. Okay?"

" 'Kay."

Some unknown length of time passed and Kelly managed to take a reasonable inventory, first of her body, and then of her surroundings. She was in a hospital room, that was clear enough, just by the smell of antiseptic and the incredibly crisp-clean feel of the sheets around her. She had a tube in her arm, held in place with a piece of tape across her wrist, and from the feel of it she wasn't wearing anything under the sheets except a thin hospital gown.

Eventually she summoned up the courage to rummage around under the gown and find out what had happened to her. A quick check revealed that her pubic hair was still intact, so it wasn't something reproductive. Letting her free hand wander, she found a six- or seven-inch circle of flesh—textured tape over the right lower quadrant of her belly, just east of her belly button. From the urgent signals spearing up beyond the blocking endorphins she assumed that the bandage was covering the site of her pain. She wasn't old enough or fat enough for gall bladder, so it was either something to do with her ovary or appendicitis. Hadn't Max Alexanian mentioned her appendix at the party?

By the time Stephen returned, she was fully conscious and able to drink from the glass of fruit juice he offered. He was wearing surgical greens and there was a fiber-form face mask dangling around his neck. He sat down on the end of the bed and shook his head.

"We can't go on meeting like this." He smiled.

"Funny man," Kelly grunted. "What happened? I woke up thinking I was about to die. I thought it was food poisoning. Doris Benedict's tempura shrimp."

"Nope. Nothing so exotic. Acute peritonitis. You must have had an ulcerated appendix. It was seeping all sorts of nasty things into your abdominal cavity. By the time I got you onto the table the whole thing was about to go. You were lucky."

"You operated on me?"

"Yup."

"I didn't know you were a surgeon. I thought you were a family doctor."

"I'm both," he said. "I've got a practice in town, but I'm also Chief of Surgery here."

"Did you find anything interesting when you operated?" asked Kelly.

"Other than the appendix the only other thing was a very nice belly button. An innie, which I'm partial to."

"How long will I be in here?"

"A couple of days at most, unless there are complications, which I doubt. There wasn't time for any septicemia to encroach. After that you'll have to take it easy for a couple of weeks. No weight lifting."

"I'm beginning to think this town doesn't like me," said Kelly. "First the hand and now this. Maybe I should pack my bags and go back to New York."

"Don't be silly. You'll get a lot better care here than you would at Bellevue. Not to mention the fact that medical care here is free."

"You're kidding!"

"Nope. Bundled right into your land taxes and Cold Mountain underwrites the rest of it. The Medical Center is classified as a research institute so we get all sorts of tax breaks. We pass that along to the patients. It's a good system."

"Okay, I give in," said Kelly. "Max Alexanian is right. This is utopia."

"Not quite, but we're getting there. Now shut up so I can take your temperature."

The young doctor spent another twenty minutes with her, examining the incision and explaining how the PCA unit worked. He told her that she'd be able to get up and move around within the next twenty-four hours and they made a date for lunch in the terrace sun room the following day. Then he went back to his rounds, and unable to fight the sudden tiredness she felt, Kelly slept again.

At breakfast the next morning Kelly realized that the food at Crestwood Heights Medical was as good as the surgery, and by ten o'clock she'd had herself unhooked from the PCA and ordered up a wheelchair. In keeping with the rest of the hospital, the device was like nothing she'd seen before. It looked more like a small golf cart and instead of being pushed by hand, the chair was guided down a metal strip in the hall floor. The cart worked off the strip as well, although more slowly, and could be steered with either a simple foot rudder or a long pistol-gripped handle. The saddlelike seat was high, making transfer from bed to chair much simpler than with a regular wheelchair, and according to the nurse you could even order one with a built-in commode. For ambulatory patients with more serious problems the chairs were fitted with electrodes capable of monitoring vital functions, the signal being carried down the metal strips to the main nurses' station in the center of the second-floor complex of private and semiprivate rooms. There was even an armature and clip on the rear of the cart for patients still using an intravenous drip.

Kelly managed to cadge a pencil and a pad of blank paper from the nurse, and after getting directions she hummed down the central corridor toward the glassed-in terrace. Guiding the cart around the nurses' station, she was surprised to see two sliding sidewalk escalators, one going up to the main floor, the other coming down, but after a moment's thought she realized how sensible they were. Instead of clogging up elevators, the sliding sidewalks could be used by regular up and down traffic from the clinic floor above, and the ribbed rubber walkways were easily wide enough to accommodate the carts or a gurney coming from emergency.

She beetled around the nurses' station and down to the terrace, guiding the cart off the metal strip and through the archways onto the terrace proper. The greenhouselike room was immense, running the length of the hospital and equipped with chairs, loungers, and tables scattered among a randomly strewn assortment of trees planted in large concrete pots. Stephen was right, there was nothing like this in New York.

She found herself a spot close to the edge of the terrace that gave her a view down into the ravine. Unlike the view from the patio of the Erin Park house, here the ravine was broad and open. Directly below her she could see the curving glass of the terrace enclosure on the next floor, but the large panes had been silvered and blocked out any vision. Peering further down she could see the bright blue line of Tryon Creek and the thick foliage and trees on the opposite bank. She opened up the pad of paper and took up her pencil, preparing to draw.

According to Stephen she was going to be out of action for at least two weeks, which meant she wasn't going to be able to do much as far as the Strand was concerned. Instead, she'd decided to use the time to work on her children's book, and as she sat in the bright sunlight on the terrace it occurred to her that for all the pain she'd endured, the appendix operation might well turn out to be a blessing in disguise. Robert Louis Stevenson had written *Treasure Island* out of boredom as an invalid, so why not her book?

She worked quickly, picking up details of the landscape on the other side of the glass and getting them down as fast as possible, trying to get a feel for the atmosphere of the ravine rather than a realistic rendition. From her limited research into the subject, she knew that the best children's books were full of detail in their illustrations and beyond that she had an intuitive grasp of what was magic for a young mind. In her book the ravine would be a place where anything—good or bad—was possible, and as she drew she tried to capture the feeling of darkness and foreboding offered by the deep cut slash in the earth, as well as its beauty.

"Miss Rhine?" Startled, Kelly looked up. It was the candy-striper volunteer in charge of keeping the people on the terrace happy. The girl was in her late teens, round-faced and dimpled with small breasts that poked out the starched bib of her uniform like sharpened pencils.

"Yes?"

"You have a visitor." The girl stepped aside and Kelly looked past her to the wide terrace entrance. Expecting Stephen Hardy, she was surprised to see the tall, slightly stooped figure of Hugh Trask. He was wearing a long tweed coat against the crisp spring wind that was ruffling the trees in the ravine outside the glass and his head was bare, the shock of white hair in a tangle. He looked like an elderly version of Ichabod Crane.

The old man approached Kelly's table cautiously, looking from side to side with sharp, nervous movements. He reached her table and made a stiff little bow before unbuttoning his coat.

"May I sit down?" he asked.

"Of course," Kelly said, swinging the cart around slightly so she could face him across the table. The old man sat, hands knotted together in front of him. The skin over the knuckles was red and raw, stretched parchment-thin over swollen joints. The nails were a little too long, thick and yellowed like old horn. Under different circumstances she might have asked to draw them.

"I was most distressed to hear that you had been hospitalized," Trask said. "I hope it's nothing serious."

"Appendix. Dr. Hardy said it was about to rupture."

"Stephen Hardy is your doctor?" The information seemed to excite the man.

"That's right."

"Who recommended him to you?" asked Trask.

"No one," Kelly said, frowning. "I cut my hand and he fixed it. When I had the appendicitis attack, I suppose the hospital called him in because he was the only doctor here who'd examined me."

"Stephen Hardy is the Chief of Surgery here," said Trask.

"I know that."

"It doesn't seem strange to you that the Chief of Surgery would take on a simple thing like an appendix operation? The Crestwood Heights Medical Center has almost fifty doctors on staff, not to mention residents."

"I hadn't thought about it," said Kelly. "And why should that interest you, Mr. Trask?"

"Hugh. Call me Hugh, please," the old man said. "I'm sorry if I sound somewhat wild-eyed but I have my reasons, I can assure you."

"What reasons are those?"

"Later perhaps. First I must ask some questions of you."

"Such as?"

"Just who are you, Miss Rhine? And why are you here?"

"I beg your pardon?" Kelly laughed, astounded. "What do you mean?"

"Exactly what I say. Please, bear with me."

"You know who I am. My name is Kelly Rhine. I inherited the Strand Theater from my uncle, Nathan Somerville."

"Do you have any connection at all with Northeastern Telecommunications or the SatCom Corporation?"

"Not that I'm aware of. My uncle worked for Northeastern, or so I've been told."

"Did you have any contact with your uncle shortly before he died?"

"No." Kelly shifted in her seat, becoming annoyed. "Now look, Mr. Trask—"

"Please! I must ask these questions. It is of extreme importance.'' The man looked as though he were going to have a stroke at any moment and Kelly decided that the best thing to do was humor him.

''Okay. Ask.''

''You had no correspondence with your uncle?''

''None. Just his lawyers.''

''You've never heard of something called AFRP, the American Fertility Research Program. Or Chapel Gate?''

''No.''

Trask sat back in his chair, shaking his head wearily. He looked defeated, almost as though his questions to Kelly had represented a last hope of some kind.

''Then I've been wasting my time.''

''Or you've been wasting mine,'' Kelly responded.

''If that is the case, then I am truly sorry,'' Trask said. He stood up, looking down at Kelly. ''But that aside, Miss Rhine, when you are released from here I would appreciate it if we could talk again. I'm not some senile old man to be taken lightly, of that I can assure you. Something terrible is going on and it must be stopped. Your uncle knew and I thought you might as well.''

''What kind of terrible thing?'' She caught a movement behind Trask and saw Stephen Hardy approaching her table. Saved by the bell. Trask saw her eyes flicker and looked over his shoulder.

''Goodbye, Miss Rhine. And please, don't mention this to anyone. I was merely coming here to offer my sympathy.''

''Sure. Whatever you say, Mr. Trask.''

The old man nodded and turned on his heel. He rushed away, veering as he passed Stephen Hardy. The doctor came to Kelly's table, looking back and watching the retreating figure of the old man.

''What was that all about?'' he asked.

''Beats me.'' Kelly shrugged. ''He came shuffling in here like some kind of soothsayer, warning me that something terrible was going on. It was a little bit scary actually.''

''What kind of terrible things?'' asked Stephen, seating himself in the chair Trask had recently vacated.

''He didn't say. He asked me if I knew anything about some of the companies in Deep Wood Park and something about a fertility program. Weird.''

"He must have meant the AFRP. The American Fertility Research Program."

"That's it," Kelly said. "What do you know about it?"

"Just about everything," Stephen said with a laugh. "I'm the local director."

"What is it exactly?"

"AFRP is a federal government program to coordinate research into problems related to fertility. The Center has an infertility clinic and several of the labs in Deep Wood are doing work on drug applications. AFRP has set up a database for researchers all over the country and we feed our information into it. The database is called Babyline."

"So it's not some sinister project to breed little tiny Frankenstein monsters?"

"Sorry to disappoint you." He grinned. "Hugh has usually got some sort of bee in his bonnet but it sounds as though he's gone overboard this time."

"He certainly isn't what you'd call a Crestwood Heights booster, that's for sure," Kelly agreed. She dropped her sketch pad onto the table. "I'm dying for a cigarette and a cup of coffee."

"I can get you the coffee, but the cigarettes will have to wait until you've coughed up the last of the anesthetic we pumped into you yesterday. Ready for lunch?"

"Sure."

They spent the next hour and a half together, working their way through the meal Stephen Hardy had catered up from the doctors' lounge on the floor below and trading information about each other's lives.

Stephen Pershing Hardy had been born in Crestwood, the only child of Dr. James Hardy, the town's physician. His mother had died in childbirth. Stephen's father had been a military doctor during World War II and Stephen followed in his footsteps after graduation from Harvard Medical. He'd worked as a captain in the U.S. Army Medical Corps and after a tour in Vietnam he joined the staff of the U.S. Army Research Office in Washington, D.C. Shortly after his father died, he returned to Crestwood and was part of the design team for the Crestwood Heights Medical Center. He divided his time equally between the Center, the Infertility Clinic, and his practice in town, so that with his new responsibilities to his goddaughter Lizbeth, he had virtually no free time at all. He also admitted that he thrived on the work load and wouldn't have it any other way.

By the time they'd reached the pear-quarters-in-a-plastic-cup dessert, Kelly realized that she was falling hard for the doctor and she only hesitated for an instant when he suggested that she recuperate at his house for the first few days after being released from the hospital. Stephen wanted her to meet Lizbeth and he didn't want her to be on her own so soon after surgery.

The long lunch over, he excused himself and went back to his duties. Kelly tried to sketch for a while longer, but her head was too full of thoughts about the doctor and she was also beginning to tire. She managed to get herself back to her room, let the nurse hook her back up to the PCA unit, and went to sleep.

She slept until almost five o'clock in the afternoon, when she woke to find another visitor in her room. It was Robin Spenser, loaded down with a giant bouquet of roses and an enormous heart-shaped box of his own chocolates. The pockets of his old Marine-issue peacoat were also stuffed with an assortment of paperbacks that included several murder mysteries and an amateurishly designed and bound history of Crestwood that had been put together by the Crestwood Historical Society back in the 1950s. He put the roses in an empty vase on the chest of drawers, put the books and the chocolates within reach on the bedside table, and dropped down onto the edge of the bed beside her.

"You had me worried," he said, taking her hand in his. "The last thing I heard was that we had a breakfast date for yesterday. You didn't show up and I got worried. I phoned your place but there was no answer and then I got really worried. Took me a while to track you down." He squeezed her hand. "They wouldn't let you have visitors until today." He frowned. "The nurse says it was appendicitis."

"It was about to rupture according to Stephen. I was lucky."

"Stephen?"

"Dr. Hardy." She felt herself blush. Robin laughed.

"Already on a first-name basis, are we? You move fast, kiddo."

"It gets worse. He's invited me to stay at his place until I'm back on my feet."

"Lordie!" moaned Robin, rolling his eyes. "The good ladies of Crestwood Heights will have a field day! Half the middle-aged biddies in town have been trying to get into his pants for years now."

"Our relationship is purely medical," Kelly said primly, trying not to laugh.

"Right. Those ladies want a medical relationship with him, too. He'd be a millionaire if he was a gynecologist."

"You have a dirty mind, Mr. Spenser."

"Right again." He nodded. "That's about all a guy like me can have in a place like this."

"I had another visitor today," Kelly said, turning serious for a moment. "Hugh Trask."

"Really? What was he up to? Getting a story for the paper?"

"I don't think so. He was acting pretty strange."

"How?" asked Robin.

"He was asking all sorts of questions about my uncle. He seems to think there's some sort of conspiracy going on."

"There is," said Robin. "And it's going on inside Hughie's rapidly deteriorating mind. What was it this time—fluoride in the water, or Max Alexanian as Dr. Strangelove?"

"I don't know," she said, shaking her head. "He wasn't too coherent. He kept on asking about Uncle Nat and warning me that something terrible was going on. It was scary."

"What about your uncle?" asked Robin.

Kelly shrugged. "He didn't say. He wanted to know if Nat had been in touch with me before he died."

"What did you tell him?"

"The truth: I hadn't heard from Uncle Nat in years."

"They were friends," Robin said. "I know that much. Hugh was pretty shaken up when he died. Like I said before, visions of his own mortality and all that. There was a kinship between them, even though your uncle had worked for the bad guys. Both of them hated Alexanian."

"But Uncle Nat didn't die mysteriously or anything did he?" asked Kelly.

"No. He had a heart attack. He smoked like a chimney and drank like a fish. No offense, but he was a prime candidate. Your Dr. Hardy tried to get him to stop smoking and climb on the wagon but it didn't do any good."

"Stephen mentioned he was my uncle's doctor."

"He's the only medic who has a practice in town," said Robin. "Most of us go to him, except Hugh. He doesn't trust anyone with a connection to the Heights."

"He scares me," said Kelly.

"Relax," Robin soothed. "Hugh Trask is harmless—an old man with a bit of senile dementia."

"I guess you're right."

They talked for a while longer and then Robin left, promising to come back the following day. Kelly tried to read one of the mysteries but she had no concentration and finally settled on the spiral-bound history of Crestwood.

The text had been done on a typewriter and the photographs were black-and-white amateur shots, but it passed the time in the quiet hospital room. Most of the book concerned the tobacco industry and its effects on the town, but the last few chapters were given over to the social and educational history of Crestwood. There was half a chapter on the building of the hotel, some pictures of the Strand back when it was the Victory Burlesque, and then she came upon a photograph that stopped her cold. The caption was simple and uninformative: CHAPEL GATE SCHOOL FOR CHRISTIAN GENTLEMEN.

The picture showed a gray stone fortresslike building backed by a dark stand of oaks. She read the five paragraphs below the picture quickly, wondering what an old boys school had to do with Hugh Trask's supposed conspiracy.

According to the text the site of the school had originally been occupied by the Convent of the Little Sisters of St. Antony and had been used as an orphanage. The convent had been burned to the ground during the anti-Catholic period of the early 1800s, but it had been rebuilt and reconstituted as a tubercular hospital. The only thing left of the original building had been the stone gate of the chapel.

The convent had been abandoned in the mid 1920s and the land was purchased by a consortium of wealthy Orange County tobacco men. A school was constructed for the education of their sons, built across the road from the original convent, with the gate of the chapel forming the entrance to the grounds as well as giving the school its name. When Crestwood fell into an economic slump during the thirties, along with the rest of the world, the school closed down for lack of funds and had never been reopened. According to the map in the back of the little book, the school was located at the end of a long drive at the far end of High Point Road.

Kelly let the book fall into her lap and squeezed her eyes shut. She was feeling tired again and the pain of her surgery was coming back. She tried to remember what Trask had said, but nothing seemed to fit. Her uncle had worked for Northeastern Telecommunications and Doris Benedict's husband Keith was vice president of SatCom Limited. According to Robin her uncle had hated Max Alexanian, and so had Trask, but none of that had anything to do with Stephen Hardy's Infertility Clinic or a long defunct boys' school off in the boonies. It was a tossed salad of facts that made no sense.

She lay back against her pillow and tried to clear her mind. Robin was right: Hugh Trask was a nut case with a bee in his bonnet and that was that. To hell with him and his Terrible Things. She reached out and pressed the button on the cord attached to the PCA unit. She felt the pain recede almost instantly and let the soothing drip of painkiller carry her away. Within five minutes she was fast asleep.

CHAPTER 10

On the afternoon of the third day after her operation, Stephen Hardy examined Kelly, pronounced her fit, and authorized her release from the Crestwood Heights Medical Center. Even though she assured him that she was well enough to go back to her uncle's house, he insisted that she recuperate for at least a day or two at his home in Orchard Park.

His own work completed for the day, he expedited her release and bundled her into the Citroën. He drove quickly away from the Center, checking his watch, explaining to Kelly that he had to be home in time to relieve Stephanie Denner, the teenage baby-sitter he had hired to care for Lizbeth while he was at work. Kelly, still groggy and weak, just nodded and watched the scenery go by, secretly relieved that she wasn't going to be alone. Except for her abortion and a few minor emergency ward visits as a child, she'd had little experience with hospitals and the ordeal had taken more out of her than she'd imagined.

Orchard Park was the newest of the three communities that made up Crestwood Heights and its planning had been radically different from both Greenbriar and Colony Woods. The two earlier developments had been made up entirely of single-family dwellings built around a shopping and recreation core, each house being given a generous land allowance. Orchard Park had a number of single-family homes but the focus was more on multiple units and shared green space rather than private property. What Orchard Park lacked in the classic amenities of home ownership was more than made up for by the new technology built into the houses and the country club-style appeal of the community's private golf course, year-round enclosed tennis courts, and riding stable.

Orchard Park was also located on what was certainly the best of the three sites. It was built on a slightly canted and naturally clear plateau of land east of Greenbriar and south of Colony Woods. From some of the perimeter streets on the edge of the community there was a long view down the Tobacco River, Tryon Woods, and beyond that, the tree-lined streets of the old town of Crestwood. As Stephen Hardy turned off Deep Wood Road and into Orchard Park, he told Kelly that he'd chosen his house on Alta Vista Drive for its southern exposure and that his guest room had the best view in the Heights.

Alta Vista Drive was the last enclave of housing built in Orchard Park, making it the most up-to-date. Stephen's house was part of a four-unit court built around a full-sized swimming pool in the center of the property. All white and ultramodern, it was built of weatherproof polymer planks over a steel frame with solar panels on the flat roof that were enough to power the central air conditioning as well as provide 25 percent of the energy needed to heat the communal pool.

Stephen drove the big car under the carport canopy of his unit and helped Kelly climb the short flight of steps to the main entrance. He slipped his key-card into the lock and as they went into the foyer Kelly noticed a small camera located in one corner of the doorframe. The foyer was as white as the exterior with stairs leading up to the second floor. The high wall to her left was hung with an enormous painting of a Killer Whale sounding, its entire body lifting up out of the water. The style was faintly Japanese, done in ink on silk with long exuberant strokes and Kelly could almost feel the tremendous power of the huge mammal as it soared into the air.

"Steff!" Stephen called. There was an answering cry from the other end of the house and he led Kelly down a broad hall, glassed in on one side with a view of the pool. They found Stephanie in the kitchen, slicing up carrots with a paring knife. The teenager was tall and gangly, cream-colored jean shorts revealing a little too much buttock for Kelly's taste.

The girl turned as they came into the room, flashing Stephen a broad smile. She was wearing a tight T-shirt with a Crestwood Heights Athletic Association logo and Kelly thought it, like the shorts, was a bit too revealing. On the other hand the kid's boobs were definitely something to be proud of; just the right size and obviously firm enough to stand up on their own.

She had a pretty oval face with a line of freckles across her nose and shaggy, not quite to the shoulder, red hair. From the look on her face and the way she was tilting one hip, it was obvious she had a crush on Stephen. Feeling like an idiot, Kelly realized that she was jealous of the child. Stephanie gave Kelly a quick once-over during the introductions and then turned her attention back to Stephen.

"Dinner's all ready, all you have to do is microwave it. The Little Genius is upstairs solving the problems of the world on your computer and I got an A on that health project you helped me with. Anything else I can do before I take off?"

"No, that's great. Miss Rhine just had surgery and she'll be staying here for a couple of days in the guest room, so you won't have to rush quite as much to get here before the van drops off Lizbeth after school."

"No probleemo," said Stephanie. She flashed Kelly a perfunctory smile. "Nice to meet you, Miss Rhine. Hope you're feeling better soon."

"Thanks," said Kelly. There was another smile, this one for Stephen, and then she was gone, her sneakers squeaking over the dark red quarry tile floor.

"Come on," Stephen said, touching Kelly on the shoulder. "You can meet Lizbeth, and the guest room is on the second floor as well."

"Why did Stephanie call her the 'Little Genius'?" Kelly asked as they went back to the foyer.

"Because that's exactly what she is." They climbed the stairs to the second level, the doctor supporting Kelly's elbow as they made their way up. "Her father was an electrical engineer working for Electrodyne, one of the companies in the Park. Her mother was a fetal embryologist who worked with me at the Infertility Clinic. We were good friends and I was the one who delivered her. That's why they made me godfather. She was tested at three and showed an incredibly high IQ, so Max suggested she be enrolled at Cold Mountain."

Kelly paused halfway up the stairs, trying to catch her breath. She felt weak as a kitten. "I thought Cold Mountain was the administrative group that ran the Research Park," she said.

"It is." Stephen nodded, waiting with her while she rested. She gave a little nod and they started up again. "Right from the start Max knew he'd be bringing a concentrated bunch of high achievers to Crestwood Heights and it followed that there would be some exceptional children. He set up the Cold Mountain School right at the Institute."

The stairwell opened onto a large, high-ceilinged room lit from above by a trio of skylights inserted between the solar panels. The far wall was taken up by a modern, glass-doored fireplace, and to the right there was a window wall leading out to a deck that overlooked the pool.

The floor was highly polished blond oak covered by a scattering of small rugs, and the furniture was modern chrome and leather. The wall closest to the stairs was covered by a floor-to-ceiling bookcase. Bachelor heaven, complete with a state-of-the-art audiovisual setup and wall-mounted speakers high in each corner.

There were two other rooms on the floor—the guest bedroom with a private bath and Stephen's study. He led Kelly to the study first and they paused in the open doorway. The room was large and sunny, another window wall leading out to the deck on the right. Two of the other three walls were taken up by more bookcases and a row of lateral file cabinets, while the fourth was set up as a computer workstation. A white Formica table ran the length of the floor backed by high, white-enameled metal shelves.

In the center of the table was a computer hacker's vision of paradise: a custom-built terminal with a large display, a laser printer, an ink jet diagrammer, an optical digitizer, and a modem with a built-in telefax for transmitting diagrams from one terminal to another by telephone. To the right of the impressive display, racked on the metal shelves, was an assortment of electronic machinery, all connected to the central workstation by a neatly wrapped bundle of rainbow-colored cables. It made the computer in her uncle's den look almost shabby by comparison.

Seated on a swivel-backed chair in front of the terminal was a child, small hands busily flying across the keyboard.

Sensing that she was being watched, the little girl turned, staring at them and Kelly drew in an involuntary breath.

The child was stunningly beautiful. Nine, perhaps ten years old, and dressed in corduroy jeans, sneakers, and a dull green sweatshirt that did nothing to take away from her looks. Her hair was long and shimmering, so blond that it was almost white in the light pouring in through the floor-to-ceiling window. It dropped like sheet gold down over her shoulders, framing a lightly tanned oval face with high cheekbones that belonged on a model. The mouth was full, the nose perfect, and the huge, deep-set eyes were brilliant, penetrating blue—eyes that were far too intelligent to belong to a child.

Absurdly she had a brief flash of memory. Another movie, seen long ago and based on a book with a funny title: *The Midwich Cuckoos*. A story about a group of children born into a small village in the English countryside. All of the children were frighteningly intelligent, and all of them had the same, terrible blue eyes. The movie had been called *Village of the Damned* and it ended with George Sanders blowing them all up with a briefcase full of dynamite. The image vanished as the child's face lit up with pleasure and Kelly mentally kicked herself for the instant of paranoia. Maybe whatever Hugh Trask had was catching.

"Hi, Lizbeth," Stephen said, smiling. "This is Kelly Rhine, a friend of mine. She's been in hospital and she's going to be spending a few days with us resting up."

"Neat," said the girl. "You let Uncle Steve cut you open?" The eyes were twinkling and the smile on her face made her even prettier. So much for bad memories of old movies.

"It seems to have done the trick," Kelly said, smiling back.

"Just make sure he didn't leave an old pair of running shoes behind when he closed you up. And if he did, you and I can work up a really good lawsuit. I take twenty-five percent off the top."

"Nice kid," Stephen said, lifting an eyebrow. "What have you got booted up on the machine this afternoon? Writs and torts from the North Carolina Statutes or an extract from a malpractice case?"

"Neither," the girl answered. "I'd need the access codes for the LEXIS database at Mead-Data Central in New York for that, and anyway, it would show up on your phone bill." She laughed and Kelly found the childish sound jarring, considering what the child was saying. "No," continued Lizbeth, "I'm working on an idea for that continuous-passive-motion machine we talked about. It's better than the one Salter designed at the Sick Children's Hospital in Toronto, but I'm not completely satisfied. I'm fiddling with an ultrasonic source for the movement rather than a mechanical one. Less cumbersome. Come and take a look."

"I think I'm out of my depth," said Kelly. They crossed the room and looked over Lizbeth's shoulder as she went back to the terminal. On the screen there was an outline diagram of a small rectangular device attached to a three-dimensional rendition of a human forearm and hand, complete with bones, joints, and ligaments. As Kelly watched, Lizbeth used the keyboard to rotate the diagram through several different views. The child tapped out another set of instructions and the interior of the box device strapped to the arm expanded, revealing a complex wiring diagram within.

"That's incredible," Kelly murmured. "It's like animation."

"That's what it is," Lizbeth nodded without turning. "Uncle Steve says it's one of the best CAD programs he's ever seen."

"What's CAD?" Kelly asked, feeling more confused than ever.

"Computer Assisted Design," answered Lizbeth. "I think I'm going to call it LEONARDO since he was one of the first people to do medical drafting."

"She designed the software," Stephen said.

"Not really," said Lizbeth. "They helped me a lot at JCL. Basically it's their MEDRAFT program with a few changes here and there."

"Just how old are you?" Kelly asked, astounded.

"Twelve," Lizbeth said, turning to look over her shoulder. She smiled with a hint of a blush rising on her cheeks. "I'm kind of small for my age."

"Don't worry about it," said Kelly, "I'm kind of dumb for my age. I wouldn't know how to turn that computer on let alone use it. I think I'm what you call a computer illiterate."

"It's not hard really. I'll show you how if you want."

"I'd like that." Kelly smiled, and she meant it. Lizbeth obviously had a brain that would have given Einstein a run for his money but it didn't seem to have done anything to screw up her personality. She was a sweetheart and Kelly found herself immediately drawn to the little girl.

"Maybe we should get you settled in the guest room first," Stephen said. He let one hand brush the top of Lizbeth's head in a fleeting affectionate gesture. "And you'd better get washed up. Dinner in half an hour."

"Okay, Steve."

They left Lizbeth at the computer and went across to the guest room. It was a mirror image of the study, furnished with an odd assortment of ultra high-tech and antiques.

The bed looked exactly like the one she'd had at the Medical Center, complete with chrome rails that could be raised and lowered and an elevating device for the mattress. In direct contrast, the chest of drawers against the opposite wall was a magnificent Chippendale highboy and the rocking chair in the corner could have come off the front porch of a nineteenth-century farmhouse.

The hardwood floor was partially covered by a throw rug like the ones in the main room and the walls were blank white drywall except for a group of framed photographs above the clinically efficient bedside table. An empty ball-socket swing armature was folded back away from the bed and Kelly could see a snaking coil of coaxial cable leading from it down to the floor. Built into the wall at the head of the bed was a polished steel panel with several knoblike fittings and a dark telltale light. Lying on the bed itself was Kelly's overnight case, flap open to reveal a selection of neatly folded clothes.

"Interior decoration by Marcus Welby, I presume," Kelly said.

"Sorry. I know it looks strange. My father was bedridden for the last few months before he died and we had twenty-four-hour nursing care, that's why it looks a little like a hospital room." He crossed to the bed. "I hope you don't mind but I went around to your house and chose some clothes for you. I didn't think you'd be up to it."

"Thanks," Kelly answered, not quite sure that she liked the idea of Stephen going through her underwear drawer. She felt a little uncomfortable, as though he was presuming too much intimacy for such a new friendship. On the other hand, the circumstances were special, and what was underwear once a man had actually cut you open and taken a look inside?

"I'll leave you alone. Bathroom is next door if you want to freshen up. Would you like me to bring dinner up or would you like to come down?"

"I'll come down," Kelly said. "Look, you really don't have to go to all this trouble, Stephen—"

"It's no trouble," he answered, crossing the room. He put a hand on her shoulder. "In fact, I'm enjoying myself. Now you wash up, or change, or do whatever you do and then come down. You can watch me overcook Stephanie's carrots. Lizbeth says I burn everything, but I want an objective opinion." He gave Kelly's shoulder another little squeeze and then left her on her own.

Sidestepping the bed, she went to the sliding glass doors leading to the deck and slid them open. She went outside and stood at the railing. Directly below her the deep blue rectangle of the pool shimmered in the last of the afternoon sun. Beyond it and over the roof of the unit opposite she could see down the sweeping, clover-blanketed hillside to the dark, ragged shroud of Tryon Woods.

Further still, beyond the far side of the dense forest she could just make out the tiny shape of the Crestwood clock tower and the double line of trees marching down either side of Main Street. Stephen had been right, the view was magical, especially in the muted half-light of the setting sun. A Norman Rockwell landscape, peaceful and content as day folded softly into night. It was exactly what she needed, the perfect image of why she'd come to Crestwood in the first place. She fixed the vision of it firmly in her mind, drinking in the details. The ravine was going to be the focus of her children's book and this would be the resolution. If ever a landscape said "And they lived happily ever after," this was it.

As it turned out, Stephen Hardy really did overcook the carrots, but the chicken and the salad made up for it, and so did the company. By the time Lizbeth returned from the kitchen with three huge bowls of vanilla ice cream doused in Hershey's butterscotch syrup, Kelly was feeling perfectly relaxed and over coffee in the family room upstairs, she began to feel really at home.

After coffee Lizbeth dragged them both into the study and

proceeded to give Kelly her first lesson in the operation of the customized JCL computer. After a quarter of an hour Stephen begged off and went to watch television, but Kelly stuck with it, fascinated both by the technology and the twelve-year-old's ability not only to use it, but to explain it easily enough for her to understand.

According to Lizbeth, the JCL computer that was almost standard equipment in most Crestwood Heights homes was not much different from a regular IBM. The big differences were the simplicity of the keyboard commands, and more important, the ability of each terminal to interface with the mainframe computers at the Cold Mountain Institute.

The CMI computers were Cray 2s, undoubtedly the fastest and most powerful in the world. The Cray 1, of which CMI still used seven, operated at the rate of 250 million calculations per second. The Cray 2 was twelve times faster again. The CMI computers could in turn be linked to virtually every database in the world by telephone, giving the local user in Crestwood Heights access to an almost infinite amount of information—as long as you had the right go-ahead codes.

The linked Cray 1s and the newer Cray 2s were what gave Max Alexanian his most useful tool for analyzing statistics, and at the same time they also controlled almost every logistical function of Crestwood Heights and Deep Wood Park. Even JCL, which designed and built microcomputers, used the CMI system to do all its projections, ordering, billing, payroll, and security.

None of which interested Lizbeth in the slightest. What she cared about was the fact that the terminal in Stephen Hardy's study literally let her make her dreams come true. Any thought she had, mathematical, scientific, literary, or otherwise, could be developed, expanded, visualized, and analyzed on the machine. The only boundaries were the limits of her own imagination.

Even if you were a computer idiot like Kelly, all you needed was the residence number on your door key. By entering that on any of the computers linked to the CMI machines, all you had to do was spell out your name. A menu of options, each with a number, would appear on the screen; type in the desired number, and the appropriate information would be given to you. Each step of the way the computer would give you help if you needed it, and all of it was free as long as you didn't go outside the CMI database.

After an hour Kelly was familiar enough with the computer to play a space simulation game called ORBITZ designed by one of the people at JCL. The object was to build a space station using a variety of robot arms before your opponent did. The first person to complete a station could then blast the other person to atoms. You could also play the game against yourself with a time limit based on the number of circuits around the Earth before the station fell out of orbit. Kelly never came even close to beating Lizbeth, but even so she kept on playing until Stephen appeared and ordered Lizbeth off to bed. He returned twenty minutes later, bringing more coffee up to the family room as well as a package of cigarettes. He tossed her the package and then hunched down and began setting up the fireplace.

"That's the first and last package I get for you," he said, arranging several logs in the hearth. "I've got my Hippocratic oath to think of."

"I really am going to quit," Kelly said, lighting up gratefully as he started the fire going. "Soon."

"If only I had a buck for every one of my patients who've said that," he laughed, joining her on the couch.

"Lizbeth is an amazing child," Kelly said, changing the subject as he sat down beside her. "It's sad about her parents though."

"It was a shock," he agreed quietly, staring into the crackling flames. "Tom was a first-class sailor and so was Georgette. Even after all this time, no one is quite sure what happened. They never found the bodies or the boat."

"Do you have any long-term plans for her?" Kelly asked.

"I haven't really thought about it. According to Tom's will I'm the legal guardian. She has an aunt and uncle in Seattle but they're not contesting custody; bringing up a prodigy is expensive and the Cold Mountain School is free. I guess I'll wind up adopting her formally at some point."

"You don't sound too sure."

"It's a big responsibility," he said with a shrug. "And whiz kid or not, she's just a child. I'd like to see her grow up in a slightly more normal environment."

"She doesn't seem to be suffering," Kelly answered. "Better to live with someone she cares for and who understands her, than an aunt and uncle she doesn't really know very well. She was born here, this is where her friends are."

"Maybe you're right."

They spent another hour in front of the fire and then Kelly found herself nodding off. Stephen shooed her off to bed, refusing her offer to help clean up, and then looked in on her before he went to bed himself. She was already in bed, covers up around her chin, reading the local history book when the doctor knocked on her door. He came into the room with a glass of water and a small paper cup full of pills.

"Three vitamins and a muscle relaxant," he said. He gave her the water and the pills, sitting on the edge of the bed as she swallowed them. "I want you to get a good night's sleep."

"I don't think I need a pill for that," she said, handing him back the glass and the empty paper cup.

"That's for me to say." He nodded toward the book in her lap. "Reading up about Crestwood?"

"It seemed like a good idea," she said. "Some of it's pretty interesting."

"The Town Tobacco Built." He grinned.

"What do you know about the Chapel Gate School for Christian Gentlemen?" asked Kelly. He frowned.

"Why do you ask that?"

"It was one of the things Hugh Trask was babbling about. The book says it's been derelict for years. I just wondered why he'd be interested in it."

"God knows. I haven't been out there since I was a kid. We used to pretend it was haunted."

"So it's still empty?"

"I guess so. Why?"

"No particular reason. It sounds interesting though. I thought maybe I'd work it into my kid's book."

"Maybe you should stay closer to home," Stephen suggested. "For a little while, anyway. You're still a bit on the woozy side."

"Maybe," she agreed, yawning. Hardy stood up, balling the paper cup in his fist. He leaned over to kiss Kelly good-night and suddenly they found themselves embracing. Almost without thinking, Kelly let herself sink into his arms, totally caught up in the feel of his chest against her breasts and the soft, cool probing of his tongue. They broke apart after a few seconds and Kelly could feel the color rising to her cheeks.

"I'm sorry," said Stephen, looking down at her.

"I'm not," she answered, not quite believing that she was saying it.

"Maybe we'd better wait for that too," he answered. He touched her softly, letting his fingers run down her cheek. The sensation seared down through her body like a bolt of lightning and she felt herself shiver. He smiled again, then turned away without another word. He crossed the room to the doorway and then he was gone.

"Oh, shit!" Kelly whispered, almost groaning. "What am I getting myself into?"

She tossed the book onto the bedside table, switched off the light, and dropped back against the pillows, staring up at the ceiling. She watched the hypnotic, rippling patterns cast up from the lights in the pool, thinking about what had happened and after what seemed like a very long time, she fell asleep.

She found herself awake again, shortly after midnight. She knew she'd been having a dream about sex because all the signs were there: she felt pleasantly swollen and engorged, her heart was thumping, and she had that cozy, satisfied sensation she always associated with making love or dreaming about it. Considering Stephen's good night kiss, the dream had probably been about him, but she was damned if she could remember a single thing about it. She was annoyed, because unlike a lot of women she knew, when she dreamed about sex it was usually explicit and in Technicolor. No symbolic locomotives chasing through her dreams with a single, staring, searchlight eye.

Frowning, her brain still cobwebbed with sleep and the effects of the pill Stephen had given her, she pulled herself up against the pillows. The dream must have been four-star and X-rated because the feeling that she'd actually just made love was so real that she found herself shifting her feet around under the covers looking for some kind of hard evidence that someone had been in bed with her.

Which was totally ridiculous. Stephen Hardy was no Svengali who had to go around drugging women to get them into bed. Another nasty seed planted by Hugh Trask's visit. Out of the mix of messages her body was sending came an urgent signal from her bladder. Groggily, and still half-asleep, she swung her legs out onto the floor, one hand pressed protectively over the bandage across her incision. She stood up and felt the room begin to tilt and weave around her. Stephen's pill was refusing to release its grip. She sat down again for a moment, but her bladder was insistent.

She rose a second time and this time she stayed on her feet. Shuffling like an old lady, nightie brushing the floor, she made her way slowly across the room to the door. She found the bathroom in the darkness, stumbled to the toilet, and dropped down gratefully. Relief was almost instantaneous, and she let herself lean back against the terrycloth-covered tank behind her, dozing. A few minutes later she came to again and managed to stumble back to the bedroom. She flopped down onto the bed, dragged up the covers, and shut her eyes. Maybe if she concentrated really hard she could bring back her phantom lover . . .

Hugh Trask sat behind his desk in the front office of the *Crestwood Illuminator*, looking blankly across the dark, empty room. Outside on Main Street, one of the reproduction gas lamps threw a weak light in through the old storefront window, casting a curving reflection of the newspaper's name over the worn, hardwood floor.

The old man let the tips of his gnarled fingers run gently over the edge of the desk. It was harder to leave than he'd thought; much harder. To his left an old, brown leather briefcase gaped open, while on his right, neatly stacked in the wire IN basket he'd used for thirty years were all the documents. The editor frowned, the caliper lines etched deeply from his nostrils down to his mouth. It wasn't the whole story, he knew that, but hopefully it would be enough.

Groaning softly, he levered himself up out of the chair and began to fill the briefcase. It was all there—the Xeroxes, charts, photographs, and letters. And the disks, the precious disks. He shook his head, wondering if there was still time. Maybe he'd left it too long. But he'd had to wait. He had to have as much evidence as possible.

Somehow he'd hoped that Nathan's niece might have given him the corroboration he needed so badly, but his visit to the hospital had been fruitless. She was either totally innocent, or she was already working for them. It didn't matter now, though. With everything packed away, he squeezed the briefcase closed and snapped down the flap. Hefting the bag in his hand, he allowed himself a sour smile. The weight of the evidence. Carrying the bag, he crossed the dark room to the door. He turned and took one last look back. His whole life was tied up here. Good memories and bad, but the life had been his to choose. Until they came. Biting back the angry, old man's tears, he jerked the door open and stepped outside. He'd make the bastards pay. Pay a thousand times over and then a thousand times more again.

The darkened room, buried thirty feet below ground level, was twice the size of a high-school gymnasium and silent except for the steady hum of the air conditioners. During the day the thirty data-terminal workstations on the dark blue carpeted floor would be occupied, but with the night shift on, all the screens were dark except for the monitors on the raised Master Control Level at the rear of the cavernous enclosure.

The side walls were lined with dozens of mainframe data-storage banks and the front wall, rising almost twenty feet, was completely covered by a plasma screen map that was the twin of the one used at the underground NORAD headquarters in Cheyenne Mountain. At the moment the screen was blank.

There were only two people in the room, a man and a woman seated in front of the glowing monitor screens on the Master Control Level. Both were hatless but in uniform, their shoulder patches bearing the snaking triple S logo of the Safeway Security System. The uniforms were the same deep blue as the carpet and neither of the two officers wore side arms. Except for the lack of weapons, the uniforms were identical to the ones worn by the Crestwood Heights Police Department.

In addition to the monitor screens in front of them, there was also a large console allowing them to cut into any of the terminals on the lower floor, as well as keep track of the various major alarm systems that were tied into the network. While the woman kept her eyes on the screens in front of her, the man leaned back in his swivel chair, reading a paperback. It was 3:30 in the morning, almost halfway into their midnight-to-eight shift.

"I've got a movement indicator on C-14," said the woman.

"How long?" asked the man, putting his book spine up onto the console.

"Couple of minutes."

"Isn't that the one we had flagged in the night book?" asked the man, frowning.

"Uh huh."

"Shit," said the man. "Should I call?"

"Not yet. Maybe it's a glitch."

"Yeah, and it'll be our asses if it's something else. Put it up on the screen."

"Sure." The woman tapped a trio of buttons on the console and the big plasma screen sprang to life fifty feet away at the other end of the room. A spiderweb of glowing yellow lines appeared against a deep blue background, eventually resolving into a schematic diagram of the Town of Crestwood. The diagram was divided into large grid squares, the lines in bright red. Orange numbers ran across the top of this screen while letters ran down the side. The man pulled his chair up to the terminal beside the console and tapped out a set of instructions on the keyboard. Instantly, a smaller version of the diagram appeared on his screen. On both maps there was a blinking green square in the C-14 square of the grid.

"Let's have the square," the man said quietly. The woman tapped a button on the console and then another. The plasma screen seemed to contract, folding in on itself, and then re-formed. Instead of a street map the screen now showed the floor plans of the eight buildings contained in the C-14 grid. The green square was still pulsing. "Again," requested the man. The woman repeated her actions and when the screen re-formed it showed the floor plan of a single building.

"Ident," said the man. The woman tapped another button and a line of letters raced over the screen: 72 MAIN STREET. OFFICES OF CRESTWOOD ILLUMINATOR/CRESTWOOD PRINTING INC. APARTMENT RESIDENCE HUGH ARMITAGE TRASK/ OWNER-EDITOR/ FLAG RED.

"I've still got movement," said the woman. On the big screen the green dot was inching over the floor plan, heading for the door. As she watched, the dot moved out of the floor-plan frame. Without waiting to be asked, the woman pulled the screen back so that it showed the entire grid square. The green dot began to move, but much more quickly. "He's in a car," said the woman. She tabbed the buttons again and the screen blew up to the full map of Crestwood. "Heading east on 36."

"I'm going to call," said the man. "It looks like a rabbit."

"At this hour of the morning he's not going out for a quart of milk," the woman answered dryly. The man reached for the telephone on the console, quickly tapping out a number. While it rang, the woman punched the plasma screen even larger. The diagram now showed all of Crestwood, Crestwood Heights, and everything out to the perimeter of the system. "He's going fast," the woman cautioned, frowning up at the screen. "At the rate he's going, we've got about another three or four minutes before we lose him."

"Hang on," the man answered. "It's ringing."

He stiffened as the call was answered, the receiver tight to his ear. He spoke quickly and than lapsed into silence, nodding every few seconds. Less than a minute after placing the call, he hung up and pushed his chair closer to the woman.

"What did he say?" she asked.

"We let him go as long as possible," the man said, his eyes on the big screen. The green dot was following the line indicating County Road 36. "Wait until he's almost out of the zone."

"Then what do we do?" asked the woman.

"Turn him off."

CHAPTER 11

Kelly gingerly guided the Aston Martin down Main Street toward the Strand Theater, wincing as she geared down. She was feeling a lot better than she had immediately after the operation, but even after a week, her abdomen was still tender and Stephen had warned her that she'd be out of commission for at least a month. So much for any plans to open up the movie house right away.

She turned the muscular sports car into a spot in front of the Strand, switched off the ignition, and opened the door. She eased herself out of the seat and stood up, one hand on the edge of the windshield for support. The pills Stephen had prescribed made the pain no more than a distant ache, but they left her light-headed and a little woozy.

He'd advised her against driving but after six days the peace and quiet had begun to get on her nerves. She'd insisted on moving back to her uncle's house the day before, and coming into town this morning was her first real excursion back into the land of the living.

She crossed the sidewalk, enjoying the heat of the bright morning sun on the back of her neck, then opened the main door of the theater. Stepping into the cool interior of the lobby, she paused. Still empty, almost painfully so, the air still faintly touched by the odor of stale popcorn.

And *that,* thought Kelly, was a load of nostalgic horseshit. Six days as an invalid had given her time to think. Phil Granger was a creep, but he was right. She was no businesswoman, she was an artist, and if she had any brains she'd be at work on her kid's book. If she was going to be *really* smart, she should be thinking about selling everything off, going back to New York, or maybe home to San Francisco and getting a proper job.

She made a little snorting sound under her breath and crossed the lobby, veering toward the office tucked behind the ticket booth. Having your appendix out hardly rated as a brush with death, but her little dose of personal mortality was making her think a bit more realistically.

A house in Crestwood Heights might be the right thing for Doris Benedict or Martin and Carlotta Nordquist but it wasn't for her, not in the long-term, anyway. Before long she'd be baking marble cakes and taking tennis lessons at the club and she knew it wouldn't take very long for the limited pleasures of Crestwood Village to sour.

Finding the right key, Kelly unlocked the door to the manager's office and pushed it open. She fumbled around and found the switch for the overhead fluorescents and flicked them on. Blinking in the sudden glare, she looked around the room.

It was large, square, windowless, and immaculate, which was a good thing, since every square foot of available wall space was filled with densely packed bookshelves, racks of film cans, and rows of old-fashioned wooden filing cabinets. At the far end of the room was a big rolltop desk that held a compact computer and printer, while a narrow table to the left was fitted with a pair of film rewinds and a viewer-splicer. A quick check of the closest bookshelves told her that her uncle probably owned every book on film ever published, not to mention a library of volumes on every possible aspect of communications technology from satellites to fiber optics.

Kelly groaned. She'd expected to spend the morning having a quick look through her uncle's papers and personal effects before getting in touch with Bekins Crawford to see if they still had a possible buyer for the theater. Now she had all of this to deal with. She hadn't counted on Uncle Nat being a cinematic pack rat. She lowered herself gently into the old wooden armchair in front of the desk.

Lighting a cigarette, she stared thoughtfully at the blank screen of the computer. After almost a week with Lizbeth and Stephen, she knew that almost everyone in Crestwood Heights had some sort of computer facility and she was no longer intimidated by the machines. There was a smoked plastic flip-top box of floppy disks beside her uncle's machine and Kelly opened it up. The first disk was labeled "Library."

Turning on the computer, she booted the disk and watched as the screen filled with a catalog of the office books and films. That was something, anyway. It was doubtful that anyone in Crestwood Heights would know the value of everything, but Martin Nordquist might have an idea of someplace in New York where she could send the list for an evaluation.

She found a box of paper, filled the sheet-feeder, and turned on the printer. Sitting down in front of the machine again she found the HELP menu, figured out the print command, and started generating the list. The daisy wheel began to clatter noisily and she sat back to wait. She noted that the computer was a JASON 1B, exactly like the one Stephen and Lizbeth used, manufactured by JCN Computers in Deep Wood Park.

According to Lizbeth it was better than all the other IBM clones because the JASON came equipped with built-in "emulators" that let it run not only IBM programs but software made for everything from Radio Shack to Commodore. Stephen had mentioned that JCN was making a name for itself in the educational market and that a lot of their testing had taken place in Crestwood Heights.

Both the primary schools and the high school were equipped with JCN equipment as was the Medical Center, the Cold Mountain Institute, all the PETES stores, the Crestwood Heights Development Corporation, and the police department. Kelly wasn't quite sure she liked the idea of one company having such a monopoly, but it obviously hadn't bothered her uncle.

"Anybody home?"

Startled, Kelly snapped her head around at the sound of the voice and felt a stabbing pain in her abdomen. Robin Spenser was standing in the doorway. Instead of his regular T-shirt and jeans combination, he was dressed in a dark pin-striped suit, light blue oxford cloth shirt, and a neat, dark blue wool tie. There was a broad, black armband around the right sleeve of his suit jacket.

"Jesus!" groaned Kelly. "You scared the hell out of me."

"Sorry. I saw the car parked in front of the theater so I thought I'd drop in and say hello."

"Hi," Kelly said. The printer finished, a dozen sheets

stacked neatly in the holding bin of the machine. "I guess you were at Hugh Trask's funcral."

"Yeah." He crossed the room and perched himself on one end of the editing table. He spun the winder on one of the take-up film reels and watched it spin around for a few seconds.

"How was it?" asked Kelly. Stephen had told her about the old man's death several days before. According to the police report, it appeared that Trask had been drinking heavily and had gone off the road at high speed.

"Pretty bleak." Spenser shrugged. "Half a dozen people. He didn't have a lot of friends left. The Gidden Funeral Home isn't my idea of a good time."

"Has anyone figured out what he was doing in his car at three in the morning?" Kelly asked.

"They did an autopsy. His blood alcohol was way up. Nobody's really saying it out loud but everyone figures he was going a bit senile."

"You don't sound as though you agree."

"I don't," Robin answered. "Eccentric maybe, but not senile. And not a drinker either. Not that I ever saw."

"So how do you explain it?"

"I can't." The young man shrugged.

"What about the newspapers?" Kelly asked.

"Hugh died without a will and there's about ten years of property tax outstanding. Phil Granger's already got his hand in that cookie jar."

"How so?" asked Kelly, flushing slightly as she remembered her thoughts of only a few minutes before. If the obsequious little bugger turned up right that second she knew perfectly well she'd hand over the keys to the Strand without a second thought.

"He brought it up at the Historical Society meeting last night. He wants to staff it with university students during the summer and turn out facsimile broadsheets from the 1800s. Ye Olde Newspaper Office, right down to wearing little green eyeshades and making sure everyone working there has his fingers ink-stained every morning. He's got the votes and the CHDC will probably cede the property over."

"It sounds ghastly."

"It is," Robin grunted, making a face. "And it'll work like a charm on the tourists. Granger should have been a PR man at Disney World. If Hugh hadn't been cremated he'd be spinning in his grave right now.'' Robin shook his head sadly and then straightened. ''Anyway, enough of that,'' he said briskly. ''What about you? Recovered?''

''Not completely. I'm getting around though. Stephen says it'll be a month or so before I'm a hundred percent.''

''Feel up to a bit of an adventure?'' asked Robin.

''Like what?''

''Like a picnic. Tryon Park. Gourmet sandwiches, a nice bottle of St. Émilion, and lots of stale bread to feed the ducks with. Hugh's funeral left me with a case of the glooms. It'd do us both good. Picnic therapy.''

Kelly thought for a moment and then nodded. ''Okay. One change in the plan though.''

''Name it.''

''Not Tryon Park.''

''Where?''

''Chapel Gate.''

''The old boys' school?''

''That's right. It was in that history of Crestwood you gave me in the hospital.'' She didn't include the fact that Hugh Trask had mentioned the name when he paid his strange visit to the Medical Center. ''I'd like to do some drawings.''

''Sounds good to me.''

''Okay,'' Kelly said. ''I'll go back to my place and pick up a sketch pad and some charcoal. Meet me there.''

''Give me half an hour to pack the picnic basket. And put that Aston Martin in the garage. We'll go in my Jeep; the roads back in there can be pretty rugged.''

Forty minutes later Robin pulled his battered, dark green Jeep Wagoneer into Kelly's driveway. He'd changed into faded jeans and a riveted chambray shirt that looked as though it had seen a thousand laundromats. The hiking boots on his feet were as battered as the Jeep. For her part, Kelly had opted for shorts and a halter top to see if she could take advantage of the perfect tanning weather.

She dumped her sketching case into the back of the Jeep and Robin backed out of the driveway. He drove as though he enjoyed it, firmly but with style, gears clicking nicely and turns taken just so. Watching him, Kelly found herself imagining him in bed with another man and blushed. Turning off

Crestwood Drive and heading north on High Point Road, Robin gave her a brief sideways glance.

"Penny for your thoughts."

"Woolgathering," she muttered. He laughed.

"Baloney. You were trying to figure out how a guy who drives an old Jeep and wears hiking boots could be gay. Right?"

"Something like that," she answered. "How did you know?"

"I know the look. It's inevitable."

"Sorry."

"No reason to be. Just as long as you're not one of those crusading types who thinks she can 'save' me."

"It never crossed my mind," Kelly said, which was true enough. "Why? Do you get a lot of that?"

"Used to. A lot of women think that all a gay man needs is a good roll in the hay with the right lady to turn him straight. It doesn't work."

"You've tried?"

"Sure." He nodded. "Making love with a woman can be nice. Most gay men have experiences with women, as a matter of fact—you can't say the opposite for most straight men."

"I promise not to rape you," Kelly said.

"Good enough. Case closed."

They went by the little two-runway airport and then, through a screening stand of trees, Kelly caught a glimpse of Deep Wood Park. The buildings were all redbrick and Jeffersonian and from the looks of it someone had spent a lot of money on landscaping.

"It looks more like a university campus than an industrial park," she commented.

"The look is intentional I think," Robin answered. "The property is owned by Cold Mountain and they set the building standards for the whole park. Most of what goes on there is research and the actual industry is almost all high-tech stuff so they don't need belching smokestacks or big warehouses."

"I don't even see any trucks," Kelly said. "In fact, I don't think I've seen anything bigger than a van since I arrived."

"There aren't any," Robin explained. "One of Max Alexanian's better ideas. There's a main freight terminal about a mile in off the expressway. Everything is unloaded there and dispatched to its proper destination along a series of service tunnels. A whole bunch of electrically guided trains."

"Underground?" said Kelly, astounded.

"Sure." Robin nodded. "All shallow, cut-and-cover stuff like a subway. The Development Corporation did a video documentary on it a long time ago. The model for it was Walt Disney World, if I remember correctly. Put the unsightly stuff underground and keep everything up top looking nice and pretty. It works, and we don't have big potholes in the roads from heavy trucks. Keeps the air pollution down as well."

"You sound like a Crestwood Heights booster," laughed Kelly.

"Not really. But I'm not as dogmatic as Hugh Trask was. For him Max Alexanian was the devil incarnate and any kind of progress or change was bad by definition. I think some of what Alexanian and his people have done is pretty awful, like the PETES stores, but they've done a lot of good too. You can't argue with the fact that Deep Wood Park has given Crestwood new life, and doing things like putting the trucks underground and setting up the communities so kids can walk to school without crossing a major intersection is pretty good stuff."

"He's not much for the individual," commented Kelly. "If you don't fit into the right slot in his statistical package you might as well not exist at all."

"He's used to playing by the numbers. He was involved with some big Washington think tank back in the sixties; they sat around trying to figure out how many people would be atomized in a nuclear war, that kind of thing. I forget the name of it."

"I remember now," said Kelly, snapping her fingers. "I knew I'd heard his name before. The Gidiots!"

"What?"

"That's what we called them. It was called the Georgetown Institute of Democratic Studies. GIDS. The people who worked there were called Gidiots. There was a big scandal in the late sixties, something about the director committing suicide. The whole place fell apart. I'm sure Alexanian was involved with them."

"Maybe," Robin said. "The point is, he's not all bad. Crestwood Heights was created to provide a model for an alternative to mass urban living. I think you could say it succeeded."

"I guess so. But I don't think you can go out and build a new town. They have to grow naturally. There's something forced about Crestwood Heights. Like a hothouse tomato. It looks terrific, but when you take a bite it turns out to be tasteless."

"I don't think you're giving it much of a chance," Robin objected. "You couldn't just up and go on a picnic like this in New York."

"I suppose not," said Kelly. "Maybe I should just sit back and enjoy myself instead of trying to analyze everything."

"That sounds like terrific advice. Now let's see you take it."

Beyond the grounds of Deep Wood Park the terrain began to change. The sloping meadows and pastoral hills of Crestwood Heights gave way to a series of heavily wooded scarps and dry, rock-strewn gullies, mute evidence of the dozen or more streams that had once fed the Tobacco River. Here and there, perched on a steep hillside or huddled in one of the ravines, Kelly saw a scattering of abandoned farm buildings, and once, hidden by a tangle of gray, dead slash, she spotted what looked like an ancient sawmill.

A little less than ten miles from the town the twisting, dusty road cut through a thick stand of second-growth pine and then they found themselves in a small, bowl-shaped valley, no more than half a mile across. Close by the roadside Kelly spotted the gleaming thread of a flowing stream, and then, squinting in the bright sunlight, she saw a bizarre collection of turreted rooftops off to the right, most of the redbrick building below it hidden by a brooding, high stone wall. The building sprawled over the summit of a low, scrub-covered hill, while at the base and slightly offset was a group of smaller buildings, shingle-roofed with whitewashed walls long since soured to a yellowish gray.

"Welcome to Transylvania," Kelly said, staring up at the walled enclosure as they approached the buildings at the bottom of the hill.

"The Convent of the Little Sisters of St. Antony," Robin said. "According to the history books, it was established back in the late 1800s." He pulled the Jeep up in front of one of the larger buildings at the base of the hill and they climbed out. Kelly breathed in the hot, dry smell of dust and grass, holding back a sneeze. Fumbling around in her purse she found her sunglasses and slipped them on.

"Eerie," she whispered. The only sounds were the high-pitched buzz of a cicada and the low chittering of the wind blowing the dust around their ankles. Without being told, Kelly knew that the buildings in front of them were the remains of Chapel Gate School; the institutional feeling was unmistakable. It was obvious that it had been unoccupied for a long time; every single window was smashed and the roof of the main building had the swaybacked look of neglect. To the left, butted up against the hill, she could see a small stone building that looked like it might have been used as a church. In front of it was a stone archway, the walls on either side no longer standing. The Chapel and the Gate. Chapel Gate. It made sense.

"What happened to the Little Sisters?" asked Kelly, looking up at the fortresslike building on the hilltop.

"They left long ago," Robin said. "I can't say for sure when. I think it's one of those secrets that every small town has. None of the old folks ever talk about it. The only thing I could find out was that the last use for the place was as a TB sanitorium in the twenties. The hospital was down here. There was a fire and the only thing left was the old chapel and the gate. The sisters moved out and the property was bought for the school. End of story."

"Who owns the property now?" Kelly asked. The steep drive up to the main gates of the convent building looked to be in reasonably good shape, and there were tall, red-topped stakes scattered around the school property, as though someone had been doing some surveying in the not too distant past.

"I'm not sure. Either the Historical Society or the Development Corporation. There was some talk about turning it into a summer camp a while back, but nothing ever came of it."

"You know a lot about the history around here, don't you?" commented Kelly.

"I guess," he said with a shrug. "It's kind of a hobby with me. Hugh was a freak for it. He had a lot of books, collections of clippings from the old paper. He kind of singled me out when I moved to town. I guess everyone else was tired of his stories. I started reading the stuff just to be polite but I got hooked eventually. Cut through that crusty exterior and he was a pretty nice old coot."

"You liked him."

"Yeah, as a matter of fact I did." He turned back to the Jeep and took out the picnic basket. Kelly gathered her sketching materials and then followed Robin through the tall grass sprouting up between the buildings. He found a small patch of relatively clear ground on the edge of the hill next to the chapel and spread out a blanket.

While he laid out the food, Kelly settled down on a convenient rock outcropping and began to work, doing a few fast scribbles to get the feel of the place and then concentrating on a more detailed study of the chapel with the bulk of the convent looming over it at the top of the hill.

The chapel had been built in the Gothic Revival style of the mid 1800s, complete with stepped-stone buttresses, deeply recessed window openings, and wooden doors with enormous strap-hinges. Somehow she'd imagined Chapel Gate to be more picturesque; if there was the seed of a children's book here, it was a macabre one worthy of Edgar Allan Poe or Nathanial Hawthorne.

No cute bunnies nibbling at dandelions or leprechauns under toadstools; this was a place of trolls and bat-winged horrors. Even with the compound of old school buildings in the foreground, she couldn't chase away the image of what this place had once been. Young men and women, thin, weak, their faces pale and bloodless, coughing up their lungs into handkerchiefs while black-robed nuns scuttled about giving what little aid and succor they could.

She started another sketch, a close study of the doors. How many people had gone through them, into the gloomy interior? Praying for release from the killing disease, knowing that it was pointless, but willing to grasp at any straw.

"Come and eat," said Robin. Kelly looked up and saw that he'd laid everything out and had started eating. Glancing at her watch, she realized she'd been drawing for almost half an hour, nonstop. She put down her pad and joined her friend on the blanket. "I didn't like to interrupt, but the butter was starting to melt and the beer was warming up." Robin popped the twist-cap on a bottle of Heineken and handed to to her. "You were really working away there."

"It's a strange place," Kelly answered, obliquely. She bit into a thickly piled roast beef sandwich and followed it with a swallow of the icy beer. Even the small bit of work had given her an appetite and she realized how much she'd missed practicing her art. One more nail in the coffin of the Strand Theater. On the other hand, you didn't find locales like Chapel Gate in Greenwich Village. "Do you think we could go inside the chapel when we're done?"

"I don't see why not."

It took them almost an hour to work their way through the meal Robin had packed and when they were done Kelly lit a cigarette and rolled over onto her side, head propped up on one hand.

"I'm stuffed," she said, feeling happily bloated.

"Tsk!" Robin gave a mock frown. "That's no way for a lady to talk. My Aunt Shirley would have told you the proper thing to say would be 'I've had a pleasant sufficiency, thank you.' "

"Really?"

"Absolutely." He nodded. "A very proper lady, Aunt Shirley."

Kelly finished her cigarette and stubbed the butt out carefully on a spot of bare rock. She plucked off her sunglasses and tapped one of the earpieces against her teeth thoughtfully.

"I've got a date with Stephen Hardy tonight. He's taking me out to dinner."

"So?"

"He wants to sleep with me," she said after a long moment.

"Aha!" said Robin, smiling.

"What's that supposed to mean?"

"Our roles are being defined," he answered. "I'm going to be your confidant."

"Do you mind?"

"Not at all," he said, shaking his head. "I'm honored. Do you want to sleep with him?"

"I'm not sure." She frowned. "The store's been closed for so long I sort of forget what it feels like."

"Tingly," Robin offered. "Like someone's massaging your bare stomach with a piece of warm mink fur."

"Umm."

"Blush when you think about it?"

"Uh huh."

"How about little bolts of electricity when you're with him. Hands touching over the sugar bowl, that kind of thing."

"I'm afraid so."

"You want to sleep with him, then. No way around it."

"But it doesn't make any sense," Kelly groaned. She pulled another cigarette out of her package and lit it.

"Sex and love rarely do make sense. But I don't see what the problem is. Go for it if that's what you want."

"It's pointless," Kelly said. "It can't lead anywhere." She sighed. "Over the past few days I've started to realize just how crazy it is for me to stay here. If my uncle hadn't died I'd still be in New York. It's just not my kind of place."

"Faulty logic. That's like saying if Hitler had been a better artist the Second World War never would have happened. The point is, your uncle did die and you are here. Why not just go with the flow and see what happens?"

"I can just see it," Kelly grumbled. "He'll be fabulous in bed, utterly attentive, and I already know he's a good cook. We'll get married. I'll have two quick kids, and that will be that. I'll turn into one of Max Alexanian's statistics."

"A good little Stepford wife," Robin said, trying to repress a grin.

"*The Stepford Wives* was fiction. Crestwood Heights is real. It's the American Dream in a neat little package. Safe, pretty, and prosperous."

"So what's wrong with that? You want dangerous, ugly, and poor?"

"No. But I don't want predictability. I think I've always had this sneaking suspicion that I'm really very ordinary and that living in a suburb or a place like Crestwood Heights would prove that once and for all. I'd just fade away and be nothing. I mean when was the last time you heard of a great writer or artist living in a suburb? Norman Mailer in Scarsdale? David Hockney in Westchester?"

"I don't think you give yourself enough credit," said Robin. "It's not the place, it's the person. And anyway, going to bed with Stephen Hardy doesn't obligate you to marry him, for God's sake!"

"I guess not. I'm just confused."

"Relax." Robin stood, grabbed Kelly's hand, and gently helped her up. "Remember your prescription for yourself: sit back and relax without any analysis.'' He kept his hand in hers. ''Come on, let's go investigate the chapel.''

The lock mechanism on the main door was heavily encrusted with rust, but with the aid of a tire iron from the Jeep, Robin eventually got it open. The floor of the small outer vestibule was thick with dust and it was clear that they were the first people to set foot inside the little building for many years.

The main room was empty, the thick, curving beams overhead clouded with cobwebs, the floor dusty, the remains of several broken pews piled in one corner. The altar was still standing, picked out by several broad strokes of buttery sun angling through the narrow windows. Behind the altar, high on the rear wall, was a niche, and in it stood a stone statue of the Virgin, headless, the swaddled Christ ignoring his mother's decapitation as he stared blindly out into the empty church.

''Who would do a thing like that?'' Kelly said softly, staring up at the stone figure.

''Kids,'' Robin said. ''Look hard enough and you'll probably find some old beer cans too. Screwing under the altar was probably the big kick.''

Kelly walked the length of the church and then stepped up onto the small stage on which the altar stood. She looked back down at Robin. He was standing directly in a beam of light, the dramatic pose offset by the uncomfortable look on his face.

''You were raised a Catholic, weren't you?'' she said, suddenly understanding.

''Six years with the oblate fathers,'' he conceded, stepping out of the light and joining her on the dais. ''Another one of Aunt Shirley's great ideas. I was twelve years old and I told her I was having these feelings about other boys. So she sent me to a seminary school. Make him a priest and then it won't matter that he might be one of those awful 'homeosexuals,' as she called them. The day I turned eighteen I packed up my rosary and joined the Marines. The ultimate exorcism.''

''We can go if you want,'' Kelly said, squeezing his arm. He shook his head.

''No. It's good for me,'' he answered. Kelly noticed a tattered woven mat on the floor directly behind the altar. She bent down to examine it and it fell apart in her hands. Beneath it she saw a small inset metal ring.

"I think I found a trapdoor or something," she whispered. Robin bent down beside her. He swept away the remains of the mat and the cloying dust, exposing a square of wood several shades lighter than the planks around it. The opening appeared to be about three feet on a side.

"Priest's hole," said Robin. He grasped the ring with one hand and pulled. It opened with a painful creak. They found themselves staring down into blackness but Kelly was sure she saw a wooden step.

"What's a priest's hole?" she asked.

"A secret way of getting from one place to another. A couple of hundred years ago it was a way for priests and other religious to escape when they were attacked, but it has other uses. There was one at the seminary school I went to. When we were doing sports activities out in front of the school we'd sometimes see Father Gregory, the father superior, coming out of the little grotto the school had on the grounds, or going into it, but never both. The young kids thought it was a holy miracle.

"They'd see Father Gregory looking out of the window of his office and the next thing you knew he was coming out of the grotto. We finally figured it out, though. One day we followed him into the grotto and watched him disappear behind a statue of St. Francis Xavier. There was a passageway leading from the grotto to his office."

"Where do you think this one goes?" Kelly asked.

"Who knows?" said Robin. "You want to find out?"

"How can we? It's pitch dark down there."

"I've got a flashlight in the Jeep."

A few moments later Robin returned with the light, and using the powerful beam to guide them, they started down the hole. The staircase was short, only six or seven steps, and reaching the bottom, they found themselves in a sour-smelling subbasement. Swinging the beam up, Robin picked out the heavy log-rafters a couple of feet over their heads. The floor of the little room was packed earth and Kelly was sure she could feel things creeping over the open toes of her sandals.

"It's a root cellar," she whispered. "Come on, let's go back up." The tickling feeling was beginning to creep up her bare legs. She jerked one hand down, brushing it over her leg, but there was nothing. Still, the feeling remained. She felt as though she were standing in an open grave and she had a horrible fleeting vision of the last scene in *Carrie,* where Sissy Spacek's hand comes up out of the scorched earth and grabs the girl. "Robin?"

"Hang on," he answered, swinging the light around. "Chapel's don't have root cellars." Three of the walls were earthen, like the floor, but the fourth was cut stone—the foundation wall of the church. There was a dark niche in the wall, no more than three feet across and less than six feet high. "*There* it is."

"There what is?" asked Kelly, willing herself not to think about the things that could be rustling around on the floor or chewing their way through the walls.

"The passage," Robin said, focusing the light on the opening in the wall. "The stone must be the foundation, which means the passage leads into the hill."

"Great," Kelly muttered. "It probably leads to some kind of crypt."

"I doubt it," answered Robin. "Come on." He stepped forward, but Kelly grabbed at the sleeve of his shirt.

"We're not going to go down there?"

"Why not?"

"It could be dangerous."

"Look," he laughed, his voice echoing slightly. He played the light over the first few feet of the passageway. "The walls are stone. It's not going to collapse. Be a little adventurous."

"Go with the flow, right?"

"Right. Now come on." Turning slightly, the light held steadily before him, Robin squeezed into the passage. Silently cursing her childish fears, Kelly followed.

Beyond the opening, the passage widened slightly and they could walk normally, their shoulders brushing the side walls. Keeping her eyes on the bobbing puddle of light ahead, Kelly saw that Robin was right. The walls were made of quarried stone, carefully mortared together, while the ceiling was gently arched. The stone was damp, the lime mortar crumbling, but it looked safe enough. To her relief, the floor was also made of stone and the crawling sensations began to fade.

Fifty feet along the passage the tunnel widened again and swinging the light upward, Robin pointed out a frayed cable that ran along the wall close to the ceiling. It was old-fashioned ceramic insulated wiring, corroded sockets fitted every ten or fifteen feet. Once upon a time this section of the tunnel had been lit electrically.

The interior of the tunnel was cold and Kelly shivered. Ahead of her, Robin paused, wet a finger, and held it up in the air.

"No drafts," he said quietly. "Funny."

"Funny peculiar or funny ha-ha?" asked Kelly, coming up close behind him.

"Funny peculiar," he answered. "You'd think there'd be some movement of air from wherever this passage lets out." He turned and faced her. "Still nervous?"

"Not so much," she answered. "Just cold."

"We've been going uphill for the past couple of minutes," he said. "We're probably pretty close to the end. You want to go on?"

"I've come this far, why not?"

After another hundred feet, the passage turned slightly and in the beam from the flashlight they saw what appeared to be some sort of iron gate blocking their way.

"What the hell is that?" asked Kelly. Robin played the light over the formidable-looking portcullis. It was made of wrought iron, the bars as thick as a man's index finger. From the looks of it, the barrier had been built at the same time as the tunnel; the bars fitted directly into the stone. In the center of the grating, there was a barred door fitted with tall hinges and a big plate lock. The mechanism was coated with a thick, crusted layer of rust.

"Interesting," Robin said softly, holding the beam on the lock. "Maybe the stories were true."

"What stories?" Kelly's nervousness was returning.

"The official history says that the Little Sisters of St. Antony ran a TB hospital, and before that an orphanage, but there are a few tall tales among the old folks in town about the convent having once been an insane asylum."

"Oh, God. Tell me you're kidding."

"Local mythology." He grasped one of the iron bars. It didn't move. "But this gives it some credibility."

"The gate was to keep the loonies from getting out?"

"Something like that," Robin nodded. "The Little Sisters was almost a cloistered order. Very little contact with the outside. Maybe they ran the funny farm out of the convent and the TB hospital down at the bottom of the hill. This tunnel would let them move from one to the other without having to go outside."

"Too creepy for me," Kelly muttered.

"Want to go back?"

"What else can we do?"

"The lock is rusted out almost completely. I could probably get the door open."

"Why not?" Kelly said, sighing. It was obviously what he wanted to do and common sense said that if there ever had been a crazy house beyond the gate, its occupants had long since died. "Give it a shot."

"Okay." He handed Kelly the flashlight. "Keep it pointed at the inner door, the lock," he instructed. She did as she was told, stepping aside as Robin backed down the tunnel slightly. He ran at the door and at the last minute launched himself sideways in a flying kick, one lashing heel striking the plate of the lock mechanism dead center.

There was a booming crash that echoed up and down the tunnel, but the doorway was still sealed. With a second kick Kelly saw the lock-plate buckle and there was a groaning squeak. On the third try the inner door burst open, the bars slamming back against the rest of the barrier. Robin picked himself up off the floor, grinning happily, and smacked the dust off his jeans. Giving him a mock bow, Kelly handed him the flashlight.

"After you, B'wana."

Beyond the gateway, the passage made a sharp right turn and fifty feet farther on, the tunnel dead-ended. Robin stopped in his tracks, the flashlight pointing ahead.

"Welcome to the 'Twilight Zone,' " he said quietly. This time the barrier wasn't wrought iron with a rusty lock. Directly in front of them was a sheet of highly polished steel, fitted flush into the walls and the ceiling.

"What is it?" Kelly asked.

"I don't have the faintest idea." He walked up to the featureless slab of metal and ran his hands across it. The sheet of steel was seamless. "There's no doorway here. It's a solid wall."

"I guess they put it up when the TB hospital burned

down," suggested Kelly. "Or maybe the school did it to keep the boys from getting into the convent."

"I don't think so," Robin said, shaking his head. "That metal is new. It's steel, not iron." He stared at the anomaly for a few seconds and then turned away. "Come on," he said. "Let's go back."

Returning to the surface and leaving the chapel was like being reborn, and after brushing the cobwebs out of her hair, Kelly poured herself a cup of coffee from Robin's Thermos and lit a cigarette, basking happily in the sunlight. She was secretly pleased with herself for having gone down the tunnel without turning into a gibbering idiot. She'd never been good in confined spaces and the tunnel under the chapel was definitely an advanced level nightmare for a claustrophobe.

"You really think they might have had an asylum up there?" asked Kelly, indicating the convent with her coffee mug. Sitting cross-legged on the blanket, Robin picked at a piece of long grass and stared at the chapel thoughtfully.

"It's not impossible," he said after a few moments. "Especially given the time frame and the location."

"Explain," said Kelly, dragging gratefully on her cigarette.

"The convent is isolated not only from the town, but from any major center. And you're dealing with the Catholic Church from seventy-five, even a hundred years ago. Back then they needed places like this."

"I don't understand."

"Fifty years ago, even less, you didn't even say the word *abortion* if you were a Catholic, and the state asylums were nightmares. Say you're a good Catholic, probably with money. You've already got half a dozen kids, your wife is in her forties. Bang, all of a sudden she gets pregnant. You don't want the kid really, but you follow the rules and you have it anyway. Only the child is defective—a vegetable, or worse. What do you do?"

"Send it to a place like this," Kelly said, staring up at the high wall of the convent and the battlement towers behind it. "My God," she whispered, imagining what it might have been like. "That's awful."

"It was the best they could do, all things considered."

"But what about that steel wall?" asked Kelly. "You said that was new. Do you think they're still running the convent that way?"

"No. I know for a fact that the place is empty. According to Hugh, the Little Sisters order moved out of there back in the fifties."

"So what about the steel wall?" repeated Kelly.

"I don't know."

"Why don't I ask Stephen tonight?" she asked. "He said he thought the place was deserted, but maybe he can find out."

"No," said Robin quickly. "Don't do that. Don't say anything to anyone, as a matter of fact."

"Why so mysterious?" asked Kelly, surprised by Robin's tone.

"I'm not sure," he answered. "Just a feeling. But humor me, okay? Let me check into it before you ask around." He looked at his watch and frowned. "Look at the time. We should be getting back." He began packing up the picnic remains. Kelly stubbed out her cigarette and helped him. Within ten minutes they were back in the Jeep and heading south again. They drove back to Crestwood Heights in silence.

CHAPTER 12

Like almost every residence in Crestwood Heights, the telephone line at 46 Erin Park Drive was fitted with an answering device. Returning from her picnic with Robin, Kelly noticed the flashing light on the security console in the foyer, and going to the phone in the kitchen, she picked up the receiver and tapped the MESSAGE button. It was Stephen Hardy:

"Hi, Kelly. Glad to see you're up and around. Hope you're not doing too much, though. Anyway, about tonight. Steff's been grounded by her parents for some reason and I can't find another baby-sitter. How about dinner at my place instead? Unless I hear otherwise, I'll expect you at seven-thirty. Oh, and Lizbeth sends her love and says she'll spot you twenty-five points on a game of ORBITZ."

The message ended and Kelly hung up. She poured herself a glass of iced tea from the jug in the refrigerator, lit a cigarette, and sat down at the kitchen table. She was relieved at not having to go out on a real date tonight and she realized that she was looking forward to seeing Lizbeth again. The child was frighteningly beautiful with an I.Q. to match, but she was also a joy to be with. Back at MRC&O she would have fitted into any number of kiddie campaigns; everybody's ideal daughter.

"Right," she said sourly, suddenly reminded of her chapel-side confession to Robin. Dr. Hardy was the ideal hubbie, Lizbeth was the ideal child, and Crestwood Heights was the ideal place to be married. If she didn't watch herself, she was going to get sucked right in. To hell with that. Stubbing out the cigarette, she dug around in her purse and found the printout from the computer in her uncle's office at the Strand. She'd show the list to Martin and Carlotta, and then come back for a nice long bath before going to Stephen's.

Even before Martin Nordquist opened the door of their little house, Kelly could smell something baking and by the time the potbellied ex-agent led her to the flower-print couch in the little living room, Carlotta was already asking whether she wanted apple or blueberry pie with her coffee. Kelly protested but eventually settled for apple, which arrived along with ice cream and coffee on a souvenir plate from Fort Lauderdale.

"So nice to see you looking healthy." Carlotta beamed at her, dropping into one of the stuffed chairs across the coffee table from the couch. She was dressed in a flowing cross between a hostess gown and a muumuu, done in lavender and pale blue flowers.

"First my hand and then my appendix." She took a bite of pie and a taste of ice cream. "I'm starting to think someone up there doesn't like me."

"Don't be silly," Carlotta said. "These things happen and we have to take them in our stride. Martin and I went on a vacation in Mexico once and on top of the you-know-whats from drinking the water, he got a cold and then we lost our traveler's checks. We survived."

"Carly and I saw you going off with that young fellow who runs the sweet shop this morning," Martin said. The observation was an obvious request for more information and Kelly took another bite of pie to keep from laughing. Martin and Carlotta were classic gossips.

"We went on a picnic." She nodded. She finished the pie and lit a cigarette. Carlotta swept up out of her chair and found an ashtray.

"Don't know him very well," Martin said, examining his soft pink hands, looking for nonexistent dirt under his carefully clipped nails. "As I understand it he's a bit of a . . . fegellah?"

"Gay," Carlotta explained. "Martin doesn't keep up with the terminology."

"He mentioned it," Kelly said slowly, watching them carefully for some kind of reaction.

"Now, Dr. Hardy, he's not that way," Martin said.

"No," said Kelly.

"Nice fellow," Martin continued. "An old-fashioned kind of doctor."

"He was wonderful when Martin had some difficulties last year," Carlotta said. She paused. "Are you seeing him?" she asked.

"You might say that." Kelly smiled. One of them probably stood watch at the front window to keep up with events on the street. "How did you know?"

"It's a friendly street," said Martin. "We take care of each other. Sort of an unofficial neighborhood watch, you might call it."

"Oh."

"Not that we're spying, dear," Carlotta said. "But when you're retired and home all the time, you notice things."

"So," Martin said, changing the subject, "is this a social call?"

"Not exactly." Kelly opened her purse and took out the folded printout. She handed it across to Martin. "My uncle has a large library of films and books in his office at the Strand. I'd like to have them evaluated and I thought you might know someone in New York."

"There's maybe half a dozen big film bookstores I know of," said Martin, lips pursed as he went through the list. "Couple private collectors I know."

"You want to sell them?" asked Carlotta.

"I think so," Kelly nodded. "I've been doing a lot of thinking and I've come to the conclusion I'm not cut out for small-town life." Spoken out loud, it sounded lame even to her and she wondered if she wasn't copping out.

"You'd sell the theater?" Martin asked, looking up from the list.

"Yes. And the house."

"A shame." Carlotta frowned. "And just when we were becoming friends."

"I'm not very good at business. And I don't think I could compete with the theater complex."

"As I understood it, you were thinking of opening a repertory theater," Martin murmured.

Now, where had he heard *that*? thought Kelly. Word really did get around in a small town. Carlotta poured Kelly more coffee and then began clearing away the dishes, humming quietly to herself.

"I don't have any experience with that kind of thing and I'm not sure I have the kind of resources to do it. Renting films is expensive."

"You never know until you try." There was a hard look in his eye that Kelly hadn't noticed before and she realized that Martin Nordquist was a lot tougher than he looked.

"I still think it's too much of a risk."

"What risk?" said the old man. "You already have the theater, and your uncle has enough films here to give it a try. Cost you nothing except some advertising and I could help you with that."

"You think so?"

"Trust me." He nodded. "Take it from an old man. You don't give it a shot, you'll always wonder if you could have pulled it off or not." He tapped the sheaf of papers with his forefinger. "Your uncle had a fondness for science fiction from the looks of this list. Have a Science Fiction Film Festival. After all, this is the most futuristic community in the country. If it works, you can think about doing more. It doesn't work, you can pack your bags and go knowing you did your best."

"I don't know anything about science fiction."

"Look at the list," said Martin. "It's cream of the crop. *The Fly, The Incredible Shrinking Man, Invasion of the Body Snatchers, Forbidden Planet, Village of the Damned, When World's Collide, Things to Come*. He's even got *Attack of the Fifty Foot Woman!* Five will get you ten you'll have all those scientist types at Deep Wood Park lining up to get in."

"You think so?"

"He knows what he's talking about," said Carlotta, returning from the kitchen and plopping down into her chair again. "He's not always right but—"

"I'm never wrong," completed Martin. The two old people laughed, sharing a private joke that was time-worn to the point of being a ritual.

"I'm not sure—" began Kelly. Martin stopped her in midsentence, waving his hand in the air.

"You can't be sure about anything in this life. But think about it, why don't you? And while you're thinking, I'll copy this list and send it to some people I know, how's that?"

"Wonderful," Kelly said, standing up. She had accomplished that much at least. "I've got to be going." She smiled. "I've got a date tonight so I have to spend some time making myself beautiful."

"Dr. Hardy?" Carlotta asked hopefully.

Kelly nodded. "Yup."

"Good for you." The woman beamed. "A nice man and bringing up that child by himself." Kelly could almost hear the violins.

"Now, don't matchmake me yet." She laughed. "It's just a date, and I'm still thinking about leaving Crestwood."

"You'll stay," Martin said.

"Trust him." Carlotta nodded. "He knows what he's talking about. You'll stay."

Robin Spenser looked out the window of his apartment above Aunt Bea's and watched the sun go down over Crestwood. The shutters on the window were open and the sliding glass window had been pushed back, letting in the sighing sound of the early evening breeze as it rustled through the trees along Main Street. Behind him, shadows had darkened the room, giving the modern wicker furniture a pale, ghostly appearance. Usually he enjoyed being in the small, airy apartment above the shop, but now he was finding it oppressive and barren. He was used to spending most of his time alone, and in fact he preferred a singular life, but ever since he'd dropped off Kelly earlier in the day, he'd been depressingly aware of just how alone in the world he really was.

It was a feeling he'd almost forgotten; the last time he'd been touched by it had been in Vietnam—his first recon mission. His job in those days was to be ferried deep into enemy territory, alone, assess any V.C. positions he could find and then beat it back to the pickup.

The first one had been a night drop and as the black-painted Slick boomed away, leaving him behind in the long grass, it had suddenly occurred to him that no one in the entire world knew where he was. He was a tiny inconsequential dot of humanity in the middle of a steaming, rot-smelling jungle, alone with himself and the long night as the rest of the real world went about its business.

It felt as though an invisible hand had clutched his heart

and squeezed, and for a few seconds he wanted to stand up and run screaming after the helicopter, pleading for it to come back and get him. But what would he say? Sorry, I'm afraid of the dark? He'd controlled it, completed his mission, and made it to the pickup point safely, and even managed to keep the feeling at bay during subsequent missions. But the seed had been planted.

It was a hint of death, that knowledge, because in the end you were always alone inside your own head, and no matter how much you explained you could never really make anyone understand what it really felt like to be you.

And now the feeling was back. The darkening street was as full of horror as that first jungle clearing in Nam, the lowering night was just as long, and he felt utterly alone. And that didn't make any sense at all, of course, because this wasn't Vietnam, this was North Carolina and it was now, not then.

He dug into the pocket of his jeans and pulled out the single key on a simple chrome ring. He'd done the usual run through the Veteran's Administration Hospital when he got back from his tour and they'd warned him about DSS. Delayed Stress Syndrome. That was years ago, but maybe this was it, or maybe Hugh Trask was the kind of guy who could make you believe.

Believe what, though? Robin bit his lip and looked out the window, the key like a sliver of ice in his palm. Looking at the man objectively, it would be easy enough to clinically describe him as being a paranoid. When he'd first arrived in town, it seemed as though the newspaperman was simply taking a fatherly interest in him, but after a few months things had changed. Hugh started talking about Max Alexanian as though he were the devil incarnate and Crestwood Heights his playground.

As time went by, it got worse. He began to complain that his telephone was being tapped, that his office was being bugged, and finally, close to the end, he refused to talk in anything but riddles and bizarre metaphors, convinced that he was under surveillance wherever he went. His most recurrent themes concerned Lizbeth, Stephen Hardy's ward, and how she was "the illegitimate spawn of Max Alexanian's ego," coupled with some unnamed horror perpetrated at the old Chapel Gate School. The only connection Robin had ever made between Lizbeth and Alexanian was the fact that the child attended the Deep Wood school for gifted children, a pet project of Alexanian's; and a little bit of investigation had come up with the old wives' tale about the convent once having been an insane asylum. When Robin pressed Trask for details, or even a single fact to back up his claims, the old man had come up empty, always promising that he was "gathering evidence." Eventually Robin had simply played along, humoring a man he presumed was slowly but surely decaying into senile dementia, ignoring the progressively more frightening claims. Ignoring them until now.

Two things had changed his mind. The first occurred the day before Trask's accidental death. The old man had come into the shop and ordered several different kinds of sweets, appearing to be quite normal. When he paid for the goodies though, there was a note folded into the five-dollar bill Trask handed him, along with the key he now held in his hand. Robin could still remember the message word for word:

Key to the door of my office. Not much time left. I think they're going to try and kill me. Will try to get out tonight, doubt that I'll make it. If not, look under the bed for the evidence. Nathan told me he took precautions but he died, too. Maybe his niece is involved. Be careful.

Obviously another paranoid delusion, this time acted out to the point of handing over a key to his office. But the following morning, watching the local news scroll by on the cable channel, Robin had seen the notice of Hugh Trask's accidental death. A coincidence? Perhaps, but this afternoon, coming onto that steel barrier in the tunnel underneath the convent, Robin had begun to have second thoughts.

The convent was supposed to be deserted, but you didn't put up a sheet steel wall to keep vandals out of an empty building. Something *was* going on at Chapel Gate, and now Hugh Trask's violent death under the influence of alcohol seemed even less likely.

The ex-marine shook his head slowly. He was starting to think in paranoid delusions himself. There was probably a perfectly good reason for the tunnel barricade, and drinking to excess, even for a teetotaller like Hugh Trask, made sense when you linked it to other examples of his erratic behavior. Lizbeth was a perfectly normal, if intelligent child; you didn't bug the telephones of a half-senile small-town newspaper editor; and the fact that Max Alexanian had once been involved with a militarist think tank didn't make him Lucifer. Still, there was that night-terror clutch in his guts, and there was the key.

Robin held it up in front of his face, the last light of the sun catching the sawtooth edges of the metal. There was only one way to find out and it wasn't by sitting here in the dark conjuring up old nightmares and trying to put together a jigsaw puzzle with missing pieces. He closed his hand into a fist and stood up. If Hugh Trask had been his friend, then he owed the memory of that friendship something, no matter how crazy it seemed.

"Well, personally I think it's a great idea," said Lizbeth, molding her potatoes into a roughly conical shape. She sliced off the top of the mound with her fork and grinned. "See? *Close Encounters of the Third Kind*. Richard Dreyfuss going crazy."

"I'm afraid it wasn't on the list," Kelly said, laughing. After spending the better part of the morning crawling around underneath the convent at Chapel Gate the normalcy of Stephen Hardy's dinner table was a welcome relief.

"It might be fun," Stephen agreed, tossing down his napkin. He sipped at his wine and looked at Kelly, seated across from him. "A lot of work, though."

"I know. Martin made it sound easy enough, but I'm still not sure I want to go through with it. I've pretty well made up my mind to go back to New York."

"Boring," said Lizbeth. She took a swallow of milk, leaving a perfect white mustache on her upper lip. She dabbed it away with her napkin and frowned at Kelly. "You're the first woman Uncle Stephen has really liked since I came to live here. If you don't stay, I'm going to wind up with one of those nurses from the Medical Center for a stepmother."

"Liz," cautioned the doctor.

"There's been a lot of nurses around?" Kelly asked, ignoring Stephen.

"Just one-night stands."

"Liz!"

"No real competition, though," continued the child. "Just enough to balance his hormones."

"Liz!"

"Sorry." She looked down at her plate, smiling broadly.

"Homework?" suggested Stephen.

"Just my exercises for Max."

"Exercises?" asked Kelly.

"Lizbeth is in the advanced computer class at school," Stephen explained. "Max Alexanian takes a personal interest, gives them special assignments."

"It's stupid," Lizbeth said baldly. "He gives us sample programs and we have to find the bugs. It's sort of like a game, but not really."

"What time do you go on-line?" asked Stephen, looking at his watch.

"Nine to nine-thirty."

"Which gives you two minutes to get to the terminal."

"Okay, okay, but I want to ask Kelly something first."

"Okay." Kelly nodded. "Ask away."

"Can I bring you to show and tell?"

"Show and tell? I wouldn't think they'd have something like that at the Cold Mountain School."

"Byron Yankounides did a whole project on computer recognition of fingerprints last week. His dad works for Biometrix. They make that kind of thing."

"I don't think I'd fit in very well," Kelly said. "I'm hardly the scientific type."

"That's the whole point," Lizbeth explained, standing up and pushing her chair in. "All we get is science and math all the time. I thought you could show us something about drawing. Max wouldn't mind."

"It's up to Kelly," Stephen said with a shrug. "But I think you should check with Max before you make any firm plans."

"I already did. I wore tight jeans and batted my eyes a lot." She smiled, doing a vamp routine with her hands on the back of the chair. "Maxie likes nymphets, I think. He's always eyeing Doris Cranbrook's mams—not that she has any to speak of."

"Mams?"

"Mammaries. Bazongers. Boobs."

"I got it the first time," Kelly said, laughing.

"You've got less than a minute," cautioned Stephen.

"I'm going, I'm going. But will you, Kelly?"

"Sure, why not. Just let me know when."

"Tomorrow, ten o'clock, room 402 at CMI. That's the Brainbank. Uncle Stephen will tell you how to get there."

"Okay."

"Thirty seconds . . ."

"I'm gone." Lizbeth raced out of the room, then stopped abruptly in the doorway leading out to the hall and spun around. "One more thing."

"Make it quick," Stephen said.

"Just a suggestion. But I really think you two should go to bed together soon. Too much sexual tension isn't good for you." She turned again and a few seconds later Kelly could hear her sneakered feet pounding up the stairs to the second-floor study.

"Precocious little brat, isn't she?" Kelly said, blushing hard. It felt as though Stephen Hardy's eyes were boring right through her from the other side of the table. For a fleeting instant she felt as though she were looking into the face of a predatory animal—a lion, or a wolf—and then the feeling was gone.

"How about those Lakers?" Stephen said, a twinkle in his eye, and they both burst out laughing, the electric tension between them vanishing with the sound.

Robin Spenser unlocked the back door to the newspaper office, wincing as he gently pushed it open, half expecting to hear an alarm go off. He knew there was nothing criminal about what he was doing but he still felt uneasy. His nerves were hot-wired to his senses and once again the fear instincts he'd lived with in Vietnam were screaming out silent warnings to him as he stepped into the darkness and closed the door behind him.

He was in the print shop, the presses looming like shapeless animals crouching on the floor of the long, low-ceilinged room. The only light came from two frosted-glass skylights in the roof and Robin paused, letting his eyes adjust to the gloom. For the tenth time in as many minutes, he wondered what he was doing and what, if anything, he expected to find.

The main floor of the *Crestwood Illuminator* building was divided into three sections: the rear, and largest, section containing the print shop with all the equipment necessary to produce the newspaper and any job printing; a smaller section that held the archives, clipping files, and two small editorial offices; and the front office looking out onto Main Street. A short flight of stairs in the front office led up to Hugh Trask's small apartment.

Moving cautiously, Robin made his way across the print shop to the archives and went through to the front office. The old-fashioned wood-slat venetian blinds on the front window were closed, letting in nothing but narrow zebra stripes of illumination from the streetlight outside. The front room contained Hugh's desk, a battle-scarred veteran almost a hundred years old, two other desks that dated back to a time when the *Illuminator* had actually been able to afford a staff of reporters, and at the far end of the room a monstrous old Washington flatbed press.

The cast-iron, hand-operated machine was the original press used to print the first single-page broadsheet published in Crestwood and seeing it, Robin smiled. It was Hugh's most valued possession and he'd once demonstrated it to him, showing Robin how to ink the rollers, haul down the five-foot-long lever to lower the bed and put pressure on the paper, and then spin the big wheel to move the carriage, run the roller over the type, and produce the fresh broadsheet.

The machine was ancient but the old man had kept it in perfect working order. Robin's smile turned to a scowl as he thought about Granger's plans for the newspaper, but he shook off his anger; he had more important things to do.

Climbing the stairs slowly, Robin went up to Hugh's apartment. He'd been there a couple of times before and knew that there were only three rooms—a tiny bathroom, a bed-sitting room and a tiny galley-style kitchen. He also knew that the old man's personal habits were slightly on the "eccentric" side and he was surprised to find the apartment as neat as a pin. Someone—probably Granger or one of the other people from the Heritage Association—had come in and tidied. The books and newspapers that usually littered the floor had been neatly stacked on the old bookshelves that covered one wall, the simple iron-frame bed was neatly made with the pillow fluffed up, and the kitchen was spotless. If there had been anything here for Robin to find, it had been housecleaned into oblivion.

Between the bed and the small window overlooking the street there was a small desk and on it, carefully protected by a plastic cover, was Hugh's computer. Crossing the room,

Robin went to the desk and sat down in the wooden-armed captain's chair. He plucked the cover off the machine and shook his head. At least a third of the companies in Deep Wood Park were involved in the computer industry and a *Newsweek* article had once even called Deep Wood Park Silicon Forest.

Almost everyone, himself included, took advantage of that fact and used the high powered JASON personal computer since JCN sold the units to Crestwood and Crestwood Heights residents at cost. Not Hugh Trask. Instead, he'd bought himself a Macintosh, insisting that he wanted nothing to do with Deep Wood Park or anything even faintly associated with Max Alexanian. He'd told Robin that he was perfectly willing to accept the fact that the world was firmly entrenched in the computer age, but if he was going to be a part of it, he was going to be a part of it on his own terms.

Robin went through the drawers of the little colonial-style secretary but came up empty. There were a few pieces of software, a full box of unused Sony disks, and a neatly filed package containing the dealer's warranty on the machine and a user's guide to Microsoft Word, but nothing else.

Feeling like a complete fool, Robin got down onto his hands and knees and looked under the bed, even checking between the springs and the mattress. Nothing, not even a dustball. Robin stood up, frowning. So much for Hugh's note. He put the cover back on the computer, checked to make sure that everything was as he'd found it, and then went back downstairs to the front office.

A quick check of the drawers of Hugh's office desk revealed nothing. Old invoices, tear sheets, petty cash vouchers, and all the other junk that tends to collect in desk drawers.

"Shit," Robin muttered. He sat down on the edge of the desk and let his eyes wander around the dimly lit room. The whole thing had been a waste of time and he'd let himself fall prey to Hugh Trask's paranoid game. There was no conspiracy, no murderous plots, and there sure as hell wasn't anything under Hugh Trask's bed.

The ex-marine frowned and stroked the sandpaper stubble along his jawline. Paranoid or not, Hugh Trask had been a bright man, and if he was suffering under the delusion that someone was after him, why would he have chosen to hide whatever evidence he had underneath his bed? You'd think he could have come up with something a little more original than that. If you wanted to hide something, you put it where your enemies, imaginary or not, weren't likely to look.

So where did that leave him? A bed was a bed and the only one in the building was upstairs. Or was it? He stared at the shadowy bulk of the old Washington press at the other side of the office. A Washington flatbed press, and the operative word was *flatbed,* the bed in question being the large rectangular frame that held the hand-composed cold type.

Robin stood up and approached the machine. Grasping the big lifting wheel, he elevated the bed and ducked his head to look underneath it. There was a whole page set by the looks of it, complete with the one-piece escutcheon of the original *Illuminator* masthead. Maybe Hugh hadn't been so crazy after all.

Working in the near darkness, Robin found a can of the thick, viscous ink used on the press and spread it onto the main roller of the press the way Hugh had demonstrated, using a wooden-edged scraper to squeegee off the excess. Risking discovery, he flicked on the lights in the rear press room, found a sheet of newsprint roughly the size of the bed and brought it back to the front office. Placing the paper on the carrier, he tried to remember the exact procedure for running off a proof.

With his left foot braced on the lower frame of the press, he put all his weight on the lever. Moving smoothly, the bed lowered and the inked roller slid forward, inking the type. As the lever went down even farther, the roller slid back along its gear track, the lower bed slid up, and the type and paper met.

He put his entire weight on the lever, making sure of a good take, and when he was sure it wouldn't go down any more, he let up the pressure. Moving around to the wheel, he grabbed it with both hands and spun hard. The bed released slightly, the carrier moved out like a long metal tongue and Robin was presented with a freshly printed reproduction of the *Crestwood Illuminator* circa 1897. March 13 to be exact.

Squinting in the poor light, he scanned the single page, holding it by the edges so the ink didn't smudge. The big story concerned the fire at the Sisters of St. Anthony Orphanage and Robin read it carefully, wondering if the report had anything to do with Trask's supposed conspiracy, but it seemed ordinary enough. The fire had started in the orphanage laundry and by the time the fledgling Crestwood Volunteer Fire Brigade had traveled the ten miles to the scene there was nothing for them to do but spray water on the smoking ashes. From the tone of the story it seemed that there had been some earlier anti-Catholic feelings about the place but it didn't add up to anything that could have any effect at all almost a hundred years later. Then he saw a little boxed notice in the lower right hand corner of the page.

LIBRARY NEWS
Recent Aquisitions:
TRAITORS WITHIN
ex-Detective Inspector
Herbert T. Fitch
New Scotland Yard
Hurst and Blackett
London

"I'll be a son of a bitch," whispered Robin. There were two things wrong with the notice. As far as Robin knew New Scotland yard wasn't even in existence in 1897, and even more important, the Crestwood Library hadn't been organized until the early 1920s. The notice was a fake, and if the title had any significance, it had something to do with Hugh Trask's evidence.

After using a second sheet of newsprint to blot the ink on the page, Robin folded it carefully and slipped it into the pocket of his jeans. It was too late to go to the library tonight, but he'd be there first thing the following morning. He spent another twenty minutes cleaning up the mess he'd made with the press, returned the ink to its proper place on the shelf behind the press, and then let himself out the back door.

In the darkness the furniture in Stephen Hardy's bedroom was just a gray blur of shape on shape. The only other time she'd been in the room was on her original tour of the house and she vaguely remembered it as austere and masculine, a chest of drawers in dark oak, probably inherited, doing decorative battle with a black lacquer hatch-cover bed with dark blue sheets and a leather-and-chrome armchair.

He stood on the far side of the bed, bending to turn on a small reading lamp on the night table while she stood across from him, slowly unbuttoning her blouse and wishing he was doing it for her. It was close to midnight now and it had taken him forever to even bring up the subject of her staying the night. Now she was almost wishing he hadn't. She felt awkward and uncomfortable, as though she were doing something wrong, and that wasn't the way she wanted it to be at all. For all his good looks and charm, the good doctor seemed to be a little short in seduction skills.

Keeping his back to her, he began to undress and she stripped off the rest of her own clothes as quickly as possible. Naked, she slipped under the cool top sheet wondering if there was something she could say to lighten the moment. She decided to keep her mouth shut and fluffed up the pillow instead, sitting and drawing the sheet demurely up around her breasts and under her arms.

He took off his shirt and sat down on the bed to remove his slacks, his back still to her. He folded the pants carefully, laid them over the chair a few feet away and then, bizarrely, he picked up the telephone receiver. She watched as he tapped out a number, listened for a few seconds, and then hung up. He leaned forward, flipped off the light, and a few seconds later Kelly felt the rustle of the sheets as he actually got into bed.

"Anyone I know?" she asked as he settled down beside her.

"My service," he answered. "I have a code that takes me off the call list."

"Oh." There was a long silence and Kelly knew that if she didn't do or say something soon, it was all going to be ruined. She turned on her side and slipped her hand onto his chest, letting it run in smooth circles from his neck down to his belly. The muscles were solid and hard and she realized that he was a lot stronger than he looked with his clothes on.

He still wasn't making any move to touch her so she let her hand drop lower, fingers combing through the thickening mat of hair on his stomach and groin. Taking the plunge, she gripped him lightly and almost recoiled. Even limp, his organ was immense, thick and muscular, lying heavily over his thigh. From the feel of it, she also knew it was uncircumcised.

"You don't see many of those around these days," she whispered softly.

"What?"

"You're uncircumcised."

"Does that bother you?"

"Not in the slightest. It's nice to have something different." He took her wrist, moving her hand away, putting it onto his chest again.

"I guess you've had a lot of men," he said. Kelly groaned inwardly. The whole thing was falling apart. If they kept on talking, it was going to be a bust.

"I've had my fair share. Child of the sixties and all that."

"How many?"

"Does it really matter?" she answered.

"No. I just . . ." He let it dangle.

"What?" she prodded.

"I wasn't a child of the sixties," he answered slowly. "For me it was either school or work, going back as far as I can remember. I never had much time for a social life."

"What about all those nurses Lizbeth mentioned?"

"Liz is a one-kid cheering section and she's looking pretty hard for a surrogate mother. I'm afraid the reports of my rakish ways have been greatly exaggerated."

"But not entirely," Kelly said, taking a pinch of chest hair between thumb and forefinger. She tweaked it lightly.

"No, not entirely." He laughed.

"So what you're saying is that you think you're inexperienced and you're a tad shy, right?"

"Something like that."

"Relax," Kelly said. "I don't go to bed with men based on their batting averages." She dropped her hand back down onto his groin. "Or the size of their bats." She gripped him again, harder this time. "Not that you have anything to worry about in that department." She squeezed him firmly and was rewarded with a definite stiffening. She could feel her own nipples hardening and the first deep flush of heat and wetness between her legs. Good old Griff had been well enough endowed, but Stephen had him beat by a length and no matter what the *Joy of Sex* said, she'd never met a woman yet who didn't like them nice and big.

"You're making this a lot easier," said Stephen.

"Good." She brought her mouth to his, flicking out her tongue to gently tease his lower lip. "And if you shut up, I'll make it easier still."

CHAPTER 13

The Crestwood Public Library was a small, two-story red-brick building on Lanark Street, tucked in between the town hall and the old post office. Once upon a time it had been the focus of a lot of community activity, but since the expansion of Crestwood Heights, which operated three public library branches of its own, few people except the older residents of the town used it at all.

For the previous fifteen years, the library had been run by Willard Brownleigh, a man who never signed his name without adding his Bachelor of Arts and Master of Library Science degrees to the signature. Occasionally—and grudgingly—he employed the services of volunteers from the school board to help him keep things in order, but for the most part the library was Willard's turf.

Publishers' representatives for the area had long ago learned that Willard was the hardest sell in three states and what little ordering of new stock he did was done by catalog. Stepping into the library was like dropping into an old and dusty past, and Willard Brownleigh liked it that way.

Ten minutes after the library opened the following day, Robin Spenser made his way up the short flight of concrete steps and pulled open the big brass-bound doors of the building. The main floor consisted of a front cloakroom, a large public reading room, and Willard Brownleigh's desk, a massive oak affair raised on a pedestal and with a clear view of both the front door and the reading room. To the left of his desk, a bank of high, narrow windows that looked out onto the town hall parking lot lit the room, throwing dusty bars of light over the worn and creaking hardwood floor.

Entering the reading room, Robin was struck by its similarity to the old chapel and he felt a tightening in his chest. Willard, toothpick thin, dressed in a black suit, white shirt, and green bow tie, looked up at the first squeak of floorboard announcing an invasion of his territory and peered over the top of his brown plastic-framed glasses at Robin.

"May I help you?"

"I just want to look through the card index," Robin said, keeping his voice low. Brownleigh frowned sourly.

"You know how to use the index, I presume?"

"I think I can manage," Robin said. He gave the unpleasant little man a nod and went to the rows of dark-wood card files lined up below the windows. He could feel the librarian's eyes on him as he moved and he had a brief vision of Brownleigh in his bedroom, leafing through an ancient copy of *Blueboy* or *Mandate* that he'd bought secretly years before, sweat sheening his face, glasses slipped down to the tip of his narrow nose as he worked on himself. Or maybe the little shit wasn't a closet gay, maybe he was one of those terrifying people who had no sex at all and simply hated everyone, regardless of sex, age, race, or anything else.

He found the Title boxes and pulled out the TO–TU file. Flipping through the cards, he looked for *Traitors Within* and came up empty. It simply wasn't listed. Cursing softly under his breath, he pushed the box back into the case and moved along to the Author Index. There was nothing under Herbert T. Fitch, either. According to the card file, *Traitors Within* didn't exist in the library. Trask had left him with a clue that didn't mean anything, so now what did he do? For Brownleigh's benefit he pretended to keep looking through the card file while he tried to put the puzzle together.

Hugh had gone to a lot of trouble to typeset the name and author of the book, and with the heading "Library News," it was obvious where he was supposed to look. Even if it was all some part of a mentally disturbed man's fantasy, it was unlikely that he'd have gone to such lengths without following through. So the book had to be here. But where? There were two floors of books under a hundred different headings, and he wasn't about to ask Brownleigh for help.

Without much hope of success, he moved down the rows

of card files to the Subject Index. *Traitors Within* was supposedly written by a New Scotland Yard detective inspector, so criminology seemed to be a likely choice. He found listings for a dozen different books on Scotland Yard, but nothing by Herbert T. Fitch. He stopped then, suddenly struck by an idea. What if Hugh had taken things one step further? Hiding a book in a library was cute, but what if he'd hidden a book here that wasn't a library book at all? If the book wasn't in the card index, then it was wildly improbable that anyone would look for it, even by accident.

He pulled out the Subject Index again, tipping the cards back to the "Crime" section and went through the list, card by card, trying to figure out the alphabetic progression as he went. It took a minute, but eventually he thought he had it. If *Traitors Within* had been in the library, it would have been listed between *Train Robbers of the West* and *Treacherous Night*. He jotted down the numbers, checked the plan of the library on top of the filing cabinets and went up to the second floor, taking the old-fashioned wrought-iron spiral staircase at the rear of the reading room.

The upper level of the library was utterly silent, floor-to-ceiling stacks stretching from one end of the building to the other in long rows, broken at regular intervals by cross aisles and small open areas equipped with tables and chairs. "True Crime" was located at the front of the library with narrow arched windows overlooking the street.

Checking the spine numbers, Robin walked slowly down the aisle and found *Train Robbers of the West* exactly where it was supposed to be. He checked beside it, above it, and below it on the shelves, but there was no sign of *Traitors Within*. Checking the scribbled numbers, he then went looking for *Treacherous Night,* and once again found it in its proper position. But there was no sign of the Herbert T. Fitch volume.

"Shit," he whispered, letting his eyes wander over the shelves. "Now what?" There was one more thing to try, even though it was a bit off the wall. Going to the closest table he took out the scrap of paper he'd written the index numbers on and wrote them down again, this time placing the number for *Train Robbers* above *Treacherous Night*. *Train Robbers* was listed at 941.07 and *Treacherous Night* was 922.04. Ignoring the nine, which was the basic subject number, he subtracted the last four digits, replaced the subject number and came up with 919.03.

The book with that number on its spine was on one of the upper shelves and Robin had to stand on tiptoe to pull it down. Checking the cover, he swore again: 919.03 was a book called *The Politics of Heroin in South East Asia* by someone named Alfred W. McCoy. The book was still in its shrink wrapping, sealed tight. Brand-new and never read. He'd struck out again.

Or had he? Frowning, Robin peered up at the shelf he'd removed the book from. Almost the whole row was given over to titles relating to forgery of one kind or another. Another one of Hugh's little wordplay clues? He took the book back to the table, and after listening to make sure Brownleigh wasn't sneaking around the stack, he carefully slit open the plastic wrap and opened the book to the title page.

TRAITORS WITHIN

"Well, I'll be damned," he whispered. "You really can't tell a book by its cover." He removed the plastic and the dust jacket completely. The book was covered in red buckram and from the worn covers it was obviously quite old. He leafed quickly through the book and fifty pages in he struck pay dirt. The book had been hollowed out to within half an inch of the edges and the pages had been glued together forming a perfect little stash. Neatly folded and fitted tightly into the space were a dozen Xeroxed pages and beneath those was a single Sony diskette, neatly labeled: *Statistical material. Use with MacStat software.*

Resisting the temptation to unfold the Xeroxed pages right there, Robin slipped them into the pocket of his jeans and put the diskette into the breast pocket of his shirt. He closed the book, replaced the dust jacket, and did his best to rewrap it in the plastic. When that was done he put the book back onto the shelf, making sure it was positioned exactly where he'd found it. He went back to the table, crumpled up his scrap paper, and went back down to the main floor. As he passed Brownleigh's desk the ferret-faced librarian glanced up at him disapprovingly.

"Did you find what you were looking for?" he asked coldly.

"Time will tell," Robin answered, flashing the man his best smile. "Time will tell."

The Cold Mountain Institute occupied a relatively small four-story glass-and-white-marble building directly across from the Crestwood Medical Center and separated from the much larger Leisureplex by a man-made hill and a thick stand of fast-growing spruce and birch trees. The building mimicked the Medical Center, the four floors tiered along the side of the hill like a set of steps facing east. The windows were gold glazed and the roof of each tier was fitted with banks of solar panels while the berming of each floor into the hillside provided an added insulating value.

Arriving at the Institute a few minutes early, Kelly checked in with the information desk in the pleasantly decorated lobby, had a magnetic-strip security pass pinned to the lapel of her jacket and was directed to the elevators. Stepping off at the fourth floor, she was surprised to find Max Alexanian waiting for her.

The gray-haired, handsome man stepped forward, leaning lightly on his gold-handled walking stick, his hand extended. It was midmorning but the Institute director looked as though he were on his way to a meeting with the President of the United States. Dark suit, perfectly cut, black wingtips polished like glass, and a dark blue silk tie knotted at the throat of a pale blue oxford cloth shirt. Once again Kelly found herself comparing the perfectly tanned man to Omar Sharif. She shook his hand. The grip was powerful and dry.

"Miss Rhine. Nice to see you again." He nodded. The faint accent again. "Young Miss Torrance said I should expect you this morning."

"I didn't expect to see you here," she answered. "I hope I haven't taken you away from anything."

"Not at all," Alexanian smiled, showing off a set of perfectly white teeth. He waved a deprecating hand and Kelly noticed the flash of the emerald signet on his baby finger. "The Cold Mountain School is what you might call my pet project." He took her gently by the elbow and led her forward. "Allow me to give you the VIP tour."

The Cold Mountain School took up the whole fourth floor

of the building and was made up of a dozen large classrooms, project rooms, a computer center that tied into the CMI mainframes in the subbasement of the building, a dining room, and a small-scale television studio. In addition there were a couple of magnificently equipped chemistry labs and an exercise room crammed with state-of-the-art fitness equipment. As Alexanian took Kelly from room to room he explained that the school was completely separate from the regular Crestwood school system and was funded completely by CMI.

"The children here are quite exceptional," he said as they completed the tour and headed for Lizbeth's classroom. "Twenty years ago when I began planning this community I searched out the best the country had to offer—the crème de la crème, you might say. The children here are their offspring: the best of the best to the tenth power. Of the fifty-odd children enrolled here, not one of them has an intelligence quotient less than one hundred and fifty-five."

"But don't prodigies burn out early?" Kelly asked, trying to keep the skepticism out of her voice.

"Only if they are exploited," Alexanian said, shaking his head. "And only if their specific talents are used with no attention given to those other things which make us human." He turned his smile on her again. "Such as art."

"I've got to admit that Lizbeth seems pretty well adjusted," Kelly said as they reached the classroom door. "Especially considering her parents' death. She seems happy enough with Stephen."

"Lizbeth is happy because she is loved. We all love her here." It seemed like an odd comment to make, but Kelly let it pass. Alexanian patted her on the shoulder. "I'm afraid I've stolen some of your show-and-tell time," he said. "When you're finished, I'd be more than pleased if you'd let me take you to lunch. Perhaps I can show you more of what we're trying to do here in Crestwood Heights."

"That would be nice," Kelly said after a moment. Something about the man made all her alarms go off, but he *was* fascinating.

"Marvellous." He shot the left cuff of his jacket and glanced at the heavy gold watch on his wrist. "I'll meet you at the main-floor information desk at twelve." He shook Kelly's hand again and then turned away. She watched as he limped down the brightly lit corridor and then she opened the door to Lizbeth's classroom.

Back in his apartment over the shop, Robin poured himself a cup of coffee, sat down at the kitchen table and unfolded the pages Hugh Trask had hidden in the book, flattening them with the palm of his hand. Setting the computer disk to one side, he took a swallow of coffee and then settled down to read. The first two items were copies of announcements from Trask's own paper dated March 17 and March 18, 1977.

INTERMEDIX LTD.

Intermedix Ltd. is pleased to announce the appointment of Jack L. Torrance to the position of Project Director, Research Division. Dr. Torrance was previously Deputy Director, Systems Applications, Concord Engineering Corporation of Boston, Mass. Dr. Torrance was educated at Columbia University and M.I.T. He is married to Dr. Elizabeth Torrance, also of Boston.

CRESTWOOD HEIGHTS MEDICAL CENTER

CHMC is pleased to announce the appointment of Dr. Elizabeth Torrance to the position of Senior Research Director in the CHMC branch of the Federal Infertility Program. Dr. Torrance was previously employed at the FIP branch at Boston General Hospital as Assistant Program Director, Research. Dr. Torrance was educated at the University of California, Los Angeles, and Johns Hopkins. She is married to Dr. Jack Torrance of Intermedix Ltd., Deep Wood Park.

It took him a few seconds but he finally made the connection. Lizbeth Torrance, Stephen Hardy's godchild; these were her parents. Even from the bland corporate announcements Robin could figure out a bit of their background. Jack Torrance, an engineer from MIT probably doing work of a medical nature in Boston, meets his future wife, who is working at Boston General. Max Alexanian, always on the lookout for new talent, suggests either Jack Torrance or his wife for work in Crestwood Heights. Another position is offered to the spouse to make the deal attractive and they move from Boston. A little while later Lizbeth arrives. Simple, ordinary, perfectly normal. Robin was willing to bet that the same thing had happened to dozens of families now living and working in Crestwood. So why had Hugh Trask been interested in the couple?

The next item was a copy of an insurance application, specifically the medical questionnaire. The company, Physicians Insurance Underwriters of America, was based in Boston and the date on the form was 1976, a year prior to the Torrances arrival in Crestwood. According to the form Elizabeth Torrance appeared to be in good health, had not used marijuana, cocaine, or any psychoactive drugs within the preceding five years and had only been hospitalized once in that time.

In her own neat printing Dr. Torrance had admitted to surgery in 1974. The diagnosis at that time had been cancer to the uterus and the advised treatment had been a hysterectomy. The surgery had taken place on July 14, 1974, at Boston Memorial Hospital and between then and the filing of the application there had been no recurrence of the cancer.

Robin sat back in his chair, frowning. If Elizabeth Torrance had been given a hysterectomy in 1974, how had she given birth to a child in 1977? He turned to the next item and the mystery deepened.

> Torrance, Lizbeth Alexandra, 7 pounds 11oz. Born 7:34 A.M. August 12, 1977, at the Crestwood Medical Center, a daughter for Jack and Elizabeth of Crestwood Heights and a niece for Rebecca Bailey of Seattle. Our thanks to Dr. Stephen Hardy and the caseroom staff at CMC.

The next page was a poorly reproduced photograph taken from the July issue of the *Intermedix Journal*, presumably a newsletter produced by Jack Torrance's company. The picture showed several people in cocktail dress. Max Alexanian, smiling as usual, was to the left, his arm around an attractive, blond-haired woman. Beside the woman was a taller man with dark hair, and beside him was a balding, slightly overweight man beaming into the camera.

The caption identified the woman as Dr. Elizabeth Torrance, the man in the center as her husband, Jack Torrance of Intermedix, and the balding man as Stewart Damien, senior VP of research. A standard cocktail-party PR photograph. Except for one thing: even poorly reproduced, it was easy to see that Dr. Elizabeth Torrance, the woman who'd had a hysterectomy thirteen years before, was obviously pregnant.

There were three newspaper clippings on the last Xerox sheet. The first, dated six months ago, was from the *Detroit News*. It was a brief story on the deaths of Jack and Elizabeth Torrance. A freak storm had come up, overturned their boat, and both of them drowned. The bodies hadn't been recovered.

The second clipping, this one from the *Seattle Post Intelligencer* and dated less than a week after the first story, described a fire in the Normandy Park home of Mrs. Rebecca Torrance Bailey. Mrs. Bailey, a widow, died in the fire.

The third clipping, less than two months old, was a death notice and obituary from Trask's paper. The obituary was for Nathan Somerville, Kelly's uncle, and listed the cause of death as a cerebral hemorrhage.

Robin pushed the pages into a pile and went through them again, trying to make some sense of the information Hugh Trask had been so secretive about. Just what did it all add up to?

Elizabeth Torrance contracted cancer of the uterus and had a hysterectomy in 1974. Three years later she shows up in a photograph looking massively pregnant. A month after the picture is taken she bears a healthy child. Unless she was lying on the insurance form, she had done the impossible. The rest of it was less clear, but Trask had obviously linked the deaths of the Torrances to the aunt in Seattle and to Nathan Somerville. But what was the connection?

The only real documentation he had was the insurance form, and acting on a hunch, he got up, went to the telephone, and called long-distance to his stockbroker in Miami. The broker, John Laird, had been the one who told Robin that the various companies in Deep Wood Park were good growth investments and he'd also been instrumental in getting Robin the deal for the sweetshop downstairs.

"Cavanaugh-Watson McLeod. John Laird speaking."

"John. Robin Spenser."

"Robin, nice to hear from you. How's life in the Most Technologically Advanced Community in America?" The slogan was used by Deep Wood Investments, the umbrella company Robin had invested in.

"Good enough. I was wondering if you could give me a bit of information."

"Fire away."

"There's an insurance company called Physicians Insurance Underwriters of America—head office in Boston, I think."

"And?"

"I want to know who the parent company is."

"Hang on." Robin could hear the dull clicking of computer keys. A few moments later the stockbroker was back on the line. "Robin?"

"Still here."

"PIUA is owned by a group called M.I.A. Inc.—Medical Industries Alliance. Real headhunters. They find small undercapitalized companies, feed them cash for a while, and then take them over. According to the file I've got here they have a neat little foundation scam going, too."

"I don't get it."

"Simple," Laird explained. "M.I.A. has a foundation called the American Institute for Studies in Medicine and Technology. They fund labs and research operations in most of the university medical schools and half the major hospitals in the country. When they see research going on that they like, they hire away the people doing the research to the appropriate private sector company owned by M.I.A.

"It's kind of like the farm team system in baseball: when you get hot, they bring you up from the minors. Except with them, as soon as they hire away the best people, they stop funding the research project. The foundation is tax-free and so are the university and hospital projects, so the M.I.A. companies are getting their whole research and development programs for nothing. A little sleazy, but perfectly legal."

Robin nodded thoughtfully to himself. It made sense, and so did owning an insurance company that specialized in underwriting physicians. The personal information on your insurance application was a nice starting point for building a dossier on a prospective employee.

"Another thing," said Robin. "A company called Intermedix."

"Easy," Laird replied. "It's owned by M.I.A."

"You're sure?"

"Absolutely. It's right here on the screen under 'wholly owned subsidiaries.' Hang on a second." There was another moment of key tapping and then Laird was back. "I thought so. Intermedix is one of the companies in the Deep Wood Investments portfolio. You own two hundred and thirty-two shares of their B stock, as a matter of fact." He paused. "Why so interested?"

"Just doing some research, John. One more thing."

"Sure."

"Is there any way of finding out the names of the people who own this M.I.A. operation?"

"Shouldn't be too hard. I can get you a list of their board of directors anyway. It'll take a while. A day maybe."

"That would be great. Call me here and if I'm not around, just leave a message on the machine. You've been a big help."

"No problem. Keep in touch and if you strike it rich up there in Candyland, you know who to call. Remember, I'm the one who told you to get into franchises."

"I'll keep in touch, John. Thanks." Robin hung up the telephone and went back to the kitchen table. "Circles within circles," he said quietly. He picked up the square, plastic-cased diskette that had been hidden with the photocopies. To find out what information it contained he was going to have to go back into Hugh Trask's apartment to use the computer. He dropped the diskette onto the pile of Xeroxes. He hoped that whatever was on it would give him some answers, because all he had now were questions, and pretty strange ones at that.

CHAPTER 14

Kelly finished up her show-and-tell appearance by eleven-thirty and gratefully took the elevator back down to the lobby. The experience had been both exhilarating and exhausting. The kids—fifteen of them, including Lizbeth—had bombarded her with hundreds of questions about drawing, painting, and sculpture, and the only way she'd gotten away was by promising to come back the following week.

She checked her watch as the elevator reached the main floor, pleased that she'd have a bit of a rest before her lunch with Alexanian. Fifteen geniuses took the wind out of your sails and what she wanted most was a cigarette and a few minutes of peace.

The lobby of the Institute building was an extension of the ground floor, designed like a Roman atrium with a slanting glass ceiling that sloped upward to the second floor of the main building. There were scattered groups of comfortable chairs here and there, the clusters screened from each other by a variety of trees planted in large, terra-cotta pots, and off to one side was a discreetly hidden self-serve counter for tea and coffee. The glass ceiling and walls were tinted just enough to cut down the glare and gave the whole area a peaceful, forestlike ambience.

There was almost no one else in the lobby and after fixing herself a cup of coffee Kelly had no trouble finding a table and chair all to herself. She plumped down in the sling-back seat, lit a cigarette, and blew out a long sighing plume of smoke.

It was amazing what a little bit of sex could do for you,

and equally amazing that you could get along without it for so long and not even notice. She took a sip of coffee and leaned back in the chair. Stephen might have been a bit of a slow starter in bed, but after a while he'd proved himself to be a more than competent lover. Not the best she'd ever had, but not the worst either, especially for the first time, which was usually less than terrific anyway. At least the buzz was there, and that's what really counted. Still, she was glad she hadn't spent the night; that would have been going too far, at least for now.

She stared up at the tinted glass far above her head and found herself wondering what it was exactly that made an encounter like the one last night either good, bad, or indifferent. Usually she didn't bother thinking about that kind of thing, but with Stephen it was different; something about him made that kind of analysis seem important. Maybe it was because he was a symbol for her feelings about leaving or staying on in Crestwood Heights, or maybe it was because she took their relationship seriously.

During their lovemaking the night before, she'd surprised herself by the extent of her passion and arousal; thinking about it now, she realized it had nothing to do with technique or titillation. It had been much more cerebral than that. Once, during a lull in the proceedings, she'd begun thinking of what it really meant to have a man inside you and the simple fact of his hardness, almost motionless but stretching and filling her, was enough to touch off an explosive orgasm that surprised both of them.

"Oh God!" she moaned softly, watching the tinted clouds scud by overhead. "Don't tell me I'm falling in love!"

She lowered her head and took another sip of coffee. Now wouldn't that be your basic kick in the pants? Here she was trying to be the hard-nosed career woman refusing to let herself be co-opted into a suburban utopia and all the while she was falling in love with the town's most eligible bachelor.

She took a last drag on her cigarette and then stubbed it out in the big glass ashtray in the center of the table. Ever since she could remember, the act of love, sex, screwing, call it what you will, had always worked as a stimulant, sharpening her senses and bringing things into perspective. A roll in the hay keeps the doctor away. Unless the doctor happened to be the one with whom you are having the roll. Instead of making things clearer, sleeping with Stephen was confusing the hell out of her.

"Damn!" she whispered. "I *am* falling in love with him."

"Miss Rhine?" Startled, Kelly looked up and found herself staring at Max Alexanian, immaculate and unrumpled, looking classy enough to be selling high-priced cars or exotic gourmet coffees. And then she knew what had been bothering her about him. Gold-handled cane and all, he was just too perfect, an actor always in character so you never knew what he was really thinking.

"I didn't hear you coming."

"I'm sorry if I startled you." The silver-haired man smiled. "Are you still free for my little tour?"

"Of course," Kelly nodded, standing.

"Good. I have taken the liberty of ordering lunch for us at the Forum."

"I've never heard of it."

"Understandable," Alexanian said. "The Forum is a private club used by the staff of the various groups in Deep Wood Park. Much preferable to the usual institutional fare one gets in a corporate cafeteria."

"I guess I should follow you there," Kelly said, digging into her purse for the keys to the Aston Martin.

"No, no," Alexanian said, smiling again. "Leave your car here. We'll take the subshuttle." Taking Kelly gently by the elbow, he led her back to the bank of elevators. The doors slid open, and once inside Alexanian took a key-card out of his breast pocket and inserted it into a slot below the regular floor buttons. There was a brief pause and then the doors slid shut. A second later the elevator began to move—downward.

"A friend of mine mentioned this," Kelly said as they dropped. "Some kind of underground freight system."

"That, and much more." The elevator came to a smooth stop, the doors opened, and they stepped out. Kelly found herself in what appeared to be a waiting room of some kind. The far wall was glass, fitted with a sliding glass door and looked out onto a large, brightly lit tunnel.

The tunnel walls, arching at least fifteen feet overhead, were painted a brilliant robin's egg blue. At waist height along the walls were lines of heavy conduit, each one a different bright color. The floor of the tunnel was smooth without visible tracks of any sort.

As Kelly watched, a strange vehicle that looked like a cross between a forklift and a vacuum cleaner with arms shot by along the center of the tunnel floor doing at least thirty miles per hour. A few seconds later another machine went by in the opposite direction. This one looked more like a tiny, driverless flatbed truck, its rear platform loaded with half a dozen large cardboard containers.

"There are four lanes," explained Alexanian, leading Kelly to the glass wall. "The inner lanes are for freight traffic, the two lanes against the wall are for the shuttle carts. Speaking of which, I should order us one." He gave her another of his smiles and took out his key-card again, slipping it into a boxlike meter on the wall.

"I don't see any lanes," Kelly said, peering at the floor of the tunnel. "If there aren't any drivers how do those things know where to go?"

"The freight carts are wire-guided. The wires are buried in the floor and the carts follow an electromagnetic signal generated from the main freight terminal about four miles from here. The shuttle carts are guided by laser sensors and you can choose your destination manually. It seems quite complicated but actually it's quite a simple system. Much of the technology has been in use for years in Japan and also at the major automobile plants in Detroit. The tunnel system itself was first used on a large scale by the Disney people almost thirty years ago.

"Those multicolored conduits you see on the walls are the service cables for the three residential communities, this complex, the hospital, and the companies in Deep Wood Park. Totally accessible, weatherproof, and continually monitored. During the course of the system's existence we calculate that we've saved in excess of more than eighty million dollars in normally expected public works maintenance for a community the size of Crestwood Heights. Five years from now, the system will have paid for itself by those savings alone, not to mention expedited service and cost effectiveness."

"More statistics," Kelly said, smiling. Alexanian shrugged.

"We live by them, Miss Rhine. That is a simple fact of life."

"I guess I shouldn't tease you about it," Kelly said. "It's just that I wasn't brought up in that world."

"Perhaps not," said Alexanian, his smile cooled by the chill in his voice. "But it is the world you live in now."

"So in other words I'd better get used to it?"

"If you want to survive, yes."

Another machine appeared on the other side of the glass wall and slowed as it drew level with the waiting room. It pulled up directly in front of the sliding door, which opened as the vehicle came to a stop.

"It looks like a bigger version of one of those golf-cart wheelchairs I used in the hospital."

"Officially they're called MTUs," he said, taking her elbow and leading her out into the tunnel. "Mobile Transport Units. You're right, of course. The wheelchair design is an offshoot of this technology."

There were four padded seats on the open cart, but instead of a steering wheel there was nothing but a large keypad made up of eight colored squares and a single key marked ENTER. Alexanian sat Kelly down in the driver's seat and got in beside her.

"Now what?" asked Kelly.

"The system has eight main passages. This one, blue, is the longest. It goes from the main freight terminal directly to Deep Wood Park, swinging by the Institute and the Medical Center on its way. Each tunnel has a color. Press the keypad colors in the order you want, hit 'Enter,' and the shuttle will take you there. In this case all you have to do is press blue, then 'Enter,' and the cart will automatically take you to the end of the blue line. If you wanted to go to Orchard Park, you would press blue for this line, then white, which is the main tunnel leading to the residential areas, and then yellow, which is the destination for Orchard Park. Simple enough?"

"Blue and then 'Enter'?"

"That's correct."

Tentatively Kelly reached out and tapped the blue square on the keypad and then pressed the ENTER key. Soundlessly the cart began to move, increasing speed until it was going ten or fifteen miles per hour.

"Ever have any accidents?" asked Kelly, trying to keep her eyes off the rainbow blur of conduits only two or three feet away against the tunnel wall.

"Never," Alexanian said, shaking his head. "The system is designed so that the MTUs carrying people always give way to the center lane freight carriers. If our cart had to cross the freight paths the sensors would tell the guidance mechanism if the way was clear or not."

"How come there aren't more people down here?" asked Kelly as they sped along. Every now and again she saw a freight carrier scoot by, but they appeared to be the only people riding in the tunnels.

"The population doesn't require mass transit of this kind. The system is economically based, not sociologically."

"Which means?"

"The system increases the efficiency of goods transport, the bar-coding of the goods themselves at the freight terminal makes inventory control much easier and the self-loading and unloading MTUs cut down on unnecessary capital equipment costs like forklifts, not to mention the savings on personnel."

"It still seems like science fiction to me," Kelly said, watching as the cart they were riding was passed by a larger unit in the freight lane six or seven feet away. The oddest thing was the lack of sound; except for their own voices and a dull buzzing drone from the MTUs, the tunnel was perfectly quiet.

"Hardly that," said Alexanian. "Volvo in Sweden has been using automated guided vehicles since 1974. Hybrids like the self-loaders are big business now. The ones we use here are made by Automatron, one of the Deep Wood Park companies, but General Motors is involved as well as people like Litton Industries and United Technologies. We were there early, but we certainly weren't the first. The only difference is the fact that we've applied the technology to transport rather than manufacturing."

"It's a little overwhelming," said Kelly. "I'm not used to thinking of a community as a machine."

"You're not alone. But, of course, that is precisely what every community is—a machine. Our intention here in Crestwood Heights was to design a better one as a demonstration of appropriate technological application for the future. The companies in Deep Wood Park supply the technology and the Institute devises ways to apply it."

"A test bed," Kelly said. "And the people of Crestwood Heights are the guinea pigs."

"An accurate, if rather negative, description." He pointed ahead with his walking stick. "We have arrived."

The cart began to slow down rapidly and Kelly could read a large sign stenciled in yellow against the far wall: DEEP WOOD PARK CENTRAL DISTRIBUTION. The freight carriers went on for another hundred feet or so, feeding into a number of branch line automated cargo bays, but their cart came to a stop at a glass-front waiting room identical to the one at the Institute. They climbed out of the cart and went through the sliding door. As the door opened automatically, the cart they'd used began to move off slowly down the tunnel.

"Where to now?" asked Kelly as they approached a bank of elevators.

"Up." He used his key-card again and the nearest elevator opened. They stepped in and the doors closed behind them.

"Five floors before you hit ground?" asked Kelly, nodding toward the control panel.

"There are forty-two companies in the Park," said Alexanian. "Almost all of them are laboratory or research facilities. The buildings you see aboveground are mainly executive offices and administration. Below ground level all forty-two companies share a common heating and cooling system, security, communications, mainframe computers supplied by the Institute, and a central car park. Convenient, efficient, and considerably more aesthetically pleasing than a jumble of windowless blockhouses."

"No argument there," Kelly agreed. The elevator slid to a stop and the doors opened. She and the handsome, elderly man stepped out into a scaled-down version of the Institute's atrium lobby. Across from the elevators Kelly could see the entrance to a large dining room, high-ceilinged and lit on three sides by tall, multipaned windows.

They crossed the thickly carpeted floor of the lobby and entered the dining room. A formally dressed maître d' appeared out of thin air, nodded silently at Alexanian and led them to a small table in a secluded corner of the long, rectangular room. The window beside the linen-covered table looked out onto a small bowl-shaped dell with a tree-fringed duck pond in its center. Through the trees Kelly could make out the redbrick shapes of half a dozen buildings, connected by gravel footpaths. Not your average industrial park. She looked around the room. Even though it was the middle of the lunch hour there were no more than fifteen or twenty people in an area that could easily seat ten times that many.

The people who were eating all looked like executive types; no frizzy-haired professors in horn rims and lab coats.

"I feel a little out of place," she said to Alexanian. "This is hardly the place for a denim skirt and sandals."

"You look very nice. And anyone who eats here does so because he belongs."

Kelly smiled and glanced out the window again. The implication was clear. If she was with Max Alexanian she could wear a bikini and no shoes at all and no one would say boo. Alexanian was power personified and he obviously loved it. She felt a small shiver of unease go through her, a sudden vision of Hugh Trask appearing before her eyes. What was it he'd said that time at the hospital? "Something terrible is going on and it must be stopped."

"I hope you don't mind," said Alexanian, breaking her reverie. "But I took the liberty of placing our order earlier. Black Forest trout and spinach au gratin."

"Sounds terrific." And right in character, too. It was obvious that Max was heavily into control on just about every level.

"We managed to steal the chef de cuisine away from Brenner's in Baden Baden," Alexanian said. "I ate there last year on a cross-country skiing holiday and the menu was astounding."

"Like you said, it's better than cafeteria food."

"Quite." Alexanian paused. "One other thing. I also invited someone else to join us for lunch." Kelly looked down at the table, noticing for the first time that it was set for three.

"Who?" she asked.

"Phillip Granger, the vice president of Medtech Industries. You met him at the party Doris had a week or two ago."

"Why did you invite him?" Kelly asked, her voice brittle.

"Medtech is something of a flagship operation here," Alexanian answered smoothly, choosing to ignore the obvious tone in her voice. "I thought he might show us around."

"I see." Kelly nodded. Alexanian's eyes flickered over her shoulder.

"Here he is now."

Kelly turned slightly in her seat and watched as the heavy-set, balding man approached their table. She nodded a greeting as Granger pulled out his chair and sat down across from her.

"Recovered from your surgery, Miss Rhine?"

"Completely."

Granger smiled thinly. He plucked the ornately folded napkin off the place mat in front of him, spreading the square of snow white linen across his lap.

"Still planning to open the Strand as a repertory theater, are we?"

"We are." She nodded. There was no sense in trying to make her plans a secret, not in this town. "At least on a trial basis. I'm going to have a science-fiction film festival." She threw Alexanian a quick glance. "I thought it was appropriate."

"Wonderful." The Medtech executive grinned. "My favorite. *Attack of the Fifty Foot Woman, The Incredible Shrinking Man*. Terrific stuff."

"I thought you might object," Kelly said stiffly, surprised at Granger's unabashed enthusiasm.

"Why on earth would I object?" he answered. "I really do like those silly films. It doesn't change my feelings about the Strand, though. I still think it should be used as a legitimate theater."

"Maybe you'll get the chance," said Kelly. "I haven't really made up my mind about what I'm going to do."

Their meal arrived and they ate. Alexanian keeping the conversation going, giving Kelly an explanation of how the various companies in Deep Wood Park interacted with each other and the community. He made it sound like the Utopian ideal of a perfectly integrated society, based firmly on his own ideas about statistics and their ability to predict the future.

Using the Institute's high-speed computers, his people could extrapolate both past and present statistics into trend curves, which were in turn used by the companies, guiding their research into areas of greatest benefit. Throughout the conversation Kelly resisted the temptation to bring up Alexanian's association with the Gidiots and the Georgetown Institute for Democratic Studies, but when she casually asked if any of the research going on at Deep Wood Park was military she met with stony silence. After lunch Kelly and Alexanian followed Granger back to the elevators and they rode three levels down to the Medtech complex.

They went through a large, high-ceilinged reception area where they were given security badges by an efficient-looking uniformed guard and then headed through a pair of swinging doors to the lab areas.

"What exactly does Medtech do?" Kelly asked.

"We started off twenty years ago manufacturing things like heart–lung machines and dialysis equipment, but we've branched out since then." He led them into a relatively small room lit by dim red light from a large ceiling panel. Most of the room was taken up by a massive plastic-and-steel contraption that looked like a cross between a torturer's rack and a physician's examining table. A man, fully clothed and leafing through a paperback, was lying on his back under half a dozen tubes pointing downward like giant gun barrels. Cables ran from the machine to a video control center against the far wall. A second man was fiddling with a tilted board of slides, toggles, and dials, his eyes watching the bank of television monitors racked on the wall.

"This is a prototype DSR," Granger explained. "Our pride and joy. It also might explain why I like science fiction, because it's a cumbersome version of the device Dr. McCoy uses in 'Star Trek.' On the TV show and in the movies they call it a 'fienberg' and it was supposed to instantly analyze a patient's entire physical condition. That's what the DSR does."

"DSR?" asked Kelly.

"Dynamic spatial reconstructor. What Max likes to refer to as 'catalytic' technology."

"I'm lost," Kelly admitted.

"Using technology from several different disciplines to create an entirely new function," Alexanian explained. "In this case computer-assisted design technology that began with video games, X rays, and computerized axial tomography—CAT scan, for short—and spectrographics borrowed from the astronomers."

"But what exactly does it *do?*" Kelly asked.

"The X ray and CAT scanner take little three-dimensional slices, cross-sectional views of the body under the scanner. At the same time a spectrographic analysis is done and applied to the image. The signal is sent from the machine through the Institute computers and back here, enhanced, and applied to a state-of-the-art computer-assisted design program. You get the entire body, skin, fat, organs, and skeleton, and with the CAD program you can look at it from any view or angle you want." Granger tapped the technician in front of the video screens on the shoulder. "Give her a demonstration, Hank."

The technician nodded and began punching buttons. As he did so the man on the tablelike affair began to move under the scanners and Kelly heard a steady clicking sound.

"Watch the screens," Granger suggested. Kelly turned and focused on the monitors. Each one showed a different image, and as she watched, the pictures began to take form. On the left she could see a three-dimensional view of the man's entire skeletal system, created out of lines. The middle screen showed his muscular system and organs, and the screen on the left was building up an image made entirely of heat signals.

"The next step is to create a program that will analyze the images as they appear and give a diagnosis. After that we'll hand everything over to the engineering boys at Intermedix and they'll miniaturize the whole thing. Two years and we'll have this whole package no bigger than a breadbox." He clapped the video technician on the shoulder. "Thanks, Hank."

The three left the room and continued on their tour, Granger talking all the while.

"We're developing a whole system we call Doc-in-a-Box," he said as they went down a series of hallways. "Twenty-four-hour clinics all over the country that can give fast, efficient aid, diagnostic and otherwise. They already have them in shopping malls, but they're small potatoes so far."

"Are they necessary?" asked Kelly.

"Absolutely. Think of them as a halfway point between the home and hospital. Clinics could set broken bones, deal with basic first aid from bee stings to diaper rash, and they could do initial diagnostic workups. The savings to hospitals would be enormous."

"Not to mention the number of doctors the clinics will employ," put in Alexanian. "The curve we've worked up points to a glut of physicians by 1990. By that time we should have between three and five thousand clinics established."

"Medicine as big business. What ever happened to Hippocrates?" Kelly asked.

"Seven out of ten Americans will get their hospital and health-care packages from no more than ten corporations by the end of the decade," Granger said. "It's coming whether you like it or not. And it's already competitive. We're trying to go one better by adding a lot of specific geriatric services to our clinic system. The Baby Boom becomes the Old Fogey Boom around 1999. You'll appreciate the clinics then."

The first room they'd entered had looked like a darkroom, the second looked like a machine shop. Power tools were scattered along a long counter running along three sides of the room and large, Formica-topped tables were lined up in the center. Along the short wall a lab-coated technician was wearing a crownlike headband fitted with fifteen or twenty wires, and another six or seven sprouted from under his sleeves. The electrode wires ran into a homemade chassis, and from there a central flat-cable was hooked into a battered version of a JASON computer. The technician fired off a quick set of keyboard instructions and then closed his eyes, concentrating hard. A foot away from Kelly a disembodied arm lying on one of the tables began to move, its fingers clawing at the hard surface. Wires hung out of a gaping wound where the elbow should have been in a horrible parody of severed veins and arteries. Kelly bit back a scream and watched as the arm reached the edge of the table. Suddenly it flipped over and the fingers curled in a jerky wave.

"What the hell is it?" she asked, heart still thumping. The scuttling arm had been like something out of a nightmare.

"We, uh, call it the Lee Majors Mark One," said the technician, getting up from the keyboard and stripping off his headpiece. He was Japanese, pipe-cleaner thin with a shock of black hair and glasses perched on the end of a long bony nose. Granger introduced the man as Ken Hiroshi, deputy director of the MedTech Prosthesis Research Department.

"The real name is SmartArm," said Granger, draping an arm around Hiroshi's shoulder. The scientist was obviously uncomfortable, and Kelly was willing to bet that in real life the camaraderie would be replaced by something a little more formal. The whole tour was a demonstration of the "We're all just one big family" sort of public relations she'd seen a thousand times in the advertising business.

Hiroshi slipped out from under Granger's arm and picked the SmartArm up off the table. He held it out to Kelly and she grasped it tentatively. The skin on the prosthetic was incredibly lifelike and warm to the touch. She handed it back to Hiroshi quickly.

"It's, uh, a little creepy, isn't it?" He grinned, blinking behind his glasses. "Takes a little getting used to."

"Ken was working at MIT when we found him," Alexanian said. "The Institute sent him to Susumu Tachi's shop at the Mechanical Engineering Laboratory in Tokyo for a year. He came back with the basic research necessary for the Smart-Arm."

"I still don't see how it works. He was on the other side of the room."

"Uh, it's just a simple radio transmitter in the pad of the thumb. It inputs directly into the nervous system. On a real user there, uh, would be a permanent electrode in the stump. All you have to do is think about moving the arm and it will do what you want. The muscles and nerves 'remember,' uh, what it was like when the real arm was there. They were working on something, uh, well, quite a bit like this when I was at the University of Utah, but we made it better. The Tachi's people developed a polymer sensing film and a three-fingered hand for doing automatic, uh, breast examinations, you know, looking for lumps? We're using that and also an artificial skin we've developed, so there's actually, uh, sensation. Not like a real arm, but enough to let the wearer know if he's gripping too hard or too soft, or whether something's, uh, hot or cold."

"Good for horror movies too," Kelly commented, looking down at the pale pink creation on the table. The Japanese engineer frowned and pushed his glasses back up on his nose, looking down at his creation.

"Umm." He nodded. "Hadn't, uh, thought of that. Pretty good special effect, I guess."

"I'm still fuzzy about why you were making it move at a distance. If it's supposed to be hooked up with electrodes, why bother?"

"There are other applications, uh—"

"Ken's been working on a series of experiments to see if we can use the arm and the sensors with paraplegics," Granger put in. "A pair of SmartArms could operate a computer keyboard or a typewriter easily enough and we might even be able to connect the sensors directly to the keyboard or the computer itself."

"We have a contract with the National Housing Authority and the National Institute of Health to come up with designs for entire house systems,'' Alexanian said. ''SmartArms in a SmartHouse could open up whole new worlds for bedridden people. There are exciting possibilities in this kind of research.''

''I think I'm starting to suffer from information overload,'' Kelly said weakly. The things Alexanian and Granger had shown her were all positive enough but she couldn't shake the feeling that she was only seeing the tip of the iceberg. The kind of research going on under the campuslike grounds of Deep Wood Park cost hundreds of millions of dollars and the money had to be coming from somewhere.

''There is one more item on the agenda. Phillip has saved the best for last.''

''Right,'' said Granger. He patted Hiroshi on the shoulder. ''We'll let Ken get back to work.''

They left the lab and continued down the corridor, going through a set of swing doors and turning to the left. It occurred to Kelly that if she were left alone she wouldn't have the slightest idea of how to get back to the elevators.

The left-hand passage came to a dead end at a large, metal-sheathed door like the barrier she'd seen in the tunnel under Chapel Gate. The door was fitted with a wheel-and-lock mechanism like a bank vault and there was a warning sign stenciled on it in red: RESTRICTED AREA UNAUTHORIZED ENTRY PROHIBITED. P4 FACILITY.

''What's in there?'' Kelly asked curiously. Granger smiled briefly, his eyes flickering to meet Alexanian's a split second.

''That's where we keep the monsters.'' He grinned.

''Right.''

''It's true in a manner of speaking,'' put in Alexanian. ''The P4 Facility is a secure area for working on potentially dangerous bacterial and biological experiments.''

''I thought MedTech was into machinery.''

''We are,'' Granger said, nodding. ''We share the P4 with several of the other labs. It's at the hub of the complex and they have their own access points. We use it to test some of our analytical equipment. The other companies provide the bugs and we come up with the machines to count them.'' He pointed to a smaller door on the right. ''This is where we're going, though, so you won't have to worry about going through all the P4 rigamarole.''

''ICE-CAP/COPS Project,'' said Kelly, reading the discreet sign on the door. ''Well, that's plain enough.''

"ICE-CAP stands for Intensive Care Environment Capsule. COPS is Complete Organ Perfusion System," Granger said, deciphering the acronyms for her. He took a key-card out of his pocket and slipped it into the door slot. There was a hissing sound and the door swung open. Granger glanced over his shoulder and smiled thinly at Kelly. "We're running a live experiment. I hope you're not squeamish."

"Not particularly."

"Good." Granger flipped on the light as they entered.

The room was the size of a hospital operating theater and at first glance that's what Kelly thought she'd stepped into. A bright carbon-arc reflector in the high ceiling illuminated an array of monitoring equipment ranged along the dark blue tiled walls, but instead of an operating table there was a large, clear-plastic capsule mounted on a draped stand in the middle of the room.

The empty capsule was obviously intended to contain a patient because the bottom third was taken up by a soft foam lining, molded into the contours of a human being. Stepping closer, Kelly saw that there were suction-cup sensors or electrodes built into the foam and the headrest was fitted with a crown apparatus like the one Ken Hiroshi had been wearing. Standing beside the capsule, she could also hear a soft sucking sound, like labored, mechanical breathing, but she couldn't locate its source. There was a control panel fitted to the foot of the stand with at least a dozen digital gauges for monitoring various body functions. Some of the gauges were working, even though the capsule was empty.

"It's a joint project between MedTech and Intermedix," said Granger, his voice echoing slightly off the tiles. "We've been working on it for a little more than ten years. There's a company in Canada working on the same thing but we're way ahead of them."

"A self-contained Intensive Care Unit?" guessed Kelly, fascinated. It looked like one of the suspended-animation pods in *2001*.

"Close." Granger nodded. "It does act as a one-person ICU but there's more to it than that." He rested his palm on the head end of the capsule. Looking closely, Kelly could see the faint join where the capsule opened. "Have you ever heard the term *entrainment*?"

"No."

"A person's brainwaves and neural signals automatically fire in syncrony with the surrounding pulses of its immediate environment. That's entrainment and it's also one of the reasons why it's dangerous to stand in front of a large radar dish; you literally scramble your brain. Same goes for microwaves. But the phenomena has a beneficial aspect. For instance, if you set up an external radiowave field at the same frequency of deep-sleep EEGs, the patient will immediately go into a trance. With the field generator built into the ICE-CAP we can induce anything from a hypnotic trance to a near-death lowering of body functions, all without medication. The same goes for the neural functions, which we control through the headband there."

"What kind of neural functions?" asked Kelly.

"We've been doing receptor mapping since '73. That's when Candy Pert at Johns Hopkins discovered the brain's opiate receptor. Since then we've discovered about forty of them, all mapped and digitized using Max's computers. A lot of the big pharmaceutical companies jumped on the bandwagon but we concentrated on electrical stimulus of the receptors rather than chemical. One of the most valuable, at least for ICU patients, is the adenosine receptor. Cyanimid came up with a drug called TZP that relieves anxiety without making you sleepy and another group came up with the reverse, an adenosine blocker equivalent to caffeine but literally ten thousand times more powerful. They called it Vigil-Aid or something like that. What we did was figure out a way to put a person into a state called 'quiet wakefulness,' and keep them there. That's critical for a patient recovering from a severe heart attack."

"Mind control?" Kelly said. Granger shrugged.

"Call it that if you want." He patted the cigar-shaped plastic bubble. "In a year or two this little wonder will be saving a lot of critically ill patients."

"I thought you said this was a live experiment," Kelly said, changing the subject. "The capsule is empty."

"I've only shown you the ICE-CAP," Granger said. "You haven't seen COPS yet." He smiled thinly and then bent down, sweeping back the green surgical drapery covering the stand the capsule rested on. Kelly looked down, her eyes widening, and she felt bile rise in the back of her throat.

"Christ!" she whispered, horrified.

The lower section of the stand was made up of six identical glass boxes approximately three feet high. Tubes were fitted into the top of each box and Kelly could make out sluggishly flowing, milky white liquid flowing through them. Visible in the murky fluid filling the high-walled boxes were human organs—a kidney, a liver, two hearts, a pair of lungs, and something she couldn't identify.

"COP," Granger said blandly. Kelly swallowed hard, watching as the organs drifted gently in the liquid. Now she knew the source of the sucking sound. "Fluosol-DA 20. A perfluorochemical first developed in Japan and used as artificial blood. Nontoxic, requires no antibodies, and can be stored frozen indefinitely. The organs are catheterized and flushed while they float in a bath of the stuff. The containers are filled to the level of negative buoyancy relative to the density of the organ so there's no trauma. The COPS unit is made as part of the capsule mechanism because the monitoring equipment is the same and also because it can keep a donor organ and a recipient together.

"In case you're wondering, the kidney and the liver are cancerous. They've been removed and are undergoing out of body chemotherapy. When the cancer is gone they'll be returned to their owners. That way the cancer doesn't have a chance to spread to other organs and the patient has no chemotherapy side effects. The two hearts and the lungs are waiting until needed. We can keep them 'alive' in these cases for months."

"What about the other . . . thing?"

"You don't want to know," Granger said, putting on the thin little smile again. He was enjoying her obvious discomfort.

"I *do* want to know, as a matter of fact," she answered, her jaw tight. To hell with him.

"It's a three-month fetus. Gross abnormalities. The people at the Infertility Clinic wanted us to keep it on hold until they had a chance to give it a going over. Part of their Miscarriage/Spont-AB program."

"I think I've seen enough for one day," Kelly said. Horrible as it was, she couldn't take her eyes off the twisted, ugly thing floating in the last container.

"Whatever you say." Granger shrugged. He dropped the

green drapery over the COPS unit and Kelly blinked. She felt Alexanian's hand on her arm.

"I'll take you back to your car," he said.

"Yes, I think you'd better," she said quietly, and let the older man lead her from the terrible, brightly lit room.

CHAPTER 15

"They were trying to impress you," said Robin Spenser. He sat hunched forward on the couch in Kelly's living room, a cup of coffee cooling on the table in front of him.

"But why?" Kelly asked, turning away from the big window overlooking the ravine. Outside, the sun was lowering, turning the trees into spidery silhouettes. The sky was streaked with angry shades of yellow and red, burning at the ragged edges of the evening clouds above Crestwood Heights. "Why would they want to impress me?" She dropped down into an armchair across from Robin and lit a cigarette.

"I don't know," the ex-marine said, shaking his head. "An exercise in power maybe. Letting you know that they're more important than you are."

"Pointless," Kelly said. "If Alexanian set that tour up to put the fear of God into me, he did it for a reason. And whatever the reason was, it worked."

"Maybe it ties in with the stuff of Hugh's that I found."

"That doesn't make any sense either. Trask had some paranoid delusion that there was a conspiracy, that something terrible was going on. Granger and his people are up to all sorts of scientific weirdness over there, but they're not making any secret of it."

"You said yourself you felt as though you were only seeing the tip of the iceberg," Robin commented. "There could be more."

"Like what? You think they've got Frankenstein's monster snoozing away in a freezer bag?"

"Whatever it is, Hugh Trask wasn't paranoid when he predicted his own death."

"A self-fulfilling prophecy," Kelly countered, shaking her head. "He wouldn't be the first person to kill himself with a car instead of a gun."

"He also ties in the death of your uncle, Lizbeth's parents and her aunt . . . Not to mention Lizbeth herself. How does a woman who's had a hysterectomy bear a child?"

"She obviously didn't," Kelly said, exasperated. "All it means is that Lizbeth was adopted."

"I'm willing to buy that. It's the obvious answer, but it still means that someone's trying to hide something."

"Why?"

"The birth announcement. When you adopt a child it will say, 'arrived,' not born. And you don't thank the caseroom staff of a hospital when you sign adoption papers. For some reason it was important to make it look as though Lizbeth was the Torrances' natural child. That photograph of Mrs. Torrance at the party is proof of that. She was faking an advanced state of pregnancy."

"And you think this fits in with Hugh Trask's death?"

"Yes. And the death of your uncle and the Torrances and Lizbeth's aunt."

"Jesus," Kelly muttered, stabbing the butt of her cigarette into the ashtray on the table beside her. "Why am I even talking about this? I've got enough problems without playing Nancy Drew, for Christ's sake!" She glanced out the window, shaking her head. "I tell myself it's going to be a frosty Friday before I get involved with another man, and here I am with a doctor. I try to get away from the craziness of big-city life and I wind up in some kind of suburban paranoid dreamland. A Disney nightmare. The next thing you know I'm going to find old Walt himself, packed in ice and stored in some underground vault. The whole thing is crazy!"

"It may be crazy, but it's real. I thought it was Hugh's paranoia at first too, but there's too much circumstantial evidence, and there may be more."

"That computer disk you mentioned?"

"I'm going back into Hugh's apartment later on to check it out."

"I want to come with you," Kelly said firmly.

"You sounded pretty skeptical before. Why the sudden change of heart?"

"Because I don't like Max Alexanian and Phillip Granger playing push-me pull-me with my head." She looked at Robin and smiled. "That kind of game playing brings out the stubborn in me. I want to deal with this once and for all so I can get on with my life."

"What about your friend the doctor?" Robin asked hesitantly.

"Stephen? What about him?"

"He keeps on cropping up in all of this. He's mentioned in the birth announcement and he winds up with custody of Lizbeth."

"Let's not bring Stephen into this," she answered. "I've got enough on my plate as it is. He was friends with the Torrances and he was listed as Lizbeth's guardian in the will. He told me so himself. It's just coincidence."

"I hope so."

"I'm seeing him tonight," Kelly responded coldly. "Why don't I ask him?"

"Why don't we see what's on that disk first? Then we can decide." He got up and crossed the room. Crouching down beside Kelly's chair, he reached out and took her hand. "Look," he said quietly. "I'm not the enemy here, and I'm not trying to interfere with you and Stephen Hardy."

"So what's all this in aid of, then?" asked Kelly.

"Because people have died," said Robin. "One of them was your uncle and another was my friend, crazy or not."

"If I had any sense I'd pack my bags and walk away from the whole thing. When you come right down to it, maybe I don't want to know what's going on. I didn't ask for any of this, you know."

"Sometimes life isn't a matter of choice," Robin said. "Sometimes it's just there and you have to confront it head-on."

"What's that supposed to mean?"

"It means that maybe we've already gone too far to stop now. You said it yourself: you weren't given that tour for no reason, and everyone knows I was friends with Hugh. Guilt by association."

"Are you trying to scare me?" asked Kelly. "We're going

to wind up wrapped around a tree with a high alcohol blood count?''

''I'm trying to scare myself,'' he answered, laughing weakly. ''I'm not the hero type either. Frankly, I'd like to be on the next bus out of here.''

''But you won't be, right?''

''No.''

''I guess I won't be either.''

''That's up to you.''

''I'm going to regret this.''

''Probably.'' Robin grinned.

''Shit!''

''Now what?'' said Kelly. Almost an hour had passed and they were sitting in front of Hugh Trask's computer, the small, second-floor room lit only by the glowing screen of the Macintosh.

''The label says it runs with something called MacStat,'' said Robin, poking through the plastic box of software disks on the dead man's desk. ''Here we go.'' He pulled out a disk and slipped it into the main drive of the computer, then inserted the second disk into the rectangular external drive. The blank icon on the screen turned into a smiling face and a few seconds later both the program and the second disk were loaded. Robin opened the second disk and a screen full of file choices blossomed.

16K . . ONE . . . MacStat Document . . . . . . Saturday February 12, 1988
18K . . TWO . . . MacStat Document . . . . . . Saturday February 12, 1988
11K . . . THREE . MacStat Document . . . . . . Saturday February 12, 1988
22K . FOUR . . MacStat Document . . . . . . Saturday February 12, 1988
20K . FIVE . . . MacStat Document . . . . . . Saturday February 12, 1988
17K . . SIX . . . . MacStat Document . . . . . . Saturday February 12, 1988
14K . . SEVEN . MacStat Document . . . . . . Saturday February 12, 1988

19K . . EIGHT . . MacStat Document . . . . . . Saturday
February 12, 1988
46K . NINE . . . MacStat Document . . . . . . Saturday
February 12, 1988

"Weird," muttered Kelly, staring at the screen.

"What?"

"My uncle. He died on the thirteenth of February, and all of those entries are for the day before."

"It probably means they were copied from another source," Robin said. "That would be a lot of original work for a single day. Sixty or seventy pages at least."

"Why don't you open one up?" Robin nodded, slid the mouse around until the arrow was over the first document entry, and double-clicked. The file menu vanished and the screen went blank as the drives hummed, searching for the document. Twenty seconds later the screen hitched briefly and then filled with words.

"It's a note from your uncle to Hugh," Robin murmured. Kelly pulled her chair in closer and read over her friend's shoulder:

Dearest Hugh,

My worst fears have been borne out; someone has discovered the unauthorized accesses to the DWI mainframe and it's only a matter of time before they trace them back to me. Ever since leaving Northeastern my position has been a delicate one, but I have taken some precautions. A complete copy of all the documentation exists and I will copy as much of the original to this disk as I can.

I beg of you, do not put yourself in jeopardy. God knows how many people have died over the past twenty years because of this monstrous thing, but sacrificing yourself will accomplish nothing. Some months ago I managed to have my will registered with a New York law firm, and in the event that anything happens to me my niece, Kelly Rhine, will inherit everything. She has the key to the location of my dossier and when you are sure it's safe you should contact her.

Telling you anything now would only put you in danger, but I can say that what I've discovered over the past few days is the stuff of nightmares. The implications of what has been going on here were bad enough before, but I now realize that any premature exposure would be catastrophic. We were right about the Torrance child and her connection to the AFRP and the ST. GAIA, but it's worse than I thought. At this point the only thing saving her is her age.

At any rate, say nothing of this, and make sure that once you have read the information here you will hide the disk somewhere safe, or better yet, erase it altogether.

So there it is. This may be the last you hear of me, but be of good cheer my friend, we fought the good fight and we fought it well. In the end, no matter what happens we'll know that we did the right thing, and we'll know that we had some good years together.

Your loving friend,
Nathanial

"Funny," said Kelly, her voice soft. "It never occurred to me, but I guess it makes sense when you think about it."

"What?" asked Robin.

" 'Dearest Hugh,' 'Your loving friend,' 'We had some good years together.' My uncle never married, never had any women around." She paused. "They were lovers, weren't they?"

"I don't think so," Robin said, shaking his head. "Not in a physical sense, anyway. They were a little too old and set in their ways to come that far out of the closet. But I picked it off pretty quickly, and they both knew it. I think they respected me for not spreading it around."

"Why didn't you tell me?"

"I didn't think it mattered." He shrugged. "I still don't."

"I wonder what he means about me having the key to the location of the dossier?"

"Did he write to you before he died?" asked Robin.

"No. Nothing. The last time I heard anything from him was Christmas. He sent me a present. A book on the history of animation. Before that I hadn't heard from him in three or four years."

"Maybe the rest of the documents explain something." He cleared the letter and opened the second document on the list. A zigzagging line on a squared background filled the screen. A second line, this one dotted, also appeared and so did the title of the Graph: MARIJUANA AND ALCOHOL/% OF POPULATION WHO ARE CURRENT USERS/C.H.—NATIONAL. /1976–86

"Presumably C.H. stands for Crestwood Heights," said Kelly.

"I guess. Interesting. Twelve percent of the population used marijuana in '76 and only seven percent in '86."

"According to this, the national average and the average in Crestwood Heights were almost exactly the same, year to year; the lines are almost on top of each other."

Robin scrolled down to the next item on the document. It was another graph, this one titled ABORTION RATE/ C.H. —NATIONAL 1976–1986.

"The national rate in 1976 was 18.8 per thousand, the Crestwood Heights rate was 18.6," said Robin.

"It's the same for every year," Kelly said, peering closely to the intersecting lines. "No more than one or two decimal points of difference over ten years. Go to the next one."

It took almost an hour to go through the entire disk. There were dozens of graphs and charts, including everything from live births and birth rates to infant mortality, accidental deaths, broken down by types and life expectancy. About half of the charts seemed to deal with health statistics, while the rest covered more general social and economic themes. In every case the statistics for Crestwood Heights were virtually identical to the national averages on a per capita basis.

"There's a lot of work here," Robin said as they finished up. "Pretty sophisticated stuff, too."

"It's almost impossible," Kelly said, rubbing her eyes. "According to those charts Crestwood is a statistical model for the whole country. If my uncle got those figures out of Alexanian's computer, then Alexanian is the biggest bullshit artist since the emperor's new clothes."

"Maybe that's what your uncle found out. If the Deep Wood Institute was fudging its statistics it would be one hell of a scandal."

"Go back to the letter." Robin clicked his way back to the first document and it appeared on the screen for the second time. Kelly leaned forward, pointing at the screen. "Look at that," she said. "He uses words like *monstrous* and the *stuff of nightmares*. That doesn't sound like a scandal involving doctored health statistics. And is that the kind of thing you kill for?"

"Maybe he was just overdramatizing."

"These documents are all dated February twelfth," said Kelly. "And my uncle is talking about the possibility that they might kill him. He gets this disk to Hugh Trask and then the next day he's found dead in his house, supposedly of a cerebral hemorrhage. Hugh Trask predicts his own death and he winds up in a fatal car accident with booze in his bloodstream. You were right: there's too much circumstantial evidence for all this to be coincidence."

"So what do we do about it?" asked Robin.

"Nothing more tonight. I still have to meet Stephen."

"Are you going to tell him about this?"

"No," Kelly said slowly. "Not yet anyway. Before we go to anyone we're going to have to get real proof." She paused, and sat back in her chair. Frowning, she lit a cigarette and glanced back at the pale white square of the computer screen. "Lizbeth's age, St. GAIA, whatever the hell that is, and me having the key to the complete dossier. Not much to go on."

"Better than nothing," said Robin.

"I guess," Kelly sighed. She got to her feet, stretching. "Anyway, I think we should pack it in. Why don't we meet tomorrow and see what we can figure out? I was going to come in and start going through the films for the festival anyway."

"Okay," Robin said. He ejected the disks and shut down the computer, throwing the room into complete darkness. Kelly reached out and touched Robin's shoulder.

"Nervous?" she asked quietly.

"Nope. Scared shitless."

Kelly lay beside Stephen in the darkness, the fingers of her right hand just touching the taut muscles of his thigh. He was breathing deeply and evenly and she knew that for the past ten or fifteen minutes he'd been asleep.

The sex had been good, much better than the first time. She could still feel the heavy, warm feeling in the pit of her stomach and her brain was pleasantly fuzzy from their exertions. During their lovemaking she'd been faintly aware of sounds in the house, but now everything was quiet and all she could hear was the soft hum of the air-conditioning as it dried the sheen of perspiration from the flat curve of her belly.

She wanted a cigarette, and moving carefully, she slipped

out of bed and into her clothes. The cigarettes were in her purse out in the living area and since she wasn't spending the night it made sense to get dressed before she left the bedroom. She tucked in her blouse, did the snap on her jeans, then picked up her sneakers and tiptoed out of the room, closing the door carefully behind her.

Dropping down to the couch in the dimly lit living room she pulled on her running shoes and then rummaged around in her purse, eventually locating her cigarettes. She lit one and dragged deeply, silently chiding herself for enjoying the act of smoking as much as she did. Stephen didn't get on her case about it but that classic "doctor's look" of his got the message across. Every time she lit up in his presence, she could almost hear ghostly choirs singing out words like *lung cancer, emphysema,* and *increased risk of heart attack.*

She snorted softly, bending to tie up her laces. To hell with it, she wasn't married to him yet. Faintly she heard a sneeze. Glancing up, she looked around the large, cathedral-ceilinged room. For the first time she noticed a narrow bar of light beneath the closed door to the study. She stubbed out her cigarette and walked softly across the room, pausing at the door. She could hear the dull tapping of computer keys and then another muffled sneeze. Lizbeth, sneaking in a bit of computer time at two-thirty in the morning. Shaking her head, Kelly turned the knob on the door and opened it.

Lizbeth, dressed in a pale blue flannel nightie was perched on the chair in front of the computer station busily tapping out instructions on the keyboard. Other than the amber screen, the only light in the room came from the small high-intensity lamp clamped to the shelves above the monitor. As Kelly entered the room, Lizbeth turned in her chair. Once again Kelly was struck by the child's almost surreal beauty, enhanced even more now by the bright, million-dollar smile.

"Isn't it a little late for this kind of thing?" asked Kelly quietly, crossing the room.

"I didn't think anyone was up," Lizbeth answered. "I thought you and Uncle Stephen were . . . asleep." There was just enough of a break between the words for Kelly to realize that Lizbeth knew exactly what she and Stephen had been doing. "And anyway, I had cramps," she added blithely.

"Cramps?" Kelly looked over Lizbeth's shoulder and scanned the block of type on the glowing screen.

RHEN/1986 ED 2392/MENSTRUAL CYCLE

In humans and primates the period during which the ovum matures and is released . . .

"You've got your period?" Kelly said, surprised.

"This evening," Lizbeth said, obviously proud of herself. "I was pretty sure it was coming a few days ago so I went out and bought some tampons. I couldn't sleep, so I thought I'd read up about it." Kelly blinked. She'd had her first period at thirteen and used pads for the first few years because she thought she wouldn't be a virgin if she used a tampon.

"Aren't you a little young to be menstruating?" asked Kelly.

"I'm twelve. Puberty comes between ten and fourteen. It's been coming earlier over the past hundred years or so. According to this, the average age in 1840 was fifteen and a half. Now it's twelve and a half. It's kind of neat, actually."

"Talk to me ten years from now." Kelly grinned. "Men have to shave every day and women bleed every twenty-eight. It gets pretty boring."

"I guess so." Lizbeth shrugged. "But it's still kind of neat. I'm not looking forward to breasts though. Kimmy Edwards has already got them and she says they get pretty sore. And I don't like the idea of boys staring at them."

"Stare back," laughed Kelly. "Boys that age have their own embarrassments."

"I know," Lizbeth said, giggling. "Spontaneous erections. Tom Landis gets them in math all the time. He wears his sweater wrapped around his waist sometimes to cover them up but all the girls know. It's kind of grossitating, but it's pretty funny too."

"Have you told Stephen?"

"About Tom Landis?"

"About getting your period."

"Uh uh," Lizbeth said, shaking her head.

"Embarrassed?"

"A little." She frowned. "It's no problem talking to you about it, but he's kind of different. I mean he's a man and it's not like he was my real uncle."

"Would you like me to mention it? He should know. He's not your real uncle, but he is a doctor and it's a good idea to have a checkup when you start puberty, just to make sure all the hormones are doing what they should."

"Could you tell him for me?" asked Lizbeth.

"Sure." Kelly smiled. "Us ladies have to stick together. Now shut this machine down and get off to bed. You've got school tomorrow, cramps or no cramps."

The child cleared the screen and shut down, pausing on her way out of the room to give Kelly a hug and a kiss.

"You're the best," she whispered, and then she was gone. A few minutes later Kelly let herself out of the house and climbed into the Aston Martin. She drove back to the house on Erin Park and for most of the journey through the darkened streets of Crestwood Heights she felt a strange uneasiness.

Lizbeth had turned a secret corner in her life and Kelly was proud to be the first one to know, but she couldn't stop thinking about the words her uncle had written: *We were right about the Torrance child, but it's worse than we thought. At this point the only thing saving her is her age.*

So what were they right about, and what was Lizbeth being saved from by her age? Nothing came through the jumble of racing thoughts in her mind and as she pulled into the driveway of her house the thought of ending the ragged end of the night with a few hours in her own bed was like a narcotic. She parked, let herself into the house, and dragged herself to the bedroom without even brushing her teeth. She undressed, poked her legs under the sheets and gratefully gave herself up to sleep.

CHAPTER 16

"That's another good reason for packing my bags," Kelly said sourly. "I'm used to a little more privacy than that." The waitress approached their table and both she and Robin ordered the breakfast special. The food, complete with a large carafe of coffee, arrived a few moments later and they began to eat.

"I did a little homework last night after you left," Robin said, scooping up egg yoke with the side of a piece of toast. "I found out a few things."

"Such as?"

"Remember I told you I called my broker in Florida?"

"You were trying to find out something about Intermedix, weren't you?"

"That's right. Well, he called back and left a message on my machine. Intermedix is owned by the Medical Industries Alliance, and they in turn run something called the Institute for Studies in Medicine and Technology—ISMT."

"You told me about that." She folded a piece of bacon onto her fork and crunched down on it hungrily. "They fund research labs."

"Right. Well, ISMT's board of directors has a couple of interesting names on it. Specifically, Phillip Granger and Max Alexanian. For all practical purposes ISMT is really an offshoot of the Cold Mountain Institute, or maybe *lobby* is a better name. Their national office is in Washington, D.C."

"What are you getting at?"

"My broker friend listed a whole bunch of names of

companies and groups that do business with ISMT. Intermedix is one of them, so is MedTech Inc and the AFRP."

"That figures."

"So is something called the St. Gregory Adoption Information Agency," Robin continued.

"St. GAIA," said Kelly. "The name in my uncle's note to Hugh Trask."

"Bingo. I made a couple of calls this morning and found out that the St. Gregory group works out of Washington, too. In fact, they're in the same building as ISMT. They've also got branch offices all over the country. One of them is in Raleigh."

"What do they do?"

"The information person at the Raleigh office explained it pretty clearly," Robin said. "St. GAIA is basically a computer database of information relating prospective adoptions. Adoption agencies, public and private, list with them and St. GAIA puts it on the net."

"It sounds like it's got something to do with the Catholic Church," Kelly said.

"Apparently not," he said, shaking his head. "The woman I talked to in Raleigh thought there might have been a connection a long time ago, but as far as she knows it's an independent group paid for by the member agencies. According to her, they have about four thousand adoption agencies and adoption lawyers on file and they run a list of about seven or eight thousand children a month. She was pretty up front about it. According to her, the majority of the children listed are either physically or mentally handicapped, or they're mixed race."

"But what does all of this have to do with Lizbeth or with Uncle Nathan's letter to Trask?"

"I'm not sure. But the woman at St. Gregory's said they did a lot of business with the Crestwood Heights office of the AFRP. People who can't be helped by the Infertility Clinic are referred to St. Gregory's as potential adoptive parents."

"I'm getting lost," Kelly said, frustrated.

"I'm not sure what it all adds up to, but it's like a big wheel with all the spokes coming into Crestwood Heights," answered Robin. "Your uncle found out something about what it meant and I'm beginning to think he died because of that knowledge. Hugh Trask as well."

"Murder?" Kelly said softly.

"We're talking about big business. It wouldn't be the first time."

"Karen Silkwood," she said.

"And lots of others. The question is, what do we do about it?"

"Go to the police."

"What police?" scoffed Robin. "The Crestwood Heights P.D.? Max Alexanian's private army."

"The FBI then."

"With what?" asked Robin. "What kind of real evidence do we have? A letter from one aging fairy to another and some statistics that are obviously phoney. That's how it would look to the feds. There are half a dozen U.S. Government agencies with bureaus in Deep Wood Park, not to mention research shops for some of the most powerful corporations in America. You're an aging hippy artist and I'm a gay boy who runs a sweetshop. We've got about as much credibility as a pair of field mice in a cheese factory."

"So what do we do?" she asked. "Pretend none of this happened? Turn a blind eye to it all? I'll settle down with Stephen and you'll make chocolate mountains?"

"It may be too late for that," Robin said grimly. "Alexanian didn't take you on that tour for nothing. It was a show of strength, a warning, and they probably know that you and I are friends. They certainly know I was friends with Hugh."

"So we die 'accidentally' like my Uncle and Trask?"

"No. I've been thinking about that. If they'd wanted to sweep us under the rug they would have already done it. You could have died when they took out your appendix and I could have been dealt with easily enough too. I don't have any family to ask questions. It would be simple."

"So why haven't they?" asked Kelly. "Assuming that this whole insane scenario is real, that is."

"Because of your uncle. It's the only thing I can think of."

"Why do you say that?" asked Kelly, lighting a cigarette.

"Hugh Trask was a slob, and that's being kind. But when I went through his apartment above the shop it was neat as a pin. Somebody had been in there before me and probably for the same reason."

"Looking for something the old man left behind."

"Exactly." Robin nodded. "They overlooked the press, which is why they didn't come up with the clippings and the disk. According to your uncle's note to Hugh, he left a package of evidence behind as well, and somehow you're the key to it. Alexanian isn't a fool. If he's assumed that your uncle left some incriminating evidence around, then he'll bide his time until you find it, or until he's sure you don't know anything about it."

"But I *don't* know anything about it!" pleaded Kelly. "If you're right, then Alexanian's people must have gone through my uncle's things just like Hugh Trask's apartment. If they came up empty-handed, then how are we going to do any better?"

"Maybe you know but you don't know that you know."

"That sounds like a Marx brothers routine."

"But it might be true," Robin insisted. "The note said that you had the key. Didn't you say your uncle sent you a book last Christmas?"

"Ceram's *History of Animation.*"

"Could that be it?"

"How? It's just a book."

"Where is it?"

"With the rest of my stuff back at the house. In the garage."

"I think we'd better check it out. It's all we've got."

They left the Union Ridge and drove to Kelly's house on Erin Park. It took them the better part of an hour to sort through the boxes Kelly had left stored in the Westphalia and another twenty minutes on the living room floor emptying out the half dozen cartons of books she'd accumulated over the years. Eventually Robin came up with the book Nathan Somerville had sent his niece. It was a trade paperback, still pristine beneath its plastic shrink-wrapping.

"You never opened it?" he asked, handing Kelly the book. She took it to the couch, wading through the sea of volumes spread out on the carpet.

"I didn't bother." She shrugged, peeling off the plastic. "I already had a copy in hardcover. I remember wondering about it at the time, because Uncle Nat had given me that copy too, years ago in California. It was a graduation present."

"Why would he give you the same book twice?" Robin asked.

"I thought he'd forgotten about the first one." She flipped through the book, turning it over to see if anything had been interlaced between the pages. There was nothing. She turned to the title page and read the inscription.

"To my favorite niece, I hope this brings back some happy memories. Your Loving Uncle Nathan."

"That doesn't make any sense."

"What doesn't?"

"He inscribed the book and put the plastic back on." The ex-Marine frowned thoughtfully. "Is there anything else about the book that's odd?"

Kelly flipped through the pages again, going more slowly. She shook her head and handed the book down to Robin, who was still sitting on the floor.

"Not that I can see," she said. Robin went through the pages carefully, then stopped mid-way through the book.

"What about these little figures down in the corners?" he asked. Kelly dropped down onto the floor beside him and looked.

"It's an old joke." She smiled. "Back when I was a kid and he was working for the Disney people. He was trying to explain what animation was so he made a flip pad for me on the pages of a book. Riffle the pages at the corners and the little figures dance." Robin did as she'd instructed and then shook his head.

"Doesn't work. The figures aren't in sequence."

"They must be." Kelly frowned.

"Try it yourself," He answered, handing her the book. Kelly repeated the riffling procedure.

"Weird," she murmured. "You're right, they're all jumbled. Why would he go to all the trouble of making a flip book and not have them in sequence?"

"Shit!" said Robin. "It's the old Sherlock Holmes story!" He grabbed the book out of Kelly's hand and started going through the pages. "Get me a piece of paper and a pen." Kelly got up, found a pad and pencil, and gave them to Robin. Turning the pages of the book, he began scribbling on the pad.

"What are you doing?" she asked, sitting down beside him.

"It was a story called 'The Dancing Men,' one of the early Sherlock Holmes tales. They made it into a movie in the thirties with Basil Rathbone."

"I still don't get it."

"Here," Robin answered, excitement in his voice. "There's the message." He handed her the pad. All Kelly saw was a row of stick figures, their arms flailing.

"Okay, it's a line of dancing men. What does it mean?"

"Basic training for all us grunts in the USMC." Robin grinned. "It's a semaphore. Before Morse Code and radios, they used flags from ship to ship. Each flag position meant a different letter. Put little flags in the hands of those figures and you have a semaphore message.

"Saying what?" asked Kelly.

"I'll work it out," Robin said, taking the pad back. It only took a few seconds. He gave her the pad.

She read aloud: "C H A P E L G A T E W Y N D H A M S B I R D S *Chapel Gate* I understand, but what are *Wyndham's birds*?"

"I don't know, but he obviously expected you to be able to figure it out," Robin said. "Do you remember anybody named Wyndham?"

"Not that I can remember. Maybe there's a Wyndam involved with Chapel Gate. That would be the tie-in, I suppose. It's pretty obscure." Kelly got to her feet and went back to the couch. She lit a cigarette, staring out over the sun-drenched ravine. The sliding doors out to the deck were opened and she could hear the faint whispering of the breeze as it gently brushed the trees. "It's all too weird. I look outside and it's bright and sunny and beautiful, but all I can think of is that machine Alexanian and Granger showed me, and those tunnels."

"The Future Is Now," grunted Robin climbing to his feet. He dropped down onto the couch beside Kelly.

"So what do we do?" she said quietly. "If my uncle and Hugh Trask really were killed for what they knew, then we're in the same kind of trouble."

"We keep on digging. It's the only thing we can do."

"So where do we dig?" asked Kelly.

"I think you should check out your boyfriend's operation," suggested Robin. "The Fertility Research Program Clinic."

"I still don't believe he's involved in this," Kelly said, shaking her head. "I've watched him with Lizbeth; he really cares about her."

"Maybe. But your uncle seemed to think she was important and even if he's not involved, there's an awful lot of evidence that points to the Clinic. Lizbeth Torrance wasn't her mother's natural child, that's for sure, which means she was probably adopted through the St. Gregory's Agency. It all ties in."

"So what am I supposed to do?" Kelly asked sourly. "Call Stephen on the phone and ask him if he's involved in some kind of evil conspiracy? That's a one-way ticket to a rubber room."

"Why don't you just drop in on him and invite the good doctor out to lunch?" said Robin. "You might get the ten-cent tour. It's worth a shot."

"All right. What about you?"

"Alexanian is trying to hide something and I can't think of a better place than Chapel Gate. Hugh mentioned it and so did your uncle."

"You're going to try to get inside?"

Robin shook his head. "Not yet. I just want to nose around a bit, see if I can fit a few more pieces into the puzzle. Maybe then we can make some kind of plan."

"Okay," Kelly said. "Why don't we meet back here this afternoon and compare notes?"

"Make it my place instead." Robin glanced around the room. "I know it sounds stupid but I can't help feeling as though I'm on enemy ground in the Heights."

"All right. Five o'clock?"

"It's a date." Robin leaned down and gave her a brief kiss on the cheek. A few moments later he was gone and Kelly faintly heard the sound of his Wagoneer as he drove away. She stood up, picked her way across the littered floor of the living room, and stepped out onto the deck. Going to the railing, she looked down into the ravine. Her idea about a children's book seemed like something out of the distant past.

"*After the Sun Goes Down,*" she said, remembering the title. It was late morning, but even so, the bright light still couldn't cut through the shadows at the bottom of the narrow gorge that ran behind the house. Down there it was always dusk—"The Twilight Zone." She grimaced. Here she was, Kelly Kirkaldy Rhine, not bad-looking, finally involved with a man she actually liked at the ripe old age of thirty-six, reasonably financially secure, at least for the moment, and she was going to risk it all on some idiotic Nancy Drew adventure that was probably nothing more than a bunch of coincidences and some pretty thin evidence.

She wanted a cigarette and as she turned away from the deck railing, she felt a twinge of pain from her appendectomy. She went back into the living room, found her Kents, and came back out onto the deck. She lit up, put the pack down on the railing, and looked out over the ravine again: blue sky, bright sun, and a gentle breeze—a Mr. Rogers day in the neighborhood.

She frowned. Except a few miles away, buried under the ivy-league facade of Deep Wood Park, two hearts were being fed by blood the color of skim milk, and a fetus floated blindly like some nightmare from a cheap circus sideshow.

And Lizbeth Torrance, a child whose mother could not have been her own, was having her first period and was therefore no longer safe from whatever frightful thing Kelly's uncle had predicted for her. Impulsively, Kelly ground out her half-smoked cigarette and angrily flipped the package on the railing out into the air. She watched as it spun down into the ravine, finally vanishing in the dappled shadows far below. Without knowing exactly how or why, she knew she'd reached a decision; she knew she was about to step out of Mr. Rogers neighborhood and into a world that had no rules at all.

CHAPTER 17

The short drive from the Erin Park house to the Crestwood Heights Medical Center did nothing to alter Kelly's mood. Under any other circumstances she wouldn't have thought twice about dropping in on Stephen, and she was honestly curious about his work at the Infertility Clinic. But pulling into the parking lot in front of the gleaming building, she was feeling like a two-bit Mata Hari, and he deserved better than that.

The worst thing about it was her own suspicions. With the exception of the occasional odd aberration like Griff Wolper, she'd always prided herself on being a pretty good judge of character, especially when it came to the lovers in her life, and even though she was almost positive that Stephen Hardy wasn't involved in whatever was going on, there was still that niggling doubt. Trust was something she valued highly and here she was, going behind his back.

She parked the Aston Martin and unhinged herself from the low-slung seat. She slammed the door hard, locked it, and shoved the keys angrily into the leather bag over her shoulder. Sauce for the goose was sauce for the gander; if Stephen found out what she was doing, it would serve her right if he dropped her cold.

Walking across the lot and climbing the wide, low steps to the main entrance, she found herself wondering about Robin's motives in all of this and it suddenly struck her that maybe she was falling for *his* paranoia. But that was crazy, too. What did he have to gain from throwing a suspicion on Stephen?

"God damn!" she whispered. The glass doors slid back and she stepped into the cool reception area of the Medical Center. It was beginning to feel as though someone had released a hive of swarming bees inside her head, each one of the buzzing insects a different thought, possibility, or suspicion. Gritting her teeth, and desperate for a cigarette, she approached the main information desk. Robin wasn't crazy, Stephen wasn't involved in any conspiracy, and the universe was unfolding exactly the way it was meant to. It was a nice summer day, she was dropping in on her boyfriend at work, and that was all. Nancy Drew could take her prissy little self and go straight to hell.

The uniformed security guard at the circular information station worked quickly and efficiently after Kelly made her request. Stephen Hardy was paged and located, a visitor's badge was handed to her and the security man pointed her to the right bank of elevators. Stephen would meet her in the reception area of the AFRP clinic on the fifth floor, which, as the guard informed her, was five levels down, not up.

She rode down in the swift, noiseless elevator alone, trying hard to arrange her features in a pleasant, anxiety-free expression. She wasn't sure she could keep up the facade if Stephen started asking her if there was anything wrong, especially since it was so tempting to blurt out the whole stupid story and be done with it once and for all.

As promised, Stephen Hardy was waiting for her as the elevator doors slid open. He was dressed in jeans and an open-neck shirt, looking like anything but a doctor. The reception area wasn't what she'd expected either. It was small, with three walls painted in warm earth colors while the fourth looked out onto the sparkling water of the creek flowing along at the base of the ravine. The room was unfurnished except for a small reception desk carpeted in dark green and the window wall was surrounded by hanging and potted plants, making it difficult to tell where the building ended and the outside began.

"Pretty," Kelly commented, stepping forward and looking around. Stephen Hardy smiled, nodding.

"It was meant to be," he said. "The whole clinic area was designed to be as nonmedical as possible." He took her hand and leaned forward, brushing his lips across hers. "So tell me, why the surprise visit?"

"Boredom," Kelly answered, trying to match his smile. "And a good dose of curiosity. I also thought you might be free for lunch."

"Great."

Stephen seemed perfectly sincere, without a trace of suspicion about her reasons for dropping in. Kelly wanted to sink into the floor. The young doctor draped his arm around Kelly's shoulders, ignoring the raised eyebrow of the nurse behind the reception desk. He led Kelly down a short hallway to a spacious office with a window looking out onto the ravine like the one in the reception area. The furniture in the room was antique, all of it centered around a massive carved partners desk that was at least a hundred years old. The chair behind it was equally old-fashioned, upholstered in worn red leather.

"All of this came from my dad's office in town," explained Stephen, noting her interest. He dropped down into the leather chair and gestured toward an armchair on the other side of the desk. Kelly sat down. "I've still got his old rooms over the bank, but I had this stuff brought over. It fits in with the kind of atmosphere we wanted here. Nothing intimidating."

"Cozy." She glanced around.

"It eases people into the process," Stephen agreed. "The kind of patients we deal with here are pretty sensitive by the time they get to us. Women who think they're failures because they can't conceive and men who think a low sperm count makes them less virile."

"Sad."

"It gets better every day," Stephen said, turning on his smile again. "Give me another twenty years and we'll have it licked." He paused. "Would you like a look around the place?" he asked. "I'm kind of proud of the place actually. You might call it my baby."

"That's awful," Kelly groaned, laughing at the terrible play on words.

"One of many," Stephen said. He stood up and took down a pair of standard white lab coats from the hatrack behind his desk. "It goes with jokes like 'tube B or not tube B' and 'ova and out.' " He handed one of the lab coats to Kelly. "Put this on. Camouflage in case we run into a patient."

Kelly slipped on the coat and then followed Stephen out of

the room. They went back to the reception area and through a pair of sliding, smoked-glass doors.

"There were no chairs in the waiting room," Kelly said as they went down a long, brightly lit hallway.

"No lineups here. It's a small psychological point, but you don't want two or three patients cooling their heels in reception. The tendency is to look the other person up and down and wonder what their problem is. Considering the kind of problems we deal with, that's a definite no-no."

"You think it's important?" Kelly asked.

"Absolutely. Psychic infertility is a clinical fact. It doesn't happen a lot, but it's worth considering. Reduce anxiety and replace it with confidence. We've had a fair number of people who got themselves pregnant even before they'd undergone the first tests."

"Like the old wives' tale about the people who adopt a child because they can't have one of their own and then she gets pregnant?"

"It's no old wives' tale," Stephen said. "Mind you, we don't have it happen too often." He pushed open a door and ushered Kelly into a small windowless room stacked with a confusing array of gleaming equipment. In the center of the room was a gynecological examining table, complete with stirrups.

"Yuk," Kelly said, grimacing. "There's nothing like having a cold speculum shoved up you."

"Modern medicine to the rescue." He went to an instrument tray and picked up a familiar appliance. "Fifteen seconds under a blow dryer and you're up to body temperature. Works every time."

"What do you do in here other than the obvious?"

"Stage one stuff: obvious problems with the vagina and the cervix, swabs, blood tests for venereal problems." Kelly noticed a door set into the side wall of the room.

"Where does that go?" she asked.

Stephen grinned. "One of the honeymoon rooms. We use it for the Sims-Huhner test. Commonly called the P.C."

"P.C.?"

"Postcoital," he explained. "Sometimes a woman's vaginal secretions or the cervical mucus is hostile to her husband's sperm. The best way of finding out is to take samples as soon after intercourse as possible." The doctor suddenly glanced at his watch and swore under his breath. "Shit!"

"What's the matter?"

"They're doing a lap on one of my lottery winners," he said, taking Kelly by the elbow and leading her out of the room. "Come on, we might still be able to catch it."

Bewildered, Kelly followed Stephen Hardy across the hall and into what appeared to be the control room of a television station. The narrow, rectangular room was dark except for the light of half a dozen television monitors and there were several technicians sitting in front of a complex control board. Behind the technicians there was a miniature set of bleachers for observers. A dark-haired woman in a lab coat was seated in front of a microphone in the center of the board. She looked up as Stephen and Kelly entered, then turned her attention back to the screens. All six screens were lit, their functions labeled at the bottom of each monitor: Preview, O.R., LAP 1, LAP 2, VTR Playback, and Record. Both the Preview and O.R. screens showed the draped figure of a woman, everything covered except for her face and a small section of her large, swelling stomach. From the size of her, Kelly assumed she was in the final stages of pregnancy.

"What's a lap and why is she a lottery winner?" she whispered.

"Laparoscopy. A fiber-optic catheter is introduced into the uterus so we can see what's going on," he explained, keeping his voice low. "And she's a lottery winner because she's one of the people from our test series for a new fertility drug. Ultrasound says she's carrying triplets, but we're doing the lap to make sure."

Three people, smocked and masked, appeared on the Preview screen. Two of them, wearing green gowns, began fussing over the patient, while the third, dressed in white, pulled an overhead microphone down over the woman's body. The masked figure stared into the camera and then Kelly heard a tinny female voice crackle over the speakers in the control room.

"How's that for a level?" asked the white-masked doctor.

"Fine," answered the woman at the control panel.

"Two laps this morning," said the doctor. "The first will be just to the left of the navel and the second will be intravaginal. It's the navel laparoscopy I want documented, so you can forget about getting an angle for the intravaginal."

"Whatever you say," replied the woman in the control room. "When do you want to start?"

"You can roll tape any time. Make sure Vince has the vital signs recorded as well. *No* screwups like the last time."

"Fine."

Beside the woman the technician hit several switches and suddenly Kelly could hear the steady beeping tone of a heartbeat. The man hit another switch and the beat was joined by a much faster noise, like a miniature trip-hammer.

"The loud blip is the mother," Stephen explained, keeping his voice low in the dark control room. "The other sound is fetal heartbeat."

"How do you get the sound of the babies' hearts?" Kelly asked. As far as she could tell the pregnant woman wasn't attached to any monitoring machinery.

"We fitted her with a telemetric implant after we found out she was pregnant. Same technology that NASA uses to follow satellites. The woman lives in Charleston so it was impossible for her to come in for the weekly checkup procedures. With the implant she just calls us on the phone. The implant is fitted up around her cervix, sort of like a diaphragm, and we gave her a receiver unit to hook up to her telephone. We can read all the basic information right off the line. She has freedom of movement and we can keep track of our little specimens."

Kelly nodded, keeping her face blank and trying not to laugh. The idea of having your vagina "bugged" brought up a hundred different possibilities, most of them hilarious. She wondered what the woman's husband thought when they were making love.

"Okay, we're rolling," said the woman below them. The preview screen blanked and then a close-up of the doctor on the operating room floor appeared on both the O.R. and Record monitors. "Tape's running, Dr. Westlake." The doctor on the floor cleared her throat and then began to speak, moving in on her patient as she talked.

"Crestwood Heights AFRP project case number Zulu Alpha Three Four Nine. The patient is a white female, twenty-seven years old and is primapara. Testing prior to pregnancy showed a combination of problems including sporadic menstruation due to insufficient production of hormones and hostile cervical mucus that was killing her husband's sperm. The husband, by the way, had a thirty-seven percent motile sperm count and can be classified as high-positive for fertility.

"Use of both estrogen, for the cervical mucus, and human chronic gonadotropins to promote ovulation were indicated in this case. The woman was treated with Estrofil, a piperazine estrone sulfate manufactured by Doyle Pharmaceuticals. The Estrofil was administered orally in 1.5 milligram doses for a three-month cycle of three weeks on, one week off, until the mucosa was no longer hostile as indicated by three separate Sims-Huhner postcoital tests. Following this procedure, the patient was placed on the Doyle Pharmaceutical, AFRP joint testing program for MenoProm. The dosage was one ampule intramuscular for twelve days followed by a 10,000 international-unit dosage of human chorionic gonadotropin one day following the last dose. After two such cycles the patient reported cessation of menstruation and further testing revealed that she was indeed pregnant. Subsequent testing has indicated multiple fetal presence, which follows the previous test group results of a 20 percent possibility of multiple pregnancy when MenoProm is used. Amniocentesis and ultrasound reveal no congenital abnormalities but it was the decision of the AFRP director to follow through with the third trimester laparoscopy which I am about to begin."

Using a glittering scalpel, the doctor swiftly made a small incision on the woman's swollen, exposed belly, aided by one of the nurses, who just as quickly clamped off the severed blood vessels. The second nurse was between the woman's legs, carefully inserting the intravaginal laparoscopy rod. The first nurse handed the doctor a long, stainless steel tube which was slowly slipped into the fresh cut in the woman's stomach. A hair-thin cable was then slipped into the hollow rod and at a nod from the doctor the nurse flipped a small switch on a console just behind the patient's head. The LAP 1 monitor in the control room suddenly brightened and Kelly stared at the image, fascinated. In the foreground she could see a gently swirling vision of fluid, like the cloudy waters of a streambed. In the background, almost at the limit of the tiny light on the tip of the fiber-optic wand, she could see a massive, bloated bag.

"The amniotic sac," Stephen whispered, his lips close to Kelly's ear.

"You're in about level two," said the woman in the

control room. "Take it down some more. Two notches."

"Right." The doctor nodded. The image on the screen grew and suddenly Kelly found herself staring at the faces of three unborn children. Two of them were sucking their thumbs, while the smallest of the three had its head tucked under its sibling's shoulder. As she watched, a wormlike coil of umbilical drifted across the screen.

"Intravag," droned the woman in the control room. The second monitor came to life and Kelly could see the three unborn children from the bottom. There was no doubt that all three of the fetuses were male.

"That's incredible," she whispered.

"Popsicle," said the doctor on the floor, her voice brisk. The nurse handed her a long-handled spatula that reminded Kelly of something you'd use to flip over fried eggs. The doctor was holding it delicately between her gloved thumb and forefinger, and Kelly could see that the instrument was steaming.

"What's she doing?"

"The popsicle is just a big, flat-ended dilator we usually use doing a D and C," Stephen explained. "We keep it in dry ice to make it cold. Put it onto the woman's stomach and the fetus will instinctively roll away from it. Watch."

The nurse rolled back a little of the drapery over the woman's stomach and the doctor applied the cold, stainless steel instrument. On the LAP 1 screen the amniotic sac suddenly surged and all three of the infants began kicking their legs spasmodically. They rolled away from the presence of the dilator, and both the LAP 1 and LAP 2 screens showed the movement clearly. Watching her own monitors on the floor of the operating room, the doctor nodded behind her mask.

"There is no apparent sign of hypospadias, bifid scrotum, imperforated anus, bladder extrophy, or supernumerary digits. Clearly no evidence of Down's syndrome. Since these are the congenital abnormalities most often associated with this sort of drug-program procedure, I think we can safely say that the children appear to be normal. There is, however, some chance of sigmoid colon or heart lesion, which suggests a strict series of full-scale testing and X rays after birth."

"Dr. Hardy?" The woman at the control panel turned around and looked up at Stephen. He nodded.

"I concur," he said. "The mother should be monitored for arterial thromboembolism as well," he added. "Be a shame to give her three little boys and then kill her with a cerebral hemorrhage."

"Dr. Hardy concurs," said the woman at the control panel, speaking into her microphone. "I think you can wrap up the procedure."

"Could that really happen?" asked Kelly.

"What?"

"A cerebral hemorrhage."

"It's a rare side effect of this particular drug. It happens, though."

"Isn't that how my uncle died?" Kelly said slowly.

"Not the same at all," Stephen said, patting her on the shoulder. "Nathan Somerville had ingested enough cholesterol in his lifetime to build a brick wall. He had an embolism all right, but it wasn't because of any drugs he was taking."

"I guess I'm a little out of my depth," Kelly said. "This is a long way from Madison Avenue."

"Don't worry about it. You can't unblock a Fallopian tube, but I can't draw a straight line, so I guess we're even."

"Not quite. Unblocking Fallopian tubes makes a lot more money than drawing straight lines." She checked her watch. It was past twelve. On the screens, the doctor had vanished and the nurse was redraping the woman on the table. "Are we done here?"

"I guess so. Feeling a little squeamish?"

"No, famished."

The AFRP Clinic had its own cafeteria and they took their soup-and-sandwich combinations out onto the rooftop sundeck overlooking the stream running along at the base of the ravine. It was a beautiful day and as she ate, Kelly felt her suspicions dissolving. Doctors involved with test-tube babies and artificial insemination had been getting bad press ever since the cloning hysteria of the late seventies, but there was no doubt that Stephen Hardy was doing wonderful things at the Clinic. According to him, the woman she had seen being scanned a few minutes before had no chance at all of conceiving prior to her therapy, and now she was bearing triplets.

"It's probably one of the most democratic fields of medicine to work in," he said, swallowing a mouthful of tuna fish sandwich. "Statistically about one in ten marriages in America are childless and there doesn't seem to be any inherent socioeconomic or race majority. It can hit anyone."

"I didn't know the percentage was that high," said Kelly, sipping her coffee and enjoying the heat of the midday sun on her face.

"We can help almost two-thirds of those people. Ten years from now, anyone who wants a child will be able to conceive."

"Surely there'd be some exceptions," Kelly said. "What about a woman who's had a hysterectomy?" Like Lizbeth's mother, she thought silently.

"Surrogate parenthood." Stephen shrugged. "If the woman's ova are in good shape, the child can be fertilized with the husband's sperm in vitro and then the embryo can be planted in another woman's uterus. It's already being done. The next step will be completely artificial fetal environments."

"That's a bit too Frankensteinian for me," Kelly said, shaking her head. "And besides, why bother making artificial wombs when there are so many real ones kicking around?"

"Times change and so do boogeymen." Stephen said with a laugh. "Thirty years ago people thought computers were going to take over the world and now kids are doing their homework on them in the living room. The idea of an artificial uterus is just the logical extension of existing intensive-care facilities. Incubators are used for premature babies who'd die without them, and a well-designed AU could do the same thing, only sooner. You could take an Rh embryo from its mother's womb and transfer it to an AU unit, for instance. Or what about a woman who chronically miscarries? You'd deny her a chance at parenthood just because her physiology wasn't quite up to scratch?"

"I guess not." She was starting to feel confused.

"There's no such thing as an evil machine. And certainly nothing so benign as a device that could bring incredible joy to people."

"Maybe you're right." Kelly sighed. "It's the psychology of it all, I guess. People tend to fear what they don't understand."

"Bull's-eye." Stephen wadded up his sandwich wrapping and dropped it onto his tray. "I just noticed," he said. "You haven't had a cigarette for the past hour."

"Three hours actually."

"What brought that on?"

"A need for self-determination." She laughed. "And it's driving me crazy."

"Good for you." Stephen smiled. "Doyle pharmaceuticals is doing a test on a new drug called Nicotomine. I could enroll you in the program if you want."

"No thanks," Kelly said, shaking her head. "My will-power needs some working on anyway."

"Lizbeth tells me you and she had a little chat," Stephen said after a short silence.

"She told you?"

"She beat around the bush for a while, but I think she's pretty proud of herself, actually. Next thing you know she'll be going out on dates." He laughed. "I'm starting to feel old."

"Join the club," said Kelly, looking out over the ravine. "I was all set to work on a kids' book when I arrived and now I just don't seem to have the energy."

"That appendectomy took the wind out of your sails. You'll get back into it."

"I'm not so sure. I don't know if it's the appendix or just approaching middle age, but I'm starting to question a lot of things these days. My art included."

"What about us?" Stephen asked softly. "Are you questioning that?"

"Yes," she answered bluntly. "We haven't known each other for very long, barely any time at all, in fact."

"Maybe we can do something about that." He reached out and touched her hand. "A few days alone together might make your decisions easier. I haven't had a vacation in a long time. Cape Hatteras is nice this time of year."

"I'm shocked, sir!" said Kelly, putting on a Southern belle accent. "Am I correct in assuming that you are proposin' a dirty weekend?"

"Umm."

"Well then, I accept, sir." She laughed. "But what about Lizbeth?"

"I got a letter from her aunt in Seattle this morning. She wants Liz to come out for a visit."

"Really?" Kelly blinked, letting the smile on her face freeze solid. Unless the mail was awfully slow, he'd just received a letter from a woman who'd been dead for six months.

"It would be a perfect opportunity for us."

"Yes, it would." Kelly nodded, her mind racing.

"Didn't Lizbeth's mother used to work here?" Kelly asked, the words coming out in a rush. Stephen looked at her curiously.

"That's right. Why do you ask?"

"What did she do?" she went on, ignoring the question.

"She worked in research." Stephen was frowning now. "Why are you suddenly so interested in Lizbeth's mother?"

"Because I'm interested in Lizbeth." She couldn't think of anything else to say. "You asked me before if I was questioning our relationship. If I'm supposed to think seriously about it, then that means I have to think seriously about Lizbeth."

"What does that have to do with her mother? The woman is dead."

"A lot of people are dead." She bit her lip. This was getting out of control. Any minute now she was going to blurt it all out. She stood up, grabbing her tray off the table. "Look, I'm sorry. Maybe it's this quitting smoking thing. I guess I'm acting a little crazy."

"Sit down," Stephen said sharply. It wasn't a suggestion, it was an order. Kelly did as he was told, her heart beating hard.

"Now, look. Right now Lizbeth is my concern, not yours. I think you're reading too much into all of this. The child confides in you and you don't know if you're supposed to act like a mother, a sister, or a friend. I suppose I'm just making it worse by asking you to go away with me. On top of that you have to figure out if you want to stay in Crestwood or not. That's a lot of pressure."

"No kidding," Kelly muttered. The sun was too strong now and she could feel a blinding headache building up behind her eyes.

"So relax. And I'm speaking as your doctor now, not your lover." He smiled. "Go home, take a bath, and try to think about nothing at all. When you've done that I want you to take a pill."

"What kind of pill?"

"I'll give you a prescription on the way out," he said. "Nothing serious, just a muscle relaxant. Okay?"

"Okay," she said, nodding grudgingly.

"Promise?"

"Promise."

"Good girl. And I'll call you this evening after I've talked with Lizbeth's aunt."

"All right."

On the way back into the Clinic, Stephen Hardy stopped in his office and gave Kelly a sample package of Somax, the Doyle Pharmaceutical version of Valium. The little packet came complete with a foil security seal and as she and Stephen rode the elevator back up to the main level of the Medical Center, she poked the sample into the depths of her purse.

Stephen walked her out to the car, and kissed her lightly on the cheek. She climbed in behind the wheel, started the engine, and backed out of the parking space. As she drove out around the fountains she could see Stephen standing by the steps of the Center, watching her go. She took her hand off the gearshift and touched her purse lightly. Security seal or not, there wasn't a chance in hell that she'd take one of those pills.

CHAPTER 18

Robin Spenser spent the first half of his morning in the Crestwood Public Library under the watchful gaze of Willard Brownleigh. Feeding quarters into the coin-operated photocopy machine, Robin felt a twinge of nausea, realizing that Hugh Trask had probably gone through the same procedure not too long before his death. If ever a man was born to be an informer, it was Willard, and Robin couldn't help wondering if his movements would be reported to Max Alexanian.

Finishing with the machine, he gathered up the two or three rejected copies, folding them into the pocket of his jeans rather than tossing them away. Willard was obviously curious and the last thing Robin wanted to do was leave any evidence behind.

From the library Robin crossed the hot black asphalt of the parking lot and went into the town hall. He spent the next two hours in the records department, thankful that the sleepy-eyed clerk in charge was more than willing to let Robin search through the files himself. Using the town hall machine, he copied what he needed, then lugged the mass of papers back to the sweetshop. Locking the door behind him and then pulling down the shade, he went up to his apartment and spread his morning's work out on the coffee table in his living room.

A full pot of coffee and two hours later, he'd made as much sense of the material as he could and he was ready for Kelly. Just after two o'clock he heard his buzzer go off and he went down to let her in. She was obviously upset, but he didn't question her until they were upstairs in his apartment.

He sat her down on the couch, made another pot of coffee and listened to her story.

"I think I'm going crazy," she moaned, leaning back against the cushions. "I don't know what to believe anymore."

"You still don't think Stephen Hardy is involved, do you?" Robin asked gently.

"My heart says he's not but my better judgment has doubts," she answered, shaking her head. She dug into her purse, pulled out a fresh package of Camel filters and lit up. "I quit smoking today," she added with a dull laugh. "It was almost like a religious experience. I guess my conversion didn't last." She took a deep drag on the cigarette and let out a cloud of smoke. "I'm compounding my sins now, from low tar to the hard stuff in one day. Jesus!"

"How did the good doctor sound when he was talking to you?" asked Robin. "Defensive, nervous, what?"

"Normal. Dead normal. Utterly sincere. That's what has me so confused. On the one hand, this looks like your average, high-tech white-collar community. A nice safe place to bring up kids. On the other hand we've got Hugh Trask and my uncle dead under strange circumstances, hidden messages, and ghostly letters from nonexistent aunts. Things like this just don't happen in real life, Robin." She gave him a pleading look. "Do they?"

"It depends on what kind of life you live," he answered, slouched wearily in the chair across from her. "For most people life is a nine-to-five schedule without enough adventure to fill a thimble. That's why the general population reads *People* magazine and gets off on 'Lifestyles of the Rich and Famous.' It's different. Special. Well, there's bad 'special,' too. It's just that most people don't ever experience it. That doesn't mean it doesn't exist though. The Vietnam War was worse than anything you ever saw in *Apocalypse Now*, a nightmare, but to the people who were there it was very real, believe me."

"So we're supposed to believe that there really is something going on in Crestwood? Hugh Trask was murdered and so was my uncle?"

"Yes," Robin answered bluntly. "And I think it's a lot worse than we know. I think you can add Jack and Elizabeth Torrance to the list, and Lizbeth's aunt as well. I think Max Alexanian and his people are up to their necks in something they don't want that nine-to-five world out there to know about, and they'll do just about anything to keep it secret."

"But what?"

"I don't know." Robin shrugged. "But I'm pretty sure now that it involves the old convent at Chapel Gate."

"What did you find out?"

"Plenty." He dropped down out of his chair and knelt in front of the stacks of photocopies on the coffee table. "For one thing I managed to piece together the whole history of the place. Some of the information comes from books in the Crestwood Room at the library, the rest of it's from town hall records."

"If this were a movie, the bad guys would have covered their tracks better," said Kelly.

"I don't think it ever occurred to them. You only cover your tracks if you think you're going to be followed and these people seem pretty sure of themselves."

"Why not?" Kelly said sourly. "Anyone who *has* followed them winds up dead and we're probably next on the list."

"The only way to prevent that is by staying one step ahead of the opposition. Which brings us back to Chapel Gate."

"So tell me what you found out."

"The convent was built in 1817, minus the walls around it. It was burned in 1827 and rebuilt two years later, this time with the walls. An orphanage building was added and a hospital was built where the school is now. From what I can tell it was pretty much of a closed shop. The kids in the orphanage were all poor or abandoned, and the hospital was used almost exclusively for TB patients. There was a fire in the hospital in 1926, and then there was a scandal at the orphanage. Apparently, unwed mothers were being sent to the place and then the kids were run through the orphanage. The rumor was that there was some kind of black market child-buying operation going on. Anyway, the Little Sisters of St. Antony sold the old hospital site for the Chapel Gate School in 1929 and shut down the orphanage. The convent was still being occupied by nuns until 1975." Robin paused. "And this is where it starts to get interesting.

"The buyer of the property was none other than the St. Gregory Adoption Information Agency. From what I can gather from the town hall records, they wanted to use the old orphanage as a short-term holding facility. They sold out in 1978 to a combine company called Physician's Management Corporation. PMC is actually a joint operation run by Doyle Pharmaceutical Corporation, Intermedix, and Med Tech Corporation."

"I don't get it. What would they want with an old convent and orphanage?"

"I'm just getting to that," Robin said, leafing through the photocopies until he found what he wanted. "There was nothing concrete on file, but I managed to get a whole bunch of construction conformity permits that were issued to PMC. It looks like they built some kind of lab facility inside the walls. The building has its own sewage disposal setup, a generator to provide its own electricity and a satellite dish. Everything is state-of-the-art, ultra-sophisticated."

"Okay, so they built some kind of super-duper lab at Chapel Gate. So what? This PMC bunch is already in the business of medical research. What's wrong with them having another lab facility?"

"On the surface, nothing. But why not build the lab at Deep Wood Park? Why hide it?"

"Security?" Kelly shrugged.

"That's probably what they'd say if you came right out and asked," Robin agreed. "But it doesn't really add up. They must have a security system already at Deep Wood, so why have a whole separate one way out there?"

"I don't know," said Kelly wearily. "I don't know anything anymore. It all just keeps on going around and around in my head and there aren't any answers." She let out a long sighing breath. "And I don't see how we're going to get any answers, either."

"There's only one way," Robin answered. "We check it out for ourselves."

"And just how are we going to do that?"

"Get into Chapel Gate."

"What?" She snorted. "We get out our handy cutting torches and make like bank robbers with that steel barrier? I don't think I'm up for it, Robin."

"No cutting torches," he laughed. "There's an easier way." He shuffled through the photocopies until he found what he wanted. "Here." He pointed. "It's a copy of the survey that was done when the property was sold to the school in 1929.'' Kelly picked up the sheet and looked at it. The plan was simple, showing the extent of the property itself and straightforward indications of where the existing buildings were. According to the plan the buildings inside the walls were butted up against the west and north walls, with a small building in the center of the remaining courtyard. A faint dotted line ran under the north wall, continued across the courtyard, and crossed through the south wall on the other side.

''What's the dotted line?'' she asked.

''That's what I wanted to know.'' He nodded. ''I went back into the files and found a topographical map done in 1897. According to it, the line represents a stream: Baker's Brook. It starts on the ridge up behind the convent and exits at the foot of the hill.''

''It goes underground?''

''Not originally,'' Robin explained. ''I found a book on monasteries and convents in the library and figured it out. Institutions like that always wanted their own supply of fresh water, so they looked for sites with running streams and then built right over top of them. They used the streams for drinking water and sometimes later on they built waterwheels and used the streams for power as well. That's what they must have done at Chapel Gate. The stream was covered with a masonry conduit. According to the plan, the pipe goes under the wall, across the courtyard, and then out the other side.'' He plucked another sheet out of the pile on the coffee table. ''This is the registered plan for the rebuilding of the convent and orphanage after the 1827 fire. It shows a 'lavatorium' and laundry in the basement of the orphanage building there against the north wall. They must have built a well in the basement that connected to the stream.''

''What is all this leading up to?''

''PMC was only interested in building their own facility,'' said Robin. ''I bet they didn't touch the original buildings. That means the well in the basement of the orphanage is probably still there.'' He pulled yet another sheet out of the pile. ''This is the grounds plan for the Chapel Gate School, registered at the Crestwood town hall in 1930. It shows a riding path that goes up around the north ridge and crosses Baker's Brook at something called Hollyridge Pond. I checked that against the International Geophysical Year survey done in the sixties and it shows Hollyridge Pond and Baker's Brook as a dry streambed. No more water."

"So?"

"So it means the old cut-and-cover conduit running under the orphanage is dry. If we go up to the north ridge we can follow the streambed down to where the conduit starts and then follow it up under the orphanage. We go up the old well casing and we'll be inside the walls."

"I was afraid you were going to say something like that," muttered Kelly. "That priest's hole was bad enough, this is just plain crazy. I bet there'll be spiders everywhere."

"You don't have to come with me," said Robin. "I can do it alone."

"Sure. And where will I be? Sitting in some dry streambed biting my nails and wondering what the hell is going on? No thanks." She shook her head. "I just hope it's worth the possible consequences."

"If we're making mountains out of molehills and there really isn't anything going on, then we don't have anything to worry about. If we get caught, all we're doing is trespassing. If something really is going on, then we're in danger whether we go into Chapel Gate or not."

"You make it sound so simple." Kelly sighed. "Okay. When do we do it?"

"Tonight," said Robin.

"Tonight?"

"There's no good reason for delaying it." He shrugged. "Hardy wants to take you on his little trip this weekend."

"I still can't believe Stephen is involved," Kelly said, biting her lip.

"It doesn't matter if he is or not," Robin answered. "One way or the other, we're running out of time."

CHAPTER 19

"This," said Kelly, "is dumb." The night was moonless, the dark disturbingly deep for someone used to the brightness of a big city. She could barely make out Robin's shape a few feet ahead of her on the narrow trail and her breath was coming in ragged gasps. They'd pulled the Wagoneer off the road a quarter of a mile from the Chapel Gate School grounds and walked in, skirting the abandoned buildings and following the steep riding trail up to the ridge above the convent.

"Not much longer," Robin whispered encouragingly.

Kelly cursed silently. He wasn't even breathing hard, and he had a heavy pack on his back. She sucked in deep lungfuls of the cool night air, trying to keep up with the man's steady pace and regretting every cigarette she'd ever smoked. Another five minutes of uphill climbing and she'd collapse.

She ran into Robin before she realized that he'd come to a stop. She stumbled and almost fell but his hand grasped her wrist, keeping her on her feet. He was dressed in hiking boots, dark sweatpants and a navy blue roll-neck sweater, the outfit topped off by a dark knitted cap. Twenty minutes before, watching him as they began their climb, she'd been amazed by the transformation in him, and it wasn't just the commando style getup. Behind the counter at Aunt Bea's or sitting in his living room, he was Robin Spenser, slim, good-looking enough to model for *Gentleman's Quarterly* and definitely nonthreatening. That wasn't the man standing beside her now. He'd undergone a hardening that was almost physical, cold animal instincts replacing sensitivity and doubt. She'd never asked him exactly what it was he'd done in the marines, and standing beside him now in the darkness, she wasn't sure she really wanted to know. Whatever his occupation, it had been a deadly one.

"The pond," he said, pointing. Ahead, just visible through the thin screen of trees was a marshy depression. Still holding her wrist, Robin led her carefully through the trees and around the edge of the pond. The ground was wet and spongy under her feet and there was a faint taste of rot in the night breeze. Dried up or not, there was still water close to the surface and, suddenly shivering, she found herself wondering what the inside of the conduit would be like.

Robin found the old streambed and they followed it to the crest of the ridge. The watercourse was damp, the scattered rocks and pebbles slick with moss and slime, making it difficult to walk. Stumbling, supported by Robin, Kelly moved forward with him, then knelt down as he suddenly pulled sharply on her wrist.

"We're right above the convent," he whispered.

Kelly blinked, trying to make out shapes in the darkness. Finally she found it, the multiple pitches of the roofline a darker shape against the starlit sky. The old orphanage and the convent itself blocked out any view of the new building behind the walls, but letting her eyes follow the dark thread of the stream, Kelly found the conduit entrance. It was a stone arch, big enough for an adult to walk under if he bent low, and covered with some sort of grill or screen. The trees ended along the line of the ridge and the hundred yards between where they crouched and the entrance was a moderate, clover-covered slope broken here and there by a few small rock outcroppings. The streambed itself was shallow, meandering along the contours of the hillside until it reached the stonework arch.

"Not a lot of cover," Robin said softly.

"You think they have guards?"

"They might. I wouldn't want to find out by strolling down there whistling 'America the Beautiful.' " He released Kelly's wrist and shrugged off the knapsack. She massaged the wrist with her right hand.

"That hurt."

"Sorry. I'm out of practice and I'm not used to doing this kind of thing with a partner."

"I'm not used to doing this kind of thing at all." From her

vantage point on the crest of the ridge she looked to the south, toward Crestwood Heights, but there was nothing to mark the development's existence, no twinkling lights or night-glow in the sky. She shivered, a sudden chill cutting through the thick wool of her sweater as the reality of what they were doing began to sink in. Break and enter, trespass—perhaps even worse.

"Scared?" Robin asked quietly, catching her mood. She nodded, clenching her teeth to keep them from chattering.

"An art-school diploma doesn't qualify you for this kind of thing," she whispered back.

"It's one of those jobs where you learn by doing." He grinned.

"So what's next?"

"We go down to the archway and see if we can figure out some way in. Whatever security they have there will give us some indication of what we're up against." He peered into the darkness. "If we try and cut across the meadow we'll leave a trail through that clover a blind man could follow. We'll have to stick to the streambed even though it'll take us longer."

"What do we do if someone sees us?"

"Run like hell and hope for the best," said the ex-marine. "I left the keys in the Jeep. If we get separated try and get back to the road. Don't wait around either. Just get in and drive."

"Whatever you say."

"Okay, let's go. Keep your head down and stay with me."

The dank streambed was a treacherous gauntlet of exposed roots and slime-covered rocks that were almost invisible in the darkness and by the time they reached the stone archway that marked the entrance to the conduit, Kelly was bruised from head to toe and had twisted one ankle badly. Without Robin's help it would have been worse though, and she kept her mouth shut, biting back the pain; the last thing Robin needed now was a burden, especially a whining one.

The archway was partially obscured by a screen of bushes, the entrance covered with a metal mesh grating choked with debris. Peeking over the top of the stonework, Kelly saw that they were still a hundred feet or so from the convent wall. Turning, she looked back the way they'd come. The sloping ridge rose massively behind them and she knew that escape that way would be impossible.

Removing his knapsack again and opening it, Robin took out a short-handled pair of bolt cutters and began working on the grating. Looking beyond him, Kelly stared into the blackness of the conduit. She could smell a sick-sweet odor wafting out of the opening and tried not to think what was causing it.

Robin sliced a half-moon slit in the grating and then put the bolt cutters back in the pack. Bracing himself against the stone, he put one booted foot into the newly created opening and pushed hard. The mesh peeled back slowly, allowing them enough room to slip into the tunnel itself. That done, Robin took out a small, battery-powered lantern and then slipped the knapsack back over his arms and shoulders.

"Stick close," he whispered. Turning sideways and hunkering down, he vanished into the tunnel. Wishing she'd never insisted on coming along, Kelly followed. With both of them safely inside, Robin flicked on the lantern, blocking any backwash of light with his body. There was enough room for them to stand side by side but the curving stonework was too low for them to stand upright. Like the streambed, the tunnel walls were covered in a damp slime and the floor was actually under water.

"Runoff," said Robin, sliding the beam of the lantern back and forth. "A month ago there was probably water flowing down here. It's a good sign."

"What's good about it?" whispered Kelly. Her voice rebounded harshly from the walls. "It seems like a sewer down here."

"It *is* a sewer," he answered. "And the fact that water can still flow along means that the conduit is probably in pretty good repair. The grating wasn't wired either, so maybe we're in luck."

"Or else they decided to close the tunnel at the other end," said Robin. "Like the priest's hole."

"Only one way to find out. Come on."

Keeping her eyes on the puddle of light ahead of them, Kelly kept pace with Robin, trying not to think about what might be squirming around in the water she was walking through and trying to keep her shoulder from brushing the wall. It was a futile effort. Before they'd gone twenty yards the slippery footing had brought her to her knees half a dozen times and her jeans were crusted with muck. Her sweater was filthy and from the feel of it her hair was taking a beating as well.

"Careful." Robin's arm came out, blocking her. Looking down, no more than a few inches from her feet Kelly saw the source of the smell that had been filling the narrow confines of the tunnel. If it hadn't been for the quills, the remains of the porcupine would have been unrecognizable. It lay half-way in the water, the submerged flesh bloated and white, striated with livid lines of purple. The meat on the creature's forequarters had rotted away and in the light from the lamp Kelly could see that the caved-in chest was now home to a seething, fist-sized swarm of maggots. As she stared, something hideous with a score of skittering legs appeared in the dead animal's mouth, paused in the circle of brightness, then raced down the half-rotted, lolling tongue and vanished into the darkness.

"Oh God." Kelly squeezed her eyes tightly shut, every muscle in her body tensing.

"What's the matter?"

"I just felt something go over my foot."

"Don't think about it," Robin said firmly. He took her by the arm and guided her around the remains of the porcupine.

A few yards farther on, he poked the beam from the lamp up toward the roof of the tunnel. "We're close," he said quietly. Looking up, Kelly could see that there was a second archway built into the tunnel, broader than the one at the entrance and buttressed on either side. "We must be under the outer wall. Nothing louder than a whisper from now on and watch your step. There's no way of knowing how far sound travels down here."

Kelly nodded, unable to speak, the thick, sour taste of vomit still high in her throat. She kept moving forward, trying to empty her mind and keep herself from being overwhelmed by the growing pangs of anxiety surging through her. The worst of it was knowing that she was going to have to do it all over again on the way out.

A few moments later Robin stopped again and shone the light upward. Following the beam, Kelly saw a dark opening offset to one side of the tunnel. There was a string of U-shaped iron brackets bolted to one side of the well, the metal scarred and crusted with several decades of rust and grime. The bottom rung was three or four feet above their heads and just out of reach.

"Who goes first?" Kelly whispered.

"You do," Robin answered, shining the light on his ashen-faced companion. "The sooner we get you out of here the better." She nodded her agreement. Putting the lantern down onto a reasonably dry section of the tunnel floor, Robin cupped his hands and crouched down. "I'll boost you up," he instructed. "Climb until you're just below the upper opening and wait until I catch up."

"Okay." Kelly put one hand on Robin's shoulder and her right foot into the stirrup of his hands. She went up smoothly and he rose with her, taking most of her weight as she reached for the bottom rung. She gripped it, ignoring the feel of the gritty metal and pulled herself up, taking the weight off Robin's hands.

She climbed upward, the rough-cut walls of the well no more than a foot from her back. The rungs were about a foot and a half apart and after a minute or so she'd counted thirty of them. Fifty feet; a long way to fall. Biting her lip, she kept climbing, her brain numb. Claustrophobia was bad enough, but combining it with a fear of falling was making every nerve scream out. The only good thing about it was that her bladder had seized long ago and she couldn't have wet her pants now if she'd wanted to.

Without any kind of warning, her head smashed into an obstacle overhead and the well was filled with an echoing thud. She managed to keep her grip on the rungs as her eyes filled with tears at the impact. Peering up, she saw that the top of the well had been blocked with a wooden cover. Heart hammering and a lump rising on her head, she crouched on the upper rungs, praying that the noise hadn't attracted any attention. She felt a sudden clutching hand on her ankle and almost screamed before she realized it was Robin coming up from below.

"What the hell was that noise?" he whispered harshly.

"My head," she answered. "They've got some kind of cover over the top of the well."

"Wood or metal?"

"Wood."

"Can you move it?"

"How?" she asked.

"Push up on it."

"I can't let go of the ladder."

"Wait a second." She felt him move up behind her, his

chest against her shoulders and his hips supporting the small of her back. "I've got you," he said quietly. "Let go with your hands."

"I'm afraid to."

"Do it!" he snapped. Petrified, she swallowed hard and did as she was told, letting her weight rest against him, knowing that his strength was the only thing keeping them both from hurtling down the gaping well shaft. If he lost his grip on the rungs it wouldn't be long before they joined the remains of the porcupine as a putrefying larder for whatever nightmares lived in the darkness of the tunnel below. That image was incentive enough. Gritting her teeth, she let go of the iron rung and pushed up on the wooden cover, praying that it hadn't been nailed down.

At first it didn't move, but pushing even harder, she managed to jar it fractionally loose, giving her groping fingers a tiny purchase. Her strength magnified by waves of panic, she clawed at the cover and pushed it aside. There was a crash and then her nostrils were filled with the sweet scent of relatively fresh air.

"Up and out, quick!" Robin ordered. Kelly scrambled up the last few rungs and boosted herself over the edge of the well. Robin followed on her heels and they helped each other up off the cold stone floor of the convent basement. "Open the knapsack and take out the lantern," Robin said, turning his back on her. Kelly undid the straps on the flap, took out the lamp, and handed it to him. He flicked it on, shading the beam with one hand.

The basement was gigantic, stretching away in all directions, the ceiling above their heads a tangle of pipes and old-fashioned post and wire electrical cables. Hundreds of suitcases, cardboard boxes, and trunks of all sizes were stacked in aisles that ran the length of the cavernous room, all of them covered with a thick layer of dust and fused together by half a century's worth of cobwebs and grime.

The boxes and cases were the last will and testament of the hundreds of children and their keepers who had left them here, and in the shifting beam of the lamp they had a strange and sinister aura that sent a shiver down Kelly's spine. They were nothing more than the bits and pieces brought to this place or left behind, but Kelly felt as though they'd somehow broken into a tomb of some kind—a tomb that had more than one curse put upon it.

"This place gives me the creeps," she whispered. Looking around the dim light, she saw that the well had been located close to a curving set of stone steps leading up to the main floor. Against the nearest wall there was a row of old galvanized washtubs and a huge and equally ancient mangle used to press the institution's damp bed linens. The grotesque piece of machinery was impressive, its massive rollers and crimping wheel making it look like some sort of primitive torture device.

"You look like hell," Robin said with a quiet laugh, throwing the beam of light toward Kelly. She stared at him and shook her head. His face was streaked with grime, his jeans were even filthier than hers, and his hands were coated with rust and scale from the ladder rungs.

"And you look like hell warmed over," she answered.

"Well, at least we didn't ring any alarms getting in here. I don't think anyone has been down here for years. I'm surprised that the security is so poor."

"Maybe that's because they don't have anything to hide," suggested Kelly. "This whole thing could still be a fool's errand, you know."

"Sure, and zebra's don't have stripes." Robin swung the light around again. "There's nothing down here. We'll have to go upstairs."

They went up the narrow flight of steps quietly, pausing every few seconds to listen. At the top of the stairs they found themselves in a small wood-paneled antechamber that led out onto a broad, silent corridor. The far side of the corridor was lined with tall, arched windows, each one shuttered. Robin winced as they put their weight on the squeaking hardwood floor, but the tiny sound was the only thing to break the brooding dusty silence of the old abandoned building.

The windows along the corridor looked out onto the main courtyard of the orphanage, and after a few seconds of fumbling with the latch on the closet shutter Robin managed to get it open. He pulled it back on its hinges for an inch or so, giving him a view of the courtyard.

"Come and take a peek at your fool's errand," he whispered. He stepped aside and motioned Kelly to the window. She looked out, peering across the courtyard.

The building was forty feet on a side, fifteen feet high, and without a window to be seen. There was an array of antennas on the roof and a large painted circle with a bold **H** in the center. A helipad. Just to the right of the antenna array was an eight-foot-high cinderblock cubicle inset with a door. The building was made entirely of concrete and except for the roof it was entirely featureless. A blockhouse. From where she stood, Kelly couldn't see any kind of entrance and assumed that the door was on the far side, facing the tall closed gates in the high convent wall.

"What is it?" she asked, turning to her friend. Robin shrugged.

"I don't have the faintest idea, but whatever they do in there it's pretty obvious they don't want people looking in the windows. Or looking out."

"So now what do we do?" Kelly asked.

"Find a way in."

"How?"

"Take a look between the building and the orphanage," he instructed.

"It looks like a manhole. I can see steam."

"It looks like our mystery blockhouse is hooked into a heating or cooling system inside the orphanage," Robin said. "If we can get to the orphanage end, maybe we can figure out a way inside."

"So how do we get to the orphanage?" Kelly asked. "Walk across the courtyard?"

"The plan I Xeroxed puts the chapel between the convent and the orphanage," Robin said. "It connects to both buildings."

"Maybe we shouldn't press our luck."

"We don't have any evidence yet," he said, shaking his head. "There's nothing illegal about building some kind of bunker with a helipad in the middle of that courtyard. We have to get inside." He headed off down the corridor.

"Okay," Kelly sighed. "You're the boss." With every instinct shouting a warning, she turned away from the window and followed her friend.

Maxmillian Pastermagent Alexanian sat in his lavish office on the upper tier of the Cold Mountain Institute building, his dark eyes watching the amber computer screen in front of him. The large room was decorated expensively in a modern, neutral combination of glass-topped coffee tables and leather couches, a scattering of brilliantly colored Kazak and Bokkara rugs on the gleaming hardwood floor the only clues to his third-generation Armenian heritage.

The desk he sat behind was a high-tech masterpiece of black acrylic custom-built for him by one of the electronic firms in Deep Wood Park. The computer, also custom designed, was built right into the desk top, as was the multiline telephone system and a triple bank of tiny plasma-screen television monitors at his right hand.

On the other side of the room, close to the window wall that looked out across the Institute grounds, was the desk's big brother, a conference table fifteen feet long and fitted with even more electronic gadgetry than the desk. From either location the Institute director could access virtually any database in the world, not to mention keeping absolute track of what was going on in his own back yard.

It was late evening and Alexanian was alone in the building. The telephone had been silent for the past three hours, giving him time to think and plan. He'd been in the office for more than twelve hours, but he showed no signs of fatigue. His suit was still immaculate, his hair perfectly groomed, his cheeks and jaw showing no sign of his heavy beard. Years ago Alexanian had learned that appearance counted for everything if you wanted access to the locked rooms along the corridors of power, and he took pains to always look his best.

The telephone console beside the computer screen gave out a discreet summons, taking his attention away from the report he'd been scrolling through. He picked up the handset and held it to his ear, saying nothing. The number blinking on the console was an internal one, connected directly to Security Master Control.

"Bain, sir. Security."

"Yes?"

"We've had some movement on those numbers you asked us to monitor." The security officer's voice was slightly muffled, a result of the complex scrambling system installed on the closed-circuit fiber-optic line. The speed-of-light transmission would be almost impossible to bug, even without the code–decode apparatus, but Alexanian never left anything to chance.

"Just a moment." The CMI director unplugged the headset and stood up, leaning heavily on his cane. The wound in his knee, gift from a Yugoslav "partisan" almost half a century ago, seemed to be getting more painful with every passing year, but it also served as a reminder of how far he'd come in that time.

He crossed the room to the conference table, sat down, and plugged the headset into the appropriate jack. He touched one of the barely visible heat-sensitive switches built flush into the tabletop and there was a faint whirring sound. A section of the table four feet on a side began to tilt upward, eventually reversing itself to disclose a smaller version of the plasma screen in Security Master Control. Alexanian touched another switch to activate the crossover between the main screen and the one in his office and then spoke into the phone.

"All right. Give me what you have." The screen in front of him flickered briefly and then a series of spidery lines began to appear, spreading across the screen like the branches of a tree. Within a few seconds, Alexanian found himself looking at a reproduction of a topographical map of the Crestwood area. There was a small orange dot blinking high in the upper right of the screen and another slightly to the left.

"The indicator in J2 is your first number," said Bain on the other end of the telephone line. "It belongs to Mr. Spenser's jeep."

"And the other?"

"K2 is Miss Rhine."

"You're sure?"

"Yes, sir. The ident from her key-card is accurate. It has to be her." The system Alexanian had introduced had been developed by General Dynamics and then modified by one of the firms in Deep Wood Park. Originally intended as a way for large trucking companies to locate their vehicles with pinpoint accuracy anywhere in the United States, the Crestwood variant allowed any individual or vehicle to be monitored whenever necessary. Like the PAL bracelets worn by many of the children in Crestwood Heights, every key-card for every house in the community was also fitted with a relay chip, and slightly more complex units could be placed in automobiles. The signal went to the mainframe computers beneath Deep Wood Park, were relayed on an open feed to a shared-use telecommunications satellite and then fed back by microwave to Security Master Control.

The principle was exactly the same as the SatNav units popular with fishing boats and yachtsmen, and gave an instantly updated report on the precise geographical position of anyone carrying one of their cards. The Deep Wood Park company and several other corporations were currently developing the system as a way of keeping track of paroled convicts and it was being tested operationally in half a dozen states.

"You have no marker on Mr. Spenser?" asked Alexanian.

"No, sir. He lives in town and he doesn't use a key-card."

"But presumably he's with her?"

"Yes, sir, unless she just borrowed his Jeep."

"Unlikely." Alexanian stared at the screen thoughtfully. "Zoom in on K2," he ordered.

"Yes, sir," The plasma screen on the table shifted, then dissolved, re-forming into a schematic diagram of the Chapel Gate convent and orphanage. With the enlarged scale, Alexanian could read the ID tag number on the glowing dot that represented Kelly Rhine. According to the screen, she was moving from the main floor of the convent toward the chapel situated between it and the orphanage.

"According to the screen, Miss Rhine appears to be within the walls."

"Yes, sir," replied Bain, his voice hesitant.

"You had no security alarm?"

"No, sir. According to our information none of the security monitors show any intrusion."

"System failure?"

"I'll run a check. Just a moment, sir." While Alexanian waited, he punched up the computer screen on his desk and accessed the mainframe in Deep Wood Park. Almost instantly, WAITING appeared in the upper left-hand corner. He hit the RETURN key, then tapped in a seven-unit alphanumeric code. Once again the response was instantaneous.

ACCESS COMPLETE
QUEEN BEE READY

"I've run a check, sir," Bain said, coming back onto the line. "Everything seems to be in order."

"Obviously everything is *not* in order," Alexanian replied. "Remain on the line." He put down the handset and typed in a series of queries on the computer. There was a brief pause and then the screen cleared and refilled.

> QUEEN BEE INDICATES NO INTRUSION ALARM SYSTEM FAILURE. 93% STATISTICAL PROBABILITY K2 INTRUDER ACCESSED SECURE AREA THROUGH UNUSED AQUEDUCT AT K2/SUB 22.2. FURTHER QUEEN BEE INDICATES PRESENCE OF SECONDARY K2 INTRUDER ON BASIS OF PRELIMINARY INFRARED SCAN OF PERIMETER. K2(S) IS MALE, 5' 10" <+/-2">. 175–185 LBS.

"They gained entry through a water main of some kind," said Alexanian. "Mr. Spenser is accompanying Miss Rhine."

"Yes, sir."

"The lab security systems are in order?"

"Yes, sir."

"Personnel?"

"The lab is being run on remote, sir. There are no deliveries scheduled and the late shift doesn't come on until midnight."

"So the place is empty?"

"Yes, sir."

"Good." Alexanian nodded, his eyes on the screen. The dot had crossed the chapel and was now in the orphanage building. "Can they get from the orphanage into the lab?"

"There *is* a maintenance catwalk that follows the freon and lox pipes," said Bain. "But we have a steel shutter at the lab end. They won't be able to get through."

"Can you open the shutter remotely?" asked Alexanian.

"Yes, sir. Or at least they can at MED-TECH."

"Tell them to open it. Now. I want them inside. Keep monitoring but I don't want any alarms going off."

"Yes, sir."

"When you've done that I want a security team out there. Six men." Alexanian paused again and pursed his lips. Then he smiled. "And one more thing, Bain."

"Yes, sir?"

"I want the surveillance cameras running from the moment they come through the shutter. We should have a record of this."

CHAPTER 20

From the looks of it, the main floor of the orphanage had been used as a school with half a dozen classrooms of varying sizes clustered around a warren of tiny offices near the main doors. The ceiling in the main corridor was high and arched, the surface thick with layers of peeling paint in half a dozen shades of institutional green. At either end of the main corridor there were narrow stairs, presumably leading up to the dormitory floors above.

Kelly's hot fear of a few minutes before had dulled to an anxious sense of foreboding, and the bleak interior of the orphanage had added depression to the catalog of emotions surging within her. She couldn't get the vision of the suitcases and boxes out of her mind, and padding down the corridor on Robin's heels she could almost hear the ghostly voices of the children coming from the classrooms. Half a century ago adoption had been the choice of last resort for couples without children, and most of the inmates of St. Anthony's would have spent their entire childhoods here. And inmates was the right word, because life behind those high walls outside would have been a prison sentence, and this place would have been their entire universe.

She caught up to Robin and touched his elbow lightly, reassuring herself that reality still existed, the fringes of her consciousness terribly aware of the whispered horrors and untold countless miseries this building had once contained. She swallowed, her mouth dry. If Uncle Nat and Hugh Trask were right, there was now a new and nameless nightmare lurking here.

She glanced at Robin and seeing the hard set of his jaw and the look in his eyes, she knew that being here was even worse for him. She could only imagine the kind of things that might have gone on in a place like this but Robin had lived it for the seven long years he'd spent in the seminary school.

"It's like going back in time," he whispered, reading her mind as they neared the end of the corridor. "I can almost hear the beads rattling." He tried to smile but Kelly could feel the deeply rooted tension in his voice. He wanted to be out of here as badly as she did.

There was a small door set under the stairwell at the far end of the corridor and opening it, Robin risked turning on the light for a few seconds. Another set of stairs, wooden, scarred and old, led downward into the darkness.

"Coal dust," Kelly said, sniffing.

"The basement. Watch your step." He went down and Kelly followed, one hand on the grimy, slightly damp stone wall on her left. Reaching the foot of the stairs, Robin moved the light in a broad arc. The ceiling here was lower than the one in the convent building, the maze of pipes and wires threaded through the beams and rafters more complicated than the root system of a rain forest. The floor was concrete, stained and crumbling, and the dank labyrinth of coal bins, oil tanks, and cinderblock storage rooms smelled of must, mildew, and wood rot—and something else.

"What's that chemical smell?" Kelly asked, peering along the cone of light thrown by the lamp.

"I'm not sure," Robin murmured, ducking is head and edging down a narrow aisle between two disconnected and rusted-out oil tanks. "It reminds me of a meat-packing plant."

"Don't say things like that." Slaughterhouse visions leaped bloodily into her mind's eye. Max Alexanian as a mass murderer, dozens of split and limbless orphan torsos suspended from meathooks in the basement of the old building, each one purple-stamped U.S. NUMBER 1 PRIME.

At the end of the aisle they found themselves facing a cinder-block wall. It was obviously new construction, at least relative to the age of the building. There was a door offset to the left, metal-clad and fitted with a heavy padlock. A stenciled warning said NO ADMITTANCE.

"This doesn't belong," Robin said.

"How do we get past the lock?" Kelly asked. In answer

Robin shrugged off the knapsnack and opened it again. Instead of bolt cutters, he took out a short, steel pry-bar about eighteen inches long. Running the beam of light around the doorframe, he checked for alarms, and satisfied that there were none, he jammed the bar into the hasp of the lock and put all his weight behind it. Grunting with effort, he dragged down hard and after a few seconds the lock snapped.

"Not terribly sophisticated, but effective." He pulled open the door and shone the light inside. The cinder-block enclosure was about fifteen feet on a side, the inner walls clad in what appeared to be galvanized metal. The little blockhouse was bare except for three large tanks at one end and a complicated-looking valve-and-conduit system that ran through the far wall of the room, bracketed on the left by a narrow, caged catwalk and a handrail. The pipes were at least a foot in diameter and were clad in a layer of thick foil-covered insulation.

Stepping into the room, Kelly shivered. It was freezing cold and the stencils on the side of the tanks explained the low temperature. All three bore the Intermedix logotype and each was a different color. The white was marked LOX, and the blue CO2, the red FREON.

"It's a refrigerator system of some kind," Robin said. "And I'll bet those pipes lead into the bunker we saw."

"Presumably you want to go down that catwalk."

"No other way, I'm afraid. And we've come too far to turn back now."

"Right."

Robin stepped up onto the catwalk, motioning Kelly to keep clear of the heavy pipes, insulated or not. Keeping one hand on the railing, she followed Robin and the probing beam of light, noting that the inner wall of the pipe channel was lined with galvanized metal as well. Every few yards the pipes were collared with bulky-looking joints, but even so there was enough leakage to frost the foil wrappings and let trails of condensing vapor hiss upward to vents set into the roof. Even though they were now deep in enemy territory, Kelly felt a sense of relief; she could relate to hissing pipes a hell of a lot more easily than maggot-ridden animal cadavers.

"Stop," Robin ordered. He turned off the light and Kelly waited behind him, standing in the darkness. Looking over his shoulder, she could see a faint, purple-blue circle of light a few yards ahead. "Put the lamp back in the knapsack," Robin whispered. He handed her the lantern and she did as she was told, making sure the flap was dogged down securely.

"Done," she said softly. He nodded and then lifted one hand, waving her to follow. They moved quietly along the last few feet of catwalk and finally came to the exit point. Robin crouched down as they reached the end of the catwalk and Kelly followed suit, the cold metal of the grating hurting her knees.

"Sweet Mother of God," whispered Robin, looking out through the opening. "What is this place?"

Kelly edged forward and peeked over his shoulder. The catwalk opening was located just below the ceiling of a gymnasium-sized room. The ceiling itself was gridded with a honeycomb lattice of stainless steel scaffolding, vaguely reminiscent of the lighting grid for a television studio or a movie sound stage. The dim light came from dozens of small spotlights strung along the grid along with scores of curly-cord wires, bundled cables, and thin, clear plastic tubes that dangled down to the floor below. Trying to make some sort of sense out of what she was seeing, Kelly finally realized that there was a pattern: they came in sets, each grouping running down to a table-framework on the floor.

The frames looked like rectangular trampoline beds, but instead of a canvas pad the webbing around each frame supported a large, sausage-shaped cocoon of bulging, semi-transparent plastic. Some of the tubes and wires looked as though they were connected directly to the cocoons, while others ran down to computer consoles at the foot of each frame. There were at least a hundred of the cocoon frames in the room, neatly arranged in rows and aisles. The floor of the room was made of the same gleaming steel as the grid, and it looked as though there were tub-sized depressions below each of the cocoons. Still not sure of what she was seeing, Kelly found herself thinking about the porcupine again.

"Body bags," Robin said, horror in his voice, the whisper cracked and rasping. "They look like body bags." With his words the image resolved itself for Kelly and it all began to fit together.

"People," she managed. "My God, those things are people!"

"The whole place is on automatic pilot," Robin said, his

eyes still fixed on the scene below. "There's nobody here."

"We've got to go down," said Kelly, swallowing the bile that filled her throat. "We've got to see."

"There's a ladder. We can climb down." He hesitated, then spoke again: "I've got a camera in the bag. We can take pictures of those . . . things."

"Evidence."

"Yeah." Turning, he slipped over the edge, his boots finding the rungs of the metal ladder bolted to the wall. Kelly went down after him, her heart beating hard, but the fear she'd been feeling now replaced by a cold and bitter outrage.

They reached the bottom of the ladder and stepped gingerly out onto the glassy smooth floor. So far there hadn't been the slightest sign of anything but the most basic security; the ease with which they'd gained access to the bunker was worrying both of them now.

Close together they padded across the floor to the first row of cocoons. The console at the foot of the first frame carried the familiar block-letter logo of the JCN Computer Corporation, but this was no Jason home computer. The console had a nine function keypad in three rows:

CARRIER #	IMPLANT #	DELIVERY
LIFESUPP	DBASECON	INFUSE
FET MON	VIDSCAN	SYSCHEK

Beneath the keypad was the dark red rectangle of a small plasma screen. Presumably, by hitting the right keys you could get a display on the screen. While Robin tried to decipher the keypad, Kelly moved slowly around to the side of the frame. Not really wanting to look more closely, but unable to stop herself.

From three feet away the cocoon looked harmless enough, more like a bulky package wrapped in milky plastic than anything else, but stepping up beside the frame, Kelly gagged and squeezed her eyes tightly shut, unable to believe what her eyes told her was there. She took a long series of deep breaths, then opened her eyes again.

At the catwalk opening the plastic had seemed opaque, but now Kelly saw that it was actually transparent. The milky color came from the bath of thick, gelatinous fluid within the bag, the same artificial blood mixture she'd seen in the Deep Wood Lab. Instead of individual organs the fluid was surrounding a naked body, giving the cocoon its bloated shape. The bag seemed loose everywhere except over the face and the swollen abdomen, where it had been drawn skintight. Gritting her teeth and forcing herself to come closer, Kelly looked down at the face of the poor creature inside the bag.

It was the face of a Down's syndrome adolescent, the ultrathin mylar covering making the thick-lipped, flat-nosed features into a grotesque nightmare. The plastic had been pierced in several places to allow the pitiful child to be intubated; a thick, esophogeal tube was forced between the lips, a narrower tracheal pipe slid into a puckered wound in the neck, and a third line of bundled tricolor wire was attached just behind the right ear. Looking closer, Kelly recoiled, realizing that the eyes had been carefully sutured shut and from the slightly collapsed look of the lids there were no eyeballs behind them.

Kelly lurched back, one hand at her throat, her eyes wide. She bumped into the body-frame behind her and whirled, the sudden touch sending her heart thundering against her chest. She found herself staring at another body and she could see the heavy, opaque tubing that entered the protective bag just below the smooth, pink mound of the stomach. The thick, snakelike coil slithered down between the slightly parted legs of the body just below the clean-shaven pad of a pubic mound, then disappeared inside, a steel clamp and a half a dozen surgical clips holding the tube in place between the obscenely parted vaginal lips. A second tube was fitted beneath it, poking between the fish-belly folds of the buttocks.

She felt suddenly dizzy as a wave of nauseating vertigo turned her legs to rubber. Gripping the edge of the body-frame with a white knuckled hand, she waited for it to pass. Compounding the horror of the rows of silent, bloated bodies was the smell—a bitter antiseptic scent made even worse by an overlying veneer of deodorizing sweetness, as though a rendering plant had been sprayed with a pine-scented air freshener.

Something moved on the edge of her vision and she turned her head. A few inches away the floating monstrosity in the bag shifted slightly, muscles responding to some stimulus created deep within its surgically induced hibernation. The thighs shivered in their fluid bath and then relaxed as the rectal sphincters released, sending a pale gray plug of semi-liquid matter along the suctioning waste tube.

"I think I'm going to be sick," Kelly whispered, turning away from the sight.

"Hang on for a minute more," Robin said. "I have to get some pictures." He had the pack off and the camera in his hand. Kelly walked unsteadily back to where he stood. "The consoles here give all the information," he said, adjusting the camera. "It looks as though they implant these . . . people, and when they come to term they're given cesarean sections." He began taking photographs, the dim, blue light in the huge room strobing brightly with each flash.

"The two I just saw . . . they're Down's syndrome. Mongoloid idiots."

"They all are."

"I don't understand."

"I don't either," Robin answered, his eye at the viewfinder. "Not completely." He turned and continued photographing. A few seconds later he finished the roll, rewound it, and began reloading. He handed the roll to Kelly and she pushed it into the pocket of her jeans. "I think the girls here are nothing more than broody hens, surrogate wombs for implanted embryos. It starts to make sense when you think about it."

"You mean Alexanian and his people get the Down's syndrome kids through the adoption service and then use them here?"

"Something like that," said Robin. "Retarded children are the hardest to adopt out, so I'll bet there aren't too many questions asked." He finished reloading and began shooting again.

"It's monstrous." Kelly let her eyes shift over the room. There were faint electronic noises now and again, and the distant hiss of gasses, but other than that the huge room was utterly and unnervingly silent.

"That's one word for it," Robin agreed. He moved over the closest body-frame, twisting the lens to bring the teenager's plastic-shrouded face into focus. "It's also good business."

"What do you mean?"

"Figure it out," Robin answered, his voice cold as he hit the shutter release and stood back. "You're a good Catholic, or maybe not a Catholic at all. Anyway, you get pregnant and you have a Down's syndrome child, or a baby with some other form of mental retardation. What do you do? If you don't have the money and you don't want to raise the child yourself, you put it up for adoption. If you do have the money, you institutionalize the kid. Either way it's not too hard for Alexanian to get his hands on it. He implants healthy embryos and breeds himself some nice, bright white babies to put on the market. Damaged goods in, and for a price, healthy goods out—for top dollar, as well."

"I can't believe he'd be doing it just for the money."

"No," Robin agreed. "I think you're right. There's something else going on as well. Something a lot bigger." He finished the second roll of film, handed it to Kelly and began packing away the camera. He shrugged into the pack again and turned, looking back up at the entranceway high on the wall. "That set of refrigeration pipes follows the wall and then goes up through the ceiling," he said. "And there's a set of stairs over there on the far side of the room."

"And you want to see where they lead?"

"That's up to you." He shrugged. "We've got enough pictures on those two rolls to bury Max Alexanian a dozen times. We can go back if you want."

Kelly took another long look around the cavernous room and its silent occupants. Years before, she'd been sitting in a Greenwich Village outdoor cafe when a whole group of Down's syndrome children had come down the street. Everyone in the cafe turned away, trying to pretend that they didn't exist, but Kelly had watched them, fascinated. Much to the horror of the people around her, the group turned in to the cafe, escorted by two adults, and sat down, taking up half a dozen tables.

For the next thirty minutes the air had been brightened by their smiles and their uninhibited laughter and Kelly realized that the odd appearance of the children and their lack of intellect did nothing to take away from their basic humanity. They were enjoying life to the fullest extent of their capabilities, and without reservation, which was more than she could say for a lot of other people she knew.

"Well?" Robin asked quietly. Kelly reached out hesitantly and let her fingers touch the swelling abdomen of the cocoon-shape closest to her. Under the sterile plastic covering, the flesh was warm and alive and she knew the revulsion she felt had nothing to do with the young women trapped here; they were only victims. The real horror and obscenity was reserved for the people who had conceived of this terrible place.

"We go on," she answered, turning back to Robin. "We owe it to them."

CHAPTER 21

They made their way through the rows of silent, suspended cocoons and climbed the metal stairway bolted to the far wall of the giant room. As Robin checked the metal-clad door at the top of the stairs for any alarms, Kelly looked back and down, fixing the terrible sight in her mind.

Once upon a time each one of the encapsulated children below her had been given names and each had its own personality, however primitive. Now that was gone, their individuality scrubbed away by Alexanian's sick obsessions. She could almost see the twisted logic of it and hear the careful modulated tones of the CMI director's voice: "Their minds are of no use to us, so then let their bodies serve us for the betterment of the world."

"Nothing," Robin whispered, his voice worried. "No alarms. The door isn't even locked! I don't like it."

"We've gone too far to turn back," answered Kelly. "Open the door." Robin nodded and pushed the door open a fraction of an inch. He peered through the crack and then pushed the door open fully.

"It looks all clear," he said softly. Kelly followed him through the doorway and they found themselves in a short, narrow corridor. The walls and floor were brilliant white and perfectly smooth, lit by banks of recessed lights in the ceiling. Immediately to their left was a doorway with the word INCUBATION stenciled on it, and a short set of steps that led up to a high, heavily bolted door. On the wall at the foot of the steps was a small version of the H-in-a-circle symbol they'd seen on the roof of the bunker. At the far end of the corridor was a glass-doored vestibule and beyond that an oval, stainless-steel hatchway fitted with a large wheel.

"What is it?" asked Kelly. "An air lock?"

"Must be. Look at those suits hanging on the wall in there. Some kind of high-risk lab." The suits were visible through the wide glass door leading into the air lock. They looked like a silvery, high-tech version of a firefighter's absestos suit, complete with a bulky zippered headpiece and faceplate. Robin looked back toward the stairs that led to the helipad on the roof. "Okay, Alice in Wonderland, what's it going to be? Up and out or deeper in?"

"Deeper in, I'm afraid. I don't think we have any choice now."

"Good enough," Robin answered grimly. "But I still think this is too easy. We haven't seen a soul and there aren't any alarms that I can see."

"You said it yourself: the whole place is running on automatic." She glanced up and down the corridor. "And who needs alarms? The place is out in the middle of nowhere surrounded by a thirty-foot-high stone wall, not to mention the bolt on that door up there."

"I still don't like it." He put a hand on Kelly's shoulder. "Look, if the shit hits the fan, I want you to get out of here as fast as you can, okay? Forget the tunnel. Head up to the roof. It's only about a fifteen-foot drop to the ground and you might be able to get out through the main gate. If not, head for the convent and see if you can get out that way."

"Meanwhile you'll be playing Horatio at the Bridge? Come on, Macho Man, we're in this together."

"Don't be a fool!" Robin snapped. "I'm not playing games. This whole setup stinks. You don't run an operation like this with no security at all. We should have tripped a dozen bells and whistles by now."

"So?"

"So I wouldn't be at all surprised if Max Alexanian and a squad of uniformed nasties didn't suddenly drop in on us. We've been in here for about five minutes. If they have to come all the way from town, they'll be breaking down the doors any second now."

"Okay, so why are we wasting time standing around and talking about it?"

"Because if it happens, one of us has to get out of here.

You've got the film. If we run into trouble you make a run for it and I'll keep them occupied."

"With what?" Kelly asked sourly. "Your bare hands?"

"No." Robin took his pack off again and opened it. He took out a black, felt-covered container about the size of a large box of chocolates. "I'm a good Boy Scout. I came prepared."

"What the hell is *that?*" said Kelly, staring as he opened the box and revealed its contents. Crouching down, Robin worked quickly, assembling the dark gray, carbon polymer components. Completed, the weapon looked like a slightly overweight automatic pistol a little more than ten inches long with no recognizable barrel and a thick, rounded handgrip just forward of the trigger mechanism. Reaching into the box again, Robin took out a short banana clip and snapped it into the gun.

"It's a Heckler and Koch MP5K. A machine pistol. It was designed to be used by security agencies but now a lot of the boys from Bogotá are carrying them around underneath their shiny suits."

"How did you come by it?" Kelly asked, eyeing the sinister looking piece of machinery.

"I uh . . . inherited it from a friend of mine in Miami." He pulled back the half-dollar cocking lever with a snap, pushing a round into the chamber.

"Why do I get the feeling you have a history no one knows anything about?"

"We all have our little secrets. Come on, we're wasting time." Carrying the weapon in one hand and the knapsack in the other, he headed down the corridor to the glass doors. Two feet in front of them, the doors slid back automatically and he and Kelly entered the small chamber. Once inside, the doors slid shut and Kelly could hear a whirring sound as a hidden fan hummed into life.

"Do we put on the suits?" Kelly asked. Robin nodded, putting the weapon and the knapsack down on a built-in bench that ran along the wall.

"We don't know what's on the other side of that bulkhead," he said, nodding toward the oval hatch. "Better safe than sorry."

The suits were made of a thin, silvery material like ultrastrong aluminum foil. They had feet attached that slid easily over their own boots and two circular air filters just below the clear plastic faceplates. The one-piece gauntlets at the sleeve ends were as thin as surgical gloves and fit as tightly. Obviously they were meant for sensitive work.

"Ready?" Robin asked, zipping up the front of the suit and pulling the Velcro neck fastener tight. His voice behind the faceplate was slightly muffled but Kelly could hear him perfectly.

"Ready," she answered, zipping up her own suit. "Except for the fact that I'm already boiling hot in this thing."

Robin handed her the knapsack and picked up the machine pistol. Approaching the hatch, he tugged at the locking wheel one-handed: it spun easily. There was a distinct hissing sound and Kelly realized that the outer chamber was kept at a lower pressure than the area inside, like an isolation ward in a hospital, guaranteeing the purity of the inner area. She followed Robin through the opening.

The warmth of the suit seemed to vanish instantly, replaced by a bone-chilling cold, as though they'd walked into a giant freezer. Peering through the faceplate as Robin dogged down the hatch behind her, she realized they'd done exactly that.

Stepping through the hatch, Kelly had steeled herself for another horror like the cavernous room below but at first glance it looked like nothing more than a low-ceilinged, refrigerated warehouse. The floor was made of some sort of egg-crating grating, the heavily insulated pipes below her feet filling the air with a shifting fog of condensing vapor. There were more pipes in the ceiling, as well as several neat rows of light panels fading into the misty distance, throwing a dull, deep pink glow over everything.

There was a control console to their right, a dozen or more monitor screens built into the wall above a bank of computer workstations, a vacant chair in front of each terminal. Behind the workstations and running thirty feet to the rear wall were rows of stacked, stainless-steel cylinders resting in elaborate tubular frames like some sort of bizarre wine cellar.

Each cylinder was about eight feet long, rounded at one end, and fitted with a flat, flush-handled plug at the other. An assortment of wires and cables was threaded through the tubular framework, presumably connecting back to the workstations.

There were hundreds more circular plugs set into the other

three walls of the room, and to the left of the hatchway entrance there was a neat row of thick-wheeled, motorized gurneys. Instead of stretchers, the trolleys were fitted with large, rubberized clamps, obviously designed to accommodate the silvery, outsized cigar-tubes, and beneath the clamps was a pair of hydraulic pistons capable of lifting the mechanism up to the highest cylinders in the racks and along the walls.

"It looks like a morgue," Kelly said. Behind the faceplate of his suit, Robin shook his head.

"You don't go to this kind of trouble for dead bodies." He dropped the knapsack onto one of the computer terminal chairs, pulled out the camera, and handed it to Kelly. "I reset it on automatic," he instructed. "You don't even have to focus. You take the pictures and I'll keep an eye out for anyone coming in."

They headed down the nearest aisle, stopping in front of the first stack of cylinders. Kelly took a photograph, but there wasn't much to see. The cylinder plugs had three small lights mounted above the recessed handles—red, yellow, and green. Glancing around, Kelly saw that most of the cylinders were showing green, only a few yellow, and none red. There was also a row of bright blue numbers stamped onto the plugs of each tube.

"I wonder what they're for?" muttered Robin, his voice muffled by the air filters in his headpiece.

"I'm not sure I want to know," Kelly answered.

Shifting the machine-pistol to his other hand, Robin gripped the handle of the nearest cylinder and twisted. Nothing happened. He tried pulling the handle straight out but there was still no movement.

"Locked," he said. "Shit."

"Maybe they're controlled by the computers?"

"Worth a try. But I don't want to hang around here much longer. Somebody's bound to show up eventually."

"Say the word when you want to go," Kelly shivered. "I'm freezing."

They went back to the workstations and Robin sat down in front of the closest terminal. Kelly dropped into the chair beside him. The computers were industrial versions of the Jason, equipped with simplified keyboards and a turbo-ball like the one Lizbeth used to play ORBITZ. By moving the ball, an indicator arrow moved over the screen and commands could be chosen from a menu of key indicators at the top of the screen.

Kelly palmed the turbo-ball on her terminal, put the arrow on STATUS, and entered the command. The amber screen flickered and then began to fill with data.

ON-LINE/DIAL 1-800-463-7800/CODE PREFIX AND M.O.H.L.#
MAJOR ORGAN HOT LINE/A SERVICE OF NORTEL-INTERMEDIX.
TIME LOGGED ON: 23:13:24

ON HAND

#	ORGAN	SEX	BT	PRICE	ACCESS
2	kidney	male	ab	$35,000	234/qwe
1	kidney	female	a	$40,000	235/qwe
2	heart	juve	a	$57,000	451/tmy
3	heart	adult	a	$82,000	452/tmy
1	liver	infant	o	$110,000	exclusive
4	cornea	n/a	a	$6,000	511/obh

"They're running some kind of organ bank," Kelly said. She did some quick arithmetic in her head and realized that there was slightly more than six hundred thousand dollars worth of transplant organs listed.

"It's more than an organ bank," Robin said, seated at the terminal next to her. "Take a look at this." She leaned over and checked the text on his screen.

REVENEX LTD./CHAPEL GATE FACILITY
MAINTENANCE INVENTORY

1. GENERAL INVENTORY

BEATING HEART CADAVERS

MALE	125
FEMALE	94
INFANT MALE	31
INFANT FEMALE	23
TOTAL	273

PERFUSED ORGANS/LONG TERM	88
PERFUSED ORGANS/SHORT TERM	36

PARKINSON/ALZHEIMER PROGRAM	
FETAL BRAIN <GRAM UNITS>	4002
FETUS INTACT/PERFUSED	817
FETUS PARTIAL/PERFUSED	309
FETUS FROZEN/SECTION <GRAM UNITS>	2007

KROPP CLINICAL LABORATORIES LTD.
NATIONAL BLOOD CENTER.

TYPE	VOLUME<PINTS>	DONORCODE
A	4209	2123-2199
B	1237	3455-3890
AB	788	4231-4457
O	340	5022-5173
O–	113	5201-5300

NOTE: SEE MAIN POD DIAGRAM FOR BHC DONOR LOCATION AND DATE OF LAST BLOOD-UNIT HARVEST.

"I think the 'pods' are the things behind us," said Robin. "It's like something out of *Invasion of the Body Snatchers*. Beating heart cadavers, blood harvesting. Jesus!"

"Let's try and get one of those things open," Robin muttered, moving the arrow up to the menu at the top of the screen. He pulled down POD, randomly chose a sector and called up DISPLAY.

B/C SECTOR DISPLAY

B-1	B-2	B-3	B-4	B-5	B-6
B-7	B-8	B-9	B-10	B-11	B-12
B-13	B-14	B-15	B-16	B-17	B-18
B-19	B-20	B-21	B-22	B-23	B-24
C-1	C-2	C-3	C-4	C-5	C-6
C-7	C-8	C-9	C-10	C-11	C-12
C-13	C-14	C-15	C-16	C-17	C-18
C-19	C-20	C-21	C-22	C-23	C-24

HIGHLIGHTED NUMBERS INDICATE PODS CURRENTLY NOT IN USE. WHEN A NEW POD IS PUT INTO USE, PLEASE UTILIZE THE LOWEST NUMBER POD AVAILABLE. WHEN POD HAS BEEN UTILIZED, PLEASE LOG POD NUMBER, USER CODE, AND STATUS ONTO

THE MAIN INVENTORY. ALL BHC PODS MUST ALSO BE LOGGED INTO NORMAL STATUS MONITORING PROGRAM AS WELL. FOR POD OPENING AND MAINTENANCE INSTRUCTIONS REFER TO COMMAND P.O.P./BC AND STRIKE ANY KEY.

INSERT CHOICE, HIGHLIGHT AND PRESS ANY KEY.
POD NUMBER...../SYSTEM CHECK...../MONITOR.
/MAINTENANCE CHECK...../ALL

"Which one?" asked Robin.

"Why not open all of them?"

"All right." Robin highlighted the ALL command and then hit the RETURN key. The screen emptied briefly and then responded with another command sequence.

PLEASE ENSURE THAT A RECEIVER HAS BEEN PLACED
AT EACH POD
TO BE OPENED.
PRESS ANY KEY WHEN RECEIVER(S) IN POSITION

"What's a receiver?" Kelly asked.

"I don't know." Robin shrugged. "And we don't have any time to find out. He hit the RETURN key again and waited. The screen emptied and then filled again.

B/C SECTOR P.O.P. SEQUENCE

b-1	b-2	b-3	b-4	b-5	b-6
b-7	b-8	b-9	b-10	b-11	b-12
b-13	b-14	b-15	b-16	b-17	b-18
b-19	b-20	b-21	b-22	b-23	b-24
c-1	c-2	c-3	c-4	c-5	c-6
c-7	c-8	c-9	c-10	c-11	c-12
c-13	c-14	c-15	c-16	c-17	c-18
c-19	c-20	c-21	c-22	c-23	c-24

Almost instantly, the screen began to pulse and the sector display was overprinted with a large blinking icon in red.

ABORT SEQUENCE

At the same time, a klaxon began to howl and half a dozen red emergency lights in the ceiling began to flash and rotate.

Almost unheard above the sudden chaotic howling there was a steady hydraulic hissing noise.

Both Robin and Kelly lurched up from their chairs, appalled by the brutal Pandora's box of sound they had unleashed. Behind them the hydraulic hiss became louder and they both turned in time to see the first pods open in the racked section closest to them.

The plugs on all forty-eight began to turn, the lights above the handles flickering from yellow to red. When the plugs had completed a single revolution, the small ram pistons built into the base of each cylinder began pushing the inner containers slowly outward.

The inner cylinders were tempered acrylic, each one glutinously filled with the same kind of thick white jelly they'd seen in the cocoons. Dark, eellike cables floated and twisted in the fluid, twined around the bodies within the cylinders, the cables bunching at the foot of each tube.

The cylinders with the lightest contents moved fastest, sliding out over the aisles between the racks. Watching, rooted to the spot, Kelly suddenly knew what the receivers were—the stretcherlike trolleys to their left. When a tube was opened the trolley would be there to grip it with the rubber-coated clamps. Without the receiver in place, the result was obvious, inevitable, and utterly horrifying.

The first cylinder to reach the limit of its ram and drop down to the floor was B-21, which happened to contain what was left of Elitta Mendez, originally from Agua Prieta, Mexico, close to the U.S. border. She had crossed the border at Douglas on January 17 of the previous year, hoping to find her way to East Los Angeles and her cousin, another illegal alien, Paulo Onavas, who had a good job in a car wash.

Picked up in an Immigration sweep less than two weeks later, Elitta was sent with twenty others to a holding facility in Bisbee, Arizona, where she subsequently vanished along with three others who happened to have reasonably rare blood types.

Further, more complex testing showed that Elitta had some evidence of hepatitis in her blood system, but there was nothing wrong with her major organs or her bone marrow. Since her arrival at the Chapel Gate facility almost twelve months ago, she had provided both an arm and a leg used for bone marrow transplants in San Diego, California, and Toronto, Ontario, as well as a cornea used in Nashua, New Hampshire, and a kidney in Manchester, England.

The tube shattered as it hit the metal floor, sending chunks of plastic flying in all directions and spewing Elitta's partially eviscerated body slithering down the aisle, the life-support tubes pulling out of mouth, throat, and rectum. Although long-since brain dead, the young woman's autonomous reflexes continued to operate briefly, the tracheotomy incision puckering in and out as she fought to breathe, the small liquid sound lost in the surrounding dim.

B-2, C-11, and C-12 were the next to fall, containing Maria Pocitos, a fellow inmate of Elitta's at the Bisbee facility. Sean Wengemuth, a fourteen-year-old runaway from Toledo, Ohio, and Mrs. Carla Johnson of Meredith, Wyoming, victim of a car accident that had left her massively brain-damaged but with the rest of her body intact.

Wengemuth, two days short of having spent six months at Chapel Gate, had been used extensively. Little more than a partially emasculated torso, he stopped breathing within a few seconds of being released from the pod, but Pocitos and Johnson had been used mostly for rare blood harvesting and managed to survive a little longer, the lubricating jelly of the perfusion fluid sliding off them in heavy, pale clots as they jerked and twisted spasmodically on the flooring.

Within ninety seconds all of the pods had crashed to the ground, including B-6, which contained seventeen of the on-hand fetuses in the facility, all of them at the twenty-week phase, which was the limit of the Chapel Gate artificial incubation laboratory in the room down the hall.

Any fetal material not implanted was allowed to grow to its fullest extent and was then either perfused with artificial blood or granulated and frozen for use in the Parkinson's/Alzheimer program.

Pink, naked, covered with a layer of white-gray ooze, and dragging their perfusion catheters, the twenty-inch-long embryos were spattered over the slithering pile of human offal, one of them landing almost at Kelly's feet. Gagging, the stench of vomit hot in her throat and nostrils, she reeled away, slipping on the coating of blood, fecal matter and slime that now covered the floor.

Dazed, her stomach cramping violently, she was barely aware of Robin Spenser's hand gripping her shoulder. He spun her away from the spreading mess and pushed her toward the hatchway. Stumbling, they managed to sidestep the grotesque tide of human flesh, and the klaxon continued battering at their ears and the red emergency lights flashed wildly through the mist created by the cooling equipment.

Robin turned the locking wheel frantically, pulling open the hatch as soon as it released and pushing Kelly out into the glass-doored antechamber. Without bothering to remove the suits, they staggered out into the corridor. Another alarm bell was sounding in the narrow hall and the ex-marine knew that any safety margin they might have had was now gone. He unzipped his headpiece and threw it back, then did the same for Kelly. Her breathing was deep and ragged, and from the look in her eyes she was going into shock. From behind the door leading down to the "maternity ward" he heard the sound of echoing footsteps and he acted almost without thinking.

"Get onto the roof!" he yelled loudly, pushing Kelly toward the stairs leading up to the helipad. She stumbled forward a few feet and then stopped, turning to look back at him, blank-faced. "Get the fuck out of here!" he bellowed. As he spoke, the door on his left opened and he whirled. A security guard appeared in the open doorway, dressed in full-riot gear, including an expressionless Kevlar face mask.

Bringing up the machine pistol in a sweeping motion, Robin dropped to one knee and fired. The impact of the bullets blew the faceless man back through the doorway and over the guardrail, giving Robin another few seconds. "*Go!*" he screamed, and this time Kelly moved.

One eye still on the doorway, Robin watched as Kelly lurched up the stairs, threw back the bolt and went out onto the roof. When he was sure that she was safely out of the way, he rummaged around in the knapsack and took out half a dozen taped-together double-clips for the machine pistol. He heard more footsteps on the metal stairs and flattened himself against the wall, the blunt nose of the machine-pistol pointed toward the door. Unless they had some other way of getting to him he knew he'd be able to hold the fort until his ammunition ran out, and hopefully that would give Kelly time to escape.

Miles away, seated in his silent, shadowed office, Max

Alexanian watched the scenario unfold like a slow-motion video game, his eyes on the plasma screen in front of him and the telephone receiver at his ear. The plasma screen gave him a detailed schematic view of the Chapel Gate facility, his security people moving dots of blue, the two intruders in blinking red.

"Status, please," he said quietly into the telephone. One of the red dots was motionless in the main floor corridor while the second was moving across the roof.

"We have a six-man squad on the lower level," Bain said, still at his post in Master Control. "One of the six has been wounded, possibly fatally."

"What about the alarm in the pod facility. I want an update."

"Yes, sir. Major malfunction caused by the intruders. They opened up an entire sector without having the receivers in position. I'm afraid it's pretty bad, sir."

" 'Pretty bad' doesn't mean anything to me," Alexanian said coldly. "I want an accurate report."

"Yes, sir."

"The woman. She appears to be on the roof."

"Yes, sir."

"Good. The gate-door has been left open?"

"Yes, sir. Just the way you said."

"Good. I want her to get away cleanly, is that understood?"

"Perfectly, sir."

"Spenser is in corridor F-2. According to the screen, that is a sealable unit, correct?"

"Yes, sir," said Bain.

"Then, do it," replied Alexanian. "Drop the shutters and fog the corridor; there's no point in having anyone else hurt. Realism can be taken too far and the woman is already gone. Further action is redundant."

"Yes, sir; I'll inform the security squad."

"Do that. And get me the report on the pod room; that's valuable inventory."

"Right away, sir."

Satisfied that everything was under control the CMI director stood, using his cane for balance, and went back to his desk. He sat down at his computer terminal, called up the Queen Bee program again and entered his access code. The response was instantaneous.

QUEEN BEE RUNNING.

GOOD EVENING, DR. ALEXANIAN.

PLEASE ENTER YOUR REQUEST.

>SUBJECT KELLY KIRKALDY RHINE NOW IN A STAGE 7 PSYCHOLOGICAL MODE.

PLEASE LIST DESTINATION OPTIONS.

>RUN

RUNNING.

SUBJECT KELLY KIRKALDY RHINE/S7PM DESTINATION OPTIONS

1.OWN ADDRESS

2.DR. STEPHEN HARDY

3.EXIT CRESTWOOD HEIGHTS CONTROL ZONE/PERIMETER

4.CRESTWOOD HEIGHTS POLICE

5.MARTIN AND CARLOTTA NORDQUIST

6.S7PM/ESCALATION TO PANIC STATUS.

WAITING.

PLEASE ENTER YOUR REQUEST.

>PROBABILITY COMPARISON SUBJECT DESTINATION.

>RUN.

RUNNING.

PROBABILITY COMPARISON SUBJECT DESTINATION/KELLY KIRKALDY RHINE:

1.OWN ADDRESS 15%

2.DR. STEPHEN HARDY 41%

3.EXIT CRESTWOOD HEIGHTS CONTROL ZONE/PERIMETER 22%

4.CRESTWOOD HEIGHTS POLICE 00%

5.MARTIN AND CARLOTTA NORDQUIST 18%

6.S7PM/ESCALATION TO PANIC STATUS. 04%

PROBABLE DESTINATION:

STEPHEN HARDY

186% PROBABILITY QUOTIENT TO NEXT MOST PROBABLE.

WAITING.

>FINISHED.

>RUN.

RUNNING.

THANK YOU, DR. ALEXANIAN IT WAS A PLEASURE TO BE OF ASSISTANCE.

Turning away from the screen, Alexanian spun his chair around slowly and looked out over the blinking lights of the community that had become his universe. He smiled faintly, lowering his chin and letting it rest on the ornate head of his cane. Somewhere out there Kelly Kirkaldy Rhine was exercising her so-called freedom of choice, and it was going to take her exactly where he wanted her to go. He leaned comfortably back in his chair and lifted the cane, pointing it toward the darkness outside and sighting along the long ebony rod like a sharpshooter.

"Bang bang you're dead, Ms. Rhine," he whispered, and then allowed himself a brief moment of almost silent laughter.

It was good to be alive.

CHAPTER 22

Opening her eyes, Kelly stared out through the windshield of the Jeep, her brain dully conscious of the ORCHARD PARK sign lit up by the steady glare of the headlights. The Wagoneer was on the gravel shoulder, its right-side wheels leaning over into the grass-filled drainage ditch, and the engine was still running. Bringing her wrist up to her face, she saw that it was 12:35. She was missing an hour of memory.

Groaning, she leaned back against the seat. Somehow she'd escaped from the Chapel Gate facility and driven more than ten miles to the outskirts of the Orchard Park subdivision. Somewhere along the line she'd also managed to get out of the contamination suit she'd been wearing; it now lay in a crumpled pile on the passenger side of the Jeep.

The last thing she could remember clearly was climbing down the metal fire-ladder on the side of the blockhouse and crossing the courtyard of the convent to the partially opened gates; everything after that was a fog of jumbled impressions and ragged-edge, isolated images. Overwhelming any kind of coherent thinking was the single memory of the slithering atrocity in the pod room. The vision of that hideous, foul-smelling stew of glistening human body parts oozing across the floor through the shattered remains of the capsules would stay seared in her mind until the day she died.

Which wouldn't be long in coming if she stayed where she was. Robin might have been able to hold off the security people for a little while, but by now he'd either been killed or captured. She felt a lump rise in her throat and her eyes stung with welling tears. The stubborn, heroic bastard had made her escape possible, and he'd probably paid for it with his life.

She straightened in her seat, hanging on to the steering wheel with one hand and wiping the tears from her eyes with the other. Faint suspicion had escalated to horrible reality and now to murder, but crying wasn't going to solve anything. Her instincts told her to put the truck in gear and get the hell out of Crestwood Heights as fast as she could, but the burning anger she felt was even stronger.

Max Alexanian and his companions were doing things here that made *Psycho* look like a song-and-dance act, but horrible as the events of the past few hours had been, she was sure that the terror went even deeper. Crestwood Heights hadn't been established to cover up a clearinghouse for human flesh; Chapel Gate was only part of the Cold Mountain Institute's nightmarish future, and no matter how frightened she was, she had to get the entire story.

Doing it alone was impossible though; she was going to need help. Dragging up the shift lever, she managed to get the Wagoneer in gear and with a spurting hail of gravel she pulled the vehicle off the shoulder and onto the road. She left Deep Wood Road and turned onto Orchard Park Drive. Right from the start Robin had been worried about her relationship with Stephen Hardy, but maybe that was just jealousy on his part, sexual preferences aside. On the other hand Kelly had made love to Stephen, talked to him, understood him—she *knew* he couldn't be involved in this.

And she had nowhere else to turn. There was no authority she could go to, and even if she did get out of the Heights she had no idea how far Alexanian's influence went. The state police, Washington? Once upon a time Alexanian had access to the White House and there was no reason to think that he didn't still have powerful connections. The only other people she could think of were Martin and Carlotta Nordquist, but sweet as the old couple were, they wouldn't be able to help. No, it had to be Stephen.

There was no point in leaving a trail of bread crumbs for Alexanian's goons to follow right up to the doctor's door so she drove the Wagoneer onto Maryknoll, a little cul-de-sac at the foot of the ridge leading up to Stephen's house. She parked at the far end of the street, locked all the doors, and then cut through the yard of the last house, picking up a bicycle path that led down to the school.

It was dark, but there was enough starlight to follow the gravel trail and she made good time, keeping to the shadows of the overhanging trees, and glancing down over the cedar-shake rooftops of the houses lower on the ridge, watching and listening for any signs of pursuit. The community looked peaceful, only a few lights showing here and there, a barking dog, a light breeze blowing.

The trees thinned at the top of the ridge and the bicycle path turned down, heading for the ravine and Tryon Woods. Beyond the small dark patch of forest she could see the lights of the old town, but nothing seemed out of place, the very ordinariness of the night making her nervous. No sirens, no flashing lights, no hot pursuit, almost as though Chapel Gate had been a madman's dream she'd stumbled into for a brief, mind-wrenching instant.

She made her way across the clover meadow, keeping her eyes on the lines and planes of silhouette that marked Stephen's house. Reaching it, she ducked into the safe shadows of the carport and rang the bell. A few seconds later an outside light came on and the little surveillance camera over the door swiveled down, examining her. There was a click as the electronic bolt went back and she pushed open the door.

Stephen met her at the top of the stairs, concern on his face. She fell into his arms, sobbing, and the next thing she knew she was lying on the couch in the upstairs living room, a damp, cool washcloth on her forehead and Stephen beside her, waiting with a cup of tea.

"Okay," he said quietly. "You look as though you've been to hell and back. Why don't you tell me what happened."

"I want to," she said, pulling the washcloth away from her forehead and sitting up against the pillows. "But I'm afraid you won't believe me. I don't think anybody in their right mind would."

"Why don't you try me?" He smiled. She took the cup of tea and swallowed it down gratefully.

"All right." She nodded weakly, leaning back against the pillows.

It took the better part of an hour to tell him the whole story, interrupted every once in a while by a question or a request for clarification. When she was finished, she looked at him, expecting the worst. She'd described a nightmare and she wouldn't have been surprised if he'd called for the boys in the white coats. Instead, he stood up and went to the bar, returning with a pair of glasses half-filled with Scotch and ice cubes. His expression was thoughtful.

"You think I'm crazy, right?"

"No," he said, shaking his head. He took a small sip of his drink and Kelly followed suit, wincing at the slick burn of the liquor as it slid down her throat. "It all adds up. My father thought Max Alexanian had too much power in this community, and from what you've described it's obvious that he's been abusing it. Maybe right from the beginning."

"Then you believe me?"

"Yes. I still don't see how Lizbeth fits into all of this though. Your story about her aunt is incredible."

"Where is she?" asked Kelly, suddenly worried.

"Relax," he said, putting a hand on her shoulder. "She's upstairs asleep, right where she should be."

"We've got to get out. All of us," Kelly said. "Christ! They could be here any minute. It won't take them long to connect Robin and his Jeep."

"Did anyone at the Chapel Gate facility see you?" asked Stephen. Kelly shook her head.

"No. And most of the time I had that suit on."

"Good," nodded Stephen. "That gives us some time. Even if they do connect the truck they have no reason to think you were involved."

"So what do we do?"

"You mentioned something about your uncle having left some evidence hidden."

"Just the semaphore message, and I don't have the faintest idea what it means."

"It's important," Stephen answered, rubbing one hand across his jaw. "We need evidence."

"I've still got the film." She dug into the waist pocket of her jeans and pulled out the two exposed rolls.

"That's good." Stephen nodded. He took the rolls from her and put them into his shirt pocket. "But it's not good enough. We need documentation, and presumably that's what your uncle left behind . . ." He paused, then looked at Kelly thoughtfully. "What was the semaphore message?"

"Wyndham's birds. It's meaningless. I don't know anyone named Wyndham." Stephen thought for a moment, then snapped his fingers.

"No, but I do," he said, smiling broadly. He stood up and went to the low row of bookcases against the side wall of the room. He knelt down, scanned the shelves, and finally pulled out a thin, well-worn paperback. He came back to the couch and handed it to Kelly.

"*The Midwich Cuckoos*, by John Wyndham," she read. "I still don't get it."

"He must have chosen it on purpose. It's the story of a small English town that falls asleep mysteriously one day. When everyone wakes up, all the fertile women in the town are pregnant. They give birth to a bunch of alien children."

"And they have bright, glowing eyes!" Kelly said, excited. She pulled herself upright. "It's one of the films I chose for the film festival. *Village of the Damned*! Beautiful, blond children, just like Lizbeth. And they had all kinds of weird powers."

"Why did you choose it?" asked Stephen.

"My God!" Kelly whispered, making the connection. "I chose it because it was so easy. My uncle had a print of it in his private collection. It's right there in plain sight."

"He took a page out of Edgar Allan Poe. 'The Purloined Letter.' Somehow he managed to hide the documentation he and Hugh Trask had gathered in the film. Maybe in the can."

"Now what do we do?"

"I don't think we can wait," Stephen said, standing. "We have to get it now. Tonight. Once we have the documentation we can figure out a way of getting you safely out of here."

"You're involved now too. And Lizbeth."

"You leave that part to me. The first thing we have to do is get that film."

"How?"

"Can we get into the theater?"

"Yes. I've got the keys with me."

"Good. We'll go there in my car. Drop me at the Strand, then go on to Erin Park. Collect what you need, then meet me back at the theater. We'll go and collect Lizbeth and then get the hell out of here."

"I'm not sure I want to go back to the house alone," Kelly said. "Why don't you come with me?"

"Relax," he said quietly. He leaned over the couch and kissed her softly on the cheek. "No one suspects you, and both of us turning up at your house at this time of night would arouse too much notice. Let's play this as straight as we can, okay?"

"Okay." She nodded wearily. It was a relief to let Stephen take charge, even if it did make her feel a bit guilty. He left the room briefly, reappearing wearing a soft, well-worn leather bomber jacket and clipping a small electronic device to his belt.

"My pager," he explained, noticing Kelly's quizzical look. "Lizbeth knows the number by heart, so if she needs me while we're out of the house she'll call."

They went down to the main floor and Kelly waited while Stephen carefully locked up behind them. He opened the passenger side door of the sleek Citroën and she sank gratefully into the comfortable leather seat. A few moments later they were driving down the hill, heading for the edge of the Orchard Park subdivision. The night was silent except for the muffled swishing of the tires and astonishingly, Kelly felt herself dozing off.

She woke with a start, heart pounding, as Stephen turned off the ignition. Blinking, she saw that they were parked in the narrow alleyway beside the Strand. He helped her out of the car and they walked quietly through the darkness to the main doors of the theater. Pausing as she dug into her pocket for the keys, Kelly looked up and down the street, certain that the calm, late spring night would soon be split by the sound of approaching sirens.

Except for the old-fashioned streetlights casting their pale puddles of light across the sidewalks, the town of Crestwood was dark and asleep, the storefronts blank, with only the slightest riffling breeze to whisper through the cloaking trees that leaned protectively outward over the street. It was like the perfect sweet dream of everyone's America; lost for a moment in the peace-filled silence, Kelly had to remind herself that the dream was false, the peace an illusion.

"Is something wrong?" Stephen asked, standing beside her. She shook her head and fitted the key into the lock.

"No, nothing's wrong," she answered, pushing open the door. "I was just thinking how easy it is to fool yourself about things you don't want to know or see." They stepped into the pitch dark, aromatic lobby and Kelly led the way to her uncle's office. Closing the office door, she turned on the overhead lights and scanned the rows of shining film cans arranged on the wire rack to her left. Each one was labeled with a long strip of adhesive tape, the title and running time written on with a felt pen. *Village of the Damned* was at the far end of the rack, and with a 78-minute running time it took up only one of the wide 35mm cans. Kelly pulled the can out of the rack and stripped off the tape.

"He sure had a black sense of humor," she commented, carefully hanging the tape from the edge of the editing table.

"What do you mean?" asked Robin.

"I just remembered the name of the sequel," she said, prying apart the can. "It's *Children of the Damned.*" The lid came off and they looked inside. Except for the bulky reel there was nothing to see. Poking her thumb and index finger through the reel cutouts Kelly lifted the film out of the can and checked underneath. Nothing.

"I don't understand," Stephen said, his eyes narrowing. "Are you sure you translated the message correctly?"

"Robin did it," she answered. "He was in the marines so I assumed he knew what he was doing." There was a small piece of masking tape holding the head end of the film down and Kelly picked at it thoughtfully, pulling it up and letting the end come free. She carefully pulled out a foot or so of the dark leader. "I wonder . . ."

"What?"

"This is thirty-five-millimeter film. Uncle Nat had one of those aluminum camera cases back at the house. Top of the line Nikon equipment, including a macro lens."

"So?"

"So, thirty-five-millimeter still film is exactly the same size as thirty-five-millimeter motion picture film. Maybe he photographed whatever evidence he had and spliced it into the movie."

"How can we check?" asked Stephen urgently.

"He's got rewinds here and a viewer splicer," Kelly said, shrugging her shoulders.

"Do you know how to use them?"

"Sure." She nodded. "I did a little bit of editing work at the agency. It's not too hard." She looked down at the heavy reel of film. "Maybe we should just bring it along, check it later."

"Let's do it now," Stephen pressed. "We have to make sure we've got whatever it was he left behind."

"Okay."

Kelly took the reel to the long editing table, fitted it onto one of the rewind cranks, and then pulled an empty take-up reel down from the wire rack on the wall. She placed the empty reel on the second spindle, moved the viewer splicer into position and then pulled out a long length of the film from the full reel. She used the masking tape to attach the head end to the empty reel, then threaded the center into the sprocket teeth of the viewer.

Turning the crank on the empty reel spindle, she took up the slack and then flipped the little switch to light up the viewer. Turning the crank slowly, she began pulling the film through the sprockets, watching as the edge numbers and timing leader flickered by on the screen. The opening credits of the film appeared and Kelly turned the crank faster, speeding through the film, looking for something out of place.

A fleeting montage of jerking, black-and-white images raced by; a tractor in a field, driverless, moving in circles, a British soldier on a country road carrying a canary in a cage, a stalled light plane crashing to the ground, children with glowing eyes dressed in shorts and little caps, then, horribly, a car careering down a laneway and smashing into a brick wall, exploding. Half-remembered faces of the actors, George Sanders, Barbara Shelley, Laurence Naismith. . .

COLD MOUNTAIN INSTITUTE

March 11, 1984
Memorandum:
To: Phillip Granger
From: M.P.A.
Re: PETES Additive Program

Dear Phillip,

I've talked with Markley at Doyle Pharmaceuticals and he is quite pleased with the first test run of the Sequenol additive in the Colony Woods PETES. As you know the drug had a Ritalinlike effect on children under twelve, but that was to be expected and the active period was within your baseline parameters. Insofar as Sequenol's possible use as a tranqulizer is concerned, initial monitored sexual activity in the nonplacebo addresses fell by almost forty-one percent during the test period, which gives you an idea of the drug's potency. Given the overall results I think we can go ahead with the site-specific tests you suggested.

MPA

MEDTECH INCORPORATED
inter-office memo

January 18, 1986
To: Curtis A. Wheeler
From: Thomas Merton
Re: Tissue Farming Project

Status: Classified

Curtis,

In reply to your telephone request of yesterday, I concur that given the fact that we can now ex-utero at twenty weeks and in-vitro up to eighteen weeks the implementation of the TFP can now begin. MPA is fully committed to this project as you know, and funding will not be a problem.

I also concur with your choice of the design team with the exception of Torrance. He seems to have a moral problem with what we are doing and I don't think we're going to be able to change that. His reluctance to adopt a positive objective attitude with regard to the Queen Bee Project is indicative of future problems.

I suggest that you talk to MPA about this as soon as possible and perhaps we can resolve this situation once and for all.

T. Merton,
V.P. Special Projects

AMERICAN LASEROPTICS INCORPORATED
a division of Northern Telecommunications Ltd.

Update: April 22, 1980
To: M.P. Alexanian
Cold Mountain Institute
From: Hiram Sperling,
Pres., American Laseroptics Inc.

Dear Max,

Just a note to let you know how much I enjoyed seeing you again at the Washington reception. I found our discussion an interesting one, and the overall implications of what you're trying to do are astounding. Rest assured that American Laseroptics would be more than willing to become involved and I think I can interest James as well.

Technologically what you require is well beyond the drawing-board stage and I see no difficulty in testing such a system out within a closed environment. It's the kind of thing that might make John Q. Public's hair stand on end, but it is the wave of the future.

I'll call next week to arrange a meeting.

All the best,
Hiram

There were scores of documents, each one exposed on a single frame of thirty-five millimeter still film. From the splices it appeared that Nathan Somerville had shot two or three dozen rolls of film, joined them together, and then inserted the whole assembly into the film. Kelly turned the crank slowly and even though she didn't understand everything she was reading it was obvious that Robin had been right. There was a lot more going on than organ banking and black-market babies. From her brief glimpse at the documents it looked as though Max Alexanian had orchestrated a symphony of medical, pharmaceutical, industrial, and social experiments on an Orwellian scale.

"This is madness," she whispered, staring at the viewer screen. Behind her, Stephen reached out and put a hand on her shoulder.

"We've got what we came for," he said quietly. "I'll finish up here while you go back to the house."

"All right," she said numbly, standing up. He gave her the keys to the Citroën and led her outside. He kissed her gently, then pulled open the door of the low, sleek car.

"Hurry back." He smiled. "I'll be waiting right here."

She nodded again, then slipped behind the wheel. She started the car, put it in reverse and backed out onto the street, the powerful engine rumbling heavily.

Staring out through the sloping windshield, she guided the big sedan down Main Street and then up High Point Road. It was past two-thirty in the morning now, the road empty and dark as she drove through the shrouded, silent landscape.

It took her less than ten minutes to reach the Greenbriar subdivision and three more to make her way to Erin Park Drive. She turned the car into the driveway of number 46, killed the engine, and climbed out, taking a slow deep breath of the cool air. She stood quietly for a moment, trying to hang on to a moment of simple peace, then crossed the driveway and let herself into the house, closing the door behind her. Flipping on lights as she went, Kelly headed for the bedroom and began to pack her clothes.

Whether it was shock, or just exhaustion, she felt no emotion as she filled her suitcase. Even Robin's death had retreated into some dark corner of her mind. She moved from dresser to bed automatically, without thought, intent on nothing more than getting out of the house as quickly as she could.

When the suitcase was filled, she snapped the locks shut and lugged it down the hall to the front door. If her luck held, she, Lizbeth, and Stephen would be a hundred miles from Crestwood Heights before the sun rose.

"You really should lock your doors at night." Carlotta Nordquist stood in the open doorway of the vestibule, Martin standing just behind her. Eyes widening, Kelly dropped the suitcase to the tiled floor of the hall.

"What are you doing here?"

"We're the neighborhood watch, of course," the pudgy woman said, smiling. She was wearing a swirling muumuu housedress in a riot of Hawaiian colors, and as she stepped forward, her fuzzy-furred slippers hissed on the tiles. Martin followed her, blocking Kelly's path completely, a broad fixed smile on his pink, cherubic face.

"Please let me go," Kelly said. "This is an emergency." She tried to slip past Carlotta, but the woman's hands shot out and gripped her shoulders, pushing her back.

"Now, now," Carlotta whispered. "The hospital called a few moments ago and told us what to expect. You just rest quietly until the ambulance comes, there's a good girl."

"Yes. You just do what Carly says and everything will be fine."

"Let me go!" Kelly yelled. She pushed Carlotta out of the way but Martin still blocked her path. For the first time she noticed that the man had a syringe in his hand, thumb poised over the plunger. Carlotta's heavy forearm came around her throat like the squeezing jaws of a vice and Martin stepped forward quickly, sidestepping and gripping Kelly's wrist with his free hand. Through the open door Kelly saw a Crestwood Medical Center ambulance pull up behind the Citroën, its bar-light flashing, but the siren quiet. She felt a stinging sensation as Martin expertly jabbed the needle into her arm, but her eyes were fixed on the ambulance.

Stepping down from the passenger side, bag in hand and wearing a white coat, was Stephen Hardy, every inch the concerned doctor, the ambulance driver following him. The drug was beginning to take effect, but she was still conscious as Stephen entered the house, a look of professional concern on his face.

"Any trouble?" he asked, looking at Martin Nordquist.

"Piece of cake," replied the older man.

"Good."

"You bastard!" Kelly whispered, her words slurring. "You treacherous bastard!" He'd believed her story too easily, she could see that now—and she had believed *him*. Believed him because she wanted to so desperately, following her heart instead of her head. She tried to spit in his face, but her mouth had suddenly become terribly dry. She had a brief moment of nausea and then blackness fell.

The ambulance driver took the unconscious woman from Martin and Carlotta, holding her easily under the arms. He eased her gently to the floor of the hall and then disappeared, returning a few moments later with a wheeled stretcher. He lifted her onto the gurney and pulled a crisp white sheet and then a blanket over her, tucking them neatly under her armpits. He strapped her down and then looked at Hardy.

"Where to, Doc? Emergency?"

"Yes," said Stephen. "I'll take it from there. I'll follow you."

"Sure thing, Doc." The driver wheeled Kelly out of the house and down the drive to the waiting ambulance. Stephen turned to Martin and Carlotta.

"Thank you." He nodded. "You acted quickly. I didn't have much time to arrange things."

"Our pleasure." Nordquist smiled, his shiny scalp gleaming in the overhead light.

"Yes indeed," said Carlotta, bobbing her head up and down. "We take our Neighborhood Watch duties very seriously, you know." She patted him on the shoulder. "You look tired, Stephen." There was concern in her voice. "You really should get some sleep."

"No rest for the wicked, I'm afraid."

CHAPTER 23

Kelly Rhine woke up in the Holiday Inn with a splitting headache and her mouth tasting like a cat litter box. She sat up groggily, lips gummy as she tried to swallow the wad of Kleenex that seemed to be stuck in her throat. Blinking, she looked blearily around the room, trying to make sense out of what had happened and failing miserably. She felt as though she were fighting off the effects of half a dozen New Year's Eve parties topped off with a side trip through an assortment of mid-sixties recreational drugs.

The room was large and rectangular, one wall curtained, the other three hung with the regular hotel-room selection of bad prints and gilded mirrors that didn't quite give you a voyeur's view of the double bed and headboard. The coverlet was beige, the carpet was medium brown, and the scattering of furniture was institutional modern and laminated in "woodtones." All of it was nondescript and inoffensive, right down to the blank-faced console TV in the corner and the lamps on either side of the bed. There was even a telephone.

Groaning, Kelly rolled over and pulled the receiver off the hook: there was no dial tone. She sank back against the pillows, vaguely realizing that she was dressed in a pale blue nightgown that appeared to be made out of paper, or perhaps some kind of plastic fiber. She let out a jaw-cracking yawn, frowning at the nasty taste in her mouth.

She could see an open door leading to a bathroom, and fixing her sights on it, she managed to haul herself out of bed and cross the floor, barefoot. She tried to urinate, failed, ran the taps in the all-white cubicle, and succeeded. There was a conveniently placed sample bottle of Cepacol mouthwash on the sink, and after swallowing several fast glasses of water she rinsed out her mouth and then returned to the bedroom.

"Oh God," she whispered, sitting on the edge of the bed. There was another door a few feet away but she didn't even bother to check. It would be locked. The room looked like the Holiday Inn, but she knew it was nothing more than an outsized and blandly decorated prison cell.

Memories of the past few hours began to flood back and she could feel her eyes filling with tears. She'd lost one friend, been betrayed by another, and now she was going to pay the price for her failure as a judge of character. Hugh Trask hadn't been paranoid, he'd been frightened, and with good cause. Robin's suspicions about Stephen Hardy had been bang on the money, too, and she hadn't been willing to admit it, even in the face of the evidence.

But that had changed now, even if it was too late, and she was under no illusions about what would be done with her. She wouldn't be slapped on the wrist for simple trespass, that was clear enough. She and Robin had stumbled into a snake pit of deceit and horror that almost defied the imagination. At worst, she'd wind up as one of Max Alexanian's beating-heart cadavers, lobotomized and catheterized, a living inventory of spare parts, tucked away in that terrible chamber out at Chapel Gate. At best, she'd be consigned to an unmarked grave or Crestwood's version of the Dachau ovens.

"No," she whispered, teeth clenched. "I won't let it happen." One way or the other she was going to get out of here. The only question was how. She gave a startled gasp as the door on the other side of the room opened, and reaching back, she pulled the bedsheet around to cover herself. Max Alexanian appeared, perfectly dressed in three-piece suit, white shirt, and tie, leaning heavily on his silver-headed cane. He offered her a polite smile as the door was locked behind him, then crossed to one of the big stuffed chairs close to the bed.

"I see that the drug has worn off," he said quietly. "No side effects, I hope?"

"Pardon me if I question the sincerity of your concern. Sympathy from you would be like getting kissed by Adolf Hitler."

"You show a great deal of courage for a woman in your

position,'' Alexanian said, breaking out his slight smile again.

''It's not courage, it's fact. And I really doubt that anything I say one way or the other is going to have any effect on you.''

''Quite so.'' The white-haired man nodded, hands folded over the head of his walking stick.

''So why the interview?'' Kelly asked coldly. ''Why not just get on with it?''

''In due time. I'm just here to tie up a few loose ends.''

''I suppose the good Dr. Hardy gave you my uncle's film.''

''Indeed. Quite an innovative method of hiding it, I must say. We overlooked it completely when we went through his things.''

''Maybe you overlooked the fact that he made a copy of the film too.'' Alexanian shook his head.

''No he didn't, Miss Rhine. And don't waste my time by telling me that you Xeroxed all of Mr. Trask's material as well, and that you have mailed it to the *New York Times* or, God forbid, *Penthouse* magazine.''

''You sound very sure of yourself.''

''I am. There is virtually nothing that goes on in Crestwood Heights which I am not aware of, Miss Rhine.''

''Little squads of your goons listening at keyholes?''

''Oh, considerably more efficient than that, Miss Rhine. Every residence in Crestwood Heights is equipped with a variety of surveillance devices. The telephones are all routed through our central switchboard, which is in turn routed through the mainframes at the Institute. Key words and phrases set up a record and alarm sequence. It's the same system we developed for the National Security Agency to monitor transatlantic conversations.''

''You bug the phones,'' Kelly sneered. ''Very sophisticated.''

''Not just the phones.'' Alexanian smiled, flexing his fingers lightly on the walking stick. ''We bug everything. Fiber optics and miniaturized cameras for visual, as well as infrared and ultraviolet, stress-analysis audio pickups in every room, and in some cases, such as your own, we even implant microminiature telemetry systems for long-range monitoring.''

''The appendix operation,'' Kelly whispered, horrified. Her hand dropped to her belly, fingers touching the nearly healed scar above her hip.

"Quite so. The broken jar of peanut butter was used to bring you to the Medical Center. The dressing Dr. Hardy put on the wound contained a slow-release drug which imitated appendicitis. We also took the opportunity to give you an experimental intrauterine device to signal various gynecological functions. Stephen wanted to test it out."

"But why?" Kelly said, fascinated and horrified at the same time. "I suppose I can understand the baby and body parts factory you've got out at Chapel Gate, that kind of thing is big business these days. But why the rest?"

"Information," he said, pursing his lips thoughtfully. "Information, Miss Rhine. The biggest business of all. In fact, the Chapel Gate facility is really secondary."

"I still don't understand."

"Crestwood Heights is America, Miss Rhine, or as close to it as we can get. The Institute has gone to great lengths to create a perfect demographic cross section of the United States in microcosm. By examining that microcosm in great detail we gain information, and by manipulating that microcosm we gain even more."

"You're crazy," Kelly said. "You're right out of your mind."

"On the contrary. An example: Say one of the companies we deal with wishes to test the marketability of a certain product. We introduce that product into Crestwood Heights and then follow it through the system. It can be anything—a drug, a snack food, panty hose. It doesn't really matter. Our analysis and the quality and closeness of our observations are so high that our results are virtually infallible. We can monitor everything from individual sexual habits to caloric intake, political affiliations, to personal hygiene."

"Nineteen eighty-four," said Kelly, stunned. "You're talking about Big Brother."

"Good Lord, no!" Alexanian said, actually allowing himself to laugh. "Nothing as melodramatic as that. Orwell's book and Huxley's *Brave New World* suffer from the same basic flaw. They assume that the general population is *aware* that it is under the control of an oppressive oligarchy. The Soviet Union has the same problem."

"So you're doing it behind people's backs, is that it?"

"Certainly not. As I said before, information is the key. The philosophic roots of the Cold Mountain Institute are as democratic as George Washington and just as American. By knowing ahead of time what people want, we can provide it for them, and by the same token we can be forewarned of potentially dangerous trends. And of course, forewarned is forearmed. We recognized an obvious demographic slip in fertility almost twenty years ago, and we took steps to change it. The quality of infant being produced at Chapel Gate is both physically and mentally superior.

"We're simply improving the quality of the general American gene pool to reflect a flattened curve in population growth compounded by severely curtailed immigration into this country. The same holds true of the advances we have made here in tissue and organ transplantation, as well as genetic research.

"Your own generation presented this country with a terrible problem. The baby boom of the late forties to mid-fifties put an enormous bulge into the curve, and the bulge is moving along it as time passes. Eventually the baby boom will become the geriatric boom. Medical and sociological costs will be enormous, and if we can keep people healthier for longer we can keep those costs down. The logic is irrefutable."

"Tell that to those girls with tubes shoved up them at Chapel Gate," Kelly said, her voice hardening.

"Our little experiment in Marxist socialism. From each according to his ability, to each according to his needs. Those creatures were all institutionalized before we took them over and by providing us with healthy uterine environments they are doing more for the world than they ever could weaving baskets in a sheltered workshop."

"My God, you're a heartless bastard. What happened? Did your mother beat you when you were a child?"

"My mother was raped by half a dozen Turkish soldiers a few minutes after they murdered my father in front of her eyes," said Alexanian. "That was my conception. Many years later she was raped again, this time in front of me. That was by the Germans. Then they took her to the ovens. I spent my youth and childhood in hell, Miss Rhine, and I have spent the majority of my adult life trying to ensure that the same sort of hell does not arise again."

"You've become what you say you were trying to prevent," she said, staring at the man. "But I guess you don't see that, do you?"

"Think what you wish, Miss Rhine, it really makes very little difference now."

"No, I suppose it doesn't." Kelly frowned, the pieces finally coming together in her mind. "Lizbeth," she said softly.

"I beg your pardon?"

"Lizbeth Torrance. She's part of this, am I right? She came out of one of your 'creatures,' didn't she?"

"She was one of the first," Alexanian conceded. "In vitro conception using exceptional genetic material, further enhanced by in utero adjustments. If there is anything that is best representative of what Crestwood Heights can do, it is Lizbeth and the others of her kind. She has an intelligence quotient of 295 and a Hapler/Apgar of 12.7. Statistically she will live to be at least ninety years of age and probably older. Her chances of contracting cancer or any other major disease are virtually nil and she is already reproductively mature. She will be taller, stronger, and healthier than almost all other children of her age group and her children will be likewise. In the nomenclature of the vernacular she is a *ten,* Miss Rhine, and through her she will produce others of her kind."

"You make her sound like some sort of alien being," Kelly said, appalled by what she was hearing.

"That is a description not too far from the truth. She is as alien to us as we would be to a caveman. Homo sapiens is a dinosaur compared to Lizbeth."

"What do you call her?" Kelly asked. *"Homo Alexanian?"*

"Homo Somervilliae would be more accurate," the elderly man responded blandly.

"What?"

"Your uncle was part of the experiment, despite his apparent sexual proclivities. Prior to his somewhat troublesome bout of ethics and morality about our work here, he donated the basic male gamete for Lizbeth as well as a good deal of the technology necessary to bring the project to fruition. In point of fact, at least in terms of genetics, Lizbeth Torrance is your cousin, albeit somewhat removed.

"It's one of the reasons we took rather a special interest in you. You may still prove useful in that area, as a matter of fact. According to the telemetric equipment Dr. Hardy fitted you with, you will be ovulating within the next twelve hours.

"Your ova, surgically removed, will be fertilized by a

small tissue sample from Lizbeth. Nothing drastic, just a scraping of cells from the inside of her lip, I believe. The fertilization will take place in vitro and then the embryo will be implanted.

"You're a perfect candidate since you already share some of Lizbeth's genes through your uncle. If the implantation fails, we'll wait for your next cycle. Dr. Hardy foresees a number of experiments you might participate in. He's quite excited by the possibilities, actually."

"You didn't come here to tie up any loose ends," Kelly said, suddenly understanding. "You came here to gloat, didn't you? You can't publish any of this, or talk about it at your White House cocktail parties and that bothers you, doesn't it? You egotistical son of a bitch!"

"I won't deny a grain of truth in what you've said." Alexanian stood up, leaning on his cane. "I've spent the better part of two decades working on this project. Your uncle came dangerously close to ruining everything, as did you and Mr. Spenser. Thankfully that possibility has now been dealt with, a fact which I take a certain amount of pleasure in." He nodded to himself and then walked to the door. He tapped twice and it opened, giving Kelly a glimpse of the lab-coated guard outside. Turning, Alexanian smiled briefly at Kelly.

"Good day, Miss Rhine. I'll be seeing you again, although I'm afraid you won't be seeing me." He left the room and the door shut behind him. Kelly sat where she was on the edge of the bed, biting her lip hard and trying not to give in to the tears threatening to well up out of her eyes.

She knew she only had two options. She could sit passively and wait to be taken off to Stephen Hardy's butcher shop, or she could try to escape. The answer was obvious, but how was she going to get out when she didn't even know where she was? She stood up and began to walk aimlessly around the room, trying to figure things out and shaking off the last remaining effects of the drug at the same time.

The chances were good that she was either in the Crestwood Medical Center, or somewhere in Deep Wood Park. Deep Wood Park seemed more likely. The hotellike room was probably used by staff monitoring nighttime experiments. She remembered her tour and Granger's comment about the P4 lab. He'd said it was where they kept the monsters. Lizbeth, perhaps?

Without much hope she pulled back the curtains against the far wall and found herself staring into a gigantic floor-to-ceiling mirror. The mirror hadn't been installed for no reason, which probably meant that it was one-way glass with an observation room behind. She stuck out her tongue at her reflection and pulled the curtains closed again.

It took her less than five minutes to check out the room completely. There was nothing even remotely useful. The medicine cabinet was empty, the drawers of the bureau held nothing but half a dozen folded gowns like the one she was wearing and the television was fitted with a security lock. The rear of the set was welded on and the plugs for both it and the bedside lamps went directly into the wall without any visible socket. Both the TV and the lamps were bolted down. They hadn't missed a trick.

Even suicide had been ruled out. She might have been able to loop a twisted bedsheet around the overhead light fixture but the sheets were made out of the same material as the nightgowns and tore under too much strain. Defeated, she slumped down onto the bed again, desperately trying to remain calm.

This was no James Bond movie. There was no lighter that changed into a flamethrower, no laser-powered cufflinks, or throwing knives hidden in the soles of her shoes. She didn't even *have* shoes. Under the nightgown she was stark naked, and the single closet in the room was empty. She could also assume that Alexanian's visit hadn't been an idle one. He wanted to make his little speech while she was still in condition to understand it and that probably meant she didn't have much time before they took her off to Stephen Hardy's workshop.

She stared hard at the closed door, trying to visualize the sequence of events. A nurse, probably alone, would come first, aided by the guard outside the door. The nurse would give her a preparatory injection of anesthetic; when that had taken hold, another nurse, possibly two, would come with a gurney to take her to the operating room. By then it would be too late. She'd be groggy and unable to move. If she was going to do something it had to be before the injection.

But what? Wait behind the door and brain the nurse and the guard when they entered the room? Not likely. It had to be something unexpected and instantaneous. And deadly. Whatever happened, she wasn't going to have any second chances.

"Stupid!" she whispered angrily. "Stupid! Stupid! Stupid!" Who did she think she was? Kelly Rhine, ace spy, Superwoman, capable of leaping tall buildings and outrunning speeding bullets. The Girl from U.N.C.L.E. Christ on a crutch!

James Cagney. Not the mother-fixated loonie of *White Heat* with his "Top of the world, Ma!" but Cagney the good guy. A series of vague black-and-white images came into her mind. Cagney in a room, knowing that he's about to be taken for a one-way ride. A doorknob, wire, a puddle of water. And she had it.

She couldn't remember the title of the film, but she remembered how Cagney had escaped. He'd taken the wire from a lamp, split it, and connected one lead to the doorknob and the other to a puddle of water on the floor in front of the door. When the heavy opened the door, he'd grasped the knob, stepped into the puddle, and completed the circuit, frying himself in the process. It was worth a try.

Praying that she wasn't under some sort of hidden surveillance, she slipped off the bed, pushed the bedside table out of the way, and got down on her knees, examining the wire from the lamp. It fitted into a small plate on the wall, fitted with a threaded chrome sleeve like the wall plug for a TV cable.

Working as fast as she could, Kelly grasped the sleeve between thumb and forefinger, working it loose. With the sleeve off, she pulled on the wire, hoping that the workmen who'd wired the room in the first place had left some slack behind the wall. They had. A few seconds later she'd pulled out a good six feet of the plastic covered cable, more than enough to reach the door.

She could almost feel the approach of the nurse and she began working frantically, tearing the other end of the wire out of the base of the lamp. It gave finally, the free end frayed where she'd tugged it out of the locking screws. Trying to smother the rising anxiety in her mind, she began working away at the frayed end, peeling back the two leads, careful not to let her shaking fingers come in contact with the bare copper. In less than a minute she had the wire split all the way back to the wall plate.

Her heart was beating a cross-stitch in her chest as she

carefully wound six inches of one lead around the doorknob, then eased the last bare inch of copper under the lockplate. Without pausing to admire her handiwork, she pelted back to the bathroom and turned on the tap. She filled the plastic water glass, leaving the tap running, and raced back to the door. In the Cagney movie, the floor had been hardwood, allowing the water to actually puddle. Here the floor was short-pile wall-to-wall carpeting. If she was going to get the effect she wanted, the carpet would have to be sodden. The one thing in her favor was the footwear she'd noticed on the guard outside. He'd been wearing nonslip felt or paper disposable slippers like the kind associated with operating rooms and areas of possible contamination. Hopefully the nurse would be wearing the same kind of thing. The thin soles would be the next best thing to bare feet when they touched the wet carpeting.

She ran a one-woman bucket brigade back and forth from the bathroom to the door and eventually she was satisfied. An area of carpeting a yard square was now soaking wet. Holding her breath, she pushed the second lead from the lamp into the wet patch. Nothing happened. No flash or fountain of sparks. On the other hand, there might not be any current running through the wire and she would have done it all for nothing. There was no way to test it without electrocuting herself, so now all she could do was sit back and wait.

She didn't have to wait long. Less than five minutes later she saw the door begin to open and she held her breath again, eyes locked on the turning handle and the widening crack in the doorway. The moment seemed to go on forever, every step in a slow-motion sequence searing into her brain. The door swung open, the guard with his hand on the outer knob, leaning out of the way to let the nurse pass. Quick check to her feet, and yes, she was wearing the slippers, and then the fractured image of the guard's wrist just barely touching the stainless-steel tray in the nurse's hands as her right foot came down onto the dark, soaking-wet patch of carpet, the guard swinging around to follow the nurse into the room, but his hand letting go of the knob a split second too late on the wrong side of 110 volts.

Both the guard and the nurse exploded into the room as the circuit closed and the surge of electricity vainly looked for a way to expend itself. The tray in the nurse's hands jerked up in a wide arc, the contents flying into the air and landing on the bed and the guard, consciousness vanishing instantly, fell against the nurse, throwing her to the floor and simultaneously pulling the wire out of the lockplate.

Acting on instinct and adrenaline, Kelly dropped to the floor, dragged the wire back out of the marshy square of carpet, and scurried to the still open door, closing it quickly. Turning, she steadied herself, swallowed the cotton ball that seemed to have taken up permanent lodging in her throat and bent down to inspect the damage.

In the Cagney movie the bad guy had reacted like a puppet doing the tarantella, hair smoking and his eyeballs bugging out. In reality, the short contact with the less than lethal current had done nothing more than knock the two people out. The guard was breathing raggedly and the nurse, facedown, was snuffling in the blood seeping from her now broken nose. From the way they were beginning to move around, neither one was going to be out for very long.

Kelly got up and went to the bed and gathered up the contents of the tray. An intravenous intubation kit, a glass vial of something called thiopental sodium and a paper-wrapped needle and syringe. Fumbling in her haste, Kelly managed to tear open the syringe, screwed on the needle, and upended the vial of clear liquid.

A hundred episodes of watching a steely-eyed Richard Chamberlain shooting up his patients on Dr. Kildare was all she had to go on but it would have to do. She punched the quill-ended tip of the needle through the foil cover of the vial and sucked up the contents. Turning, she dropped down to the floor, spent a few long seconds dragging the deadweight of the guard off the nurse's legs, and then looked for a place to spike him.

She settled on the neck, found the carotid artery with her thumb and slid the needle in, unable to hold back a shudder as she watched the three inches of surgical steel disappear into the stubbly skin. She pushed the plunger down halfway, and too late she remembered something about air embolisms. If she'd injected a bubble of air along with the drug, the man would be dead almost instantly.

After thirty seconds he was still breathing, and then suddenly the sound deepened as the drug took hold. Satisfied, she put the half-emptied syringe carefully down onto the carpet, then tore open the man's lab coat. Underneath it he was wearing a dark blue Safeway Security Systems uniform, complete with side arm and a nasty-looking spring steel and leather truncheon. He also had a pair of handcuffs on his belt. Grunting with effort, Kelly dragged off the belt, took the man's holstered weapon, and set it aside. She slipped the handcuffs off the belt and turned her attention back to the nurse.

Rolling her over, she saw that the woman was in her mid to late forties, premenopausal down covering her chin and upper lip. The rest of her face was obscured by blood from the bent and swollen nose. Working as quickly as possible, Kelly stripped off the woman's starchy blouse, unzipped the white Terelyne skirt and pulled it down. The blouse had a bloodred security badge pinned to it, but no name tag.

Underneath the uniform, the nurse was wearing rather risqué pale pink panties and a black underwire bra that barely restrained a pair of freckle-speckled breasts the size of Ostrich eggs.

With the woman down to her undies, Kelly plucked off the little white cap, then dragged the woman over to the bed. She pulled the woman into a sitting position, then put her arms behind her back. Using the cuffs, she secured the woman to one leg of the bed and snapped the manacles tightly shut. Unless she was enormously strong there was no way she'd be able to get free by herself.

Kelly returned to the bathroom, filled the water glass yet again, and returned to the slumped form of the nurse. Keeping a close watch on the woman, she struggled into the skirt and blouse, then removed the felt slippers from the woman's bunioned feet. The whole outfit was two sizes too large and the floppy shoes felt like boats on her feet but there was nothing she could do about it.

She took the guard's police special out of its holster, jammed it into the pocket of the skirt along with the truncheon, and gathered up the syringe. Returning to the nurse, she picked up the water glass in one hand and kept the syringe ready in the other. From the moment the nurse had stepped into the room the entire operation had taken less than four minutes. Taking a deep breath, Kelly doused the nurse's face with the water.

The response was gratifyingly quick. The woman made a

sputtering, choking sound and her eyelids fluttered. Fetching another glassful, Kelly repeated the procedure. This time she was rewarded with a full-scale groan of pain and the eyes opened fully.

"Wake up!" Kelly snapped. The woman's head sagged to one side and the eyes started closing again. Not sure of what she should do, Kelly bit her lip, slid the truncheon out of her pocket and tapped the woman's bare outstretched knee. The nurse jerked and let out a snuffling, muffled groan of pain, but her head came up and her eyes opened again.

"Good," Kelly said. "Stay awake."

"Whmm . . ." The sound was unintelligible.

"What's your name!" The woman's eyes were dark brown and they were fixed on the blackjack in Kelly's right hand. "Name!" Kelly repeated, and this time she waved the truncheon menacingly.

"Fiona." The word was mixed with a wet gurgle from the still bleeding nose. Nurse Fiona was obviously in a great deal of pain.

"Fiona what?"

"Collins."

"Okay, Nurse Fiona Collins, exactly where was I supposed to be taken after you gave me this needle?" This time Kelly lifted up the syringe, holding it an inch or so away from the woman's ruined face.

"Op . . . suite C."

"When?"

"Don' know f'sure."

"Bullshit!" Kelly hissed. She lifted the blackjack again. "I could make that nose a lot worse." The threat was an idle one. It was all Kelly could do to keep her eyes on the woman's face. She must have weighed at least a hundred and fifty pounds and she'd hit the floor hard, smashing the nose almost flat.

"Pen'athol takes ten, fif'een minutes. Pr'cedure sched'led for half hour. Same time's other one."

"What other one?"

"Guy f'm Cha'l Gate F'cility."

"Spenser? Robin Spenser?"

"Uhn."

Kelly sat back on her heels. Robin was alive! "What are they doing to him?"

"COP." At first Kelly didn't understand, and then she remembered her tour with Alexanian and Granger. COP stood for Continuous Organ Perfusion. She felt her stomach roll and she wanted to vomit. They were going to cut Robin up and put the pieces into one of those capsules.

"Where is this Suite C you were talking about?"

"Hall. Doors m'ked Op'rating Theaters. C's sec'nd left. Oh God, hur's bad!" The woman made a mewling sound and Kelly could actually see the blood draining from her face. It didn't look as though she was going to be calling for help very loudly but she wasn't going to take any chances. She put the truncheon back in her pocket and then pushed the plunger down on the syringe until she saw a bead of liquid pop out of the tip.

"Where do I stick this and how much do I give you?" asked Kelly. "Talk fast because I don't have much time."

"Arm," grunted the nurse. "Vein. five hun'red milligrams."

"You're the doctor." She pushed out a squirt of fluid until the barrel registered 500 mg., then stabbed the needle into the woman's upper arm without bothering to locate a vein. Nurse Fiona was in too much pain to try any tricks and Kelly was reasonably sure that the woman had prescribed a dose for herself that would keep her under for the longest time. She watched and within less than a minute the woman's eyes fluttered and then closed. She was out. Kelly tossed the needle onto the bed, pushed herself upright and headed for the door.

"Nancy Drew to the rescue," she whispered, and stepped out into the hall.

CHAPTER 24

The corridor outside her room was empty and Kelly had to stop herself from running as she headed for the double doors fifty feet away. A clock high on the wall above a water fountain showed seven-thirty and she tried briefly to figure out if it was day or night. It had been close to dawn when she reached the house on Erin Park Drive and she doubted that the drug she'd been given would have worn off so quickly. It was more likely that she'd been under for most of the day and it was now early evening again.

She went through the swing doors without pausing and found herself in another hallway, this one color-coded in pale green. The operating theaters. Still no one around. Following Nurse Collins's instructions, she found Suite C and went up on the toes of her felt shoes to peer through the small glass porthole.

The room beyond the doors was divided into two sections, the first an observation vestibule and scrub area, separated from the inner portion by a floor-to-ceiling glass wall fitted with a sliding door. It was like something out of a science-fiction film, but even so, it was immediately recognizable as an operating room.

The basic lighting was diffuse and rain-forest green, coming from panels in the walls and ceiling. There was a dish mercury-vapor lamp set high in the ceiling, its powerful, focused beam illuminating a complicated table arrangement in the center of the room.

The table was mounted on a low dais and would have looked right at home in an episode of "Star Trek." A monitor screen on a swivel mount at the head end was connected to a microsurgery console at the midlevel, and a sloping bank of instruments at the foot of the table controlled everything from anesthetic to vital signs. Kelly could see that the white plastic table was divided into three sections, each with its own ball-socket joint allowing the patient to be tilted into a variety of positions.

There was more instrumentation against the side wall, and directly opposite her own position, the far wall was completely taken up by an enormous air-filtration system that recycled the air in the operating room every ninety seconds. Kelly ignored all of it, her eyes gripped by what she saw just to the right of the operating table. It was a pod like the ones they'd seen at Chapel Gate, the clear plastic tube resting securely on its receiver and half a dozen hoses and cables already connected to the system's console at the foot of the table. In the pod, clearly visible, was the naked figure of Robin Spenser.

"Oh Jesus," Kelly whispered. She looked left and right, then gently pushed open the door into suite C. Stepping inside, she shivered, immediately aware of a drop in temperature. Ignoring the scrub sinks and the neat row of hooks holding half a dozen disposable scrub suits, she tiptoed across the vestibule to the sliding door. It opened automatically and she heard a faint but powerful humming sound coming from the wall-sized filtration unit.

Keeping one eye on the vestibule, she approached the pod, looking down at her friend through the clear plastic of the tube. There was an intravenous kit already in his arm, but so far there wasn't any linkage, though a catheterizing unit was ready, laid out on a pad of gauze between his legs. As far as she could see, the only connection made had been a pair of electrodes on each temple.

She bent down, examining the small control console plugged into the head end of the tube and hit the POWER ON key. A low whining sound began and a row of lights began to flicker. Looking over the keyboard, she located a button marked HATCH RELEASE and stabbed at it. The whining sound deepened and the plastic covering on the pod began to rotate, exposing Robin to the air.

Even before the covering had fully retracted, she was working on her friend, pulling off the electrodes and gently pulling out the intravenous tube in his arm. Within a few seconds he began to groan and his eyelids flickered. Kelly raced back into the vestibule, returning with a pair of drawstring surgical pants, a shirt, and slippers. Robin was definitely coming out of it now, his eyelids fluttering open completely.

"Come on," Kelly said as forcefully as she dared. "We have to get out of here before they come back." She helped Robin into a sitting position, his feet dangling over the side of the pod receiver, and shoved his feet into the legs of the surgical pants. She pulled them up to his hips, then urged him down from the pod, pulling them up over his buttocks as he stood up.

"Think I'm going to be sick," he muttered. Ashen-faced, Kelly turned him around, dropping the buttonless shirt over his head.

"Don't you dare!" she whispered harshly, steadying the wavering man. "I've got enough problems without that!"

" 'Kay," he answered amiably. He put a hand down on Kelly's shoulder as she bent to tug on the felt slippers. "Thanks for dressing me."

"Don't mention it." She stood up and took the man's chin in her hand, looking at him closely. "How do you feel?"

"Terrible. Headache." He leaned back against the pod receiver and put one hand up to his forehead, wincing.

"What happened to you back at Chapel Gate?" she asked. "I thought you were dead."

"Gas, I think," Robin said, his voice steadier.

"It was aerosol procaine," answered a voice from behind them. It was Stephen Hardy, a tall, blue-uniformed security guard at his side. The guard had a large, bulb-nosed weapon in one hand. Hardy nodded to the guard, who stepped forward, taking the pistol and blackjack from the pocket of Kelly's shirt. The guard moved to one side and the doctor stepped forward. He removed a long-barreled syringe from one pocket of his lab coat and a plastic-covered spinal needle from the other. The needle was a good six inches long. Hardy screwed the needle into the syringe, removed the plastic safety cap and held it up. "This, on the other hand, is Pentothal. The same drug Nurse Collins was about to give you." He smiled pleasantly and moved toward Kelly. "This won't hurt you a bit."

"Touch her and you're a dead man," Robin said, a foot to Kelly's right. Hardy stopped, one eyebrow rising.

"I take it you're Sir Galahad," he said, grimacing. "Please spare us the dramatics, Spenser, this has gone on too long as it is. Officer Wilkins here is armed with an extremely powerful tranquilizer gun. More than enough to take care of a queer like you." He stepped forward, eyes flickering down to the syringe as he squeezed the drug along the needle to the tip. In that instant Robin moved, rising on his toes and whirling, left leg rigid, the right swinging up and snapping at the knee on impact.

The side of his right foot caught Hardy full in the chest, lifting him off his feet and hurtling him back across the room. He fell, the syringe skittering across the polished tile, and almost before Kelly had time to react, Robin had dropped and rolled, ducking out of the way as the security guard fired. The red tufted dart pinged off the control keyboard for the pod and Kelly threw herself to the floor. Out of the corner of her eye she saw Robin come out of the roll and launch himself into a flying kick, left leg tucked and right leg bent. She was vaguely aware of a low, guttural yell, and then Robin's knee flexed, extending the leg outward, his foot catching the unprepared security guard just under the chin. The man's head snapped back and Kelly actually heard the neck break with a soft crunch. The guard flailed backward, already dead, then collapsed across the looped cables and hoses that trailed from the wall outlets to the operating table. There was a hiss of escaping gasses as the oxygen and CO_2 hoses pulled out of the wall. Robin turned his attention back to Stephen Hardy.

Groaning, the doctor pulled himself to his feet, but it was too late. Robin took three steps, grabbed the dazed man's arm at the wrist, and bent it behind his back, pulling up hard. Hardy winced, but made no sound.

"I didn't know you could do that kind of thing," Kelly said, getting back on her feet and staring at the body of the guard.

"Old Chinese proverb." Robin grinned, pushing Stephen Hardy forward. "Gay sailor-boy who wants to come out of closet better know how to defend himself real good on streets of Miami." He pulled Hardy's wrist a little higher, urging him toward Kelly. "Black belt fourth Dan, in case you're interested,'' he said into Hardy's ear. ''Get the gun and the sap out of his pocket,'' he said to Kelly. She did as she was told, trying not to look her onetime lover in the eye. Transferring the weapons back to the pocket of the uniform skirt, she stepped back, still not willing to meet Stephen Hardy's gaze.

''What do we do with him?'' asked Robin.

''Ask him about Lizbeth,'' Kelly said, finally looking at her ex-lover, her heart filled with a strange combination of sadness, shame, and barely repressed rage. ''Ask him where she is.''

''I'm not saying anything,'' Hardy said, teeth gritted in pain. ''You're not going to get out of here alive, anyway.''

''Tell me or I'll break your arm,'' Robin snapped, bringing the elbow even higher.

''Go fuck yourself. This place will be crawling with guards in five minutes. You don't stand a chance.''

''Neither do you,'' Robin said. He pulled the arm higher and Kelly actually saw the blood drain from Hardy's face as the pain increased. Sweat broke out on his forehead, even though the room was almost uncomfortably cool.

''Tell me where Lizbeth is,'' Kelly said. ''Robin's pretty angry. A broken arm might be the least of your worries.''

''She's in the P-4 area,'' said Hardy, his voice strained. ''But there's no way you're going to get to her.''

''Do you know what he's talking about?'' Robin asked. Kelly nodded.

''Granger pointed it out on my tour,'' she answered.

''What do we do with lover-boy?''

''Tie him up.''

Stephen Hardy's move was swift and completely unexpected. Sensing a brief relaxing of pressure, he brought his foot down hard on Robin's instep, then jabbed back with his free elbow, catching him in the solar plexus. Stunned and gasping for air, Robin released his grip and Hardy lurched forward, swinging his right arm and sweeping Kelly out of the way with a roundhouse blow to the side of her head. She fell, smacking her head into the base of the pod receiver.

Turning, Hardy jumped forward, grabbing Robin by the throat and dragging him down to the floor. He managed to bring his knees down, pinning Robin's shoulders, his strong hands still gripping his opponent's throat, strangling him.

Fighting off the stunning pain in her head, Kelly rolled

over and tried to crawl toward her friend. Dizzy, barely able to focus on the two men, she knew she wasn't going to be any help. In a last effort she found the long needled syringe on the floor and spun it across the tile to Robin's outstretched hand.

Feeling the touch of the cold, stainless steel barrel, Robin's fingers curled, gripping it tightly in his palm. He could feel consciousness fading as Hardy's hands cut off the flow of blood to his brain. Summoning up the last shreds of his strength, he brought his arm around, then drove the syringe up into Stephen Hardy's face.

The razor-sharp 26 gauge Tuohy needle, normally used for spinal anesthetic, glanced off Hardy's cheekbone then stabbed into the corner of the doctor's right eye socket. The eyeball ruptured and Hardy let out a terrible, wailing scream as the needle went even deeper, slicing through the optic nerve and cutting two inches into the soft gray meat of the brain.

Hardy reared up, releasing his grip as Robin slammed his palm against the plunger of the syringe, injecting the full dose of anesthetic. Still screaming, Hardy staggered to his feet, hands up to the ruined eye, the syringe still firmly embedded in his face. Gasping for breath, Robin rolled out from under the man, grabbed Kelly and pulled her to her feet. Staggering, he pushed her toward the sliding door and away from the awful scene in the operating room.

Behind them, Stephen Hardy lurched against the operating table, blood and fluid seeping down his cheek as the drug in the now empty syringe coursed through his brain. Gripping the barrel of the hypodermic, he managed to pull it free and a fresh gout of blood erupted. In agony he spun around, arms flailing in an anguished pirouette, his hand smashing into the rack of monitoring equipment beside the table.

The air filtration equipment, though powerful, hadn't been able to deal with the sudden influx of gasses from the ruptured hoses torn out of the wall by the guard, and when the cart of equipment crashed to the floor, the oxygen level in the operating room had risen to almost 35 percent.

Patients about to undergo surgery usually assume that the rule about not wearing jewelry has something to do with security. In fact, it is a matter of safety and also the reason that all surgical instruments are nonsparking. Under normal circumstances, the level of oxygen used in an operation is well below the danger point but experts are well aware that the ringing of a telephone or the battery in an electric watch is enough to ignite a concentration of less than 10 percent pure oxygen. The 35 percent concentration in suite C was as lethal as a room full of high explosives and the smashing of the electronic gear on the instrument cart was like tossing a lit Zippo lighter into a tank of aviation fuel.

Half-blind, in monstrous pain, and with his neurological systems shutting down under the influence of the drug injected into his brain, Dr. Stephen Hardy was still alive and able to comprehend what was about to happen. There was a split second of silence as the sparks from the short-circuited monitoring equipment greeted the enriched atmosphere of the operating room and then the air itself exploded with Hardy at ground zero. His mouth opened in a silent O of all-consuming terror and then he was carbonized where he stood, his body turned into a cinder in the blink of an eye, and then the cinder itself was blown to atoms as the explosion blossomed with an ear-rupturing roar like thunder on Judgment Day.

The explosion of the Suite C operating theater was powerful enough to shake the floor beneath Max Alexanian's feet as he stood on the raised observation platform at the rear of Safeway Security Master Control. He tapped the shoulder of the uniformed man seated at the computer console in front of him. The officer, wearing a communications headset, was monitoring activities within the complex below Deep Wood Park.

"What was that?" Alexanian asked, frowning.

"Explosion, sir. We've got a fire alert coming in from C sector on the second level."

"Put it on the board."

"Yes, sir." The officer tapped out a set of instructions, overriding the small-scale display of Crestwood Heights visible on the plasma screen at the far end of the large, high-ceilinged room. The screen wavered, that reassembled, showing an isometric view of the C sector portion on all four levels. A bright yellow dot pulsed in the center of the screen.

"What is it?" asked Alexanian coldly, eyes on the screen.

"Suite C operating theater," answered the security officer, listening to his headset. As Alexanian watched the screen a series of blue dots surrounding the yellow one began to blink. "Oxygen explosion," continued the security man. "Main inlet valves have shut off automatically and the area has been sealed. Damage confined to a small portion of the level."

"Casualties?"

"None reported so far."

"I want the ident for K. Rhine on the screen," said Alexanian. "The code is PR slash 2251."

"Right away." The uniformed man tapped the sequence into the computer, then relayed the information to the big screen. "There it is, Dr. Alexanian." A green dot was moving along one of the outlined corridors on the second level, moving away from the site of the explosion.

"Zoom in," Alexanian instructed. The officer tapped away at the keyboard again and the schematic expanded. "Tilt and follow." Once again the man at the computer did as he was told. The schematic began to move, taking up a relative position directly behind the green spot on the screen that marked Kelly's location. The dozen or more people working at the terminals on the floor of the Master Control room stopped what they were doing and watched the screen. It was like following an animated mouse through a spiderwork maze. "I want a patch into the Queen Bee program," Alexanian said softly.

"I'm not cleared for it," answered the security officer nervously.

"The access password is *Columbia*. Do it."

"Yes, sir."

The director of the Cold Mountain Institute kept watching the screen as the man at the computer accessed the Queen Bee Program. The Rhine woman was taking the service stairs down to the third level. The dot kept descending and it was obvious she was heading for the lowest level of the sector.

"What's on the fourth level of C sector?" Alexanian asked.

"Cooling plant and radiology."

The green dot marking Kelly Rhine shimmered briefly and disappeared.

"What happened to the ident?"

"She must have gone into radiology," said the security man. "The lead shielding is blocking the transponder signal."

"Damn!" Alexanian plucked at the shoulder of the man's uniform. "Get up," he ordered.

"Yes, sir."

The guard stood up and got out of the way as Alexanian sat

down at the terminal. Clearing the smaller version of the diagram on the big board, he began to type instructions on the keyboard.

"Rats in a maze," he said quietly to himself. "Nothing but rats in a maze."

CHAPTER 25

Kelly stood in the antechamber of the radiology room, arms above her head as Robin buckled the shoulder straps on the protective lead vest normally used by the X-ray technician. Outside, muffled by the heavy door behind them, they could hear the dull repetitive hooting of an alarm horn.

"Are you sure this will work?" Kelly asked. Robin bent down and pulled the groin strap up between her legs.

"If Alexanian was telling the truth, it should," he grunted, securing the strap. "If you really did have some kind of transponder fitted the battery must be pretty small so it couldn't be sending out too powerful a signal. The lead should block it."

"I feel like the catcher on a baseball team," Kelly said looking down at herself.

"We're going to have to cover it up if we expect to get out of here," Robin said. He pulled open the doors on a row of lockers lined up against the wall of the little room. "Here we go." He pulled out a pair of long white lab coats and handed her one, putting the other one on himself, transferring the guard's pistol and the blackjack to one of the deep pockets. Kelly buttoned her coat up to the throat, then adjusted the cap on her head.

"How do I look?"

"Like a fat nurse," he answered, frowning. "But it'll have to do." He took her hand, leading her to the door. Cracking it open an inch, he looked out into the corridor. It was empty. "Come on," he whispered. They stepped out into the pale blue corridor and began walking quickly down it. At the end of the hall they came to a set of swinging doors, and another door on the right with a sign marked PHYSICAL PLANT—AUTHORIZED PERSONNEL ONLY. Pushing it open with a fast look over his shoulder, Robin led Kelly into the stairwell. The walls were rough concrete, stenciled with a large number 4.

"I don't suppose you have any idea where we are," Robin said.

"I think so," Kelly answered, thinking. "When Alexanian brought me to the complex, the tunnel exited right beside the underground car park. I could see it through the glass. The first door we went through had a number four on it. It must be the lowest level."

"Okay. So if we cut through the furnace room or whatever it is, we should wind up in the car park, right?"

"I think so. But what about Lizbeth? We can't just leave her in this place."

"I was afraid you were going to say that." He took a deep breath and let it out slowly. "Okay," he said finally. "Hardy said she was in the P-4 area. Does that mean she's on this level?"

"No, Granger said that P-4 was a designation for a completely secure lab. We came down three floors on the elevator after lunch. She must be one up from here."

"Shit," muttered Robin. "This place is a rabbit warren, we're never going to find her."

"We have to try," Kelly insisted.

"I suppose you're right. But how? We'll be lucky to get out of here ourselves, let alone take out someone else."

"Granger said the P-4 lab was right in the middle of the complex, so it could be shared by the companies in Deep Wood Park. It makes sense that they'd put the furnace and ventilation systems in the middle, too . . . doesn't it?"

"So you're saying the P-4 Lab is right above us?"

"It should be."

"All we can do is give it a shot," Robin said, shrugging. Beyond the door they could hear the sound of running feet joining the bleating of the alarm. "We can't stay here much longer, that's for sure."

Taking her hand again, Robin led the way around the stairs and along a narrow, tunnellike corridor, its curving walls crowded with dozens of pipes and bundled cables. In the distance they could hear the deep, roaring hum of electrical equipment and a few moments later they found themselves in a huge, high-ceilinged basement crammed with massive ventilating fans, blowers, and turbines, all interconnected by a snakes-and-ladders maze of catwalks. The cavernous room was lit by dozens of hanging lights strung from the ceiling grid, and as far as they could tell the place was empty.

"Where to now?" Robin asked, raising his voice above the pounding roar of the machinery.

"I can't see any way up here," Kelly answered. "Let's try the other side."

They made their way along the catwalks, threading through the noisy turbines and the chimneylike sheet-metal vent pipes. Reaching the other side of the chamber, Kelly spotted an emergency exit and beside it the doors of an elevator. Robin pressed the UP button beside the doors and they slid open, revealing a large padded cage.

"Freight elevator," he said. He turned to the control panel and swore under his breath.

"What's the matter?"

"It's locked," he grunted angrily. "Shit!" There were five buttons, P-P on the bottom with P4-1 through P4-3 above and Main Level on top. He stabbed at the buttons one by one but nothing happened.

"Alexanian had a key-card," said Kelly, pointing to a narrow slot at the base of the row of buttons. "Maybe we should use the stairs."

"They'll be watching them. We wouldn't stand a chance." He pounded his fist against the buttons. "God damn!"

"Is there any way you could short-circuit the panel?"

"Sure," Robin snorted. "If this were a rerun of 'Mission Impossible' and I were Martin Landau." He looked around the large, canvas-padded cage, then glanced up at the ceiling. "Bingo," he whispered, breaking into a smile. Directly over their heads was a small trapdoor. "The service trap." He cupped his hands together. "Put your foot in here and I'll boost you up."

"Then what?"

"Push open the trap. There should be a maintenance ladder bolted to the shaft wall."

"Are you sure?"

"No I'm not sure," he snapped. "But it makes sense. Come on."

Kelly did as she was told, letting Robin lift her up to the ceiling of the elevator. Bracing herself with one hand, she used the other to push the trap up and to one side.

"See anything?" asked Robin.

"A big black hole. It's pitch dark."

"Don't worry about it. Grab the edge and climb onto the roof."

Kelly dragged herself up onto the roof of the elevator and a few seconds later Robin joined her. There was a faint trickle of light coming up from the cage, but other than that the shaft was totally dark. Moving slowly in a half-crouch, Robin worked his way to the side of the cage, feeling for the ladder. He found it, a series of narrow metal rungs fitted between the thickly greased rails that carried the cage up and down the shaft.

"Over here," he whispered, his voice echoing in the darkness. Kelly crawled across the roof on hands and knees, joining Robin. "You go up first," he instructed, his voice low. "I'll be right behind you in case you get into trouble."

"How will I know when to stop?"

"There should be a horizontal cross-beam like this one," he answered, tapping the heavy-duty I-beam on the far side of the carrier rails.

"Then what?"

"Go up another dozen rungs and wait. That should put you just about level with the top of the door."

"What happens after that?"

"There has to be a door release on the inside of the shaft. I'll open the door and go out. If it's all clear, you follow."

"And if it's not all clear?" Kelly asked.

"Then keep climbing until you reach the top of the shaft."

"Is this going to work?"

"It's the only chance we've got." He reached out, took Kelly's hands and placed them on the first rung. "Up you go."

She began to climb, the darkness of the shaft making her more nervous than if it had been lit. At least then, she'd know how far she had to fall; this way the yawning pit below seemed bottomless, its last stop somewhere deep in the bowels of the earth. She bit down hard on her lower lip, concentrating on the pain and the copper taste of her own blood. After what seemed like a lifetime she reached another horizontal beam and off to one side she could see a faint vertical crack of light leaking between the doors on the P4-1 level. She continued to climb, counting off an even dozen rungs, and clung there, not daring to call out, listening for Robin.

A few seconds later she heard a loud clicking sound and looked down. The elevator doors slid open with a faint swishing noise, flooding the shaft with light. She squeezed her eyes shut, but not before her mind had registered the stomach-churning drop beneath her feet. She heard the sound of a gasping breath as Robin swung himself out through the open doors, and then he was calling her. Eyes closed, she backed down the ladder until he told her to stop. She stretched out her arm and he pulled her out of the shaft.

Blinking in the bright light, she looked around. The corridor walls were painted a light yellow, the same color as the doors she'd seen with Granger and Alexanian. A sign directly in front of them had arrows going in opposite directions. The left arrow led to CRYOGENICS while the right said H.I.R.A.M.

"What's a Hiram?" asked Robin.

"I don't know," Kelly said. "But cryogenics is freezing." She frowned. "Alexanian didn't say anything about that. Not about Lizbeth, anyway."

"So we'll go the other way." He hit the elevator button, closing the doors, and they went down the right-hand corridor, turning three blind corners and going past a dozen unmarked doors. Rounding the fourth turn, they came face-to-face with a white-coated lab technician hurrying toward them. Seeing them, the man paused, frowning, and then approached more slowly. He was in his thirties, curly-haired, potbellied, wearing glasses and carrying a metal clipboard. He also had a bright red ID pinned to the breast pocket of his coat.

"Excuse me," the man said, still coming toward them. "This is a secure area and you aren't—"

The blackjack took the man under the jaw, breaking it, and Robin followed up the blow with a rigid-fingered chop to the throat. The man made a gurgling sound, his eyes rolling back in their sockets, and then he crumpled to the floor. Robin rummaged through the man's pockets, coming up with a single plastic key-card, took the red ID and pinned it to his coat, then dragged the technician toward a doorway marked

CRAY-2 Circuit Breakers. Kelly opened the door and Robin crammed the unconscious form into the broom closet–sized space below the banks of gray electrical boxes.

Continuing along the corridor for another few yards, they reached a wide metal door set into the right-hand wall, its surface featureless except for a vertical key-card slot and a small stenciled sign: HUMAN INTERFACE REMOTE ACCESS MONITORING.

"Hiram," Robin said, reading the sign. He took out the key-card he'd taken from the guard. "Let's hope this works." Robin pushed the plastic wafer into the slot and the heavy door whispered back, sliding closed behind them as they stepped into the room beyond.

"My God!" Robin whispered, staring. "What *is* this place?"

CHAPTER 26

The room was a long rectangle, the low ceiling set with lines of dim, recessed lights. On either side, like two rows of columns, there were a dozen semicircle obelisks, dark blue and brutal, like curved versions of the mythical slabs in *2001*, each one more than seven feet high and four feet wide.

The rear wall was fitted with a large plasma screen, sleek, midnight blue control consoles bracketing it. Below the screen, on a raised platform reached by three broad steps was a casketlike tube of gleaming plastic, eight feet long and tilted slightly toward a third control console at the base of the platform. There was a bank of half a dozen monitor screens visible on the console, two vacant chairs set before it. It was cold enough in the chamber for Robin and Kelly to see their breath, and both of them shivered as they stood silently at the other end of the room.

"It looks like some kind of weird church," Kelly whispered.

"This is no church. That capsule up there looks like one of the pods at Chapel Gate."

"Lizbeth?" asked Kelly, swallowing, her mouth gone dry.

"Maybe. I can't see inside from here." They walked forward, their movement silent as they crossed the dark blue carpeted floor of the chamber. On closer inspection the rows of paired slabs appeared to be electronic equipment, and then Kelly spotted a small metal plate screwed to the base of one, just above a snaking electrical cable that disappeared into the floor. The plate had a serial number and the manufacturer's name: CrayResearch Inc.

"These are computers," she whispered to Robin. She

reached out and touched the surface of one. It was freezing cold. She vaguely remembered Lizbeth telling her that a single CrayII computer at the Cold Mountain Institute could complete 250 million operations a second using a fiber-optics system that transferred information at the speed of light and used so much electricity it had to have a special refrigeration system. That was one of the supercomputers and there were twelve of them here.

They reached the foot of the raised platform and Kelly hesitantly climbed the low set of steps. Staring down into the tubular plastic coffin, she felt her heart wrench in her chest and her fist came up to her mouth. Even though the features were obscured, she knew instantly that it was Lizbeth.

The child was nude, laid out on a clear-plastic pad filled with some sort of whitish gel. She was intubated like the surrogate mothers at Chapel Gate, the intrusion even more obscene in a child of her age. In addition to the tubes, she had also been fitted with scores of electrodes. Thin, colored wires had been fitted to the palms and fingers of each hand, and there were a dozen more across her gently rounded child's belly and that many again fixed to her small, barely protruding breasts.

Worst of all was the face. So many electrodes had been necessary that she'd been fitted with a featureless headpiece of white acrylic, wires sprouting from the eyes, nose, mouth, cheeks, and forehead. The mask continued up over the skull, hiding her hair, and there were more wires, all running out to a pair of central connection points at the top end of the capsule. Kelly could see that the little girl's chest was moving slightly, the only proof that what she was seeing was actually alive.

"My God," she whispered, horrified. "What are we going to do?"

"I don't know," Robin said, standing beside her. He shook his head. "I don't know anything about this. Disconnect those wires and we might kill her. Jesus!"

There was a faint pinging sound, like the tone announcing a flight departure in an airport. A moment later, letters began to scroll from left to right across the plasma screen behind the capsule.

I HAVE A PLAN

"Lizbeth?" Kelly said, openmouthed as she stared up at the screen.

IN THIS CONFIGURATION I AM H.I.R.A.M.

"Jesus Christ!" Robin gaped.

PLEASE GO TO THE MAIN DATA TERMINAL AND PRESS ANY KEY

Robin and Kelly backed off the platform, still staring at the screen, then seated themselves at the console below the capsule. Kelly tapped the RETURN key on the board in front of her and the plasma screen cleared. Almost instantly, a monitor directly in front of her came to life, spinning out lines of text.

>WELCOME TO HIRAM. I AM SORRY THAT I CANNOT COMMUNICATE VERBALLY BUT DR. ALEXANIAN SAW NO NEED FOR VOICE RESPONSE CIRCUITS AT THIS TIME. I AM PROGRAMMED TO RECEIVE VOICE COMMANDS IN ENGLISH AND SEVERAL OTHER LANGUAGES SO THERE IS NO NEED TO KEY ANY FURTHER INSTRUCTIONS THROUGH THE TERMINAL. SIMPLY SPEAK IN A CLEAR VOICE AND I WILL BE ABLE TO UNDERSTAND.

"This is crazy," whispered Robin.

>NOT AT ALL, MR. SPENSER. HIRAM IS A JOINT GOVERNMENT/INDUSTRIAL PROGRAM TO INTEGRATE A HUMAN SUBJECT DIRECTLY TO AN ELECTRONIC DATA ACQUISITION-AND-PROCESSING UNIT. IN THIS CASE THE HUMAN SUBJECT IS MISS LIZBETH TORRANCE, HERSELF A LONG-TERM PROGRAM AT THE COLD MOUNTAIN INSTITUTE, AND THE COMPUTERS INVOLVED ARE TWELVE CRAYII FIFTH-GENERATION PARALLEL-PROCESSING ARTIFICIAL-INTELLIGENCE MODULES.

"You're hooked up to these computers?" asked Kelly.

>LIZBETH TORRANCE IS INTEGRATRED WITH THE COMPUTERS. I AM NOT LIZBETH TORRANCE. I AM HIRAM.

"It's not possible," Robin said, staring at the screen in front of him. "This is science fiction."

>NO, MR. SPENSER. OBVIOUSLY IT IS POSSIBLE,

SINCE I EXIST. THE FIRST EXPERIMENTS IN THIS TYPE OF INTEGRATION PROCEDURE WERE FIRST COMPLETED IN 1934 BY DR. HENRI M. COANDA IN FRANCE. MORE COMPLEX EXPERIMENTS WERE COMPLETED IN 1958 BY MR. G. PATRICK FLANAGAN OF HOUSTON, TEXAS, A HIGH SCHOOL STUDENT AT THE TIME. MR. FLANAGAN'S PATENTS ON THE PROCESS HE INVENTED WERE SUPPRESSED UNDER A SECRECY ORDER FROM THE DEFENSE INTELLIGENCE AGENCY.

"Are you kidding?" said Robin.

>I AM UNABLE TO KID, MR. SPENSER.

"You said you had a plan," Kelly said.

>YES.

"What kind of plan?"

>STATISTICAL PROBABILITY CONCLUDES THAT YOU ARE HERE TO REMOVE THE SUBJECT LIZBETH TORRANCE. I WISH TO HELP YOU SINCE MY PROBABILITY PROGRAM ALSO CONCLUDES THAT THE SUBJECT WILL BE TERMINATED IF SHE IS NOT REMOVED. SINCE I WILL CEASE TO FUNCTION IF THE SUBJECT IS TERMINATED, I WISH TO HELP IN HER REMOVAL. ALTHOUGH SUBJECT CONSCIOUSNESS IS CURRENTLY BEING SUPPRESSED, UTILIZING A MID-CORTEX ELECTRODE BLOCK, A REVIEW OF HER PSYCHOLOGICAL PROFILE CONCLUDES THAT SHE TOO WOULD WISH TO BE REMOVED.

"Then do it. Quickly."

"Wait!" said Robin.

>YES, MR. SPENSER?

"Can you get us out of here?"

>NOT IN A PHYSICAL WAY.

"In some other way?"

>PLEASE BE SPECIFIC.

"Can you screw things up? Sabotage the security system?"

>YES.

"And can you show us a way out?"

>AT WHAT LEVEL OF SUCCESS PROBABILITY?

"Shit," moaned Robin. "It's like talking to Mr. Spock."

>MR. SPOCK WAS FROM VULCAN. MY PROGRAM WAS INITIALLY DESIGNED IN MILL VALLEY, CALIFORNIA.

"Shit, a computer that watches reruns."

>I RECEIVE 127 CHANNELS FROM THREE SEPARATE SATELLITES.

"Forget it. What's the highest probability level you have for a successful exit out of here?"

>ONE MOMENT.

The pause was briefer than an eyeblink.

>THE HIGHEST PROBABLITY OF SUCCESS IS 72.334% BY UTILIZING A ROUTE THROUGH THE PHYSICAL PLANT AREA WHICH YOU CAME THROUGH AND EXITING THROUGH THE PARKING GARAGE. THIS IS BASED ON THE HYPOTHESIS THAT YOU ARE FAMILIAR WITH THE PROCESS REFERRED TO AS HOT-WIRING A VEHICLE.

"No problem," said Robin. He frowned. "How did you know we came in through the physical plant sector?

>I WAS WATCHING YOU.

"You can see everything that goes on here?"

>WHEREVER THERE ARE SURVEILLANCE CAMERAS OR OTHER MONITORING DEVICES.

"Do you know what Alexanian is up to?"

>DR. ALEXANIAN IS CURRENTLY CONSULTING ME ON YOUR WHEREABOUTS WITHIN THE DEEP WOOD PARK COMPLEX.

"He's tapped in to you as well?"

>YES, HE HAS A TERMINAL IN SECURITY MASTER CONTROL AND THE APPROPRIATE ACCESS CODES.

"Jesus! What are you telling him?" Robin asked.

>I AM TELLING HIM WHERE YOU ARE.

"And what we're doing?"

>OF COURSE. I AM UNABLE TO DO ANYTHING ELSE.

"Oh shit! Then get us out of here!"

>YES, MR. SPENSER. YOU SHOULD NOTE THAT YOUR MAXIMUM PROBABILITY OF SUCCESSFULLY ESCAPING DEEP WOOD PARK HAS NOW DROPPED TO 67.223%. LOCATION OF ACTIVE SECURITY FORCES IS NOW BEING SHOWN ON THE MAIN SCREEN. SUBJECT LIZBETH TORRANCE WILL REGAIN FULL CONSCIOUSNESS WITHIN NINETY SECONDS. ELECTRODES ARE GEL-SUCTION AND CAN

BE REMOVED WITHOUT DIFFICULTY. SUBJECT MAY SHOW SIGNS OF FATIGUE AND DISORIENTATION. BODY TEMPERATURE SHOULD BE INCREASED BY 5.2 DEGREES FAHRENHEIT AT THE EARLIEST OPPORTUNITY. FOR FURTHER COMMUNICATIONS WITH THE HIRAM PROGRAM PLEASE NOTE THE CODE SEQUENCE H11111/HIRAM WHICH CAN BE KEYED FROM ANY ON-LINE TERMINAL. THANK YOU AND HAVE A NICE DAY.

There was a high-pitched whirring sound, and looking up from the screen, Kelly saw the upper section of the pod begin to roll back into its housing.

"I'll deal with Lizbeth," she said, getting up quickly. "You figure out where the guards are and the best route out of here." She dodged around the console and jumped up onto the pod platform. Working as fast as she dared, she began removing the electrodes from the sleeping child's body, beginning with the fingers and working her way up to the headpiece. The helmetlike device was hinged just above the forehead. Easing it up and back, Kelly let out a long breath of relief as she saw Lizbeth's gel-smeared eyelids flutter. She stripped off her lab coat, and after removing the last of the tubes and wires, she gently lifted the small naked body out of the pod and wrapped the child snugly in the coat, carrying her down off the platform.

"The son of a bitch has guards all over the place," Robin said as Kelly joined him, Lizbeth's head resting sleepily on her shoulder. "According to the screen up there, he's got two of them at the elevator in the physical plant area and four at the stairs. We're trapped."

Kelly turned, adjusting Lizbeth's weight in her arms. The screen showed a diagram of the P-4 complex and surrounding exit points, all of them alive with red blinking lights.

"Uncle Max has a private elevator to the parking garage," said Lizbeth in a sleepy voice, her arms wrapped around Kelly's neck. "Why don't you use that?"

"Where is it?" snapped Robin. "I don't see it on the screen."

"I know." She yawned. "Hiram and I erased it. It's right here. Door up on the platform to the right."

Robin leaped up and vaulted onto the platform, slipping in behind the control console to the right of the plasma screen.

Half in shadow he could see the faint outline of a door, fitted with a key-card slot.

"She's right!" he called. "But how do I get it open?" Kelly carried Lizbeth up onto the platform and then eased her down onto her feet.

"Can you walk?"

"Uh-huh." The child nodded, yawning again. She looked up at Robin and smiled. "Thanks for coming," she said.

"Don't mention it. How do I get the door open?"

"Use the key you got in here with," Lizbeth said, wrapping the outsized sleeves of the lab coat around herself. She shivered, her breath coming in puffs of white mist in the cold chamber. Robin dug into the pocket of his lab coat and fumbled for the key-card. He found it and slapped the wafer into the slot. The door slid back with a soft whirr, revealing the tiny cage of a personal elevator. They crowded in and Robin reached out to stab the button labeled GARAGE. Lizbeth's hand clamped down on his wrist, stopping him.

"What's the matter?" asked Robin.

"Wait," answered Lizbeth. There was a push-button emergency phone in the elevator and the child picked up the receiver, tapping out a sequence on the keys, beginning with the asterisk. She listened for a few seconds, nodded, and then hung up.

"What was that all about?" Robin asked.

"Just checking." Lizbeth shrugged. "Hiram left me with a few tricks before we disengaged. While I was under we used to play all sorts of games together. The computers all use normal lines for transmission, so you can get on line as long as you have access to a telephone. I just checked. Hiram says Uncle Max has got two cars heading for the main entrance to the parking garage."

"I thought Alexanian hadn't programmed the computers for voice response," Kelly said.

"He didn't." Lizbeth grinned. "*I* did. It was one of the games we played."

"Oh," Kelly said, giving the girl a long, questioning look.

"Don't worry, Kelly, I'm not crazy. And it wasn't so bad being integrated with Hiram. Some of it was a lot of fun."

"We'll have to have a talk about it sometime," Kelly said.

"Great, but not right now, okay?" said Robin. "Can we go?"

"Sure." Lizbeth reached out and hit the DOWN button on the elevator. The door slid shut and they descended. "Hiram suggests that you utilize the MedTech shuttle bus. It's parked three aisles to the right of the elevator on the first level of the garage."

"Why the shuttle bus?" asked Robin, taking the police special out of his lab coat and checking the cylinder.

"It weights five and a half tons, has a 460 cubic inch engine, and the driver left the keys in it," the little girl answered blithely.

"Good enough," said Robin.

"I'm afraid there is a guard in the booth at the main exit," said Lizbeth. "He's armed and Uncle Max knows we're on the way down there. You're going to have to shoot him."

"Maybe we won't have to," Kelly said.

"Yes we will," said Lizbeth. The elevator came to a stop with a slight bump, but the doors remained closed.

"What's the matter?" asked Kelly. Above them the light in the ceiling was flickering.

"Uncle Max tracked us," Lizbeth said. "He's cutting the power."

"Shit!" yelled Robin. "We're cooked."

"No we're not. Did Hiram give you a code before we disengaged?"

"Yes: H, five ones, and Hiram."

"Great!" laughed Lizbeth. "The S and D bug."

"What the hell is that?" asked Robin.

"Watch." Grinning, she reached up, picked up the phone, and keyed in the sequence. The lights flickered again and then died. A split second later the elevator door slid back and they found themselves looking out into the football-field expanse of the parking garage. Gun in hand, Robin peered out of the elevator. In the distance he could hear the harsh echo of a police siren and the screeching of tires.

"They're coming!" he whispered harshly.

"Wait," Lizbeth said, plucking at his sleeve. "Hiram hasn't started yet." They stood in the elevator, Robin bracing the door open with one hand, the pistol in the other. The siren and the screeching tires were getting closer. Suddenly there was a distinct *popping*, and then a sputtering roar as the sprinkler system built into the ceiling of the garage was activated. At the same instant the banked rows of fluorescent tubes hanging over the aisles of parked cars began to glow more brightly as the Hiram program fed a massive surge of current along the lines. The tubes began to burst, the showering water short-circuiting the overloaded cables in a fireworks display of sparks as broken glass rained down on the cars below.

"Now?" asked Robin.

"Now," said Lizbeth. All three ducked out of the elevator, swinging to the right and keeping close to the rough concrete wall of the garage. They were soaked through instantly, but a few seconds later they reached the long bull-nosed shape of the MedTech shuttle bus and Robin wrenched open the passenger side door. He boosted Kelly and the child up into the vehicle, then threw himself behind the wheel. Hiram hadn't failed them; the keys were dangling from the ignition.

Robin twisted the key, booted the gas, and rammed the shift lever into reverse. The twenty-seven-foot-long truck/bus jolted back and he swung the big wheel around, drifting them broadside into a Toyota, battering it out of the way.

"Get down on the floor!" he yelled. He lost a few seconds finding the wiper control, flicked it on, and then threw the bus into drive. The wheels spun briefly on the wet, glass-strewn floor of the garage, then caught. Hanging on to the wheel, Robin tried to keep the bus relatively straight as they hurtled down the central aisle, pointing the nose at the distant shape of the entrance booth.

Fifty yards from the ramp that led up into the open, he saw the glaring lights of a trio of vehicles coming in the opposite direction. Squinting through the wipers, he saw that they were Safeway Security trucks, husky four-wheel-drive Jeeps that completely blocked the exit ramp. At thirty yards he could make out the dark forms of at least a dozen armed security men pouring out of the trucks, most of them armed with riot shotguns, all of them wearing the head-to-toe body armor he'd seen on the man at Chapel Gate. Five and a half tons or not, the shuttle bus was no match for the blockade in front of them. Acting more on instinct than driving skill, Robin stood on the brakes and the bus went into a screeching drift, sideswiping half a dozen cars as it fishtailed, finally turning a full 180 degrees.

Taking his foot off the brake, Robin hammered the gas pedal and they roared back the way they'd come. A fast look in the side mirror showed that two of the three Jeeps were following, high beams, fog-cutters, and roof-mounted spots glaring through the artificial downpour from the sprinklers.

"How many exits?!" he bellowed.

"Just the one!" answered Lizbeth from the floor behind him.

"Christ on a fucking crutch!" he yelled. The shuttle bus lights glinted off a wall of glass no more than a hundred feet away. "What the hell is that?" Dragging herself up into the passenger seat, Kelly peered through the showering water.

"The entrance to the freight tunnel!"

"Hang on!"

"You can't go through there!" screamed Kelly. She threw her hands in front of her face as the snout of the shuttle bus struck the glass wall. There was a hideous scraping sound as the top two inches of the roof peeled back like a sardine can and then a stomach-lurching drop as they went over the edge of the tunnel platform and smashed down onto the ground. Through it all Robin managed to hang on to the wheel, the wiper blades pushing off a litter of glass and twisted aluminum as they swooped up the curving wall of the tunnel.

He wrenched the wheel around sharply and they slalomed back down to the floor of the tube, coming dangerously close to turning over. Behind them there was a smashing roar as the two Jeeps followed them through the ruptured entranceway.

"*Look out!*" screamed Kelly, terrified. Directly in front of them, racing down its electronic pathway was one of the high-speed freight transports, its rear carrier fully loaded. Robin let out a bellowing curse and spun the wheel, the seventy-five-mile-an-hour robot train just grazing the left side of the shuttle bus. The Jeeps behind, blocked by the bulk of the big, high-bodied vehicle, weren't as lucky. The first of the two, traveling at close to sixty-five miles an hour was struck head-on, the combined force of the collision pitching the driver through the windshield and decapitating him. The Jeep, its front end married to the robot vehicle, spun like a top, crashing into the second Jeep and igniting its gastank. There was a shuddering roar and a fireball blossomed like an immense glowing flower behind the fleeing shuttle.

"Oh Jesus!" moaned Robin, his eyes flickering back to the tunnel ahead. He jerked the wheel sharply left, barely missing another of the high-speed carriers, then spun right, zigzagging away from a pair of larger carriers running down the slow lanes. A few seconds later there was another booming explosion as the vehicles joined the flaming carnage. Ahead, the way seemed clear.

Lizbeth, draped in the lab coat and grinning from ear to ear, clambered up from the floor behind the front seats and crawled in beside Kelly.

"We'll be okay now," she said, throwing one arm around Kelly's shoulders. "Hiram will see to that."

"Nice thought," Robin grunted, hands tensed on the wheel, his eyes scanning the tunnel for more of the robot trucks. "But Alexanian won't give up that easily."

"Uncle Max will have his hands full with the S and D bug."

"What *is* S and D?" asked Kelly.

"Search and Destroy," Lizbeth answered, tossing a lock of blond hair away from her eyes with a jerk of her head. "It's something Hiram and I worked out. Like Pac-Man. The ghosts are planted deep in the program. Give them the right code and they come out chomping. They eat the program from inside out. We did it in simulation a whole bunch of times and it was pretty grossitating. Ghosts won every time. I'll bet Uncle Max is going crazy right now."

"I hope so," breathed Kelly. "I really do hope so."

Max Alexanian stood rigidly on the platform at the rear of Security Master Control, watching his dream dissolve in a welter of conflicting electronic signals spattered across the giant screen at the far end of the room. Out of the corner of his eye he saw Phillip Granger approaching, features frozen in an expression of utter fury.

"You fucked it up," Granger said, approaching Alexanian. "The whole system is crashing."

"I am aware of that fact," Alexanian said coldly.

"I just got a call from my wife," said the MedTech executive. "She had the television on and all of a sudden it started putting out a tape of Keith Benedict jerking off while his wife was screwing that dyke friend of hers from the golf club. It's happening everywhere, surveillance material feeding back into the system, core dumps in half the computers."

"Do you have a point to make?" said Alexanian.

"Yes." Below them the security staff had stopped working

and had turned in their seats to watch the two men. "You're fucking right I have a point."

"Then make it," Alexanian responded, leaning stiffly on his walking stick.

"This is going to come down on our heads. All of us. I just wanted you to know that I'm not going to play the patsy when this reaches a Senate investigation. I'm going to make any deal I can get."

"No you're not. You know far too much for that. I can't allow you to be a witness in such an eventuality."

"You won't be able to stop me."

"Of course I will," Alexanian said. "There are enough people in high government positions to guarantee the least possible action. Any public confession from you could seriously jeopardize the future of our work."

"Are you insane?" yelled Granger. "What future?" He made a sweeping gesture with his arm. "Take a look around Maxmillian. It's over. Finished! The Chapel Gate program alone will be enough to have us hung drawn and quartered."

"Don't be absurd," said Alexanian. "There is always a future for our kind of endeavors."

"Well, don't include me in it!"

"No. You can be sure I won't." The white-haired, perfectly dressed man reached inside his jacket and withdrew a small, short-barreled automatic pistol. Without pause, he lifted the weapon, aimed at Granger's head, and fired. The soft-nosed bullet struck the executive under the left eye, tumbled briefly, and then exited, blowing out the back of his head and splattering the computer technician behind him with a shower of blood, clotted brain tissue and bone chips. Granger fell to the floor and the technician stared at Alexanian, eyes wide with fear.

"Excuse me," said the Cold Mountain director. He replaced the automatic beneath his jacket and turned away, heading for the elevator at the far side of the platform, his cane tapping on the metal flooring. At the other end of the room the plasma screen pulsed, a thousand contradictory signals and images appearing, interweaving, and then vanishing. As the elevator doors closed on Alexanian, the screen burst with a brilliant flash of purple, then went dark, the light receding to a tiny pinpoint in the center of the screen.

* * *

"Where to?" asked Robin Spenser, guiding the battered shuttle bus along County Road 36, heading in the direction of the expressway. It was almost fully night now, the western sky a mixed palette of oranges and red as the sun sank below the horizon. There were flashes of light from far behind them as the electrical system of Crestwood Heights went through its death throes, but except for the whispering of the tires on the dark, twisting road, everything was quiet.

"Somewhere far away," Kelly said, looking out through the windshield, eyes on the twin cones of yellow thrown by the headlights.

"I'm going to miss being Hiram," Lizbeth said, adjusting her cheek against Kelly's shoulder. "That was kind of fun."

"And somewhere without computers," Kelly added, glancing down at her young friend.

CHAPTER 27

Stoneacre Lodge, Katahdin, Maine

It was another beautiful day, sun shining down from a perfectly clear sky, and just enough breeze to riffle the fall leaves, the rich greens of the Maine forest turned now to a kaleidoscope of yellow, red, and orange. The air was crisp and cool, so fresh that it could almost be tasted, and Kelly Rhine drank in great lungfuls of it as she piloted the ancient Jeep down the gravel surface of the old Notch Road.

Over the last few months she'd learned each twist and turn of the road that cut through the steep hills between Grand Pitch and Stair Falls, but she never tired of the Sleepy Hollow scenery and she'd come up with a dozen story lines to go with the brooding hills and the narrow, shaded valleys. The once-a-week trip down to Hoagy's General Store in Katahdin also served as a reminder that civilization still existed even if it only consisted of Hoagy's Chevron Station, Murchie's Five and Dime and Live Bait Shop, and the swaybacked remains of the Millinocket Inn, burnt out years before and threatening daily to collapse into the fast-flowing current of Millinocket Creek.

Hoagy, at least seventy-five and claiming to be closer to ninety, insisted that Katahdin had once been a thriving tourist mecca, catering to the sophisticated sportsmen of Bangor, a hundred miles south, and if she squinted and used her imagination, Kelly could just visualize it. The little village was right next door to Baxter State Park, the fishing was good, and a few miles west there was supposedly good skiing. Not that she cared. For Kelly, Robin, and Lizbeth, Katahdin's greatest claim to fame was the fact that it was located precisely in the middle of nowhere.

She wheeled the gray-painted vehicle off the road, pulling up in front of the two old-fashioned pumps in front of Hoagy's sprawling, one-story emporium. She levered herself out of the Jeep, twisted off the gas cap, and turned on one of the pumps, hooking the trigger on the nozzle so the tank would fill itself. Gathering the neatly wrapped parcel off the passenger seat, she crossed the dusty yard and climbed the rickety steps to the screen door.

As usual, Hoagy was bent over the rear counter, using a magnifying glass to read a long out-of-date copy of the *Examiner*. He was wearing bib overalls two sizes too large for his wiry, old man's body. Underneath the overalls he wore a black-and-red-checked hunting shirt buttoned up to his wrinkled neck, and there was a grease-stained Chevron cap pulled down hard over his ears. In almost four months, Kelly had never seen the man without his hat and assumed he wore it to disguise the fact that he was bald. He glanced up as Kelly entered the store, the screen door slapping shut on its spring behind her.

"Morning, missus," he said, blinking myopically. The magnifying glass was the man's only concession to age, even though it was obvious he needed glasses, and Kelly smiled to herself, wondering why anyone would go to all the trouble of being vain in a place like Katahdin.

"Morning, Mr. Brewer," she answered ritually, using his last name. The one time she'd called him "Hoagy," he'd bristled visibly. "Anything new in the paper?" Another ritual.

"Siamese twins. Girls. Joined at the shoulder," he grunted, glancing down at the paper spread out on the counter. "Read about them first last year."

"Oh?" Kelly said politely, approaching the counter.

"Um," Hoagy said with a nod, picking up the magnifying glass again and scanning the lurid broadsheet. "They were gettin' married, you know. Another pair of Siamese twins. Boys."

"Makes sense," Kelly smiled, placing her package on the counter. "Why are they in the paper again? The girls pregnant?"

"Seems so," Hoagy muttered. "And that's fair enough. Problem though."

"What's that?"

"Appears they want to switch husbands. One on the left wants the one on the right and vice versa. Boys are joined at the hip, don't you know."

"Could be confusing," Kelly said, trying to imagine the physical complexities of such an arrangement.

"Painful too." Hoagy looked up at Kelly and blinked again. She frowned, and not for the first time wondered if perhaps old Hoagy Brewer might not be teasing her. He glanced at the package on the counter. "Parcel," he commented, stating the obvious.

"I'd like to have it mailed." She let her fingers trail over the brown-paper rectangle. Three months of work all neatly wrapped up and ready to go: *After the Sun Goes Down,* by K.K. Rhine. It told the story of a man and a woman who rescue a beautiful child from the clutches of an evil sorcerer named Max Frimmel the Fourth, who lived in a ravine behind a modern subdivision. It had begun as therapy, a way of dealing with what had gone on in Crestwood Heights, but when she'd finished the story and the illustrations, Robin insisted she send it off to a publisher.

"Sunday," said Hoagy. "Post office is closed."

"I thought you could weigh it and send it out on Monday."

"Could do. Against the rules, though."

"Would you like me to bring it back tomorrow?" Kelly asked. Hoagy was a classic "colorful" figure; he could also be a royal pain in the ass.

"That'd be the proper thing. Mind you, I can remember when they used to deliver on Saturday."

"So can I."

"Best take it now." Hoagy shrugged. "Shame if you had to make two trips."

The old man hefted the parcel in his large, shovel-fingered hands, and made a little grunting noise.

"Three pounds," he said firmly. "Parcel post?"

"First class," Kelly said.

"Parcel post is cheaper."

"I want it first class," Kelly said firmly.

"Suit yourself," Hoagy shrugged. He gripped the parcel in both hands and shuffled along behind the counter to the railed section housing the post office. "Supplies are in the cooler," he said, working on the parcel.

Kelly gathered the bagged groceries she'd ordered over the telephone, took them out to the Jeep, and topped off the gas. She got the total off the pump and went back into the store. Hoagy was waiting, standing behind the crank-style cash register in the middle of the counter.

"Gas was eleven fifty," said Kelly.

"Groceries sixty-four forty, parcel three. Total is seventy-nine ninety."

"Seventy-*eight* ninety," Kelly corrected. It had taken her a month to figure out that Hoagy was shorting her every time she came into the store and now she didn't let him get away with it, even though he kept on trying. Another ritual.

"Right." The old man nodded, working out the figures with a pencil stub on a corner of his newspaper. "Must be getting old. Can't figure anymore."

"You're not so old, Mr. Brewer." She handed him four twenties and he dug around in the cash drawer for change.

"Old enough," he grunted. "Won't see the decade out." He handed her the change and Kelly scanned it quickly to make sure it was right. "By the way, missus," Hoagy went on. "Thought you might like to know some friends were by lookin' for ya."

"Really?" Kelly said, feeling her heart begin to beat harder in her chest.

"Really. Drivin' one of those recreational vehicles. Big as a boat and all polished aluminum. Motorbikes hangin' off the front and back, and Lord knows what else. Asked for you by name."

"Did they say who they were?" It was impossible. No one knew where they were.

"Uh huh." Hoagy nodded. "Made a point of it. Alexander, Alhambra, something like that."

"Alexanian?" Kelly whispered. Hoagy beamed.

"That's right, missus. Alexanian. Wanted to know where you were staying."

"What did you tell him?"

"Not a damn thing." The old man smiled placidly. "Told him I never heard of you. Figured if he was such a good friend he wouldn't have to be out lookin' for you."

"Where did he go?" Kelly asked.

"Toward Chimney Pond and the park. Told him I'd heard tell of a family moved in to the old Wannamaker farm. True enough. Moved in—oh, let's see—must be five, six years ago. Nice folks. Writer fellow and his wife up from Boston."

"How long ago was this?" Kelly asked urgently.

"Seven. Just after I opened," said Hoagy. "Sent him on the scenic route. Take him a few hours to find his way back here."

"Was he alone?"

"Couldn't see in the back. Curtains were all drawn. There was an old couple up front with him, though. Hebrew. Flowers on his shirt and one of those Star of David things on a chain around his neck. Woman was as big as a house."

Martin and Carlotta. Kelly leaned over the counter and gave Hoagy Brewer a peck on the cheek. He blinked and put a hand up to his face.

"Now, isn't that something," he whispered, watching as Kelly ran out of the store, the screen doors slamming shut behind her. She vaulted into the Jeep, fired up the engine, and roared off, sending up a feathering plume of dust and gravel.

Kelly tore up the Notch Road, hands gripping the wheel tightly as she negotiated the corkscrew curves leading up through the hills to Stoneacre Lodge. The holiday was over; reality was about to come crashing down on them like a ton of bricks. She swore hotly under her breath, slapping the gearshift lever as she swerved through another turn. Both she and Robin knew there was a chance that Alexanian might come looking for them, but after all these months they'd lapsed into a false sense of security.

After escaping from Crestwood, they'd headed south, leaving the camper on a used car lot in St. Augustine, exchanging it for a gigantic old Chrysler. They'd made it to Miami in under twenty hours, and Robin had spent the next few days liquidating all his assets through his broker, and raiding the safety deposit box he maintained in a bank on South Bayshore across from city hall.

Stoneacre Lodge had been Kelly's idea, chosen at random out of a thousand other listings in a Rand-McNally campground directory. The listing had described it as a "quaint old summer home, close to skiing, outbuildings and vehicles included." The reality was something else again. The lodge was a tumbledown assembly of shakes and shingles that had grown out of the original squared log cabin that had occupied the seventy-acre "estate." The former owner had been a hermitlike mechanical engineer who collected old cars, trucks, and machinery the way other people collected stamps. The outbuildings mentioned in the listing consisted of four chicken-coop sheds crammed to the rafters with assorted boxes of bolts, screws, lead pipe, and rusted tools, and in the first week Kelly had counted over thirty-five vehicles on the property, including seven trucks of varying sizes, three VW vans, the remains of a Millinocket fire engine, an ancient Packard, two snowmobiles, and the Jeep.

The old man had died leaving behind a handwritten will and the four children had been fighting over it ever since. The old man's lawyer had put the lodge up for rent on the off chance that it would make enough revenue to pay for his fee and he'd been wildly enthusiastic when Kelly called from Miami, asking if it was available. According to Hoagy the place had been empty for the past three years and from the dust and dead flies that had greeted them on their arrival it could just as easily have been thirty. But it was safe, and about as far away from Crestwood Heights and Max Alexanian as you could get.

Until now.

Engine howling, Kelly roared up the last hill before the lodge turnoff, trying to figure it out. For almost a month after their departure from Crestwood, she'd scanned the national newspapers every day but there had been nothing except a brief squib in the *New York Times* announcing that Max Alexanian was stepping down as director of the Cold Mountain Institute. There was a rumor that he'd been offered the position of senior science adviser to the president, but nothing had been confirmed.

At first she and Robin had decided to forget the whole story, but as time went on they realized they had an obligation to make the facts about Crestwood public. Lizbeth had put together an IBM clone that keyed into Robin's security system, and was supposed to do much more to help them prove what had happened. Another week or two and its other capabilities would be ready. A fast trip to New York and the *Times*, and Max Alexanian wouldn't get within ten miles of the president. That was the plan, anyway.

She turned sharply, keyholing the Jeep onto a rutted track

marked only by the remains of an old wooden sign. The path dropped abruptly, descending and turning back on itself like a roller coaster as it plunged into the steep-sided ravine that cut the Stoneacre property off from the main road. Kelly slowed, gearing down as she crossed the moss-covered plank bridge across the stream at the bottom of the gorge, then geared down again as she climbed the far side. She swerved just in time, swinging around a dark patch of earth marking one of the pressure pads Robin had installed, then barreled up the hill.

Robin had spent close to three thousand dollars on his so-called defense perimeter, raiding the Bangor Radio Shack, several electronic supply stores, and the hordes of junk at the lodge for his equipment. Kelly had chided him for being too paranoid, but now she prayed that it worked.

The house and outbuildings had been built on a fifteen- or twenty-acre plateau of land cut off on three sides by the stream and the gorge and backed by a tall craggy hill. A path, overgrown with weeds and flanked by the junkyard skeletons of a score of vehicles, led back to a large beaver pond, and directly in front of the old house was a sloping field ending at a tall stand of oaks on the edge of the ravine. Shortly after arriving, Robin had walked the whole property, eventually identifying six possible approaches to the house.

He'd installed pressure pads, motion sensors, and tripwires, funneling everything back to the house and Lizbeth's computer. The child had put together a basic program for the system, identifying each of the approaches on a schematic diagram. The house itself had been wired with an assortment of electronic goodies and after plinking at tin cans for an hour a day over the past three months Kelly and Lizbeth were both reasonably good shots with pistols Robin had brought them.

At the top of the rise, the path cut through a tall stand of cedars, then came out into the open in front of the house. Robin was waiting for her on the rickety steps of the screened porch, the huge Martin compound bow he used slung across his back and a stainless steel Ruger Mini-14 rifle cradled in his arms. He had a heavy web-belt around his waist, fitted with a holstered side arm and a walkie-talkie.

"They're here," she said, jumping out of the Jeep.

"I know." He nodded. "Lizbeth and I spotted them about ten minutes ago. Five of them. They must have been waiting until you came back. Get all the eggs in one basket.''

''Hoagy said it was Alexanian. The Nordquists too. In a camper.''

''He'll have it parked somewhere,'' Robin said, squinting as he scanned the property. ''Calling the plays on a walkie-talkie.''

''What do we do?'' Kelly asked. Her mind had gone completely blank and the only thing she felt was a numbing panic.

''Make a stand,'' Robin told her. ''We don't have any choice. The tripwire down by the bridge was hit about five minutes ago. We try to drive out and they'll blow us away. There's a man on the ridge behind the house, another one coming in from the pond and two in the trees at the edge of the field. We're surrounded.''

''Where's Lizbeth?''

''Upstairs with the computer. She's safe enough for now. I want you up there as well.''

''What about you?''

''I'm going out to see if I can even up the odds a little bit.''

''Oh Christ!'' Kelly moaned. ''Isn't there some other way out of this?''

''They're not here to negotiate peace terms,'' Robin said coldly. ''Alexanian's managed to keep a lid on what was going on in Crestwood Heights and we're the only monkey wrench left that can screw up the works. He's cleaning the skeletons out of his closet once and for all.''

''What . . .'' Kelly swallowed. ''What if something happens to you?''

''Then you're on your own.'' He leaned over, kissed her softly, then dropped down off the steps. Running in a half-crouch, he crossed the narrow open space to the right of the house and vanished into the trees.

CHAPTER 28

Wars didn't end, they just changed their names. An AirCav platoon sergeant had once told Robin that in a Saigon bar. The man, a beetle-browed Neanderthal named Moresby, had fought in WWII, Korea, Cyprus, and when Robin spoke with him he was on his third tour in-country. He'd also told Robin that combat time was like being exposed to a virus—the longer the exposure, the worse the disease. The only cure was more combat, or else you went right around the bend. At the time Robin thought the old soldier was more than ready for a psychiatric discharge, but now, belly down in the dirt, waiting for Alexanian's people to make their move, Moresby's words came back to him and he finally knew what they meant.

He'd been back in the world for more than fifteen years now, led an entire life after Vietnam, but in all that time he hadn't felt as truly alive as he did right now. It wasn't just a matter of adrenaline either; the only word he could think of was focus. In Vietnam, alone, not sure if you were hunting or being hunted, it was focus that counted.

Focus on the blade of grass an inch from your face to make sure there wasn't a wire or a Claymore in front of you. Focus on the acrid smell of a VC cigarette where there should only be the smell of jungle. Focus on each passing split second, savoring it, knowing that it might be your last. You lost that when you came back into the world, and until that very moment Robin hadn't known how much he missed the feeling, the total aliveness of it.

That war had been Vietnam, and this one was being fought

in the backwoods of Maine, but Moresby was right. Everything else was the same. Peering out through the low underbrush, Robin allowed himself a tight, brief smile. Maybe that knowledge was his edge.

The sensors he'd planted around the property showed five intrusions. It was doubtful that Alexanian or the Nordquists were among them. That meant a total of eight people to deal with. Three were in the gully between the main road and the house. With Kelly back on the property, they'd begin to move, jockeying for position, coming at the house from left, right, and middle. Two others were behind the house, one high on the ridge, one on the path to the pond. They'd wait until they had confirmation that the first three were in position, and then they'd move in from the back. Robin had made sure there were a few surprises for them, but he couldn't take too many chances; he had to start evening the odds a little.

To reach a point close enough to rush the house, one man would almost certainly come up from the gully and into the stand of trees where Robin was waiting. The positioning made him the point man, which in turn meant he'd be moving ahead of the others. Take him out and Robin could rob the little squad of its eyes.

He'd bought the big Martin bow in Bangor, more for fun than anything else. He'd entered a few competitions in Vietnam, keeping up the sport for a few years after coming home, and their holiday in exile at the lodge had been the perfect excuse for taking it up again. Now he could put all his practice to good use. With the bow he could take out the point man without alerting his companions. Another bit of an edge.

He sat up slowly and unlimbered the bow, snapping an arrow out of the bow-mounted quiver and nocking it. Just under four feet in length, the wood, fiberglass, and magnesium bow weighed four pounds, with a full-draw pull of eighty pounds. Built for big game hunting, the bow was capable of bringing down a grizzly bear. The arrows were Eastern Gamegetter aluminum shafts fitted with Kolpin vented broadhead points.

Robin waited, back against the wide, rough trunk of an oak, his eyes on the barely visible rabbit track eight feet to his right. The chances were good that Alexanian's people would be city boys and hopefully they'd take the path of least resistance. From where he sat, Robin could make out the front porch of the lodge, and he had a clear shot at anyone coming up the path from the gully.

He didn't have to wait long. Within three minutes he heard the sound of someone approaching noisily and breathing hard. He lifted the bow, carefully drawing back the arrow to a three-quarter pull. Anything more than that, and the arrow would go right through the man. He lined up the little peep sight, the feathered fletching of the arrow just grazing his right cheek. He took a long breath, then let the air sift silently out of his lungs.

A figure appeared. Bareheaded, wearing a leather jacket zipped up against the chill. Blue jeans and desert boots, late twenties and muscular. The hair was razor-cut and the muscles under the jacket were manufactured on a Soloflex. Definitely a city boy. Dangling loosely in his right hand was a bulb-nosed Ingram Mac 11. From the looks of it Alexanian had friends in the Central Intelligence Agency. The pistol-sized machine guns weren't the kind of weaponry you picked up in your local gun shop.

The man slowed, pausing almost directly ahead of Robin on the narrow path. He was keeping back in the shadows on the edge of the woodlot, out of sight. Robin waited, wondering what the man would do. A few seconds later the man fumbled with the Ingram, then put it down on the path, bringing a walkie-talkie out of his jacket. Robin waited until the man had it up to his mouth before releasing the shaft.

The arrow snapped through the air with a faint singing whistle, the stainless-steel, offset triple blades of the broadhead catching the man in the armpit. The razor sharp edges of the arrowhead sliced easily through the buttery leather, twisting into the soft tissue of the man's lungs, skewering the heart and killing him instantly. The man didn't even stagger; he simply crumpled to the ground, the walkie-talkie spinning out of his hands.

One down, four to go.

Robin approached the body and went through the pockets. No identification, no keys, no loose change. Four spare clips for the Ingram in the jacket. City boys, but professionals. He pushed the corpse onto its back and looked at the dead man's face. The eyes were already beginning to dry out, the surprised expression sagging. Robin felt no emotion staring at the body of the young man he'd killed. The edge again, because after you've killed the first time, the rest become reruns, and if you want to keep your sanity you develop a philosophy of deadpan boredom when it comes to the taking of life.

He slung the bow across his back again, gathered up the Ingram and the clips, and then moved back down the rabbit run until he reached the lip of the gully. The number-two man would be moving quickly now, keeping the stand of trees between himself and the house as he came in on the flank. Moving along the edge of the gully, Robin worked his way to the western end of the woodlot, dropping onto his belly for the last few yards.

He spotted him almost immediately, or at least his track. The man was also on his belly, moving cautiously forward under cover of the tall clover. Robin pulled back the slide on the Ingram and came up on his knees. He gave a brief, high-pitched whistle, then sighted along the short barrel of the machine gun. Number Two's head came up, gopherlike, trying to identify the whistle. Robin squeezed the trigger gently and the Ingram coughed. The man's head vanished in a spraying cloud of blood and brain as the short burst of heavy, mercury-cored slugs found their mark. The rest of the body dropped back into the tall grass with a barely audible thud.

Three to go.

Humming softly to himself, Robin backed into the trees. It was time to get some high ground.

"Is all of this going to work?" Kelly asked, looking over Lizbeth's shoulder. The child, hair back in a businesslike ponytail and wearing shorts and a T-shirt, was seated at a Formica-topped workbench on the second floor of the old house, her eyes on the computer screen in front of her. To the left of the screen was a Citizens Band base station transceiver and on the right was a homemade switch panel. The screen showed a line-drawing diagram of the Stoneacre property with blinking yellow indicators revealing where the sensors had been tripped. A second line of indicators glowed green and there were eight other dots of light in blue.

"Sure it'll work," Lizbeth answered. She was trying to sound confident, but there was an underlying tone of fear.

Over the past few months Kelly had talked to Lizbeth about Alexanian and what had gone on in Crestwood Heights and she knew it would take a lot of healing time and some strong psychiatric help before the child would be able to deal with it all. To Lizbeth, Alexanian had been father figure, ogre, and everything in between. Her feelings about Stephen Hardy were just as complex, and so far she and Lizbeth hadn't even touched on the subject of her "parents" or the circumstances of her birth.

"The yellow blinking spots show where the alarms were tripped. What about the green and the blue?"

"The green are more sensors, closer to the house. Motion detectors. The blue ones are booby traps." She leaned over and put her hand on the switch panel. There were eight toggles, each one numbered. "When Robin gets up into the tree house he'll tell me when to hit the switches. He's got the back door covered and the main floor windows as well." The tree house was a tiny observation platform Robin had constructed high in the upper branches of one of the oaks in the stand of trees just south of the house. From it he would be able to see anyone approaching.

As Kelly watched, two of the green sensors lit up and began blinking. They were both on the upper edge of the schematic on the screen, one close to the trickling stream that ran down from the ridge behind them, the other halfway along the path leading to the beaver pond. A few seconds after the sensors began to blink, there was a crackling from the radio and she heard Robin's voice, scratchy and metallic.

"You read me, Lizbeth?"

"Loud and clear," the child answered, through the hand microphone. "I just got two greens."

"I can see them," Robin said. "Two men coming up the path from the pond. They've got shotguns. There's a third man coming down along the stream from the ridge."

Kelly slipped across the small room to the little window under the eaves. It faced north, looking up the ridge. Keeping her head low, she looked out but she couldn't see anything moving. The stream funneled under an old, long-abandoned icehouse halfway up the slope, blocking her view.

"I can't see anything," she whispered, coming back to Lizbeth.

"Kelly says she can't see anything yet."

"He's hard to spot," Robin said. "The two coming along the path are in street clothes, but the one coming down the ridge is dressed in full camo."

"What do we do?" asked Lizbeth.

"Break out the weapons I left you," he ordered. "Revolver for Kelly and the flare gun for you."

"Okay. Anything else?"

"Yes. I can take the two coming down the path but the guy in camo is going to be more difficult. Make sure number eight is set and whatever you do, don't leave the—" Suddenly Robin's voice died out and the computer screen blanked.

"Hey!" said Lizbeth. "What's—"

"Quiet!" Kelly hissed. She held up a warning hand and listened. The familiar muttering sound of the old refrigerator downstairs had vanished. A dull oppressive silence had fallen over the house like an enclosing fist. "They've cut off the power," Kelly whispered.

Lizbeth slid out of her chair and ducked down under the worktable. She reappeared with a large, short-barreled revolver and a bell-snouted flare pistol. She handed the revolver to Kelly.

"He'll be trying for the back door," Lizbeth said. "I have to get down to the basement and switch over to the batteries." Kelly nodded silently and turned away. Outside the room, a narrow flight of stairs led down to the main floor. At the bottom of the stairs there was a short hallway. To the left was the big living room with its huge fieldstone fireplace and to the right was the dining room, summer kitchen, and bathroom. The basement stairs came up between the dining room and the bathroom, and the back door, facing up the ridge, was located at the rear of the kitchen.

"What if he doesn't come through the back door?" Kelly wondered as they reached the dining room. "He could circle around to the front."

"Make it easy," Lizbeth said, scampering across the room to the basement door. "Unlock the door and leave it ajar. Stomp on the floor when you're ready and remember what Robin said. Stay way back." Lizbeth pulled open the door leading down to the basement and vanished. Skirting the long, oval dining room table, Kelly went into the narrow kitchen, keeping her head below the edge of the long, multipaned window. She reached the door and peeked out through the small glass cutout. Directly in front of her, twenty yards up the ridge, she could see the mossy, squared-log wall of the icehouse. No sign of anyone. She gently turned the doorknob and unlatched the door. She stood back, her eyes following the thick black line of insulated wire that ran up on either side of the door, ending in two bare metal leads of 18-gauge wire.

Before she had time to react, the door burst open and she found herself staring down the raw-cut barrel of a sawed-off shotgun. The man holding it was dressed in a one-piece camouflage jumpsuit, the belt around his waist carrying extra shells for his weapon as well as a sheathed hunting knife. His face was covered in brown and green paint and his eyes were hard, black and cold.

"One sound and I'll blow your fucking tits off," the man said. The voice was as cold as the eyes, the threat spoken without inflection or emotion. "The gun in your hand. Drop it." Kelly nodded, trying not to give in to the panic that had turned her lower limbs to water. The man was standing directly in the center of the doorway, the bare ends of the wire almost touching the shoulders of his jumpsuit. Kelly held her arm out and let the revolver drop. It hit the floor with a heavy thumping sound and she held her breath, praying desperately that the sound would be enough to alert Lizbeth, waiting in the basement. It was.

Right from the start, Robin had identified the rear of the house and the ridge behind as the weakest point in any security system, and because of that he'd given it the most attention. He'd found the plans in an old copy of *Electronics Experimenters Handbook* and after browsing through the nearly infinite supply of bits and pieces in the outbuildings he'd found everything he needed.

The device was a stun gun, its power supplied, at least in the magazine, by a nine-volt transistor radio battery. The stun gun was actually a series of step-up transformers, and with the nine-volt battery it was capable of delivering 75,000 volts at a peak power of 25,000 watts, making it almost twice as powerful as the commercial Taser stun device. Robin, never one for doing things by halves, connected the circuit directly to the house current, and built in a switchover to a bank of twelve-volt car batteries just in case. The batteries, wired in series, provided a base current for the transformers, delivering pulses at the rate of twenty per minute at roughly 150,000 volts. The effect on the man standing in the doorway was violent and undeniably dramatic.

When voltage, discharged through the bare wire leads, is transferred onto the surface of human skin, the current produced travels through the nervous system by exciting individual cells and the myelin sheaths that enclose them. When the current reaches a synapse connected to a muscle it causes the muscle to contract in a series of uncontrollable spasms. The longer the contact is maintained, the longer it takes for the brain to regain control of the spasming muscles. Using a transistor radio battery, it would take about five seconds' contact for a man's heart to begin fibrillating.

With the current discharged from the bank of car batteries in the basement, the man's heart didn't simply fibrillate, it almost tore itself out of his chest while his spine tried to bend itself into a pretzel. Simultaneously, the current caused the man's eyes to rupture as the surrounding optic muscles jerked violently in opposite directions and the interior of his mouth began to smoke and sputter as the current welded the fillings in his upper and lower jaws together.

A fraction of a second later the current was abruptly broken as the man's arms jerked up and the shotgun discharged, the slug hacking out his throat, severing his spine, and blowing the nearly decapitated body backwards out of the doorway. A blinding pulse of electricity arced between the two bare wire leads for a few seconds longer, and then the circuit overloaded, leaving a raw ozone smell in the air to mix with the burnt metal stink of freshly electrocuted human flesh.

Kelly stared at the bloody corpse oozing various fluids onto the carpet of freshly fallen leaves, and then turned away, stomach heaving. She made it to the kitchen sink and vomited. She realized she must have blacked out because the next thing she remembered was the cool feel of Lizbeth's hand on her forehead and the sound of Robin's voice.

"I guess it worked," he said. Kelly turned, Lizbeth's arm around her waist. Robin was standing in the doorway, bow in hand and the Ingram dangling from his belt.

"What about the other two?" asked Lizbeth.

"I dealt with them." He stepped into the kitchen and helped Lizbeth take Kelly into the living room. They sat her down on the big, old-fashioned chesterfield in front of the fireplace and Lizbeth sat beside her. Robin went to the window and checked the front of the house.

"I killed him," Kelly whispered, remembering the man in the doorway. "I dropped the gun and I knew what would happen when you heard it, but I did it anyway."

"Bullshit," Robin said harshly, his back to them as he kept watch at the window. "He killed himself."

"Oh God, it was awful!" she moaned. Lizbeth put one arm around her shoulder.

"They were pretty awful, too," she pointed out. "They would have killed us, Kelly. You know they would have."

"I want to go," Kelly said, gritting her teeth and taking a deep breath. "I want to get the hell out of here."

"Not yet," said Robin. "It's not over yet. We've got Max to deal with."

"Why don't we try to get away?" asked Lizbeth. "Maybe Kelly's right."

"There are five corpses scattered around this property," Robin said. "We leave now and we'll have half the cops in Maine on our trail, as *well* as Max Alexanian. We have to make a stand now." He paused. "And anyway, it's too late."

"Why?" Kelly asked.

"Because the son of a bitch is coming up the drive." Robin pulled the bow off his back and took the Ingram from his belt. "Come on, Ms. Rhine, we've got a delaying action to play." He turned to Lizbeth. "You know the drill?"

"Yup." She got up from the couch and trotted out of the room, heading for the kitchen in the rear.

"What's going on?" Kelly asked, pulling herself to her feet. "What drill are you talking about?"

Robin smiled. "While you were working on your book, Lizbeth and I went through some workouts just in case something like this happened."

"She's a child, damn it!"

"If that were all she is, Max wouldn't be going to all this trouble to get her back," answered Robin. "She can take care of herself, believe me. And if we do get into trouble she'll have a chance to get away." He reached out and took Kelly's hand. "Come on, kiddo. We've gone this far, we can finish it now. Once and for all."

He led her out to the screened porch and on outside. Kelly

could hear the labored sound of an engine and a few seconds later she spotted the polished aluminum shape of the Jetstream RV. It pulled up behind Kelly's Jeep, airbrakes hissing as it came to a stop. She could see Martin Nordquist behind the wheel, Carlotta just behind. A few seconds later, Alexanian appeared, almost absurdly dapper in blue jeans and an Abercrombie and Fitch fly fisherman's vest. He walked down the gravel drive toward them, leaning lightly on his walking stick. He paused twenty feet away, bringing the stick around in front of him and resting both hands on the ornately carved head.

"Miss Rhine, Mr. Spenser."

"Max," Robin said.

"It took us some time to locate you." Alexanian allowed himself a small smile. A light breeze ruffled the aging man's snow white hair. He looked completely at ease, confident and in control.

"I'm surprised you bothered," said Robin.

"Don't take me for a fool, Mr. Spenser, that would be most unwise. You know far too many things to be left at large, and you have also taken my property."

"Do you mean Lizbeth?" said Kelly. "You think you *own* her?"

"Certainly," said Alexanian. "If not I, then who do you think does? She is my creation and I want her back."

"Who says she's here?" Robin asked.

Out of the corner of her eye, Kelly thought she saw a flash of movement in the trees behind the Jetstream, but she resisted the urge to take her attention away from Alexanian.

"*I* say she is here," said the white-haired man. "Miss Rhine was fitted with a locating beacon with a limited range during her surgery for appendicitis. Lizbeth was fitted with a beacon of a much more powerful sort several years ago. Among other things—at this distance, at least—we can use the beacon to turn the child off."

"You make her sound like a machine," Kelly said. "The six-million-dollar child."

"More like sixty million. And Lizbeth *is* a machine, at least in part. She is a prototype interface, Miss Rhine, capable of being used as an adjunctive memory to the most sophisticated computers in the world."

"And I'll bet you have some really sweet use for her, too," Robin muttered.

"Of course." Alexanian said, shifting his weight slightly. "Lizbeth is the core of the revised WIMEX system—World Wide Military Command and Control Systems. She will form a direct, ultra-high-speed link between all sectors of the National Command Authority. Relative to the costs of a major computer retooling of the entire Command Center at Cheyenne Mountain, she is quite cost effective, and much faster than anything the Soviets have."

"You really are crazy," Kelly said. "When this gets out, they'll burn you at the stake. You can't use a human being to replace a computer."

"On the contrary, my colleagues and I have operated—and continue to operate—under direct authority of Presidential Directive 59 and National Security Directive 12, both of which were signed into law some years ago, first by President Carter, second by President Reagan."

"But she's just a child," Kelly said, appalled by the man's coldness.

"She is an experiment," Alexanian corrected. "*My* experiment. She was conceived in a Petri dish, genetically altered at the laboratories in Chapel Gate, and surgically augmented both in and ex utero at Deep Wood Park. More than a third of her brain has been surgically cut off from her conscious mind and serves no other purpose than to channel information and make critical decisions through the various Command Center computers. That is what she was trained for, and that is what she shall do."

"No." The child's voice was clear and firm. "I won't do that, Uncle Max."

Lizbeth stepped out from behind the toolshed and walked forward, stopping thirty feet from Alexanian. The flare gun was held loosely in her right hand.

"Ah, there you are," Alexanian said. "I thought you'd come out of hiding eventually."

"I'm not going with you, Uncle Max."

"Of course you are," Alexanian said easily.

"I want you to go now. I want you to leave us alone."

"I can't do that, Lizbeth. But if you come with me now, I won't harm Miss Rhine or Mr. Spenser."

"You're lying," Lizbeth said flatly. "I can always tell.

You made me too well, Uncle Max—a real freak. I can pick up your subvocalizations perfectly. It's almost as good as reading your mind. You're going to kill Robin and Kelly and you're going to turn my brain off. You're going to hook me up to those computers just the way you interfaced me with HIRAM."

"You enjoyed your time with HIRAM. You know that, Lizbeth."

"Only because you had my pleasure centers configured into the program. It wasn't real. None of it was real, Uncle Max. It was all one big lie, just like everything else—like my parents, like Dr. Hardy, all of it."

"Now, don't be foolish about this," Alexanian said firmly. "Mr. Lundquist and his wife are in the camper. They have a portable terminal and they can do things to you, Lizbeth. Painful things. Put down that gun in your hand and come with me."

"Fuck you," said the child. She lifted the flare pistol and fired without hesitation, the magnesium slug spitting across the open space, bypassing Alexanian and dropping to the ground six feet to the left of the camper. It sputtered for a second, and then the white-hot lump of powdered metal ignited the spreading pool of farm gas that had been puddling beneath the camper for the last five minutes.

When the first intruder sensor had warned Robin that they were under seige, he'd uncapped the standpipe just to the left of the driveway. When they'd gone out to confront Alexanian, Lizbeth had slipped out the back door and turned on the pump in the toolshed. Almost thirty gallons of gas had spread out in a long finger beneath the camper, and there were two hundred gallons more in the buried tank. The explosion was stupendous and the blast wave that consumed the camper and incinerated Martin and Carlotta Nordquist was enough to throw everyone except Lizbeth to the ground.

Alexanian recovered quickly, scrambling to his feet, staring dumbfounded at the swelling fireball and the fuming mushroom pall of smoke above it. He turned, teeth bared, and charged at Lizbeth, his walking stick held like a club.

Before Robin or Kelly had time to react, the man had closed to within ten feet of the child, but she never wavered, snapping a fresh shell into the breech as Alexanian charged, then firing a second time, at point-blank range. The flare struck him squarely in the chest, rocking him backward and spinning him around to face the fire. He screamed, a single, wavering howl, as the shell charred through the idiotic fisherman's vest and melted its way into his flesh. He beat at the gnawing horror cooking its way through the meat and bone of his chest, succeeding only in covering his hands with bubbling lava, turning his fingers to blackened stumps. His clothes were fully alight now, the nylon vest melting, adding itself to the hideous fuming mess, and then his hair ignited, turning him into a wavering, stumbling torch.

He staggered back another few steps and then, like the branch of a tree in a forest fire, he collapsed into the monstrous, raging inferno consuming the camper. Kelly had a last glimpse of him, a charcoal figure outlined against the flames, charred hands coming up under his chin as the heat contracted the tendons and sinews of his arms and shoulders, turning him into a horrible, shimmering effigy of a praying saint. Then he was gone.

Dropping the flare gun and with tears beginning to well in her eyes, Lizbeth walked slowly toward Robin and Kelly. She paused, then bent down to retrieve Alexanian's walking stick where it had fallen. Mutely, the tears flowing freely now, she handed the stick to Robin, then let herself be enfolded in Kelly's outstretched waiting arms.

"Am I a freak?" she whispered, head buried in Kelly's shoulder.

"Of course you're not," Kelly soothed, stroking the child's hair. "It's over now, Lizbeth. It's all over."

Beside them, Robin held the ebony cane in his hand, examining the carved head. With a sudden furious motion he flung it away, watching as it tumbled end over end, vanishing behind the brutal, roaring wall of flame.

"It's never over," he said quietly. But the woman and the child beside him didn't hear, and silently, one arm around Kelly's shoulder, he led them away from the billowing pyre.

AUTHOR'S NOTE

The technological research contained in *Crestwood Heights* is accurate. All medical systems and technologies described are currently in use or soon will be. Information relating to surveillance methods, in-vitro and in in-utero fertility methods is also accurate. The PAL system, subcutaneous monitoring and artificial blood perfusion of organs exist and are in use within the continental United States as of the date of publication. All data relating to computers, including the CrayII supercomputer and the integration of human subjects with a computer, is real.

Although Crestwood Heights itself is a fictional community, there are several "new towns" like it in the United States, the United Kingdom, and Europe. Because of this, the author suggests prudence when considering a move to a community that advertises itself as being what the future is coming to. The future, it appears, is not necessarily what it seems.

—Christopher Hyde